Dangerous wrong-side-of-the-tracks bad boy Jake Carter is definitely Eve Shawcross's *Mr. Wrong*. She's been playing with fire, and only after getting burned has she learned a painful lesson—no-strings-attached sex ain't for her, no matter how sizzling it is. Craving a *real* relationship with the promise of a future, Eve vows to find her *Mr. Right*, a man who can give her what she so desperately wants—love, marriage, and children.

Ten years later, Eve is left reeling when *Mr. Right*'s sordid secret life is exposed. Shattered by his bitter betrayal, she tries to pick up the pieces. When his duplicity jeopardizes her safety, survival becomes her sole focus. Just when Eve thinks she's avoided peril, she comes face-to-face with sexy *Mr. Wrong*—and their complicated past.

The tables have turned. Now wealthy and powerful, Jake's determined to tempt her back into his bed. He proposes *an arrangement*, but she's thrown by the terms in his contract. The stakes are high. Knowing her traitorous body and how persuasive Jake can be, Eve isn't sure she can play the game by his rules. Her gut cautions that all is not what it seems, but the passion she once found with him can no longer be denied.

Can Eve abide by Jake's terms? Or will desire evolve into love?

Meeting the Past
Copyright © 2020 Anne Lucy-Shanley
ISBN: 978-1-4874-3005-4
Cover art by Martine Jardin

Published by eXtasy Books Inc or
Devine Destinies, an imprint of eXtasy Books Inc

Look for us online at:
www.eXtasybooks.com or www.devinedestinies.com

MEETING THE PAST

BY

ANNE LUCY-SHANLEY

DEDICATION

For my mother, who loved a good story.

CHAPTER ONE

Ten Years Earlier

"Oh, God."

Eve Shawcross dashed to her bedroom to flip through the calendar tacked on the wall above her desk. There was that bout of flu she'd suffered, and the occasional nausea since. Thoughts racing and her pulse jumping in her throat, she told her father she was going out and sped to a drugstore on the other side of town.

Locked in the store bathroom, Eve stared in bewilderment at the two pink lines. Her hands shook when she paid the salesclerk for additional tests, but to her chagrin, the results were the same — positive. She put her head in her hands. She thought they'd been careful.

She'd have to quit college and find a job. *Shit*. What would she tell her dad? What would she say to Jake? Eve ignored the insistent knocks on the door and hoped the floor would open and swallow her. *A mother at nineteen. My life's over.*

She met Jake that night and broke the news. Clearly shell-shocked, he stood at the window for several minutes, staring out over the inner-city landscape. Eve heard drunks brawling on the sidewalk below. A police siren whined. Through paper-thin walls came the wail of a child from the adjacent apartment. She waited for Jake's reaction, wringing her hands.

Once, she'd encountered his neighbor and her passel of

ragamuffin children in the hall. Not much older than Eve, she appeared middle-aged. Hair lank, her printed shift faded from washing, the woman stared vacantly, her snot-nosed children fussing and pulling at her. Eve imagined a scenario where she lived with Jake at the Maxwell Arms Apartments, raising her baby with an unwilling father poorly suited for domesticity. Was that Eve's future? It was unthinkable.

Jake combed a work-calloused hand through his shaggy jet-black hair, his stance radiating tension. Even now, in her despair, she felt the sexual tug. She shook her head to free herself from it, tearing her gaze from his muscular back and lean hips in the dusty jeans he'd worn to work. He turned from the window and offered to marry her. Eve laughed. It was a preposterous notion. "So I can end up like Wanda in 2B? Talk about my worst nightmare."

Jake's wounded male ego was obvious from the reproachful look he hurled at her. "I can take care of you and anyone else that comes along. That's a promise."

"As a laborer? Come on, Jake."

"Maybe I don't wear a suit and tie like your father," he snapped, his eyes icy. "You didn't care about my job when I was fuckin' your brains out."

"That's exactly it—you know what we have isn't a proper relationship. We don't date, we fuck. And that's all it ever was gonna be."

"Is that so?" Jake challenged.

Eve swore under her breath and rubbed a hand over her eyes. "This is pointless. I'll call you after I think."

The following week, after class, Eve drove across town to meet Jake at his apartment. Her stomach was queasy from nerves as much as hormones. When she parked her car in front of the grubby complex, she made sure to lock the doors.

Sway by *The Rolling Stones* drifted into the hallway. As Eve approached Jake's unit, she detected the skunky odor of weed. He sat at the battered dinette table in his minuscule kitchen holding a bottle of beer when she let herself in with her key. The fixture on the ceiling cast little light, making the room shadowy. He wore dirty work clothes and dusty boots. His leather jacket hung on the back of the chair, and a half-smoked joint rested on the edge of a chipped green ashtray.

Jake glanced at her and lazily lifted the beer bottle to take a drink, squinting through the smoke wafting from the ashtray. He finished the beer with one long swallow, turning down the volume on the record player when *Wild Horses* began.

"You didn't return my calls, Angie," Jake said coolly, using his pet name for her. He brought the joint to his lips to take a deep drag.

"I lost the baby." Eve tried to sound unconcerned, propping against the hallway wall to stay in the shadows. She bit her lip to keep it from trembling. In seconds, Jake was out of his chair and beside her.

"Did you see a doctor?" he asked, palm cupping her cheek. His hands were roughened by work, smelling of dirt and gear oil overlaid by pot. She moved out of his reach, though it took effort. *If we don't have a* real *relationship, why is this so difficult?*

Eve feigned detachment. She mustn't cry. She must be strong. "I started bleeding. I went to the hospital. They told me it was a miscarriage."

Pushing past him, Eve opened the door of the old-fashioned refrigerator. She grabbed a bottle of beer, twisting the cap off with the hem of her shirt and taking a drink. She swallowed her threatening tears with beer.

"I meant what I said about getting married." Jake slouched against the wall opposite her in the darkened hallway, thumbs tucked in his belt loops. The easily identifiable riff of *Can't You Hear Me Knocking?* played on the turntable. The shadows hid Jake's expression. "There can be babies in the future, Angie. When the timing's better for us."

Eve knew she looked as dubious as she felt. *We don't love each other. Why is he pressing for marriage? It doesn't matter.* She took a deep breath. "I'm sorry, but it's over."

"*What?*" Jake straightened and leaned forward to grip her forearm.

Calmly as she could, Eve placed her beer on the counter and pulled away. "I met someone."

"What the fuck?" Jake slammed his fist down hard on the counter beside her, making her flinch. "In the space of a damn week?"

"We only went on one date, but he's nice. He's older. Settled. I-I think I can possibly have a future with him." Eve met Jake's green eyes, lifting her chin in defiance. "We both know marriage and babies aren't your thing."

"I can't believe this shit."

"It was never going anywhere. We were never meant to last," she whispered. "You know it as well as I do."

"The fuck I do." When Eve attempted to leave, he grasped her wrist. "What we have is special."

"It's chemistry. Period. We have nothing else in common. We've never had a real conversation before now." She jerked away, knowing she'd cave if she listened to him. Being involved with Jake was playing with fire. *Learn from what happened or get burned.*

Eve put the apartment key on the hallway table when she left. *Sometimes you have to be cruel to be kind.* He would lead her down the road to ruin. She heard Jake's howl of frustration and the repeated bangs of him punching a wall. Her cheeks wet with tears, she quickened her step.

4

CHAPTER TWO

Present Day

The pungent scent of charred bacon and scorched toast lingered in the air. Eve switched on the exhaust fan above the cooktop, humming *Chris Stapleton's Tennessee Whiskey*. She plated the eggs, frowning when she spied a sliver of eggshell she'd missed. Plucking out the shell, she tossed it in the trash while her gray cat, Wally, wove a figure-eight pattern through her ankles.

"Who's this I see at the stove? *Julia Child?*" Martin teased, giving her a perfunctory kiss. Eve caught a whiff of toothpaste, and she smiled at her husband. He wore his usual suit, his close-cut sandy hair damp from a shower.

She laughed. though it wasn't the first time she'd heard the joke. "Very funny."

"Where's Addy?"

"She has an appointment. I gave her the morning off." Eve lifted the plates and set them on the tray. "I thought we'd eat on the terrace."

"Did she prepare my lunch before she left?" Martin asked, negotiating the tray through the patio door she held for him. Eve gave him side-eye. His words were innocuous enough, but she read between the lines.

"Yes, she made your lunch. FYI, I make a damn good ham and cheese sandwich," Eve grumbled, sitting at the wrought iron table and unloading the tray.

Blue eyes twinkling with amusement, he put his hands up in surrender. "I didn't say anything."

As she nibbled her breakfast, Eve grimaced. How was it possible her food tasted burned and raw at the same time? Pushing her plate away, she sipped her coffee, shrugging. "I guess I should've stuck with my usual toaster pastries."

Eve pretended not to notice Martin using his butter knife to scrape away the blackened surface of his toast, instead watching Wally, who had sneaked out with them. She grinned when he focused with intense concentration on a monarch butterfly fluttering past a rose bush. The early morning sunshine glinted on the dew spotted grass, and a gust of Santa Ana wind blew down from the mountains. Star jasmine grew wild and unchecked on the pergola above them, making a flowered canopy that shaded the patio. Eve pulled her sweater closer and shut her eyes, breathing in the sharp, sweet smell of jasmine.

"Mort mentioned a new tennis pro was hired at the club," Martin said, overly casual, putting egg on his toast.

Eve opened an eye.

"Supposedly he's excellent."

"Let's not get into that again." Despite Martin's urging to learn tennis, Eve had no aptitude for it. Her anxiety made her tense up. She was a disaster on the court. Groaning, she remembered her humiliation as she missed serve after serve. Her instructor's huffs and clenched teeth made his feelings clear. "Isn't it enough I've learned to play golf?"

"You've become a fine golfer, but—" Martin's mouth turned down. *Here we go.* Eve bit back irritation. "The problem is you refuse to play a round with anyone other than Hitch Grant."

"Because I prefer a friendly game with my best friend—one where *Mulligan* isn't a four-letter-word—rather than with Mort Weston. He's pedantic. He acts like he's at the *PGA*

Championship." The morning had begun pleasantly. It was a shame. "Mort's *handsy*, too."

As Martin chewed, Eve heard the crunch of eggshell. She felt her face prick with heat when he frowned and swished a mouthful of juice to cleanse his palate. His voice was full of censure when he spoke. "The Westons are important socially."

"I should let Mort *feel me up* so you can win a spot on the board at The Palms? Really, Martin?"

"I never said that, did I?" Too soft-spoken and circumspect a man to raise his voice, Martin didn't *fight*. He led *discussions*, making rational points to flay Eve's arguments with his brand of logic. "Mort comes from a different generation, but he's harmless."

"Stop sticking up for that dirty old man." Eve shook her head, adding through clenched teeth, "If that creep guides my hips *to model a proper golf stance* again, he'll be on the receiving end of my seven iron."

"You know how important it is that you cultivate friendships with the right sort of people." Martin sounded disappointed. "Mort has influence in Santa Beatriz. The least you could do is call Bianca and suggest a twosome."

"Bianca Weston bathes in eau de parfum. My throat closes up anytime she's within five feet." Eve put a finger on her eyebrow to stave off a headache behind her eye socket. "And she's no intellectualist. Listening to her makes my IQ drop two points."

Martin sat his cup on the glass-topped table with a decisive clink. "You're unreasonable. And unkind. Bianca's nothing but cordial to you."

Eve tamped down the gush of frustration. She pictured Bianca's swollen duck-lips and silicone-enhanced chest and argued, "She's a *Stepford Wife*. She rotates three topics of conversation—her plastic surgeon, *The Grapefruit Diet*, and

Mort's ex-wife, *the crypt keeper*. Remember when Jillian Caldwell brought up *The Oedipus Complex* at our last dinner party? Bianca thought Jillian was talking about the new Japanese restaurant in town, and *Freud* was a way to prepare fish."

Feeling the weight of Martin's disapproval, Eve refused to meet his eyes. She was sick of hearing about Mort and the club. She took a calming breath before continuing, "The Palms has been a source of friction since you registered us when we were newlyweds. I have nothing in common with the trophy wives there—and I don't feel comfortable pretending I'm something I'm not."

"Sometimes we have to do what we don't feel like doing." Martin crossed his arms and gave her a hard look. "I understand you'd rather remain at home with Addy or work at that preschool than volunteer with the Junior League, but certain things are expected of you as my wife. I think I've been exceedingly patient with you over the years."

"You've been *patient* with me?" Eve's mouth parted. "What do you mean?"

Martin sighed, his face set. "You wanted to take art classes. I had no problem with that or finishing your degree. But the job at that preschool . . ."

"*That preschool*?"

"The point is I've always supported you. Is it too much to ask you to provide me what I need?"

"My *education* was a hardship for you? My *job* is a hardship?" Eve's throat ached with tears. "Boy, I guess I'm failing my balancing act."

"You know my feelings. I've always made my stance unambiguous."

She bit the inside of her cheek. "Aren't *I* good enough for you?"

"I didn't say that. Please try to remain calm."

Eve blinked back her tears. Martin hated it when she cried.

He handed her a napkin, and she blew her nose. She met his eyes and made her tone conciliatory. "I know you prefer I don't work . . . it's . . . I value my independence." She paused and took a deep breath. "I'll give my notice today if you agree we can try IVF."

The silence was palpable. Eve twisted the napkin she held. When Martin answered, his voice was regretful but firm. "I'm fifty-two. I'm too old for a child."

"After my miscarriage nine years ago, you promised — we'd go to a fertility specialist if we didn't conceive by the time I turned thirty." Eve sounded shrill but didn't care. "You *promised*."

"Be reasonable. Your obstetrician said with your scar tissue and fibroids that it's unlikely you'll conceive even with IVF." He added in a placating tone, "I know it's difficult, but you must accept we aren't meant to be parents." He checked his wristwatch. "I'm late for work."

Eve shook her head when he rose to leave. "But — what about adoption? You know I've always wanted children, Martin. You can't change your mind like this — blindside me like this — out of nowhere. It isn't fair."

He leaned down and brushed his lips against her forehead. "I'll likely be late tonight. No reason for you to wait up for me. I'll sleep on the sofa in my office at the lab."

"Don't leave," Eve begged. "Let's talk more about this. Please."

Martin tilted his head toward Wally, where he was stalking a speckled gecko on the far side of the flagstone patio. "You better fetch your cat before he disappears up the mountainside after that lizard."

CHAPTER THREE

"Sorry, Jaws, but it's Noah's turn," Eve said the next day, removing the colorful board book from Stella's chubby fist and giving it to Noah. Eve hoisted the toddler to her hip. Despite her innocent appearance, Stella was apt to attack when provoked. When Stella's expected indignant howl didn't materialize, Eve sighed with relief. It had been a trying morning at Santa Beatriz Preschool. It didn't help that Martin hadn't returned her calls. Swallowing the lump in her throat, she pushed her marital problems from her mind.

"Eve? Can I see you?" Denise, her boss, stood in the doorway. Shoving down her irritation, Eve nodded. The class had finished an art project and were headed to the playground. The transition was always chaotic and the *worst* time to leave the classroom.

Nicole, her teacher's aide, shot her a look that said *What now?*

Eve shrugged a shoulder in answer, lowering Stella to the carpet. Rolling her eyes heavenward, Nicole collected jackets from cubbies.

"I'll try to hurry back before stuff spirals out of control, Nic."

Nicole winked. "Girl, I got this."

Denise stood in the corridor, wide-eyed. "The police are here to speak with you."

"With *me*?" Eve shook her head, wondering if she'd misheard. A frisson of fear tickled her spine.

Two detectives, a man and a woman, waited in Denise's

office. The woman wore a button-up shirt that had seen better days and well-creased chinos but possessed an air of grim authority. "Evangeline Pierce?"

"Y-yes?" Eve asked. The man was young and nervous. He averted his gaze. *That's a bad sign.*

"I'm Detective Janice Carolla. He's Sergeant Wise." Eve's attention skittered back to the woman. Carolla pointed to the armchair positioned in front of Denise's desk. Legs jelly, Eve sank into it. *What is going on?* She gripped the arms of the chair and braced for ugly news.

What was the detective saying? *Husband, found dead,* and *stabbed* made little sense. Eve homed in on the bleach stain on the collar of Carolla's rumpled shirt, her heart thudding in her ears so loud it drowned out the woman's voice.

"Breathe in through your nose and out your mouth." Carolla put a steadying hand on Eve's back.

She did what Carolla instructed, but became light-headed. Her vision dimmed. From the fringes, Eve saw Wise step from the room. When he returned with a tepid tumbler of water, she'd regained a degree of composure.

Eve accepted the glass with clumsy fingers, murmuring, "There must be some mistake."

"I'm afraid not. We're investigating every avenue, but it appears to be a mugging gone bad." Carolla did the talking. Wise loitered by the door as if poised for flight. "Did your husband have any enemies?"

"W-what?" Eve shook her head, dumbfounded. The tumbler slipped from her hand. Water soaked her jeans and dribbled into her sandals. Carolla knelt and picked up the shards of glass from the tile, depositing them in the trashcan.

Nodding to Wise, Carolla gave Eve's shoulder a squeeze meant to be comforting. "Wise will find a co-worker to drive you home. We'll talk tomorrow."

Feeling every second of her twenty-nine years, Eve

screwed her eyes shut and concentrated. *Breathe in, breathe out. Breathe in, breathe out.*

Wise and Carolla steered Eve out to the parking lot. Nicole trailed behind with Eve's leather purse swinging from her arm. Getting behind the wheel of Eve's SUV, Nicole searched in the purse for the key fob. With robotic movements, Eve climbed into the passenger's seat, neglecting to fasten her seatbelt. She was barely aware of Nicole starting the vehicle and pressing *navigate home* on the GPS.

As they drove past the playground, a group of kids gathered at the chain-link fence. Denise joined them, her face full of curiosity. "Where's Miss Evie going?" One of the older toddlers asked, the sound of his voice carrying through Nicole's open window.

Breathe in, breathe out. Breathe in, breathe out.

The journey seemed a never-ending pilgrimage. Hysteria clawed at her throat as Eve struggled to remain in control. Conversation was impossible. All she could manage was breathing. She wrung her hands and stared numbly at the scenery.

Perla Blanca, the blue-collar section of the city, was a blur. The tightly packed apartment complexes and rows of shoebox stucco homes stretched on. Nerves jangling, she wondered if she'd *ever* get home. The careless cloudless blue of the California sky mocked her.

The close confines of Perla Blanca gave way to Vista la Montana, the upscale part of town. Eve's stomping grounds. The outdoor café where she and Martin drank espresso Sunday mornings, *The Times* spread open to the crossword puzzle on the tabletop between them. The gated entrance to the country club. Ramon was in the guard shack. *How can people carry on normally? Martin's dead — murdered!*

Eve experienced a pang of bone-melting relief when the GPS commanded, "Turn right onto Jacaranda Trail. In point thirty-eight miles, you will reach *home*, at one forty-seven

Jacaranda Trail."

"This is *your* house?" Nicole asked as she parked in the driveway, but Eve didn't answer. She staggered from the vehicle and made her way down the curving flagstone path on autopilot. She wasn't aware of Nicole lagging behind to scrutinize the Arts and Crafts-style home or to admire the bougainvillea vines, blooms riotous with color, threaded through the pergola above the garage doors. The air was heavy with the scent of potted gardenias. Eve pursed her lips, repelled by the fragrance.

Turning the corner, they were met with a panoramic view of Santa Beatriz below and the cerulean waters of the Pacific beyond. Today Eve surveyed it with dull eyes.

The front door flew open. Addy, a plump woman of fifty-five, hurried to draw her into a warm embrace. Eve wilted against her. "Luv." Tears muddled her English accent. "I just learned about Martin . . . I can't believe it."

"*Murdered.*" Eve's lips were rubbery. She stumbled over the word. Simply uttering it left a nasty metallic tang on her tongue.

"I know. I know," Addy murmured brokenly, holding tight. After a minute, she pulled away and gave Nicole a watery smile. "Please come in for a cup of tea."

Addy put an arm around Eve's waist and helped her inside to the sofa in the living room, Nicole following behind. Eve curled in a corner, pulling her knees to her chest without taking off her sandals. *What does it matter if I get dirt on the upholstery? Does anything matter?*

Nicole sat on the edge of a chair and regarded the surroundings with interest until Addy brought a tray of tea.

"Evie? Take the cuppa." Addy held a mug of steaming tea. Eve roused herself and accepted it, wrapping her hands around the mug for warmth. "My, but you're shivering, pet."

Her face troubled, Addy arranged an afghan around Eve. Once she was satisfied that the blanket was well-tucked,

Addy lowered her bulk into an armchair across from the sofa. She said to Nicole, "I can't thank you enough for driving Eve home."

"I'm happy to help. Are you Eve's mom?"

"No, darling. I'm her housekeeper."

"Oh." Nicole's eyebrows rose and she glanced to where Eve sat on the sofa. "Is there anything I can do? Make calls? Prepare food?"

"I'm not sure yet—I can't think. This is surreal." Addy dabbed at her eyes with a tissue. "I assumed Martin worked late and slept in his office when he didn't come home . . ."

The solemn cadence of their voices and their sorrowful expressions made Eve's eyelid tic. She needed action, needed to move. Placing the mug on the side table, she got unsteadily to her feet, afghan draping around her shoulders like a shawl.

"I'll go upstairs and change." Her voice sounded funny, even to herself. Nicole sprung up to offer assistance, but Eve motioned for her to stay. "It's okay."

Her movements were halting when she made her way up the stairs. *It's not okay. Nothing will ever be okay again.*

CHAPTER FOUR

Eve shut the door to the master bedroom, let the blanket fall, and stepped from her leather sandals. She peeled off her damp jeans and wrinkled shirt with haste, staring at the pile of clothes on the floor, her mouth tight. The peasant blouse was one of her favorites, but every time she saw it in her closet, it would bring her back to the moment she learned Martin was murdered. *Murdered. My God, what a hateful word.*

The clothes were defiled. Eve wouldn't be able to wear them again. She decided to throw them in the garbage, adding bra and panties to the pile. Pulling her robe from the closet, Eve let her gaze skim over the bed. A pair of Martin's folded reading glasses were beside an unfinished glass of water on the night table. She blanched, chest constricting. Whirling away, Eve steadied herself against the closet door, trying to curb her panic.

The argument she and Martin had the morning before haunted her. Shuddering, Eve remembered asking herself, while drifting off to sleep last night, if it had been a mistake to marry him. Frustrated with his rigidity, she'd contemplated divorce. Now, she felt guilty and disloyal.

Sagging into the overstuffed chair in front of the window overlooking the terra-cotta tiled roofs of neighboring houses, Eve ruminated. From the beginning, she'd accepted Martin for what he was, a scientist, not an empath. But he'd grown colder and more unyielding each year. She'd chafed at his controlling ways. *Last night I'd decided to give him an ultimatum — either agree to adopt a child, or it's over.*

15

Eve shook her head, thoughts turning to calls she needed to make. Her first instinct was to phone her father, but he was on a cruise and wouldn't have cell service. Shoulders slumping, she realized she ought to ring Martin's friends, and his family in Monterey, too. It filled her with dread. *Not today. I can't.*

Hitch. Eve longed to hear her best friend's voice. She lifted the receiver of the vintage style landline phone on her dressing table, dialing his number by heart. After one ring, voicemail answered.

"I'm in Mykonos or on a yacht in the Aegean. Leave a message, and maybe I'll get back to ya before I head to Corfu. *Adio!*"

She hung up, staring out the window, remembering their initial meeting like it was yesterday.

Eve spent most of her first summer in Santa Beatriz at the pool with her sketch pad. It was there she'd met Hitch, a trust fund baby summering in town before jetting off to Germany for Oktoberfest. Emerging from the pool, he'd shaken his blond curly hair of water and collapsed in an empty lounger beside Eve. Noticing her drawing, he asked what she was working on. Shyly, she'd showed him her rough sketch of a toddler playing in the splash pad.

"Hey, that's good. Can you do my portrait?" Hitch posed on the edge of his chaise, modeling in jest as *Rodin's The Thinker.*

Eve surveyed him for a moment, considering. He had a patrician face with a knife-blade long nose and cornflower blue eyes. Not conventionally handsome, his lean surfer looks lent him appeal. With a chuckle, she'd flipped to a fresh page and scribbled. When Eve tendered Hitch the sketch, her eyes danced with amusement. She'd drawn him in caricature, arm around a surfboard, his head oversized. Nose beak-like, his mouth was opened extra wide in a toothy grin. After throwing his head back and howling with laughter, he held out a hand. "Hitch."

They bonded over their distrust of collagen injections, a loathing for tennis, and an affinity for tropical drinks with umbrellas. He was a terrible flirt, and Eve briefly wondered if he was pursuing her, but he'd come out to her before he left that autumn. He wanted to stay closeted, so she kept the fact he was gay a well-guarded secret.

Wally whined outside the door, pulling her back. Making the mistake of looking at the bed again, Eve gasped at the quick zap of panic. She scrambled across the room and whipped the bedroom door open, hurrying out. The hallway was neutral. Safe. She leaned her forehead against the cool wall. *Now what?*

Wally stretched and patted her hip with his paw. Eve bent and scooped him up for a cuddle. When he wriggled from her grasp, she walked with him down the carpeted hall to his favorite guest bedroom.

He vaulted to the bed and sat on his haunches, his golden eyes unblinking. Bones aching, Eve flopped beside him and stroked his ears. She yawned, overcome by fatigue that made her head pound. Eyelids drooping, she moved Wally to his preferred spot on the pillow and peeled back the comforter.

"Luv?" The setting sun made the shadows long on the walls. "You've kipped hours. You've not had anything to eat since this morning. You must be starving."

Eve asked, her voice hoarse, "Did you take Nicole home?"

"She arranged a ride."

"I should've thanked her for bringing me home." She clicked on the bedside lamp. A tray of toast and tea was on the nightstand. Before placing the tray on Eve's lap, Addy straightened the bedclothes. Well-buttered toast cut into *soldiers* were arranged on the plate. A fragrant bloom from Eve's

17

garden was in a bud vase. Her heart swelled with gratitude. Addy was the mother she never had. Clearing her throat to stave off the threatening tears, Eve lifted the mug of tea.

Addy pulled a chair up to the bed to keep her company. "Nicole brought in your purse. Your phone's been ringing and chiming all sorts."

As she chewed a soldier dripping with honey, Eve studied Addy. The woman's eyes were red-rimmed, her mouth tense. Martin and Addy weren't close, but he was a considerate boss. He often gave Addy extra time off for church activities, or to visit her cousin in Sausalito. Every year he bought her first-class airfare to spend Christmas with her sister in Northeast England.

"You look done in." Eve squeezed Addy's plump hand.

"I'm worried about you, pet. Your father's across the country, and your best friend doesn't sit still long enough to finish a cuppa."

"He's trying to outrun his restlessness," Eve said. Hitch clowned around, hiding his sadness, but Addy was a shrewd character and people liked confiding in her. She was one of the few people who knew Hitch's sexual orientation.

"Once he comes out, I'm sure he'll find peace, though I can't imagine how scary it must be." Addy snagged a piece of toast from Eve's plate, munching thoughtfully. "Have you contacted your father?"

Eve put her empty mug on the tray. "I couldn't. Remember, he's on a ship in the middle of the Atlantic."

"We can message him through the cruise line," Addy said, brushing crumbs from the skirt of her nightgown.

"I'll send him an email." Eve yawned, and Addy took the tray from her lap. Eve stilled her with a hand on her arm. "Will you help me move my clothes in here tomorrow? I can't face going back into my bedroom — it's too much."

"Of course, pet."

Bright light streamed through the sheer curtains. For a moment, Eve forgot where she was. Then it came back to her. Unease floated over her like a gauzy shroud. Martin was dead, and she needed to face reality. There were calls to make, details to attend to.

Body aching as if she'd been flattened by a truck, Eve sat on the edge of the bed and rubbed the grit from her eyes. She needed a hot drink. Tightening the sash of her robe, she padded downstairs.

Eve found Addy in the kitchen, drinking coffee and watching the morning news, wearing her usual uniform of t-shirt and dark slacks, her brown hair damp from washing. As Eve sat, Addy poured her coffee. Then, frowning, she switched the TV off with the remote. "It's a headline this morning."

"Did they mention his name?" At Addy's nod, Eve's heart plummeted to her feet. Everyone would know what happened. She put her hands over her face and reminded herself to breathe. "I'm not ready for this."

"Remember when I told you about my fiancé, Reg?" Addy asked gently.

"He died in the Falklands War. Nineteen eighty-two, wasn't it? How did you get through it?" Fighting tears, Eve's voice came out a plaintive whisper.

"I muddled through, as you will. Nobody, and I mean *nobody*, knows what it's like to lose someone they love until they go through it themselves."

Eve contemplated returning to her bed and hiding under the covers.

Addy continued, "Detective Carolla rang. She wants us to meet her at the police station at eleven for questioning. She asked you to bring Martin's laptop for the investigation."

When Addy pulled a carton of eggs from the fridge, Eve's stomach curdled. She warned, "I can't eat."

"Try you must," Addy said firmly. With a practiced hand, she cracked eggs into a bowl.

CHAPTER FIVE

Eve picked at her omelet. The smell of bacon lured Wally. He sat expectantly at her feet. She tore bacon into tiny pieces for him. With a glance at the clock on the microwave, Eve cleared the table, but Addy shepherded her to the stairs. "Go shower. I'll wash up."

Wanting to rinse away the muck of the last twenty-four hours, Eve turned the water hot as she could stand. She scrubbed her skin, her throat clogging with the tears she hadn't allowed earlier. Sounds muffled by the spray, Eve lost it, giving in to her anguish. She slid down the tiled wall of the shower, not noticing the needle-like sting of the jets.

The water turned cool. Wally paced outside the stall, yowling. By the time she finished shampooing her hair, Eve was numb. Wrapped in a towel, she watched Wally lap the water around the drain. Martin hated it when he did that.

Eve's reflection in the mirror revealed a pinched face and dazed expression. Today her eyes were enormous, her blue-gray irises more gray than blue. She bit her lip to keep it from quivering. As brittle as glass, she reckoned all it would take was a nudge and she'd splinter into a thousand pieces.

Addy knocked on the bathroom door, supplying a stack of clothes. There was a moss green blouse, a matching knit cardigan, and jeans. Stylish cranberry flats were on the top of the pile. Eve needed the diversion of getting ready. She rummaged through the vanity drawer for the spare makeup she kept there. Dusting her face with powder to cover her pallor, she shakily applied mascara and lip gloss. Her pearl earrings and her wedding rings were her only jewelry.

The police station was a utilitarian concrete building two blocks from the beach. Addy parked her tan sedan in a visitor's spot in the empty parking lot. While Addy locked the car, Eve let the sun warm her upturned face for fortification before meeting with Carolla.

After consulting a directory in the lobby, they made their way up the stairs to the second floor, Martin's laptop tucked under Eve's arm. Carolla met them in the hallway outside her closet-sized office. Wearing a polo shirt and jeans, she was neater than the day before but as authoritative.

"Thanks for coming in, Mrs. Pierce, Ms. Dennis. Coffee?" Carolla gestured to a crusty carafe. Addy shook her head to refuse. Eve looked dubiously at the tar-like liquid but nodded, thinking it might be nice to have something to hold. "Creamer, sugar?"

"Black's fine," Eve murmured.

"I'll have you wait here while I talk to Ms. Dennis."

She observed the exchange between Addy and Carolla through the plate-glass window, the closed door muting their voices. Tears spilled from Addy's eyes and her hands gesticulated while she spoke. Eve pressed her fingertips to her temples, then opened her purse to find her phone.

There were several texts and voicemails. Bianca Weston had rung to offer condolences. Angelica Fellows, who was married to Martin's friend, Ted, promised to stop by.

Nicole had called to check on her. Flor Martinez, whose child was Eve's pupil the year before, wanted to know what she could do to help. Denise asked when Eve would be back to work. *Ugh. Has she no clue?*

The office door opened. Addy stepped out, her cheeks tear stained. Eve embraced her before joining Carolla, forewarning tingling. She was happy to have the cup of coffee to occupy her hands, though they were trembling, as were her lips.

Sitting back in her swivel chair, Carolla asked Eve to tell her about Martin.

Eve's voice was tentative when she said, "He was Ivy-league educated and from an upper-class family. He founded his lab three years ago, using a bequest from his grandmother. Med Tech has several big-name pharmaceutical clients. Martin was proud of that."

"Yesterday, I asked whether he had enemies. Had he quarreled with anyone recently?"

"He wasn't the type to quarrel. I can't imagine him angering anyone enough to want to *kill* him. Maybe he had issues with someone at the lab, but I doubt it." Eve paused, worrying at her lip with her teeth. "He didn't discuss his work with me."

"Not at all?"

Eve shakily lifted her coffee and took a tiny taste. It was awful. "Very little, though we often entertained clients."

"Networking?" Carolla inquired, consulting her steno pad of notes.

"Yes. We had dinner parties at our home, or we entertained at The Palms of Santa Beatriz."

"Membership there's exclusive, and you reside in an affluent area, with a live-in housekeeper. You're *comfortable*."

"Comfortable, certainly not rich. I maintain a simple life-style. As a preschool teacher, I don't make much money. I have my own accounts for my bills. Martin's income covered our household expenses."

"Martin was the family money-manager?" Carolla asked, and Eve nodded. "Would you say he was proficient?"

Eve nodded again, wondering where Carolla's line of questioning headed. "I don't often use our joint checking account, but it's kept at a twenty-five-thousand-dollar balance. There's also a savings account, and stocks and bonds for retirement."

"I reviewed the financials. Frankly, I'm concerned,"

Carolla said in her measured way.

Alarmed, Eve moved to the edge of her chair. "*Concerned?*"

"Martin made large cash withdrawals these last few weeks, draining accounts. Savings, retirement, even credit cards. I assume you're not aware of this?"

"No! He emptied accounts? Why?" As she met Carolla's sharp eyes, blood drained from Eve's face. She placed the cup on the edge of the desk. Coffee slopped over the sides and on her hand, but she didn't notice. "Where's the money?"

"Presumably, the killer stole it. According to his charge card, last week Martin booked two plane tickets. The flight departs from LAX at seven *tonight*." Carolla paused. "What's noteworthy is both tickets are solely in his name. Maridien Airways allows name transfers of accompanying guests at check-in. It's like Martin didn't want anyone to know who'd be traveling with him."

Eve wrung her hands, speechless. Any equilibrium she'd reclaimed in the last hours evaporated.

Corolla consulted her notes. "Destination Cape Azul, an island country off the West coast of Africa. Establishing residency is simple and the cost of living low. There aren't diplomatic relations between the US and Cape Azul. It's perfect for those needing to . . . vanish."

CHAPTER SIX

Eve needed help walking to the car. Her legs wouldn't hold her weight. Carolla conferred with Addy while Eve waited in the passenger's seat, head in hands. *I'm gonna end up in Santa Beatriz Hospital's psych ward.*

Addy opened the driver's door and dropped into her seat. Her fingers tight on the steering wheel, she didn't speak while driving. Pulling into her stall in the garage, she said, "I don't bloody believe it."

Eve turned to her friend, not bothering to hide her misery.

Addy sighed. "Come on, luv."

She pushed Eve into a dining room chair and snatched a bottle of whiskey from the drinks cart, along with two rocks glasses. Sinking into the chair beside her, Addy uncapped the bottle and poured them a shot. Eve lifted the tumbler to her lips, shuddering when she drained it. She whispered, "This can't be happening."

Addy poured them a refill, repeating, "I don't bloody believe it. Of all men . . . I'd not expect Martin capable of such chicanery."

"Stockpiling funds to take with him when he left *tonight* for *fucking* Cape Azul. Who was he taking with him?" Eve smacked a hand on the table, making their glasses jump and Addy yelp. Eve leaped from her seat, white-hot betrayal coursing through her body. "That treacherous, vile, cheating sonofabitch!"

Eve ran upstairs to the master suite. Wally sat on the landing, grooming his back claws. The bedroom door crashed

25

against the wall, and he darted away, his ears flattened. Grabbing her tablet, Eve hustled back downstairs, chest heaving from emotion as much as exertion.

She prayed Carolla was mistaken. With rubbery fingers, Eve logged into their joint checking account. The balance was five hundred dollars. Their savings account was empty.

"Fuck," Eve cried. It took three attempts before she was able to access Martin's retirement account. Zero balance. Moments later, she confirmed his credit cards were maxed, hefty cash advances made in the last week. The airfare purchase had posted the week before. She checked his email, but there were no clues about his plans. Eve leaned back in her chair, abandoning the tablet on her lap. She was numb. "How will I pay bills? I have *nothing* but my piddly checking account."

"He had life insurance, didn't he?" Addy asked after a moment.

Eve straightened, hope surging. "Santa Beatriz Mutual. I'm not thinking straight." She signed into their online account. Her brow furrowed. *Policy surrendered for cash value.* Eve lowered her head to the table.

What will I do?

Eve spent the rest of Saturday and most of Sunday locked in the den with a bottle of booze. She heard the doorbell ring when people stopped by. Drinking whiskey straight from the bottle, she ignored Addy's knocks and the requests to join her for meals.

Bitterness twisted in Eve's belly. Who had Martin been having an affair with? Was it one of their friends? Which one was he planning to run away with? Had they laughed about how easy Eve was to dupe? *Bastard.* She paced the room, her hands balled into fists.

She remembered Martin kissing her hair after gifting her a diamond bracelet and necklace, eager to *show her off* at the club. And then there was the horse for their anniversary kept stabled at a local farm, because he *loved* her. Love? Love wasn't leaving her penniless and broken while he tootled off to an island paradise with his floozy. *He was a liar.*

What was the point of giving her guff about the Westons and the club the other morning if he was leaving? Why bother telling her he no longer wished to be a father? And what if they did have a child? Would he have walked away from his flesh and blood as easily as he was willing to walk away from his wife?

I'm a trusting fool. How could I have been so naïve to not see what was happening under my nose?

Perhaps Eve should've married Jake when he proposed. At least they'd had sexual chemistry. She'd made a mistake trusting the wrong man, believing Martin was a solid choice. That he was a good catch. Eve growled in frustration. Martin was lucky someone else got to him before she did — she was angry enough to kill him herself.

CHAPTER SEVEN

O n Monday, Eve met with Martin's lawyer and made arrangements with a realtor to put the house on the market. Stopping by the farm where her horse was stabled, she spoke to the stable manager. He would organize the horse's sale. Once home, she collapsed into a rocking chair on the porch beside Addy. Carolla called with an update as she poured a glass of iced tea.

"Martin's body will be available for release tomorrow. You'll need to choose a funeral home."

"Who should I call?"

"Any mortuary in town will do. The funeral director will walk you through the process," Carolla assured her.

"Any developments with the investigation?"

"No, sorry. The scene had little forensic evidence, and the security footage was scrambled. I'll keep working, and if there's anything helpful on Martin's technology, the geeks'll find it."

Muttering her thanks, Eve disconnected. She leaned her sore neck against the rocker's headrest for a minute before turning to Addy, her lips screwed into an ugly smile. "I need to find a mortuary."

"I'll do an internet search," Addy said, taking her phone from her pocket. "I know there's one on State Street."

"I'm so damn mad at Martin right now that I don't *care* what happens to his remains." Eve's voice was laced with fury, her fists curling involuntarily. She made a concentrated effort to quell her anger.

Addy put in the call. "They can see us now, if you'd like."

Eve nodded, rising. Good thing she hadn't changed from her navy suit.

Thursday morning, Eve prepared rooms. Lila, Martin's aunt, would arrive that afternoon with Martin's sister, Maureen, and Maureen's children. She was putting fresh towels in the guest bathrooms when the doorbell rang. She hurried to the foyer, smoothing her hair while she walked. Half-expecting a neighbor with a casserole, Eve was surprised to find Jillian Caldwell, Martin's friend and work colleague, at the door.

Once, at a party, Eve had overheard Jillian remark to another woman that Eve was Martin's *starter wife*. Martin disliked drama, so Eve had bitten down a sharp retort rather than make a scene. *Let her make a snide comment today.*

"Coffee," Jillian demanded. Always impeccably dressed, she wore a dove-gray suit and cashmere coat with a wide fur collar that matched her silvery eyes and steel-colored hair. Jillian strode into the kitchen like she was the hostess and Eve the guest. Eve swallowed irritation at the woman's high-handedness. *What is it about her that makes me feel small?*

Jillian sat at the marble-topped kitchen island, watching Eve grind coffee beans. Footsteps approached from the stairway and Addy turned the corner, dressed in a long-sleeved t-shirt and jeans. "I'm sorry. I didn't hear the bell."

"I thought you were sleeping," Eve said. "Coffee?"

"No, luv. We need groceries. I'm off to the market."

After Addy left, Jillian sniffed, "I don't understand how you can be so familiar with the help. It isn't seemly."

"Addy's one of my closest friends."

"Whatever." Jillian waved a dismissive hand.

Ignoring her exasperation, Eve set a cup of coffee in front of Jillian, and asked, "To what do I owe the pleasure of your visit?"

"Have you seen the news?"

She shook her head, battling to keep her emotions under control. Jillian reminded Eve of the big-shouldered broads of 1930s cinema. Brash, ambitious, outspoken. Never pretty. Handsome with a tinge of frigidity. She always suspected Jillian wanted more from Martin than mere friendship. *Was she fucking him?*

Jillian used the remote on the countertop to switch the TV to a cable news network. Eve took a sip of coffee, forgetting to blow on it. It was bitter without sugar and too hot. She swallowed anyway.

A commercial for toilet paper finished and one for cat food began, then a reporter was onscreen, posing outside a familiar concrete and glass building. Eve started. Could there be a break in the case?

"Last week research scientist Dr. Martin Pierce was slain in a mugging here at prestigious Med Tech. Today, astonishing allegations of fraud have surfaced, causing ripples of shock through the industry. Stocks plummet as sources predict—" Eve's vision became hazy. She stumbled into a chair. *Oh my God. Oh my God.*

Jillian squinted at her. "What do you know?"

"N-n-nothing." A wave of dizziness engulfed Eve. She put her head on the table. Jillian swore and abruptly left the room, her heels tapping. She returned with a bottle.

She added a slug of scotch to Eve's cup. "Drink."

By the time Eve finished the coffee, she'd pulled herself together. Her voice trembled when she said, "You're CFO. What do *you* know about the allegations?"

"What do *I know*? I know Martin was a man, and men can be weak creatures prone to making reckless choices." Jillian's gaze swept over her blouse and jeans, stopping at the diamond-encrusted rings on her left hand.

Eve spotted a flash of movement from the corner of her eye.

Someone aimed a camera through the kitchen window, taking their photo. In seconds, Jillian snapped the blinds closed. Splotches of scarlet spread across her cheeks to match the red of her lips. Eve whispered, "This *cannot* be happening."

"Don't you get it? Your precious Martin was a lying sonofabitch."

Hadn't Eve thought the same? If Martin's plan had come to fruition, he'd be sunning on a beach in Cape Azul. *He's left me to clean up his mess.*

"This house, your vacations, the jewelry. Where do you think that kind of money comes from, little girl?"

"I didn't ask for any of it!" Eve ground out through gnashed teeth.

Jillian's mouth set in contempt. "Blonde, tight body. I told him you'd be high maintenance before he married you, but he refused to listen to reason. It's *your* fault he's dead."

Outrage swelled in Eve's chest. Her whole body shook. She stood abruptly, chair tipping. It took all her restraint to keep from striking Jillian. "Get the fuck out of my house."

"You better have a plan for survival. I have a feeling you'll need one." Jillian stalked out. The front door slammed.

This isn't my fault . . . is it?

Bile burned Eve's throat. Clapping her hand over her mouth, she dashed to the bathroom.

CHAPTER EIGHT

Carolla answered on the first ring. "I've been expecting your call."

"This is a nightmare! *What is happening?*" Eve sobbed into the phone.

"The Feds took over the investigation. They think the stabbing's related to the fraud uncovered at the lab."

"There are reporters in my yard."

"I'll send a black and white over to warn them off your property, okay?"

Eve swiped at her nose with an impatient hand. "Okay."

"I suggest you retain a lawyer."

"But I didn't do anything—I don't know anything. I swear." Eve sniffled.

"The report I submitted to the investigators made it abundantly clear I don't believe you're involved in any of this, but you should protect yourself in case they interview you. Get representation."

Eve thanked Carolla and rang off. Blowing her nose, she got a drink of water before dialing Martin's attorney, who she'd seen earlier in the week.

"Sit tight and stay calm. If they want to meet with you, call me, and I'll be there to represent you."

Addy walked through the service door moments later, arms full of grocery bags. Brow knit, she asked, "What's the palaver? News vans are in the driveway."

"Wait 'til you hear the latest." Eve shook her head. "You will *not* believe the morning I've had."

They rushed to prepare appetizers. Eve arranged slices of cheese on a platter. Addy emptied a box of crackers into a basket.

"I have crab puffs ready to go in the oven." Addy drooped against the kitchen counter, mopping the perspiration from her face with a paper towel. "Phew. The carpet needs hoovering yet."

"I'll do it. You're exhausted."

"And you're not?" Addy shooed her up the stairs to shower. "There's a dress on your bed for you to wear."

Forty-five minutes later, the doorbell rang. Eve took a bracing breath before opening the door. Lila Pierce, an ordinarily spry octogenarian known in the family as *the velvet steamroller,* looked withered. She placed her cane on the threshold and extended her papery-skinned cheek for a kiss. Eve, dutiful, kissed her, then ushered the group into the foyer. Five years younger than Martin, Maureen shared his sandy hair and dark blue eyes but carried extra weight around her waist and hips. Brian and Stephanie, Maureen's children, were in their twenties with the same stout figures.

"I can't believe Marty's gone," Maureen blubbered when she hugged Eve. "How can this be happening?"

"I've asked myself the same question," Eve said. *You don't know the half of it, Mo.* "Please, let's sit in the living room."

"Come along, Mom." Stephanie put an arm around Maureen's shoulders.

Eve passed appetizers, and Addy materialized with a tray of tea, wearing the salmon-colored apron she donned when they entertained. Brian mixed a pitcher of martinis at the wet bar. He handed a cocktail to Eve, and asked, "What's with the reporters camped down the road?"

Eve plucked at the skirt of her retro swing dress. *How much should I tell them? Not about Martin's Cape Azul plans, that's for sure.* She murmured, "News broke this morning. The lab's been accused of fraud."

After a beat of silence, Maureen exclaimed, "What? This can't be happening! Thankfully our parents aren't alive to see what's become of poor Marty." Wailing, she buried her face in her hands. Stephanie sat her cup on the table and held her mother.

"Nonsense." Aunt Lila asserted in her strident voice, "Marty didn't have a larcenous bone in his body. I ought to know. I raised the boy. Most likely, the true fraudster killed him to prevent him from going to the authorities."

Eve stayed close-lipped, hoping her face didn't divulge her feelings concerning Martin's treachery. *If it looks like a duck and quacks like a duck.* Bitterness bloomed in her breast, as it often did these days. She pushed it down and finished her drink.

"Maureen made an appointment with a Pastor Clayton from Hope Presbyterian. Tomorrow morning we'll help him write Marty's eulogy." Lila tilted her head toward Eve, manner pointed. "Since Marty didn't belong to a church."

Religion was a sore spot between Martin and his family. A man of science, he was an atheist. Eve was a non-practicing Christian, but to mollify Lila, she'd persuaded Martin to agree to a consecrated wedding ceremony.

Stephanie asked, "Who will sing at the service?"

"Pastor Clayton said he'd find someone from the church choir." Maureen blew her nose with her hankie.

"I should think he'd be accommodating, considering the size of my donation," Lila declared, positioning her cane to rise from her chair. "Evangeline, please chaperone me to my room. I need to rest before dinner."

Eve got Aunt Lila settled in the master bedroom. Maureen and Stephanie had rooms adjacent to Eve's, and Brian was set up in the den where there was a sofa bed. Relieved to shed her hostess role, Eve scurried to her bedroom. As she picked up her phone from the table where it was charging, her heart skipped when she discovered a missed call.

"Life ain't the same with Ol' Hitch outta town, is it, doll?" Hitch asked upon answering. Eve smiled at the sound of her friend's voice. "Sorry I've been incommunicado. Blame a hunky sailor named Stavros."

"Are you in Corfu?"

"Affirmative. Stavros left, so back to reality." Eve heard the tinkle of ice cubes over the line as Hitch made a drink. His flings were a diversion. She knew when he and a lover parted, his depression cycled.

"What time is it there?"

"Late. I gotta hit the sack soon. I have an early flight to Boston. Grandfather Caulfield's ninety-seventh birthday's Saturday, and there's a celebration at his Nob Hill house." She heard Hitch take a long swallow of his drink. "To say I'm dreading it is the understatement of the century."

"Hitch—" Eve's voice broke. She gripped the phone harder to keep it from slipping through her clammy fingers.

"What's wrong?"

Eve told him about Carolla's Friday morning visit to the preschool and Martin's death. The hopelessness over not being able to get ahold of her father was in Eve's voice. She didn't share how Martin had stripped their accounts and planned to flee with an unknown companion—or Jillian's harsh words. Shame like scalding water hit her. *Why do I feel ashamed? I did nothing wrong.* Yet shame was what she felt, along with smoldering anger.

"I'll change my flight and come back to Santa Beatriz."

"You *cannot* miss your grandfather's party."

"You need your BFF."

"I can't ask that of you. It's okay," Eve lied, knowing Hitch's Grandfather was a cranky fellow and difficult to please. "I have Addy, remember?"

"Addy's a peach, but—"

Eve interrupted, "I expect a call from my father any time and he'll offer to come out." *Not that there's enough time for him to get here for the memorial service.*

"If you change your mind . . ."

"I've chartered a yacht," Lila stated, putting her silverware across her half-eaten plate of roast beef.

Eve, mind occupied elsewhere, looked up from her untouched food. "Sorry?"

"I've made plans Saturday morning to scatter Marty's ashes at sea—as there will be no *proper* interment." Disapproval dripped from Lila's voice. Addy came around the table to clear the dishes, clasping Eve's shoulder in encouragement as she walked by.

Fighting back a gush of frustration, Eve remained silent but was unable to keep the pained expression from her face. What would they say if she told them about their beloved Marty's plane tickets to Cape Azul, where he could dodge extradition? She imagined Aunt Lila clutching her pearls and demanding smelling salts. *That wouldn't do at all.* Instead, Eve lifted her glass of wine.

"Come on, Auntie," Brian chided. "We've all heard Martin's views on the subject. He was vocal enough."

"We need to respect *his* wishes," Stephanie said, and Eve gave them a smile of thanks from across the table.

Addy brought a tray with a coffee carafe, but Lila shook her head. "The meal was delicious as ever, Ida. Though I prefer my beef rare."

"Addy," Eve reminded Lila, refilling her wineglass.

"Right. Addy. Delicious, regardless." Lila used her cane to push up from her chair at the head of the table. "Maureen, let's take a stroll around the garden before retiring. Fetch my sweater, will you, Stephanie? It's quite cold tonight."

"Yes, Auntie."

Thankful that the meal was over, Eve sipped her wine.

As she prepared for bed, Eve's father called. She repeated what she'd told Hitch about Martin's death, knowing it wasn't admirable that she was too proud to confide her problems. "As soon as I get the go-ahead from Martin's lawyer, the house'll be listed for sale." Eve sounded glum. She *was* glum. She'd guzzled too much wine, which made her maudlin.

"I'll arrange for a helicopter to bring me to port tomorrow. From there, I'll book a flight to California, my dear," her dad said in his formal way, his voice faint over the poor connection.

"No," Eve protested, alarmed at the cost. "Aren't you due ashore in a couple of days?"

The line crackled. "Yes, but I don't mind cutting my cruise short."

"You saved for three years to take your trip, Dad. And there's no way you can make it in time for the memorial service anyway," Eve argued. "We'll figure out a time for you to visit later."

"Are you sure? You need your father during this trying time."

"I'm sure."

Her dad's voice was laced with apology when he said, "I regret not checking my email sooner."

"I'll be all right, Dad. Really." Eve swallowed the emotion in her throat. It was a pity she couldn't volunteer to pay for his transport, but Martin's cremation had depleted her savings. She now had less than two thousand dollars to her name.

"Perhaps you should return home to Old Hillbury. Do mull it over," Dad said before they hung up.

Eve sat back against the headboard, gnawing her fingernail. It felt selfish to ask others to go to expense and hassle to be with her. She wanted to beg Hitch and her father to come to her. Instead, Eve had pushed them away, reassured them she'd be fine, and isolated herself. *Why? So I can be brave? Suffer alone?*

Perhaps it was from habit as much as pride. Even as a child, she was independent. *Am I too independent?* She'd always been careful to make the right choices, but here she was — a penniless widow. What was the *right* thing to do now?

Eve buried her face into her pillow to drown out the sound of her sobs.

CHAPTER NINE

The dark morning sky guaranteed rain. The wind buffeted the branches on the trees outside Eve's window. It would be a cold, miserable day, unseasonable for September, but fitting for a funeral.

Reaching for the box of tissues on the side table, Eve blew her nose. She'd cried herself to sleep, and between the wine and her tears, her face was puffy. Wally slunk from under the bed, allowing her to scratch his chin. She heard Martin's family in the hall, leaving for their appointment at church. Ears pricked at the unfamiliar sound, Wally dove back under the bed. "Lucky," Eve muttered, yearning to join him.

She opened the closet door to choose an outfit for the memorial service. She often thought of her two lives while dressing for the day. This morning was no different. *Two lives.* Down to earth preschool teacher? Or upper-crust wife? *Was I a fool to think I could live in both worlds?*

Raised in a respectable middle-class neighborhood by her accountant father, Eve often felt woefully inadequate around Martin's wealthy family. Her seething anger at his betrayal had changed her. She was glad to be plain, ordinary Eve, with her humble roots.

Once dressed, she scrounged in the desk drawer for her spare scrapbook and pencils. Eve took a seat on the swivel chair, exhaling. Finding a clean sheet to doodle on was therapeutic, and it relaxed her instantly. *Why didn't I do this sooner?* Her hand moved of its own accord, fingertips rubbing against the thick paper to shade. Soon a man's face looked up at her.

Classically handsome. Square jawed, pale eyed. Black hair slicked back from a strong forehead, nose aquiline.

It was *him*. Jake.

Eve's conscience nagged. It was mere hours until Martin's service. How could she be thinking of Jake now? *Because you always wondered if you'd married the wrong man, and faced with Martin's duplicity, you* know *you did.*

She tore the sheet from the pad, ripping it into tiny pieces. He haunted her, never far from her thoughts. Eve shook her head. It was futile. Most likely, Jake was no longer the bad boy on the motorcycle who drank whiskey and got into bar fights, exciting and dangerous. And able to ignite her desire with one glance. He was probably married with kids, balding and chubby, and working a job he hated. A minivan would've replaced the chopper. *You've romanticized him. He wasn't right for you.*

Eve dawdled in her room, flipping through the sketch pad. The drawings were there somewhere, ones she hadn't shared with anyone. Finding what she sought, Eve stilled, her mouth curving into a sad smile. She traced the lines with a fingertip. The round-cheeked toddler was dark-haired, like his father. How else would the child resemble him? Would he have possessed a similar clever mind, good not only with his hands but with figures, too? Though she'd lost him to soon to know for sure, Eve always thought Jake's baby would've been a boy.

"I didn't have the opportunity to know Martin personally. By the attendance today, I can tell he was a well-liked man." Pastor Clayton, all teeth and polyester, beamed in benevolence at the mourners seated in the neat rows of chairs. His praise of Martin bordered on excessive, and Eve wondered how substantial Lila's donation was. "His aunt told me about his important research. His most successful endeavor was the development and testing of the skin cancer treatment,

Clyanar."

Edgy from her crowd anxiety, Eve couldn't focus on the eulogy. Her attention strayed to the front of the room as if magnetized. Centered on a pedestal, alongside a poster-sized portrait of Martin wearing his lab coat, was an urn. His ashes. *Requiescat in pace, bastard.*

A soloist sang *Amazing Grace.* Lila sniffed daintily into a lace-edged handkerchief. Eve patted her hand. The service was never-ending. *How can this be real life?* At last they formed a receiving line to accept condolences. First in line was Flor Martinez, the mother of one of Eve's former pupils. A soft-spoken woman, she grasped Eve's hands and squeezed. "I'm sorry."

"Thank you." Eve smiled at her. "And thanks for the casserole. Addy said you stopped by when I was out."

"I can never repay you for your generosity when I lost Antonio last March . . . the babysitting, bringing food, diapers." Flor's eyes shone with tears, and Eve felt her throat clog in response.

Eve said, "Give the kids my love." Flor nodded, sniffling, continuing on to Aunt Lila. The receptionist and lab assistants from Med Tech came through the line. Eve thanked them for coming, shook their hands, and accepted their sympathies. Somehow, she said the right words.

"I can't believe Martin's gone," Bianca Weston whispered, air-kissing Eve. Her strong perfume hung suspended in the air like vapor.

Eve suppressed a sneeze. Were Bianca and Martin fooling around?

"Evangeline." Angelica Fellowes wore a somber suit, her ash-blonde bob as smooth as her nipped and tucked face. Her voice was kind, but Eve wondered what she thought, what they all thought. Had they heard the news? Did they think Martin was a crook? Angelica patted Eve's shoulder before moving away. "You poor darling. You have my sympathy."

Eve excused herself and hastened to the bathroom, locking the door. *It's too much.* She desperately wanted to put on her sunglasses and slip into the limo, which was waiting to whisk her away. Hands braced on either side of the sink, she took restorative breaths and evaluated herself in the mirror. Her blue-gray eyes were huge in her ashen face. Her fitted black silk jacket with its oversized pussy bow and matching trousers was chic. She tucked her hair behind her ears, tidying her chignon.

Eve's lips contorted in a ghoulish smile. *I look good – the portrait of a tragic young widow.* Pulling the tube of crimson lipstick from her trouser pocket, she relined her mouth. *Remember the anger. It'll help.* She squared her shoulders before returning to battle.

"Who are those oddballs?" Aunt Lila asked in a low tone, nodding to the far corner of the room. The couple sat at the furthest row of chairs. They made no move to join the receiving line, though it dwindled. The man wore shorts and a Hawaiian shirt, his gray hair in a ponytail. The woman was more noteworthy. Her 1980s style red and black leather ensemble with its deep cut neckline and skimpy skirt was wildly inappropriate for the occasion. Skin orange from spray tanning, her shoulder-length blue-black pageboy was an obvious wig.

As Eve shook the hand of the last mourner, she noticed the couple was gone.

CHAPTER TEN

The sun was bright in the sky, but the sea choppy and the air frigid. Eve shivered and pulled her pashmina wrap tighter, glad she'd worn pants. Lila had chartered a pristine white sixty-seven-foot yacht, and despite the vessel being stabilized, Pastor Clayton grew green around the gills performing his chaplain duties. *Brace yourself and think of the size of that donation, Pastor.* The man's face belied relief when he finished his sermon. Closing the cover over his bible, he invited Stephanie to the bow, raising his voice to be heard over the wind.

Tendrils escaped Stephanie's braid, and she held her hair back with one hand while reading a poem. Eve listened with half-attention. *Will this ever end?* She groaned under her breath, thinking of the reservations for lunch at The Palms. Playing hostess wore thin.

Balancing his weight on the deck, Brian unscrewed the urn's lid. A pair of squawking seagulls landed near where the group sat on benches, their beady eyes alert. Brian tilted the container, and the ashes swirled away. Adjusting her sunglasses, Eve stiffened her spine.

Brian's expression was stoic, but Maureen sobbed, and Lila and Stephanie wiped tears with their handkerchiefs. Misery was contagious. Dry-eyed, Eve coiled the handful of unused tissues she held in her lap. Tears or no tears, she *was* devastated. She mourned the man she once thought she knew, not the loathsome stranger he'd become.

They dropped roses into the sea. The flowers bobbed on

the surface of the gray water before being carried away by the current.

"Good riddance," Eve whispered to the wind when the captain piloted the boat back to shore.

Martin's family left early the next morning and Addy headed to church. Eve ate a solitary breakfast at the kitchen table, lingering over a crossword puzzle. Wally waited at her feet. She held out her spoon and he lapped the remnants of her yogurt.

The mid-morning sunshine and blue sky beckoned. Eve gathered her hair into a ponytail and put on a ratty pair of jeans. When she opened the French doors leading to the terrace, Wally sneaked out. He flopped on the flagstones and rolled onto his back.

Once in her garden, Eve felt like herself for the first time in over a week. With the drama, she'd neglected to water her flowers. The soil was dry and cracked. She pulled out the garden hose, becoming subdued when she realized the oasis wouldn't be hers much longer.

Giving the soil under her persimmon tree a thorough soaking, Eve thought it was a shame she'd no longer be there when it finally bore fruit. Watering her bed of delphinium, she saw Wally rise from where he lay in the sun, his back arching. Hissing, he slinked behind a terra-cotta pot. Eve whirled to find the unusual couple from Martin's memorial service.

The man wore a yellow and orange Hawaiian shirt, a gold chain nestled in his gray chest hair. He was hairy from his ears to his toes, which peeked out from flip flops. The pate of his head was bald and sunburned. What little hair was left on the back of his head was scraped into a thin ponytail.

Eve put a hand to her chest, where her heart thumped.

"I'm Sal." He smiled, but it didn't reach his eyes. Something felt off, but Eve didn't understand her wariness. Sal jerked a thumb to his companion. "This is Iris."

Iris's frame was skeletal except for her massive, enhanced bosom. Dressed in another leather ensemble, Eve noticed the bright blue matched the unnatural hue of her eyes. Today's wig was shoulder-length, with a fringe of bangs. Her stilettos sank in the ground between the flagstones.

"Would you like to sit?" Eve indicated the wrought-iron table and chairs, her intuition urging prudence. She lowered into a chair across from them. "You were at the funeral. Did you know Martin?"

"No." Iris spoke with an unexpected clipped inflection. Russian, Polish, Ukrainian? Eve wasn't sure. "We're friends with someone knowing your husband."

"Mr. Barbee." Sal's wide jester-like smile never slipped. Eve looked back and forth between them, unable to identify her unease. *What is going on?*

"I'm wanting your hair." Iris's neon gaze fixed on the golden ponytail over Eve's shoulder.

Eve touched her hair. "Uh . . . thanks?"

"Iris, now ain't the time." His retort was sharp, but his smile didn't slip. "Your husband borrowed money from Mr. Barbee. We're here to collect."

Fuck. You've got to be kidding. Eve shook her head dumbly, but bile rose in her esophagus.

"Barbee wants his money," Iris snapped.

Eve flinched. *Do not freak out. Stay seated.* Taking a deep breath, she met Iris's eyes. "Where's the paperwork?"

Sal produced a document from his shirt pocket. Eve unfolded it, skimming the text. She gasped, blood draining from her face. It was a copy of a promissory note bearing Martin's signature. Payment of one hundred fifty thousand dollars was due the beginning of October.

"You got money?" Iris sneered.

Be cool. Lie. "I'd have to make arrangements." Eve's voice didn't shake, but her hands sure did. She fastened them in her lap. "You're here to collect? It's not even due yet."

"We're wanting you prepared. Barbee don't do no payment plan," Iris said with a braying laugh ending in a choking cough. Sal tapped his fingers on the table until Iris caught her breath.

"Now, Iris, I'm sure this nice gal understands her husband's debt must be paid in full by the due date. She'd not want to involve others, such as the authorities." Sal directed his words to Iris, but he winked at Eve. "Or friends. Didn't you see Flor Martinez and her kiddos at the Save-a-Bunch yesterday?"

Eve frowned, alarmed at the direction the conversation took. "What do they have to do with anything?"

"Flor suffers terrible last year," Iris tutted.

Sal's smile was saccharine. "The thing about accidents is they're . . . unexpected. I mean, what if something happened to little Antonio? It would shatter Flor."

"What are you saying? Are you actually *threatening* me?" Eve bit the inside of her cheek, tasting blood.

After a moment, the pair stood. Sal said, "*This is an attempt to collect a debt, and any information obtained will be used for that purpose.*"

CHAPTER ELEVEN

Springing from her seat, Eve tiptoed across the flagstones and peered around the corner of the house. A yellow SUV turned left out of the driveway. She grabbed the sheet of paper from the table and stuffed it into her pocket. Scooping up Wally, Eve sprinted to the safety of the house. She set the alarm with tremulous fingers.

In her phone's internet search bar, Eve typed, *Am I responsible for my late husband's debts in California?* With a sinking heart, she read aloud, "In community property states both husband and wife are responsible for debts incurred during the course of the marriage. The surviving spouse assumes the decedent's debt as their own."

Eve did a search of the lender's name, Sylvester Barbee, and sorted through the results. Her stomach made unhappy noises, and she wondered if she'd have to race for the bathroom. *Sly the Skillet* had been brought up on charges over the years, but nothing stuck, because key witnesses recanted, or vanished. The charges ranged from racketeering to money laundering. These days, he was an *entrepreneur* who owned a string of pawnshops.

Sal and Iris gave the impression of being weird, harmless. *If I ever expected a shakedown, I'd have expected two shady mob types in shiny suits, not those two knuckleheads.* But they were menacing. *Dare I risk going to the police?*

Answering on the first ring, Carolla listened as Eve described the visit in a halting voice. "Did they claim to represent Barbee?"

47

"Well, no. They said they were *friends*," Eve admitted.

"Did they threaten violence, use profanity, or imply threats?"

Sal and Iris weren't novice goons. They were wily enough to make their statements ambiguous. Now she felt foolish. "Yeah, they *implied threats.*"

Carolla's measured breathing made her impatience clear. "Bill collectors are intimidating. You probably don't realize since you've never been in that situation before." Eve heard people in the background and Carolla say, "In a second."

"They confronted me in my garden. I mean, coming to *my house*? That's harassment."

"Eve. One visit isn't harassment. Have your lawyer send Barbee a letter stating communication needs to go through him and debts will be settled during probate."

Face flaming, Eve's embarrassment turned to aggravation. "They were at Martin's service. What if they show up again?"

"If you sincerely feel harassed, you can apply for a temporary restraining order through the court, but it can cost several hundred dollars. Do you even know their last names?"

"No." Eve gritted her teeth. *This is beyond pointless.*

"Well, there aren't grounds for police intervention. Your lawyer can make it clear creditors have to wait until Martin's estate is settled. Simple as that." *Sure, simple.*

"All right. I'll have my attorney send a letter. Thanks." *More like thanks for nothin'.*

After leaving a message for Martin's attorney, Eve curled up on the sofa, absently petting Wally when he nudged her hand with his nose. Though her demeanor was tranquil, internally she fumed. She tried to watch a rerun of *The Office*, but it was useless. Switching off the TV, she paced instead. Sal was a caricature from a cheap B movie. And that weirdo, Iris. Eve rolled her eyes. How *dare* they threaten her? Her fists curled. Consumed by a mixture of rage and fear, mid-step, she stopped.

That's it. I'm done dealing with Martin and his shit. I'm getting out of Santa Beatriz. I'll go home to Dad. Hopefully, the house will sell before they track me down. Maybe they'll never find me. Screw Sal and Iris. Screw Barbee, too.

Driving to the nearest office supply store, Eve made sure she wasn't being tailed. She began packing right away. Her focus was on flight. She indiscriminately piled belongings into boxes. When Addy arrived home later that evening, she had finished packing china from the hutch in the dining room and was working on the den.

"In here," Eve yelled, stacking paperwork in a document box.

Addy stayed in the doorway a moment before speaking, purse in her hands. "Hmm. Matters have gone even more pear-shaped since I've been out, haven't they?"

Eve sat back on her heels and wiped the sweat from her forehead. She'd packed nonstop for hours. "Yeah."

"You look woozy. I think you need to eat. Come on."

The concept of food repelled her, but Eve followed. Heart palpitating from low blood sugar, she flopped into a chair. She accepted a steaming mug of tea a few minutes later.

"There's a girl. It's plenty sweet. It'll do you a power of good." Addy assembled chicken salad sandwiches, joining her. Eve lifted a sandwich hesitantly to her lips. Once she'd taken a bite, she realized she was famished. Soon the plate was empty, and they were on their second cuppa. "Now, spill it, pet."

The hollowness in Eve's gut eased, but not the terror. She described the visit, handing Addy the promissory from her pocket. "You know what's strange? Although I'm petrified, I also feel . . . defiant."

"Good. That means your fire's back."

"Since Martin's death, I've been through a full gamut of emotions. From shock to grief, then rage to fear. One thing I know — I can't sit here passively letting stuff happen to me.

I'm *over* feeling powerless."

"Every day there's a new issue, isn't there?" Addy scanned the promissory note, shaking her head. "What I can't understand is Martin accepting these terms. Are you sure this is legitimate?"

"It's his signature." Forehead creasing, Eve asked, "Why would he care about high APRs? He wouldn't be repaying the loan — *I would*."

"Right. But you're broke. They can't get blood from a stone."

Eve volleyed her side-eye. "Have you seen *The Sopranos*, Addy?"

Expression sympathetic, Addy said, "I've got savings. It isn't enough, but it's yours. Perhaps you can ask Hitch to lend the rest."

Eve groaned, contemplating going to Hitch, hat in hand. She thought of the *Ben Franklin* maxim her father was fond of, *the devil wipes his breech with poor folks' pride.* "No, not unless I absolutely have to."

"You need to go to the police if these people are bullying you."

"I did." Eve shot her friend an aggravated look. "Carolla recommended Martin's lawyer send *a letter*."

"You've been packing, so . . ." Addy lifted her mug to drain the last of her tea, eyes shrewd over the rim. "What's the plan?"

"To get away. To evade Martin's creditors. There's no better solution in the short term, but you shouldn't know details. I'm sure Sal and Iris can shake the truth loose from people."

"I'll come along."

"They were clever enough to keep their threats veiled, but I *know* they're dangerous —"

Addy held up a hand. "If they'd confronted me, I'd be in bits, too. Take a breath and tell me your plan."

"What about church? Your cousin in Sausalito?"

"I can visit her, and I can find a new church." Addy clucked, putting her hands on her hips. *"The plan?"*

CHAPTER TWELVE

They toiled late into the night, finishing the rooms on the main floor, then packing their bedrooms. They stacked boxes they wouldn't take in the garage, staging the house for real estate showings. Eve filled her luggage with clothes and shoes, placing the rest in garbage bags. It didn't take long to fill her SUV.

"I'll rent a cargo trailer tomorrow, under my name." Addy pushed her chestnut brown hair back from her flushed face. "We'd better exercise caution, don't you think?"

Addy took water from the fridge. As Eve drank, she squinted at the clock on the microwave, her vision blurry. Putting her empty bottle on the counter, she said, "We need sleep."

The insistent pealing of the doorbell woke them mid-morning. In robes, hair disheveled, they met in the foyer. Skin blanching white, Addy whispered, "I peeped out the kitchen window . . . it's two men, one tall and scary and one in a horrid Hawaiian shirt."

Eve was glad the solid carved wood door concealed them. Fists pounded, the door bouncing against the jamb. She pulled Addy from the foyer toward the dining room.

"Evie," Addy hissed. A swarthy man was outside the French doors. He hadn't seen them. He was on the phone. Eve put a finger to her lips and, out of his line of sight, sidled into the dining room along the wall. She wanted to hear his conversation.

52

"Iris, I told you to leave Pierce to me. You're great with the guys, but upper-class broads need soft cajoling." His voice was as big as his frame and totally frightening. When he tried the doorknob, Eve suppressed a squeak of alarm, clapping a hand against her mouth.

"She must be out. I don't wanna trip the security system." He paused, listening to the voice on the phone. "Rich bitches can always scrounge up dough if they gotta. She's probably at the bank now." He chuckled. "Barbee'll have payment by the first. I'll be back tomorrow for assurances. Hold off a minute before implementing Plan B."

Footsteps receding, he left via the flagstone path. Eve bent to fight the encroaching blackness making her eyesight swim. *Plan B? What was Plan B? A kneecapping?*

Addy clutched her arm, her voice reedy. "Should we call the police?"

"Why bother? We're on our own."

An hour later, when Eve opened the front door to check the mailbox, she found a naked doll lying on the mat, the scalp conspicuously missing. Quickly glancing around the yard, she slammed and locked the door, leaving the *calling card* where it lay.

Driving Addy's sedan to Crown Federal, Eve picked at a hangnail, cursing when she made herself bleed. Grabbing a tissue from the box on the dash, she wound it around her finger, impatience etching her brow. With little sleep, she was fueled by caffeine. She touched the key in her trouser pocket. She'd come across it in Martin's desk. It unlocked the safe deposit box they rented years earlier, at his insistence.

At a red light, Eve put on her sunglasses, checking the traffic for any sign of a tail. She vibrated with nervy energy, fingers drumming on the steering wheel while she waited for a pickup to leave a parking spot in the crowded lot. Claiming the space, Eve felt a rush of victory. *So far, so good.*

The vault was beyond the lobby. Tiny and fusty, the room made her nose twitch. The manager put in her key and waited for Eve to insert hers in the lock below. At last, she was alone in the vault with the box. Long and shallow, it was perhaps two inches high and a foot long. She laid a hand on the hinged cover. *Please, Lord, prove I was right to bring my big purse. Let there be something good in here. Please don't let it be empty.* It wasn't. Eve gulped.

There were gold cocktail rings set with gemstones, a diamond tennis bracelet, brooches and earrings, four necklaces with glittering pendants, and a strand of pearls with a diamond clasp. Dazzled, Eve picked up the bracelet and tested its weight in the palm of her hand. Under the fluorescent lights, the diamonds sparkled. No paste copies, they were quality pieces, worth a small fortune. Were they Pierce family heirlooms? If so, would Aunt Lila demand their return?

With sweaty, shaking hands, Eve stowed the jewelry in her purse and pushed the metal box back in its slot. She wiped her hands on the seat of her pants before exiting the vault. Putting her sunglasses on and tightening the sash of her coat, Eve strode through the bank, poker-faced. Her heart thudding against her sternum, she sped home. When the garage door rumbled closed behind her, she finally breathed.

CHAPTER THIRTEEN

Through the kitchen window, Eve saw Addy park the SUV, a rented cargo trailer hitched to it. She tied the garbage bag of perishables from the fridge and freezer and disabled the alarm. Before taking the bag to the bin at the end of the drive, Eve scanned the yard.

Addy met her, holding a sheet of paper and looking troubled.

The message was handwritten in red ink. *You'll pay, bitch.*

"Crap." Eve worked the back of her neck with her hand.

"What shall we do?"

Gritting her teeth, Eve took the note, crumpling it. "Pack and get the fuck out of here."

For two hours, they darted from the house to the trailer. By the time they finished, they were drenched with perspiration. Addy pushed her hair back from her face and wiped the moisture from her lip with the sleeve of her t-shirt. "Walk through the house for anything we may have missed, pet."

As they cruised down 101 through Thousand Oaks, Wally made his discontent clear with throaty yowls from his carrier in the backseat. Flapping her hands in the air, Addy declared, "I can't take any more of that moggy yelping."

Unbuckling her seatbelt, Addy balanced her ample rump against the dashboard and leaned into the backseat. Wally in her arms, she turned and slid back into her seat. Wally rubbed his whiskers against Addy's hand and purred.

"Make sure he doesn't jump down by the gas pedal," Eve

cautioned, sweeping a tuft of fur from her shirt.

Addy studied the GPS and groaned. "Forty-one hours until we make it to Old Hillbury."

"We'll drive in shifts. You know I love your stories of growing up in England. Why don't you share some to pass the time?"

"I don't want you falling asleep at the wheel listening to my tiresome yarns," Addy said. "I want to hear some of *your* stories. You never say much about your mother. Why?"

"Not much to say. She died in a car accident when I was a toddler. I don't remember her." Eve's smile was tinged with regret.

"How tragic."

"I coped. I always felt worse for my father than myself. I know he was lonely when I was a child." Eve lifted a pragmatic shoulder and changed the subject. "Wasn't your dad a milkman?"

"Yes, he was. He was a gigantic man with a personality to match. I take after him." Addy grimaced.

Eve glanced away from the road for a second at Addy's creamy complexion and button nose. She was rotund but hardly ugly. "I'll bet you had plenty of boyfriends in school."

"Oh, some." Addy's brown eyes twinkled. "Did I tell you Gerald from church asked me on a date last month?"

"Isn't he in his seventies?" Eve shook her head. "You need a man your own age, Addy."

"The men my age want forty-year-olds. Reg was my soulmate. No man seems good enough in comparison."

"He was a war hero." Eve clasped her friend's hand.

Addy smiled. "There are worse legacies, I suppose."

"What's Martin's legacy?" Eve snorted. "Liar? Crook? That wasn't who I married."

"He had me hoodwinked, too. I thought your marriage was solid. I never even heard you two fight."

"Because I kept my mouth shut and did what Martin wanted." Eve confessed, "I haven't been happy for a long time. Our relationship had turned stale."

"Not like with *him*? Your old flame?"

"You're making me regret telling you about him." Eve chuckled, glad her inborn sense of discretion prevented her from oversharing.

"Sometimes, you're too reticent. Don't you trust *me*?"

"Of course, I do. You and Hitch are my best friends. Look, there wasn't any future with Jake. I have regrets, but why bother wasting time thinking about the past?"

"Because you're going home. What if you run into him?"

Eve kept her voice light. "Who knows if he's still in town?"

Later, after Addy fell asleep, with just the radio to keep her company, Eve's thoughts strayed. *What if Jake is still in town?*

CHAPTER FOURTEEN

Eleven Years Earlier

"Come on, Eve," Suzanne cajoled. "How often does the gang get together these days?"

Amber put her arm around Eve. "With everyone home for Thanksgiving, this is our chance."

Eve looked back and forth between her friends, resolve fading. Suzanne almost levitated with expectation and Amber gave her an imploring smile. Eve put her hands up. "You win. I guess I can work on my research paper tomorrow."

"We're gonna have so much fun. Tonight's the night." Suzanne did a shimmy. "I'm gonna wear a slutty dress."

Eve shook her head. Suzanne was on her way to the Navy classifying her as a friendly port. "Where are we going?"

Amber lifted an eyebrow. "The Roadhouse."

"Are you kidding?" Eve's face showed her incredulity, and her friends found it hilarious. She shot them a glare. On the wrong side of the tracks, the club had a reputation, and it wasn't a good one. Subject to frequent drug raids, it catered to a rough crowd. Her father would kill her if he knew.

"You need to walk on the wild side once in a while, Evita," Suzanne scolded, opening the door to her closet. "Like I do."

"How will we get in? They check ID, don't they?"

"Sean knows the bouncer." Amber pawed through her overnight bag and drew out a red body con dress with peek-aboo panels. "I'm wearing this. What do you think, Eve?"

"That you need a psychiatrist," Eve deadpanned. "At least wear a jacket."

"I know you're freaking out, but Sean and Steve will take care of us. We'll be fine. Here, Amber, this'll be amazing with your dress." Suzanne chucked over a military-style bolero.

Amber stripped off her clothes and yanked the dress down her curves. Checking herself in the dresser mirror, she cautioned, "No jeans allowed tonight, Eve."

"You got a hot body," Suzanne told her, waving a camisole and a miniskirt. "Why not show it for once?"

"Yeah, right. It's freezing out. I'm not wearing *that*," Eve scoffed, thumbing through the closet.

Suzanne was at her elbow. "I have something for ya."

"I'm trembling with anticipation."

Suzanne put a palm to her hip. "Do I detect a note of sarcasm, Eve?"

A note? More like a symphony.

Eve heard the music pumping when she and her friends exited Steve's antiquated van. Before continuing to the nondescript cinderblock building with the unlikely moniker of *The Roadhouse*, they waited for him to lock the vehicle.

"I thought a roadhouse was a biker bar off a highway, not a neo-metal club in the warehouse district." Eve avoided the cracks like spiders' webs on the sidewalk. She wore sky-high open-toed pumps and didn't want to face-plant.

"Cool choppers," Sean enthused when they passed rows of bikes crammed in a parking lot.

A cat streaked across her path, and Eve stifled a shriek. Embarrassment heated her face. *Ugh, grow up.* She was freezing in her scoop-necked striped shirt and black pencil skirt. Suzanne insisted the pin-up look was all the rage. Curling Eve's hair and lining her lips in scarlet, Suzanne had said, "Channel *Wanda Woodward* from *Crybaby*. You need some of her sass!"

Sean and the beefy bouncer did a complicated routine of

handshaking and fist bumping. Once in the building, Eve ascertained the unmistakable fragrance of weed and the saccharine stink of old spilled liquor. The place throbbed with too-loud music. On a stage directly ahead, a band dressed head to toe in black performed, the lead singer screaming into the microphone. Eve cringed while trailing behind her friends.

Suzanne furnished a plastic cup of beer and Eve took a mouthful, nose wrinkling. It was lukewarm and flat. Sean and Steve did shots of cheap rotgut. Amber held a handful of pastel-colored pills. Eve refused with a shake of her head. *What am I doing here? This isn't my scene.*

Eve tossed the beer in the trash as the crowd swallowed her friends. She leaned against the wall. Sentience raised the hairs on the back of her neck. *Am I being watched?* Her gaze roamed until she found her quarry. *Oh, hello, hottie.*

He lounged against the bar, tall, broad-shouldered, wearing jeans and a motorcycle jacket. He held a beer bottle by the neck. Posture relaxed, he stared at her with lazy insolence. It was as if he didn't care that Eve caught him. *No, he likes that I know he's watching.* His easy confidence intrigued her. She threw him what she hoped was a come-hither expression, then looked away, heart hammering. She glimpsed back at him under her lashes, biting her lower lip. His mouth curved in a half-smile. Was that a dimple in his cheek? *Oh, shit. I'm in trouble.*

Arousal tugged. She squirmed, and his smile deepened like he discerned his effect on her. A flush spread over her from the roots of her hair to the tips of her toes, leaving Eve breathless. She'd never experienced anything like it.

"C'mon," Suzanne said, suddenly beside her, pulling her to the dancefloor. Eve's mind was on Hottie at the bar. Why hadn't he joined her? She wondered if he wanted her to go to him. He must know she would.

"I want you to dance with me." A hand fastened on her forearm, dragging her from Suzanne, who now grated against some rando. Eve shook her head at the heavily tattooed man in leather vest and chaps. His eyes were dilated to black pools. She tried in vain to signal Suzanne, then sought Steve or Sean, but they were gone. *Great. Thanks a lot, guys.*

"Let go, creep!" Fear rose in Eve's chest. Struggling to extricate her arm, Eve felt the biker's grip tighten. He laughed at her feeble kicks at his shins. Creep was wrenched away, and Eve was released, scrambling to stay upright. Hottie punched Creep in the jaw. Creep dropped like a sack of potatoes, and Hottie loomed over him, his expression dark.

When Creep remained prone, Hottie turned to her, nostrils flaring. The unleashed violence stirred something in Eve she didn't understand — something primal. She absently massaged her sore arm, holding Hottie's gaze. He was dangerous and sexy. *Is he a knight in shining armor, or an asshole in aluminum foil?*

Drawn to him, Eve took his hand without hesitation when he held it out. It engulfed hers, sending a jolt of electricity up her arm and through her body. He pushed through the crowd, leading her to the dirt parking lot.

"I'm Jake." His voice was deep and he towered over her. She brazenly tipped her head back to meet the fire of his green eyes. Her body was brought to life, humming with sexual awareness, skintight. She'd never felt a craving *need* like this before. Now, she could focus on little else.

"Evangeline — Eve," she said huskily.

He lit a cigarette, shielding the match from the wind, the flame illuminating his classically handsome profile. He took a drag and exhaled, offering her the cigarette. Tongue-tied, she shook her head. Eve's body burned. His manner promised *something,* and she wanted it. She ground her thighs together, but the ache increased until it was unbearable. Jake flicked the cigarette butt into the gutter.

Compelled by a sensation she didn't understand, Eve

reached up to bury a hand in the hair at the nape of his neck. She guided his head to hers. When their lips met, she lost herself in him. He was intoxicating, tasting of beer and heat. Jake backed her against the rough cinderblock of the building, his tongue entangling hers.

When he drew away, they were both panting. Eve felt the rapid beat of his heart through his shirt where her palm rested on his chest. He leaned his forehead to hers until they caught their breath, his hand under her blouse, fingers caressing her ribcage. He ran the tip of his index finger along the waistband of her skirt, making Eve shiver.

"Wanna get out of here, Evangeline?"

CHAPTER FIFTEEN

Present Day

After several days of travel, Eve and Addy closed in on their destination. Friday night, they checked into a hotel an exit off the New Jersey Turnpike to sleep before completing the final leg of their trek. By eight AM they were up and showered, sipping coffee from the carafe in their room. Not wanting to waste time stopping at a diner for breakfast, they chose a doughnut from the continental breakfast bar when they checked out.

Mid-morning, Eve navigated through the traffic on the Tappan Zee Bridge, entering Old Hillbury city limits. Addy surveyed her surroundings, eyes inquisitive. "What's this river?"

"The Hudson. We're fifteen minutes from Dad's. Finally."

"How far is Manhattan? I always wanted to see the Statue of Liberty."

"An hour by train." Eve smiled at Addy's enthusiasm, finding it catching. She turned left on Elmwood and Addy pointed to a hand-painted sign. *Welcome to Rockwater Neighborhood.*

"You've mentioned Rockwater."

Mature trees lined the quiet streets. Houses were a mixture of early to mid-1900s Colonial, Tudor, and Cape Cod-style homes with single car garages. American flags were displayed by front doors or mounted on flagpoles in neatly mowed yards. Though it was comprised mainly of pensioners now, Eve saw evidence of younger families by the tricycles in driveways and swing sets in backyards.

"Rockwater's pretty as a postcard," Addy remarked in her chatty way. "Where are *Opie* and *Aunt Bee*?"

Turning onto Yankee Drive, Eve laughed, but Addy was right. It was idyllic. Approaching her father's beige stucco Tudor with its stone accents and mullioned windows, she slowed. The manicured lawn was landscaped with hostas and shrubs. During her last visit, Eve had painted the door red and planted geraniums in pots on the front steps. "Here we are."

"How charming," Addy said as Eve carefully backed the trailer into the paver driveway. "Why don't you greet your father and I'll put Wally on his leash for a wander?"

Hearing his name from the backseat, Wally chirped, arching in a luxurious stretch. Eve turned off the ignition. "Thanks. I'll come get you."

Eve grabbed her purse from the center console and fished for her key to the front door. She made her way across the yard, a breeze lifting her hair. Unlocking the door, Eve asked, "Dad?"

He poked his head from the arched entryway of the living room, his smile warm. Stepping in the foyer, he held out his arms. "Welcome home."

Her father was a reserved man, and his hugs were stiff, but Eve clung to him. She blinked back tears when she pulled away and considered him. He wore khaki slacks and a sweater, his casual at-home uniform. He was suntanned from his cruise, and his golden hair was cut in its usual crew-cut style. "Dad, you look great."

"You look pallid and wearied. Where's your friend?"

"Walking Wally."

"Come have a drink." In the cheerful yellow kitchen, her

dad poured Eve a glass of lemonade from the pitcher on the enamel-top table. "How are you coping, my dear?"

Eve smiled. When others heard the way he addressed her, they thought it prim, but to her, it was endearing. She put her hand in his and exhaled. "I'm glad to be home."

"The investigators still haven't found who's responsible for Martin's death?"

Eve sighed. "It's my understanding there wasn't much evidence."

"Losing a spouse is difficult enough—but to murder. That adds a gruesome dimension."

Eve flinched at *murder* but nodded. She bit her lip, admitting, "There's a twist. The Feds are investigating allegations of misconduct at Med Tech."

"What nature of misconduct?" He tilted his head, his blue-gray eyes narrowing.

"I'm not exactly sure." A flush bloomed on her cheeks, but Eve ignored it. *I did nothing wrong!* "I'm waiting to see if the investigators contact me."

"Thank the Lord you hadn't anything to do with Martin's lab." He squeezed her hand. "Do you need a lawyer? I can retain one."

She shook her head. "Dad, it turns out Martin racked up more debts than I originally thought."

"Oh, no." Her dad's eyes softened. "He was always so steady and reliable. It makes one question whether the misconduct, debts, and his death are connected, doesn't it?"

"It sure does." Eve laughed without humor. "I wonder if the truth will ever come out."

Dad's mouth turned down. "You know Martin loved you. Never in a million years would he have wanted to hurt you."

Yeah, well, you don't know about the humiliation of Cape Azul, Dad. She changed the subject. "I've got to find a job—fast."

"I can help with finances."

"No," Eve said firmly. She stood and bent to kiss her

father's cheek. "Letting Addy and me stay here is help enough. I'll go get her so you can meet."

She watched with curiosity as her father and Addy sized each other up. An odd tension filled the air. Dad introduced himself, bowing and tendering his hand to Addy, which was his way. The ceremony seemed to amuse Addy. She sniggered, which made Eve's taciturn father bristle ever so slightly. To those who didn't know him, it would go unnoticed, but Eve could tell by the set of his lips and ramrod straight deportment that Addy offended him.

"I'm peckish." Addy rifled through the refrigerator. "Let's have a sarnie before unpacking."

Short, plump Addy moved pots and pans from the cabinet by the sink to the one by the stove and reorganized the refrigerator. As she sniffed a takeout container of Chinese, Addy's nose scrunched. She dumped it, with flourish, in the trash. If she noticed the frown of displeasure on Dad's face, she didn't show it. Dicing onion and celery, Addy opened cans of tuna to mix with mayo. She pronounced over her shoulder, "Slim pickings in this house. Tomorrow I shall go to the market to get some proper food in."

Entertained by the expressions flitting across her father's face, Eve noted surprise, irritation, and fascination. Addy placed plates of crustless sandwiches cut into orderly triangles on the table. Settling into a chair, she lifted a triangle as Dad clamped his meerschaum pipe between his teeth. The familiar mellow scent of tobacco tickled Eve's nose. To her, the fragrance was a remembrance of her youth, but Addy put her sandwich down, glowering in Dad's direction. Not saying a word, he left the room.

"Poor manners for someone toffee-nosed," Addy remarked before taking a hearty bite.

CHAPTER SIXTEEN

After lunch, Eve checked on Wally. Cowering behind the living room sofa, he hugged the wall. His eyes were accusatory. Emitting a low cry somewhere between a whimper and a growl, Wally apparently said *Move along, sis. I've had enough for today.*

When Eve came into the kitchen, she found Addy wiping the counters. "How about a tour of the house?"

In the dining room, Addy pointed to the paneled wall opposite the glass doors leading to the terrace. "What's this?"

"*The Wall of Eve*. I didn't want my friends to see it when I was a teenager—I was embarrassed. Now, I understand. This is Dad's way of expressing how much he loves me."

"My goodness, what chubby cheeks." Addy nodded to toddler-aged Eve wearing a red sweater and taking a bite from a juicy apple, her blonde hair wind-tossed. She paused at each photo—Eve in a tutu at a recital. Playing in the leaves in the yard, Eve caught in joyful mid-laugh. Eve with a fishing pole, her fair brow furrowed in concentration as she reeled a fish. Addy lobbed her a cynical look. "*Your father* took these?"

"Yeah. And developed them. He's got a darkroom in the basement."

"Hmm."

"Rendered speechless? That's a first," Eve teased. She gestured to her dad's bedroom and bathroom at the back of the house before ushering Addy up the stairs to the two rooms tucked under the eaves. The guest bedroom faced the street, and her father, in his considerate way, had made up the wrought iron bed with clean linens and a blue quilt.

"How twee." Addy put her hands on her hips. A diminutive wardrobe was built into the wall by the twin-size bed, and there was an antique lamp on a pie-crust table. "I don't need much space."

Indicating a door, Eve said, "There's a Jack and Jill bathroom there."

"Let me peek at your room."

Eve crossed the hall and opened the door to her bedroom. The walls were papered in lavender flowers, a matching comforter on the twin-sized canopy bed. A white desk was beside a window overlooking the backyard.

"Quaint."

"That's realtor-ese for minuscule," Eve said dryly. "I don't feel like unloading the trailer yet. Let's sit outside."

She poured lemonade while Addy settled on the wicker settee, kicking off her sandals. Accepting her glass, Addy said, "There won't be many more days this pleasant. We better relish it while we can."

Eve tilted her head to a sugar maple in the neighbor's yard. "I know. The leaves are already turning."

"I recognize that tree from the photos of you when you were little."

"Ah, those were the days," Eve mused, tucking her feet beneath her, tone wistful. "Life sure was uncomplicated then."

Addy's keen gaze held hers, and she leaned over to pat Eve's knee. "This is a whole new beginning for both of us."

The fresh green smell of the backyard brought Eve back to the many hours she'd played there as a child. She nodded to the shed in the corner of the fenced yard. "I used to have a playhouse there. Dad built it for me. It was purple with white shutters and gingerbread trim."

"*Your father* built it?"

Eve laughed at her tone. "Yes. Why not?"

"He doesn't seem the type."

"Maybe not," Eve conceded. "But every summer we'd camp and fish and take nature hikes. He even led my *Girl Scout* troop. When you get to know him, you'll see—he's a marshmallow."

"Hmm." Addy put her empty glass on the table. "We'd better unpack."

"Dad will help."

CHAPTER SEVENTEEN

A s October approached, all was quiet. Remaining vigilant for Sal and Iris, Eve began to think she'd escaped them. By degrees, her anxiety waned as she realized she was safe to move about freely.

Rising from her childhood desk, Eve stood at the window, pulling her cardigan sweater tighter. The morning had been blustery, a thin layer of frost blanketing the lawn. Frost melting, the chill in the air lingered the rest of the day. Eve's stomach grumbled. She didn't need to check the clock to know it was almost dinnertime.

Voices raised in argument floated up the stairs. *Dad's home. What are he and Addy bickering about now?* She hurried downstairs. Her father's face was purple. Addy's eyes snapped fire. Hands on her hips, she looked like an angry little hen. A chuckle burbled from Eve's lips.

Her father turned to her, sputtering with indignation. "She threw away a whole stack of my magazines. When will she kindly keep out of my personal belongings? Isn't it enough she's reorganized this whole house?"

"Those magazines were months old," Addy retorted. "If you've not read them yet, I daresay you shan't!"

"I'm going for a walk," Eve told them, then muttered under her breath, "Off a damn cliff . . . in hopes of escaping you two." She took her coat and scarf from the closet, but Dad and Addy didn't seem to care. They continued quarreling.

Strolling around the block, Eve wondered if she should sell some jewelry and lease an apartment. Her father clearly irritated the usually easy-going Addy. She often complained bitterly about his strait-laced ways, calling him a *toff* under her breath. Eve stayed out of it, figuring they were adults, but she was mighty sick of their squabbling.

Nose lifting at the drifting smell of wood smoke in the crisp air, she took in the happy little homes and the orderly yards, inhaling. Across the street, children played tag. Down the avenue, a mother hollered to her child for dinner. The normalcy of the scene was comforting, making Eve's problems distant and unimportant.

By the time she came back, the tension in the air had disintegrated. Her father was in his club chair with his favorite magazine, a hot toddy in hand. Addy posed demurely on the sofa, knitting project in her lap. The only sound was the clicking of her knitting needles and the crackling of the fire in the grate.

"Everything okay in no man's land?" Eve cautiously asked after hanging her coat in the closet. "Did you manage a cease-fire?"

"We're fine, pet. Dinner in ten minutes."

"We're having chateaubriand," her father said over his magazine.

The way to a man's heart.

At the dinner table, Addy put meat on Eve's plate. "Here's a well-done piece. You're pensive. No luck job hunting?"

Eve laughed. "You made finding a job look easy, Addy."

"I was lucky to find the teacher's aide position at Sycamore Avenue School," Addy said. "What have you applied for?"

"Directorships, but I haven't had any callbacks. I guess I don't have enough administrative experience to stand out among the other applicants. I'll have to settle for another teaching position."

"That reminds me." Her father cleared his throat. "Mrs. Davenport from HR mentioned openings at the daycare center. You can go in tomorrow morning for an interview."

"Daycare? I thought you worked for a construction company, Dad."

"I work at Consolidated's corporate headquarters. They launched a daycare last year for employees."

"Oh." Eve twirled her wineglass, pondering. "But, how does HR know your daughter's looking for work?"

He swallowed, shrugging. "I must've mentioned in passing. What the exact position is, I'm not sure. You'll learn more tomorrow."

"So, is it a construction company, Jim?" Addy asked.

"Holding company. Consolidated buys the stock of struggling construction companies and controls the company after the takeover."

"Takeover? As in hostile?" Addy asked. "Ooh, cutthroat."

Dad agreed. "Takeovers *can* be. The company formed eight years ago. Carter's a gifted businessman for someone young. Ruthless when needed, but gifted."

"*Ruthless?*" Eve pulled a face. "Yikes. I'm not sure I'd mesh with a boss like that. Maybe I'll pass."

"Where's your confidence?" Addy chided.

"Addy's right. You're well-qualified and bright. You'll be fine."

Eve put up her hands in surrender. "All right. You've convinced me. I'll give it a shot."

Addy winked at Dad. "There's apple strudel for dessert."

CHAPTER EIGHTEEN

Hair wet from a shower, Eve opened her closet and rummaged for an interview-worthy outfit. Wally supervised. Pulling a sweater dress out and laying it across her bed, she foraged through her chest of drawers for matching tights. Nervous butterflies fluttered in her stomach while she put on makeup.

Once dressed, Eve surveyed herself critically in the long mirror on the back of the bathroom door. The gray dress, tights, and suede booties were good, but she needed to break up the monochromatic color scheme. Hauling a cardboard box from the top of the closet, she seized a patterned scarf to loop around her neck. She blew Wally a goodbye kiss when she left.

Using her GPS, Eve easily found the contemporary glass structure in downtown Old Hillbury. After parking in the ramp attached to the building, she checked the map in the stairwell. She shivered and tightened the sash of her raincoat. *Is it nerves or the cold?* At ground level, the sidewalk wrapped around the building. Eve followed it until she was at the main entrance. Taking a deep breath, she pulled the doors open, stepping into the marble lobby.

An arrangement of leather furniture was in front of a fireplace. Flowers flanked a wet bar with coffee and pastries. A splashy abstract painting hung above the fireplace. Eve spotted security cameras in the corners of the lobby and the guard at his post by the bank of elevators. A well-groomed Asian woman in a conservative suit sat behind a sleek glass reception desk, answering calls via headset. She held up a manicured finger, giving Eve a smile. Ending the call, she asked, "How may I help?"

"I have an interview with Mrs. Davenport."

"May I see ID?" After Eve showed her driver's license, the receptionist paged Mrs. Davenport. "It'll be a few minutes. Help yourself to a pastry."

Eve's stomach growled. Needing a sugar rush, she poured a cup of coffee and added a healthy dose of cream and sweetener before choosing a raspberry Danish. Eve was chewing the last bit of her breakfast when a willowy black woman appeared, extending her hand in greeting. "I'm Gwendolyn Davenport, Evangeline."

"Eve, please." Hoping she didn't have any remnants of Danish on her face, Eve shook hands. The middle-aged woman wore a long print dress, chunky silver jewelry, and clogs. Her dreadlocked hair was piled high on her head, accentuating the swan-like curve of her neck. The effect was glamorous.

"And call me Wendy. Everyone does. Let's go up to my office." Preceding Eve past the guard to the staff elevator, she swiped a key card. Wendy explained as the door slid open, "We're security conscious, and protocols are strict. Our computer mainframe and servers are in this building."

The pastry settled like a stone in the pit of Eve's stomach when she took a seat in Wendy's office. Pulling a tablet from a desk drawer, Wendy said, "The application's on here. Did you bring your resume?"

Eve nodded, removing an envelope from her purse. She handed it to Wendy in exchange for the tablet. Filling out the application, she asked, "Can you tell me about the position? My father didn't know the details."

"We have multiple openings." Wendy examined the resume. Eve felt the woman's scrutiny while she finished the form. "You completed your bachelor's in education last year. Why not teach school-age children?"

"I adore kids of all ages, but have more experience with younger students." Eve confided, "I'm seeking a director-ship."

"I see."

"I'm okay with teaching, if that's all you have available," Eve assured her. "But I need full-time employment."

"I think we can work something out." Wendy's smile was amiable when she mentioned compensation far more than Eve expected. "Follow me. I'll show you around the center."

As she trailed Wendy, Eve's step was light. She was amazed at how her fortune seemed to be turning. *About bloody time.* On the ground floor of the building, the daycare was in a bright, light-filled atrium, the playground visible through the windows.

"Parents leave their children on their way into the office, and fetch them on their way home." Wendy pointed to a door down a hall. "A nap room's through there, and an indoor gymnasium's on the other side of the building."

The well-equipped space was divided into zones. There was a kitchenette with tables and chairs for lunch and art pro-jects, areas for story time and quiet play, and cubbies with hooks for coats. Eve took in the shelves of educational toys and puzzles, the play area with a mini kitchenette, and child-sized furniture. *They spared no expense here.*

"Delightful," Eve said.

Wendy preened. "Thanks. I set it up."

A ginger-haired child presented a play telephone. Eve grinned, bending and pretending to answer it. Once Eve gave the phone back and the little girl wandered away, she told Wendy, "No matter how badass you think you are, when a toddler gives you a play phone, you answer it."

Wendy chuckled. "Eve, I think you're what we're looking

for in a director."

"Really?" Eve's mouth curved into a smile.

"Can you start tomorrow?"

CHAPTER NINETEEN

October first came and went without a hiccup. Eve loved her new job. She wrote lesson plans and conducted morning and afternoon circle, where she read stories and sang with the kids after snack-time. While the teachers oversaw activities in the playground or gym, Eve performed administrative duties. The yearly licensing inspection was due in November, and she was determined to pass it with flying colors.

At the end of October, Eve was in the staff canteen when she received a call from Ellen Sanders, the listing agent at Santa Beatriz Realty. Eve had e-signed paperwork the day before to put the house on the market and the listing went live that morning.

Ellen's voice was thick with apology. "I'm sorry to be the bearer of bad news. I brought clients in for a showing and discovered the house vandalized."

"What? The house was vandalized?" Eve exclaimed, drawing attention from a man at a nearby table. She lowered her voice. "What happened?"

"The vandals broke through the doors in the dining room. Sofa cushions and mattresses were cut open."

"I sense hesitation. What else?"

"They left a nasty message in red spray paint on the foyer wall. I can send photos via text, if you want to see the damage."

"No," Eve blurted. *No, I do not want to see Barbee's handiwork.* Icy fingers of dread gripped her throat. "I must've forgotten to set the alarm when I left. Damn. Can you arrange clean up and repairs and invoice me?"

"Certainly."

After the realtor rang off, she gathered her lunch and pitched it in the trash. When she'd sat to eat, Eve had been starving. She'd helped with the Halloween party that morning and hadn't had time for breakfast. Now, she couldn't face food. Returning to her office off of the atrium, she sat with her head in hands. She'd have to scrounge money to pay for the repairs. And the break-in was a stark reminder Barbee hadn't forgotten about her. A visit from Sal and Iris seemed imminent. The serenity Eve had relished over the last weeks vaporized.

She chewed the inside of her cheek. The familiar edginess returned. She had to move. The clock showed that twenty minutes remained of her break. Slipping into her pumpkin-colored peacoat, Eve buttoned it with restless fingers.

Winding the scarf Addy had knit for her around her neck, Eve walked around the campus. The brisk air was invigorating, untangling her mind. Kicking acorns from her path with more force than necessary, she liked the crunching sound of the leaves under her leather boots. Overcast and gray, with the promise of rain, it was like Halloweens of her childhood and fit her gloomy mood.

The rest of the day moved at a glacial pace. All Eve wanted was a cup of tea and a hot bath. Wendy knocked on the door of her office as she prepared to leave at five. "Glad I caught you. The boss wants to see you. His office is on the top floor."

Eve bit back irritation. *I've worked here a month. Why today?* "I use the staff elevator?"

"Yes. His assistant left for the day. Knock on the double doors behind her desk."

Shucking her coat, Eve opened a mirrored compact. She applied lip gloss and let her hair down from its clip. Adjusting her tweed skirt and the V-neck of her frilly cream-colored blouse, she left her office, her coat over an arm.

Swiping her keycard at the staff elevator, Eve tapped a foot while waiting. *Why am I being summoned?* Then she remembered her father's description of their boss. *Ruthless.* She chewed on her thumbnail. Had she made a mistake? Was she going to be reprimanded? Fired?

The unease low in her stomach intensified when the elevator doors opened at the penthouse suite. It resembled a pricey art gallery. Modern metal sculptures were artfully posed on pedestals and a series of paintings were on the wall above the receptionist's desk. She didn't recognize the scrawled signature, *Lex*, but Eve figured the pieces didn't come cheap. At the double doors, she lifted a tentative hand to knock.

"Enter."

Eve stepped into the well-appointed office. Recognition dawned within seconds. Blood rushed from her face. The shoulders encased in the tailored jacket were broader, more muscular, and the set of his full mouth more cynical. Jake.

"Oh my fucking God."

"Sit down, Angie," he said, lip curled, gesturing to the chairs facing his desk.

She sat before her legs buckled.

CHAPTER TWENTY

"Am I in *The Twilight Zone*?" Eve cried, half-expecting *Rod Serling* to materialize. "You're *the* Carter of Carter Consolidated?"

This cannot be happening! Memories flashed of the first time they met. The scorching heat. The undeniable pull. It was still there, humming below the surface. The knowledge terrified her. His smirk told her he guessed what she felt. *Move,* her brain squawked. "This isn't right . . . I'm leaving."

"Stay where you are," Jake ordered. Always intense, now he was downright imposing. "I'm in charge *this* time."

Her voice was strangled when she asked, "Why am I here?"

"I have a business proposition for you."

Eve's breath came in gasps. She was sinking, as if in quicksand. "I already work for you. Or I *did*."

"Wendy says you're a wonderful addition to the center," Jake said in a sensible tone, his expression mild. "I've no intention of firing you."

"You think I should continue working here? With *you* as my boss?" Eve managed a dry laugh, remembering how angry he'd been when she broke up with him.

"It would be exceedingly foolish for you to throw away a perfectly good job because you want to avoid me, wouldn't it?"

Eve framed and rejected several rejoinders, sensing resentment simmering beneath Jake's controlled façade. *What is he playing at?* He chuckled, leaning back in his chair. The crooked smile exposed his dimple. They locked gazes, and the tension in the air ratcheted. Eve made the mistake of looking at his mouth. She moistened her lips with the tip of her tongue, remembering the pleasure his mouth brought her once upon a time. Her body remembered, too. She shifted in her seat.

"You're exquisite. That hasn't changed," Jake purred, expression turning predatory.

Eve quashed the urge to run from the room. "Did you hear I was back in town and engineer this?"

"*This*?" he mimicked, his head cocked to the side, as if having fun at her expense.

"Yes, the *job*. This *meeting*. Is it a setup?" She waited for his response, pulse racing, but his face was impassive. "I don't know what you have in mind . . . but, whatever it is, it won't work."

Jake nodded to the rings on her left hand. "Because you're married?"

"Yes," Eve said, defiant, clasping her hands in her lap. *Keep your cool. Don't let him see he's rattled you.*

"Martin Pierce. A topic we should address." His tone glib, a muscle worked in his jaw. *He's still pissed at me, after all these years.* Eve shook her head, stomach churning. No, she didn't want to talk about Martin, especially not with Jake. "I know your husband's dead."

Eve's lips parted. A myriad of emotions blossomed in her chest. She struggled to decide which was the strongest, which to latch onto. Fear? Confusion? Anger? Frustration?

"And, I know about the mess you're in."

"Explain," Eve demanded, her teeth gnashed.

"I've kept tabs on you the last ten years, Angie. I've waited for you to be free again."

Eve moved to the edge of her seat. "Did you have something to do with Martin's death?"

Tipping his head back, Jake laughed. "Don't be ridiculous."

"That's reassuring," Eve snapped. "I'm comforted by your declaration of innocence."

"You're delectable, but you flatter yourself if you think I'd assassinate your husband to get you back. Your marriage wasn't destined to last. Widow or divorcée . . . it makes no difference to me." Jake raised a hand in a placating gesture. "Don't be angry with me. Pierce got himself in trouble."

Eve bit her tongue to keep from arguing. She'd get nowhere lashing out. Sitting back in her seat, she crossed her arms. "Tell me what you know."

"I don't know *why* your husband needed money, but he borrowed a lot from the wrong people." He shrugged.

"A lot?"

"Into the millions," Jake said with grim satisfaction.

Oh, why not? I should've figured. I'll bet Barbee's the tip of the iceberg. Darkness closed in. Defiance gone, Eve put her head between her knees, her coat and purse falling to the floor.

"I'm surprised you haven't been leaned on yet."

Eve sat up, rubbing her temple with shaking fingers. "Who says I haven't been?"

"So you know the characters Pierce borrowed from are mobsters. They'll make your life unpleasant until they receive payment."

Eve gulped, insisting, "My house *will* sell and I'll chip away at the debt."

"You think the type of people you owe will be patient?"

"Then my father will help . . . I have friends who'll help."

Jake's smile looked smug. "I doubt your pride would allow you to ask him—or your friends—for the astronomical amount you need."

"You have all the answers," Eve snarled. "What do *you* suggest?"

"You need a benefactor. I need someone to manage my home and accompany me on social occasions with none of the obligatory romantic rubbish. No syrupy sentiments, no

expectations or proclamations of love. A business arrangement free of entanglements. I propose marriage."

CHAPTER TWENTY-ONE

A ddy wore a lilac-colored shirt with a ghost graphic that said, *I May Be Short But I'm Fa-boo-lous!* She poured individually wrapped candies into a pumpkin-shaped bowl. Engrossed by Addy's actions, Wally stretched and swatted a paw.

Picking at a hangnail, Eve went to the front window. The cold drizzle hadn't hampered the enthusiasm of the costumed children working their way down Yankee Drive. Last Halloween she'd volunteered at the party at The Palms, passing cups of punch beside Martin. She'd been carefree, secure in her future. Tonight, Eve wasn't carefree, nor secure. Her reunion with Jake gnawed at her, haunting her. *Halloween's a fitting day for old ghosts.*

"What happened at work today? You look tense."

Eve turned to find Addy staring at her. "No, I'm fine. I . . . I have a headache."

She fled to the privacy of her bedroom and lay on her childhood bed, hugging a pillow. Eve's mind replayed the meeting with Jake on a continuous reel. *Lord, he's sexy. That dimple.* She groaned. There'd been a time when she would've put the tip of her tongue to it before moving to capture his mouth. Willing the arousal in her core to pass, Eve squeezed her thighs together around the pillow.

Jake's proposition was tempting but *wrong*. The type of marriage he sought went against everything Eve valued. A traditionalist, she believed in the institution of marriage. Perhaps it was idealistic, but she thought a couple ought to at least *like* each other before entering into it.

He was no longer a reckless guy on a motorcycle but an executive behind a desk in a fancy office. How had Jake gone from laborer to successful captain of industry so quickly? He hadn't given the impression he possessed ambitions. Working long hours, he also liked to party. *We were together months, but we didn't know each other, not at all.* When not in bed, they drank whiskey, listened to music, and got high. They didn't have conversations about goals and dreams.

I'll bet these days Jake's used to buying whatever he wants. Well, I'm not for sale. The idea was offensive, especially when Eve remembered Jillian Caldwell's words. She didn't have a vain bone in her body. Nor was she a social climber. *Do I give that impression?*

Marriage to Jake seemed perilous. Could she maintain detachment? *What if I fall in love with him?* Loving a man dismissive of *syrupy sentiments* sounded downright bleak. Eve believed in romance. Her marriage to Martin hadn't blazed with fiery passion, but they'd built a foundation of affection and mutual respect.

And where's that gotten you?

She and Jake were chalk and cheese. They couldn't be more different. During their meeting, he hadn't broached the subject of sex, but he wanted her. His office crackled with it. Could he tell she felt the same? He must. But he was bitter. Did he want to punish her? Maybe. Eve figured desire overpowered all else. Was sex expected? *C'mon, you know his plans don't include us being pals and playing checkers to pass a blustery winter's night.*

Eve shook her head. It was indecent. She couldn't see a future with Jake when he'd proposed ten years earlier, nor could she now. *If I marry again, I want love. I want children. Matters that obviously don't appeal to him.*

He'd dismissed her with *I'll be in touch.*

Eager to flee, she'd bundled her purse and coat and bolted

from his office, wishing she could as easily outrun the feelings he'd stirred up.

CHAPTER TWENTY-TWO

E ve waited for Jake to make contact. Continuing to work at Consolidated, she didn't see him, though he worked just upstairs. After the licensing assessment, she had more time to dwell on her predicament. A whispery voicemail from a blocked number made the walls close in.

"This is your friend. We're on our way to Old Hillbury. See you soon, Mrs. Pierce." The phone slipped from her hand, crashing to the floor.

Convinced her pursuers were lurking, Eve left the house only to work, becoming reclusive. The stomachache she suffered from the night she received the threatening voicemail hadn't gone away. Unable to sleep, she subsisted on coffee.

Addy was much too astute not to notice. At first, Eve pushed aside her concern, but after an exhausting day at work and in a moment of vulnerability, she broke down and told her about Jake—and the phone message. Relief coursing through her when she shared her burden, words spilled from Eve's lips. Addy placed a plump hand on hers. "What will you do, luv?"

"Consider Jake's offer. What else?"

"You say the attraction's still there." Addy said, her voice full of speculation, "You're adults. Why not explore it?"

Could Eve explain how hazardous Jake was to her peace of mind? How she lost control in his arms? Should she confide in Addy about miscarrying his baby? No, she wasn't strong enough. Instead, Eve said, "Because it's not wise to trust him. Jake was a hothead. He lashed out if wronged. I doubt he's changed."

"What do you mean?"

"Once, there was a fistfight at the poolhall when Jake thought he was hustled. Another time, a confrontation with a guy at a bar who'd been *disrespectful*. I wounded his male pride and he hasn't forgotten."

Addy's expression was shrewd. "You're concerned he's planning some sort of retaliation."

"Possibly." Eve gave her a glum smile. "If only the universe will give a sign telling me what to do."

Addy put her arms around Eve, enveloping her in a hug. "My advice is to proceed with extreme caution."

Eve took a sick day the next day. Loafing on the couch, she watched TV and dozed. Addy got home from work mid-afternoon, the opening of the front door waking her.

"Brr!" After hanging her coat in the closet, Addy said, "You look better."

"I can cook dinner tonight." Eve pretended not to see Addy's grimace.

"I told Sylvie I'd babysit the kids at her place while she's working late at the salon." Sylvie Ferris was in her mid-twenties, divorced, and mother to two precious children. Aiden was in Addy's kindergarten class, and she often babysat him and his sister.

Preparing a cuppa, Addy joined her. When Eve's phone rang, she rejected the call, dropping the phone back on the coffee table with a scowl.

"Was it *them*?" Addy asked, and Eve nodded.

"I didn't tell you, but I sold two pieces of jewelry. I needed money to cover this month's mortgage." Restless, Eve made a sound of aggravation in the back of her throat. Folding the afghan, she laid it over the arm of the sofa. "That house better sell fast, or it'll be a small turkey this Thanksgiving."

"Let me finish my tea, and we'll go for a walk."

"No, I'm too jumpy." Eve picked up her cup to put it in the dishwasher. "Sal and Iris could be lying in wait."

The doorbell sounded, and they both recoiled. Eve gazed at Addy, finding her dismay mirrored. Putting her cup down jerkily, she peeped out the front window. Jake was on the stoop, wearing a black wool overcoat, the lapels turned up against the wind. He pressed the bell again, the set of his mouth impatient.

"It's Jake!"

"Heard you were sick," he said by way of greeting after she opened the door, his manner curt. He entered the foyer without invitation, skimming over her patterned pajamas and messy hair. His large frame shrank the size of the foyer, changing the atmosphere to something between steamy and boiling. Nodding to where Addy sat in her chair, Jake asked, "Aren't you going to introduce me, Eve?"

Face flaming, Eve made introductions, etiquette prompting her to invite him to sit. When she took his coat, his cologne wafted, making her weak kneed. Jake and Addy nattered about the weather while Eve slouched against a wall.

A casual ankle crossed over his knee, seeming perfectly at ease, Jake was charm personified. He rested an arm along the back of the sofa.

Spellbound, she watched his suit jacket part, displaying a flat stomach evident through his tailored shirt. *I'd bet my eyeteeth those abs are the washboard variety.*

"Pet? I said, why don't you make Jake a coffee?" Addy's tone indicated she was tickled.

Oh, great. This is all I need. Eve noted Jake's smirk when she scurried past.

From the kitchen, she heard Jake inquire about Addy's job, sounding engrossed. Addy gobbled it up. Eve puttered, in no hurry to return to the living room. *Coward.* Spooning fresh grounds into the coffeemaker, she waited for the coffee to brew and eavesdropped on the lively conversation. Eve's stomach did somersaults when Jake laughed at what Addy said.

Unable to stall any longer, Eve returned to the living room. As she handed the mug to Jake, their knuckles brushed. Awareness zapped through her and she avoided his eyes, suspecting he felt it, too.

"Lovely meeting you, but I must do errands before my babysitting job," Addy said.

Realizing she and Jake would soon be unchaperoned, Eve felt her throat collapse to her stomach. Addy had mentioned nothing about *errands* earlier. It took clapping her eyes on Jake once for her to forsake her own sage advice, Eve noted with chagrin. *That crafty little stinker.* She gaped, helpless, as Addy donned her parka and left.

You're gonna get it, Addy Dennis!

"Alone at last," Jake said in an almost deprecating way. "Have you missed me?"

CHAPTER TWENTY-THREE

"I've been counting the days." Addy's machinations had made Eve flippant. *Extreme caution, my foot.* Even Addy wasn't immune to Jake's allure. Flopping into Addy's vacated chair, Eve crossed her legs, unable to keep a frown from her face. "I can't marry. Martin *just* died."

"I don't want to hear about Pierce and I don't care about conventions," Jake snapped.

"Then why suggest marriage?" Eve raised a judicious eyebrow. "You can't get much more conventional than holy matrimony."

Jake's expression turned mulish. "It's what I've decided I want."

"I hate to break it to you, but marrying a widow whose husband's barely cold will cause gossip."

"I can weather it."

"Maybe I can't." Eve took a meditative breath. "Stop for a minute and consider my position. Martin—"

"I told you I don't want to discuss Pierce," Jake ground out. "That man came between us."

"We've been over this. There was no *us*." Eve shook her head, failing to conquer her annoyance. "He didn't steal me away from you. *I* made a choice."

"It was a poor one. A matter of time until you came to that conclusion yourself."

She removed imaginary lint from the sleeve of her pajama shirt. He'd hit too close to home. "So you've said, but I did love my husband."

Jake's laugh sounded nasty. "You ought to think about the quandary he's left you in rather than waxing poetic about love." He put his cup on the side table. Eve bore the weight of his perusal for several minutes.

"I could've handled our breakup better, I admit that—"

Jake held up a hand. "Save it, Angie. We were together months." He shook his head. "You meet a wealthy older man, and within a week, you move on. Hell, I suppose I can't blame you for not taking your chances with me. I wasn't exactly cultured and refined in those days."

"Our relationship was strictly sex." Eve argued, "You couldn't expect I'd accept your proposal when that was all you offered."

"Things are different now."

She snorted. "Believe me. I'm well aware of that."

"Martin Pierce had his turn. I've waited long enough for mine."

"I don't like what you're implying. My husband married me because he loved me." Cheeks burning, Eve remembered Cape Azul, which took the wind from her sails.

"If that's your brand of love, then the concept doesn't interest me. I prefer a direct and honest approach." Jake got up and strode toward her.

Was he always so tall? Eve shrank into her chair.

The masculine tang of his cologne invaded her senses when his strong, tanned fingers closed over her upper arms. Jake hauled her from her chair like she weighed nothing. He bent his head, bringing his lips to hers.

Eve pushed against his chest, stunned. She couldn't think, couldn't breathe. His fingers cupped her chin, forcing her to meet his captivating green eyes. It was as if he stared straight to her soul. Her resolve dwindled. It was terribly draining to be strong, always making the right choices. She wanted to feel good for the first time in a long time. *Oh, hell. It's useless to object. I want this.*

She nodded her assent. Jake's mouth was explorative, persuasive. His tongue pushed against her lips and she granted him access to the contours of her mouth. Eve made a sound, part whimper, part approval. Twining her arms around his neck, she buried her fingers in Jake's hair, happily drowning in him.

His experienced fingertips traced her spine, making her shiver. Eve admitted to herself in those reckless moments that if he laid her on the sofa to have his way with her, she would welcome it. It was madness, but she *welcomed it.* Then Jake pulled away, and she moaned in frustration. He raked a hand through his hair, his breath in gasps.

Reality slowly came back, and with shaky hands, she fixed her clothes and her hair, mortified by her behavior. *Wanton.* She was a naive eighteen-year-old virgin again, willing to give Jake everything. *You've learned nothing.* Eve put her hand to her cheek. Her face was on fire.

"See?" Jake's voice was mild, but his smile mocked. He appeared in control again, but Eve couldn't claim the same. She remained breathless. "We still have it after all these years. It scares you. It's always scared you."

She shook her head. Huskily, Eve said, "It doesn't matter. It's not enough."

"That kiss was an experiment, Angie. It's proven I want you."

"What if *I* don't want *you*?"

"Your body never could lie to me." Jake let his words sink in. "I wanted to know if the spark remained. It does. But it's up to you whether we hit the sheets."

Eve squinted. "Wait—are you saying sex isn't part of your offer?"

"No, my offer's marriage. Sex is up to you."

Bullshit. "I don't believe you."

"Do you think I get my jollies blackmailing women into my

bed? Don't insult me. You'll be in my bed because you want to be."

"You'd accept my refusal?"

"Yes." His expression turned roguish. "But I can be *very* persuasive."

"Okay, *Romeo*," Eve muttered, crossing her arms over her chest.

"I know if I'm patient enough, you'll come to me of your own volition." He laid a business card on the table and slipped on his overcoat. "I *will* have you."

Trailing him to the foyer, she intended to knock his ego down a peg. "Maybe you won't."

"You know I will, baby." Jake opened the front door. "There's no denying what we have. It's stronger than both of us."

CHAPTER TWENTY-FOUR

Saturday morning, Eve received a text from Hitch.
Hey, doll. Long time no talk. How's it hangin'?

She laughed. Her fingers itched to type, *Not much going on, Hitch. I owe millions to loan sharks, but that's no problemo since my old flame will pay the debts if I marry him. By the way, he's hot as hell and says whether we bump uglies is up to me, but . . . I don't dare trust him. How 'bout you?* Instead, Eve replied she was fine, asking if he remained in Munich, where he'd spent Oktoberfest.

Bumming around Monaco now. Not coming back to the states 'til the holidays. If you followed me online, you'd know!

Eve shook her head, grinning. Ever since she'd deleted her social media accounts two years earlier, Hitch had teased her about reactivating them. They traded texts until Addy stepped from the kitchen. Today's t-shirt proclaimed *Life Is Short & So Am I.*

"Luv, would you run to the market for me?"

Eve reluctantly nodded, unwilling to tell Addy no. She couldn't stay a recluse forever, could she? "Let me wrap up my conversation with Hitch first."

"Tell him hallo from me."

During the drive to the neighborhood market, Eve watched for anything unusual, but her mind centered on Hitch. Their friendship was often a distant one. Hitch sought adventure, losing himself in his escapades. She saw in him what others didn't, a man struggling to live his truth. She didn't ask more from him than what he gave, and Hitch accepted her for who she was. *Will I ever see him again?*

At the store, Eve compared laundry detergent. After putting back the more expensive option, she continued to the butcher counter. Addy wanted ground beef. Placing the package of meat in her cart, she caught sight of a man in a garish shirt and an emaciated woman in violet leather. *Oh, please, no.* Shutting her eyes, she hoped they were a figment of her overactive imagination.

Sal wore his usual mawkish grin and a long-sleeved turtleneck under his Hawaiian shirt. Iris's curly wig was stringy, like a black mop. They walked down the cereal aisle in slow motion, Iris bringing the purple-painted tip of her finger across her neck in a throat-slit gesture. *That's it. I'm fucked.*

Thoughts topsy-turvy, Eve pushed her cart to the front of the market to the checkout. She loaded her purchases onto the belt with erratic movements. Sal and Iris were at the express lane. The blood drained from her face when she realized they'd bought a pair of oversized kitchen shears. *What are they planning?*

When the cashier told her the total, Eve found her debit card in her wallet, fingers unsteady. Inserting the card, she bumped an elbow into her purse. It tumbled to the floor, contents scattering.

"Shit. Sorry," Eve stammered to the cashier. Kneeling to retrieve her wallet, she stretched for her lip gloss. Before getting to her feet, she spied the black card wedged under the wheel of her cart. Grabbing it, she ran an index finger over the embossed silver digits. The number was to Jake's cell. *I wished for a sign to help me decide . . . well, here's my sign.*

The duo waited outside. Iris was fondling the scissors, her gaze zeroing in on Eve's hair. Eve brought a hand to her braid, wheeling the trolley through the automatic doors. She stopped several feet from them. *Do it. Deal with the consequences later.* She held out Jake's business card. "Call this number. The guy who answers will take care of it."

Iris sneered, dangling the shears. Sal snatched the card, pulling a phone from his shirt pocket as he walked away. Eve couldn't hear his words, but lasered by Iris's glare, she didn't dare move closer to listen.

Joining them again, Sal stowed his phone, his smile jester-like. Handing the card back to Eve, he said, "Pleasure doing business with you, Mrs. Pierce."

As they left, Iris turned to give Eve a dirty look. She flung the shears into the bushes as if incensed. Eve stared at their retreating figures, clinging to her cart and expelling a breath she hadn't realized she held. It couldn't be as simple as that, could it? Seconds later, her phone rang. *Decide in haste, repent in leisure.*

"Meet me for dinner tonight to finalize our transaction."

Eve couldn't speak at first. *Christ, you've agreed to become Mrs. Jake Carter.* Her voice wobbled when she beseeched, "Another night?"

"I've wired two hundred thousand dollars for you. It's the least you can do."

"I-I need time—"

"Come on, Angie, you knew what you were doing when you gave that guy my number." He sounded irritated.

"Tomorrow?" *Mrs. Jake Carter!*

"Tonight," Jake said firmly. "I've waited for ten years. I'm tired of waiting."

"I don't think I can."

"You can. You will. I'll send a car for you at six."

Time to pay the piper.

CHAPTER TWENTY-FIVE

Eve took pains with her outfit, choosing a pewter-colored angora sweater that brought out the silvery flecks of gray in her irises. She burrowed in her bag of jewelry for diamond earrings. Slipping on ballerina flats, she wondered if she should put her hair up. But Jake liked it loose. He'd wind the golden strands around his palm, pulling her head to the side to nuzzle her neck, his breath branding her. *Stop it, fool.* She coiled her hair into a clip.

"Addy says you've got a date," her dad said while Eve waited for her ride.

The aroma of his tobacco reached her nose, and she sniffed in appreciation before answering, "Actually, I'm having dinner with Jake Carter." Her father put his newspaper down, his blue-gray eyes narrowing. Playing with the lapel of her cashmere coat, Eve admitted, "I knew him when I was a teenager."

"Is that so?"

Uhh. The doorbell rang. *Saved by the bell.* "Bye, Dad."

Scanning the restaurant entrance for Jake, Eve fiddled with the stem of her glass of Chianti. Moments later, his tall frame filled the entryway, and the restaurant suddenly seemed tiny. When he walked through the restaurant, his confident gaze held hers. Eve couldn't look away. She was drawn to him like a moth to a flame.

Jake's demeanor fit a man of his wealth. He wore his tailored suit as easily as an old pair of jeans. *Charisma.* He had it

98

in spades. Women at other tables viewed him with open appreciation, their expressions greedy. Eve understood. She dabbed at her chin to make sure she hadn't drooled.

"I hope you haven't waited long," Jake said, and she shook her head. Lifting a finger to signal the waiter, he requested a bottle of champagne.

When they were alone, Eve asked, "Champagne?"

"We're celebrating our engagement." He tossed her a lazy smile, delving in his pocket for a jeweler's box. Flicking open the lid, he revealed a gaudy emerald cut diamond ring. Eve's stomach clenched. *What have I done?*

"Stone not big enough?" Jake mocked.

A rustle of displeasure brought her back. She shot him a look. Their waiter arrived with their champagne. Noticing the ring, he congratulated them, and diners at the other tables called their best wishes. Eve was obliged to suffer through the unwanted attention gracefully.

When everyone went back to their meals, Jake purred, "You're beautiful."

"Gee, thanks. You're swell, too," Eve muttered, gulping her champagne. The flickering candlelight made the diamond blaze. She couldn't drag her eyes from it. Alarm compressed her chest. She was in too deep now. Snapping the lid shut, she assessed Jake's reaction from beneath her lashes.

He smirked, lifting his flute in salutation.

She exchanged her champagne for a glass of iced water, thrown off-kilter by his smug self-satisfaction. "How can I wear *that* to work?"

"Appearances matter," Jake said easily.

"It'll alienate my co-workers. It'll change how they treat me."

His voice was cool. "You wanted a man who could provide. Baby, you got it."

"Jesus. You have an ax to grind, don't you?"

"I have no idea what you mean, Angie."

I'm playing right into his hands, aren't I?

The waiter approached for their order, though the last thing on Eve's mind was food. Choosing a salad, she settled back in her chair. The pounding in her head made reason elusive. Things moved at breakneck speed. She scrambled to keep up.

"You look wary," Jake remarked after the waiter left. There was hunger in his eyes that had nothing to do with food.

Eve was his quarry, and he had her cornered. She leaned forward, keeping her tone glib. "Grandmother, what big teeth you've got."

Jake tipped his head back and laughed, but the predatory gleam remained. "All the better to eat you with, little girl."

"Yep," Eve said under her breath, ignoring his wolfish countenance. "That's what I figured."

"You'll fare much better with me than with your creditors. I can guarantee that." The sensual timbre of Jake's voice insinuated as much. He reached to stroke her palm with a thumb. Frissons of electricity surged through her.

Extricating her hand from his, Eve gave him side-eye. "I'm swooning. I hope nobody asks if you got down on bended knee."

"I'm sure you'll handle any questions with aplomb," Jake assured her, acknowledging, "I'm not a man to pledge romance, and I never will be. But you'll get the best fucking of your life."

She snorted at his cool confidence, evaluating him over the rim of her glass. "Your ego's grown with the size of your wallet."

"I wouldn't say that." His mouth quirked at the corner, making the dimple in his cheek emerge.

"Right," Eve agreed. "You've always had a colossal ego."

"It's self-confidence, baby, and it's gotten me far."

The waiter set their food down. Jake demolished his steak

while Eve picked at her salad. When he finished, he wiped his mouth with a napkin. "I'll take you to my house, and we'll discuss the details of our arrangement."

"That *all* you have in mind?" Eve asked, but he simply smiled.

Jake signed for the meal, then ushered her outside. The valet brought his vehicle, a racy black sports car with tinted windows. Jake held the passenger door open for her, but Eve hesitated. "I'd rather go home, if it's all the same to you."

"It's not all the same to me," Jake's said brusquely. "You're trying to delay the inevitable."

He had a point. "Fine."

As he got behind the wheel, he remarked, "Aren't you docile as a lamb all of a sudden?"

Like a lamb led to slaughter. Eve gnawed at her nail and remained silent.

Jake maneuvered the powerful car away from the curb and into the busy downtown traffic. On the radio, *Billie Holiday* crooned soulfully about the man she loved. On the outskirts of the city, he placed a warm hand on her thigh.

His caressing fingers seemed to leave invisible scorch marks. Eve was treading dangerous waters. Remembering how readily she'd succumbed during their last encounter, she shoved his hand away with unmistakable firmness.

Jake chuckled.

CHAPTER TWENTY-SIX

"Wow," Eve said. The sprawling stone, brick, and wood dwelling was a contemporary interpretation of mid-century design. Tall brick walls bordered the grounds. "This reminds me of *Fallingwater*."

"It lacks the obligatory water feature. For now." At the wood and glass doors, Jake positioned his palm on a mounted scanner. The lock clicked open. At Eve's frown, he explained, "It's a biometric lock system. Everyone has a unique vein pattern, like a fingerprint."

Their footsteps echoed in the foyer. Jake used a touchscreen on the wall to disengage the security system. With a few taps, lights turned on throughout the house—an elaborate fixture of bronze and stained glass illuminated above them, catching Eve's eye. A work of art, it fused modern and mission styles.

"I commissioned a prairie-school artist from Chicago to design that," Jake explained. "*Otis Redding* okay?"

These Arms of Mine reverberated. It was one of Jake's favorites. Memories stirred of their past. The sizzling nights when they'd not been able to get enough of each other. Eve's throat tightened. She found his smoldering gaze on her, as if he read her mind. Coughing, she turned away, the spell breaking.

Eve took in the open floor plan, the staircase of metal and wood, the stone floors. She wandered from room to room while Jake considered her, a curious expression on his face. A wall of wood-framed glass doors overlooked a patio. Craftsman style cabinetry lined the kitchen. Raising an eyebrow, she recognized the sleek range. Hitch had installed the same model in his California condo. "This stove costs fifty thousand dollars."

Propped against the pocket-door to the pantry, Jake stood with arms crossed. "Thanks for noticing. Why don't we go upstairs?"

"I bet there's a bed you'll try to introduce me to," Eve muttered.

There were several spacious bedrooms and bathrooms, painted builder white and empty of furnishings. Jake's office was spartan, outfitted with a desk, chair, and a lamp. "As you can see, the house needs a woman's touch."

Eve paused at the door of the master bedroom, a plain room with a king-size bed. Her heart banging like a drum, her gaze sought and found his. "Is this the bed you'd like me to become intimately acquainted with?"

Jake smiled.

She indicated the glass doors opening to the second-floor balcony. "May I?"

The night was nippy, smelling of impending winter. Leaves scattered and swirled over the grounds. They stood at the metal railing for several minutes, occupied with their own thoughts. Eve's headache eased. She counted the security lights posted every several yards along the brick wall bordering the property, losing count at thirty. *If this were my house, I'd . . . stop it. This isn't real. Playing make-believe is too risky a game.*

Jake moved behind her, resting his hands on her hips, but Eve scooted away. *Remember why you're here.* "Don't we have business to discuss?"

"Business before pleasure," he readily agreed, preceding her to the kitchen.

She sat at the island while he got bottled water from the commercial fridge.

"You said you need someone to run your house," Eve

prompted when he joined her.

"And decorate."

"Hiring an interior designer would be far cheaper than paying my debts." She sipped her water not because she was thirsty, but because it was something to do.

"I can afford it. What I require is arm candy."

Eve rolled her eyes. "There are plenty of attractive women. Why *me*?"

"A mutually beneficial transaction suits us both. On my end, as a billionaire, traditional dating's a minefield. Most ladies don't appreciate the concept of sex without strings. They grasp for more." Jake wrinkled his nose. "It's predictable. I don't have time for nonsense."

"Who does?" Eve agreed, flippant.

"I literally don't have time. I'm a workaholic. I wouldn't be where I am if I wasn't."

"I'm intrigued by your meteoric rise to titan of industry." She put a hand under her chin, resting an elbow on the countertop. "The Maxwell Arms is a far cry from this castle."

Jake pinned her with sharp eyes. "You think I lived the way I did because I liked it? That I didn't have aspirations? Fuck, I had thirty grand in the bank when we met."

Eve's lips parted in surprise. It was news to her. "How'd you manage that?"

"By working my ass off. I finished my bachelor's and was in an accelerated MBA program when we met. I graduated the year after you left Old Hillbury."

"You were a student? When did you study?"

"When I wasn't working, or with you." Jake's smirk told her he relished her shock. "I took night classes and worked during the day. Not easy, but I was young and hungry."

"I can't believe what I'm hearing."

"Believe it or not, it's the truth. I completed my first takeover at twenty-four."

"*At twenty-four?*" Eve asked, sitting up in her chair. "How's that possible?"

"It wasn't an important company." Jake shrugged. "And I had help from my mentor, who's more father to me than my old man ever was. He introduced me to the right people, and loaned me money when I needed it."

"I didn't know you before, and I know you even less now." Eve groaned. "How will this *ever* work?"

"You know me as well as any woman could." Jake loosened his tie and unbuttoned the top buttons of his shirt, then rolled up his sleeves. "Our pact will work—if you don't develop an attachment to me."

What nerve! She snorted at his loftiness. "I'll try to avoid falling in love with you."

"Good. Because I won't be falling in love with *you*," Jake said firmly. It stung. *Touché.* "There'll be a monthly stipend for clothes. I'll furnish cars, vacations, jewelry—whatever you require. You can keep the job at Consolidated, or not. It makes no difference to me."

Eve bristled. "The agreement is you pay my debts. Nothing further."

"As my wife, you'll wear designer apparel, and that ain't cheap."

That old, familiar feeling returned, reminiscent of Martin pushing her to dress and act a certain way. Eve narrowed her eyes, her voice shrill. "Let's get something straight from the outset, Jake. I am what I am, and I've got plenty of clothes that suit me fine. If it's a special occasion I need an outfit for, that's its own thing, but I won't have you telling me how to dress. That's non-negotiable."

"As you wish. Nevertheless, the money will be at your disposal. And I expect an extravagant wedding. Hire an event planner if you'd like, but spare no expense."

Eve's brow furrowed. "Why?"

"It's what's expected for someone with my wealth."

"Precisely how long is this marriage to last?"

"Twelve months, renewing on a year-by-year basis. If the arrangement's amenable, it can continue for a lengthy interval." Jake smiled. "I prefer a good return on my investments."

Eve pulled a face. "What if I decide I no longer wish to be married before the first year's up?"

"You'll be required to repay a percentage of the money I've paid on your behalf. Each month the amount reduces until the twelfth month when there will be a zero balance." Jake went to the screen on the wall. With a few taps, *The Rolling Stones* sang *Under my Thumb*.

Well, isn't that fitting?

"Of course, I may tire of you before then. In that case, same rules apply."

Your instincts are correct. Jake Carter's a scoundrel. Don't trust him. Eve scoffed, "So I'm captive to your whims?"

"As I am captive to yours." It was like he read her thoughts when he said, "I'm sure you trust me as little as I trust you. A contract will protect us both."

Wanting to wipe the smirk off Jake's face, she said, "I'd like to see you try to collect that two hundred grand from me if I walk out of here tonight and refuse to marry you."

"I made that payment in good faith, Angie." His eyes were ice-cold. "Until you've signed the contract and we're married, don't expect me to satisfy any more of your debts."

"Fair enough." Her headache was back. Eve lifted a hand to her temple. She needed time to think about what she'd learned during their conversation. "I guess my lenders will have to wait 'til we're married to get their money."

"I have a solution for that." He rubbed his hands together. "We're marrying at the courthouse on Tuesday afternoon."

CHAPTER TWENTY-SEVEN

"What?" Eve gripped the metal arms of the stool. "You *cannot* be serious!"

"I've never been more serious." Jake lifted his water, his manner unconcerned, finishing it in one swallow. "We'll apply for the license on Monday morning and sign the prenup afterward."

"Oh, no, we won't." Eve shot off the stool, finding her legs gelatin.

"Do you want your debts paid?" He lasered her with a cold stare, and she became subdued.

"Why so fast?" Her brow furrowed. "Wait—you want an *elaborate* wedding."

"Yes, I do. Sit." Jake pointed to her seat. "Let me continue."

Jaw clenched, Eve sat. "Ugh, my brain hurts."

"By marrying quickly, you have my protection, and you're upholding your end of the agreement. Nobody needs to know we're married until the wedding, which can be after the New Year."

"That's scarcely a long engagement."

"Perhaps, but I fancy a winter wedding."

"Haven't you contemplated everything? What about my father? How do I explain it to *him*?"

"However you wish." Jake looked bored. "Tell him we've been seeing each other since you started at Consolidated. Hell, tell him the truth for all I care."

"As if," Eve muttered, crossing her arms. She was sure her blood pressure hovered in the danger zone.

"Your first assignment's tomorrow evening. My sister has an art exhibition at the Fenton Drew Gallery. Wear something pretty."

"You have a sister?"

"Hold still, pet. How can I do this when you're twitchy as a blue-arsed fly?" Addy asked around the bobby pins in her mouth while arranging Eve's hair into a chignon. After a few minutes, she stood back and admired her handiwork. "Lovely."

"Thanks." Eve rooted in her makeup pouch on the kitchen table. "You can't tell Dad. You have to let me handle it my way. I mean it."

"So, the official story is you corresponded platonically for years and it was a happy coincidence when you met up again at the end of September at Consolidated." Addy plopped down beside Eve at the table. "All this conspiracy. I feel like a modern-day *Mata Hari*."

Eve stowed her lip gloss in her vintage sequined clutch. "Didn't she die by firing squad? I'd pick a different hero."

"Hmm." Opening a can of soda, Addy fixed her with a thoughtful look. "When *will* you tell Jim about the engagement?"

"Soon, because we need to plan a wedding. You'll help me, won't you?" Hearing her father, Eve put a finger to her lips.

Dad came into the kitchen, his cheeks wind-burned and his favorite *Nikon* around his neck. "My word, you're fancy. Where are you off to?"

"To a gallery downtown to see Jake's sister's exhibition." Standing, Eve smoothed the skirt of her black dress, feigning nonchalance.

Addy asked, "Did you find anything photograph-worthy, Jim?"

"I got some shots. Last of the season." Addy nudged Eve

with an elbow while her dad added grounds and water to the coffeemaker. Bringing his hands together to warm them, he turned to Eve. "*Another* date with Jake Carter?"

She fiddled with the beads along the neckline of her dress. *Do it.* "Jake and I have seen each other often since I've been back."

"You never mentioned."

Eve swallowed her misgivings and flashed her father a smile. "I thought you'd feel it was too soon after Martin's death. Now that we're serious . . ."

He frowned. "How serious?"

"Fairly."

"I haven't exchanged more than a dozen words with the man at Consolidated. Don't you think it wise to bring him to the house so we can get to know each other?"

Oh, boy. Eve thought fast. "I've invited him to dinner tomorrow night, Dad."

"That's a beginning," he said, opening the cabinet for a mug.

At a crosswalk a block from the Fenton Drew Gallery, Eve spotted Jake waiting on the sidewalk. A cashmere scarf around his neck, his hands were in the pockets of his overcoat. Heartbeat speeding, Eve noticed, again, how attractive he was. *Keep it together, girl, and hurry.* She'd underestimated how busy downtown would be on a Sunday afternoon and had to park several blocks away. As she darted across the street, her high heels clacked on the pavement.

Jake's hair was wet. She experienced a twinge of guilt when she saw his breath in the frosty air.

"Sorry I'm late. Why not wait inside?"

He studied her full-skirted black swing coat and the heels with the sexy ankle straps. "I haven't been here long. I came straight from the gym."

Sculptures similar to the ones at Consolidated were behind the plate-glass windows, along with canvases of nude female forms drawn in crayon. *Meet Lex,* a poster advertised on the door Jake opened, and the penny dropped. *Ah.*

He escorted her to the well-lit lobby. They checked their coats at the counter and entered the gallery proper. Looking around, Eve was keenly aware of Jake's hand at the small of her back. Crowd anxiety made her pulse jump in her throat. She hadn't expected wall-to-wall people. It wasn't like other exhibits she'd been to with Martin. This one was loud with the roar of spirited conversations. Face hot, Eve toyed with the beads at her neckline.

"I'll fetch us drinks if you want to wander," Jake said from the periphery. Paintings from watercolor to abstract lined the walls, showcasing the artist's range. Eve lost herself in the art, working her way around the room. She stopped at a grouping of informal pencil drawings on paper. The subject was one she'd often sketched—Jake. Smiling, pensive, and scowling Jake, which she was well-acquainted with.

He appeared at her elbow, holding two glasses of wine and looking cross. "Christ. I told her not to include these."

Amused, Eve hid a smile. "They're terrific. I draw, but I'm not as talented as your sister."

"Bankroll her education at Pratt," Jake muttered. "And this is the thanks I get."

Eve sniggered and was rewarded with a scowl, much like the artist's rendering. She sipped her wine and slipped through the crowd to consider a mixed media sculpture of a mermaid on a square base, Jake close behind.

A woman with a shaved head and multiple piercings on her gamine face stepped in Eve's path. She had Jake's green eyes, but they were narrowed. She snarled, "You must be the infamous Eve. I'm Lex Carter."

The ire in Lex Carter's expression unnerved Eve. For a

second, she remained silent, wondering what tales Jake had spun. *You're not a bitch. You just played one in his version of events.* She ignored the bees buzzing in her belly and gave Lex a droll look. "My hair's cleverly arranged to disguise my horns. Pitchfork's in the car."

Lex's posture relaxed to something less hostile. Eve had the impression she'd risen in the woman's estimations. Before Lex could speak, Jake interrupted in a stern tone, "I told you not to include those sketches, Alexandra."

"Then buy them, big brother." Lex winked. "If you do, I'll have 'em removed from the wall and packaged."

Eve watched the exchange, fascinated. This was a side to Jake she'd never witnessed. With a grumble, he took a black credit card from his wallet. Lex plucked it from his fingers with a crafty grin, sauntering away.

Jake griped, "I've been swindled out of a thousand bucks."

CHAPTER TWENTY-EIGHT

They met downtown at the steps of the courthouse the next day. Eve tugged her stocking cap further down her forehead, shivering. The sky was hazy with a hint of snow and dark as her aura. She'd gone to bed fretful she'd made a mistake and woke with apprehension low in her stomach confirming it.

Eve was glad both her dad and Addy were at work when she came downstairs, dressed in skinny jeans and an oversize sweater. She'd decided there was no reason for them to know she planned to apply for a marriage license. That evening Eve would tell her father she and Jake were engaged, and she dreaded it.

"I'm returning to the office for a meeting after we sign the prenup. I've let Wendy know you wouldn't be coming in today or tomorrow," Jake said while they waited for the elevator in the lobby.

"You'll definitely be over early tonight to schmooze my father, right?"

"I said I would," Jake said as the elevator dinged. "You look troubled. Relax, Angie. It'll be fine."

Right. Relax. She dug in her pocket for a tissue, hoping her dripping nose didn't foretell a cold. On the third floor, Jake guided Eve to the city clerk's office. They didn't speak while waiting in line. The couple in front of them seemed too young to marry, wore matching parkas, and were handsy. For some reason, they irritated Eve, but she couldn't put her finger on why. Was she envious they were in love? She tried not to

112

notice them French kissing. What a contrast she and Jake were with the couple.

Eve hoped *their* marriage lasted more than a year, because she had doubts hers and Jake's would.

Later, shirt dampened with sweat and spilled broth, Eve pushed a lock of hair from her cheek. Distracted with mixing dough, she'd neglected the pot on the stove. Broth bubbled over the sides of the pan, extinguishing the burner flame, and leaving the air acrid. Turning off the gas and flipping on the exhaust fan to high, Eve blew a frustrated breath through clenched teeth. *I'm a disaster.*

Stop perseverating about the prenup you signed. Still, the fact she'd soon be Mrs. Jake Carter weighed heavily on her. She'd become adept at compartmentalization over the last months. Now she relied on that skill, deciding to mull over her feelings later. *The* Scarlett O'Hara *of Old Hillbury. Fiddle-dee-dee.* Eve rolled her eyes.

Grabbing quilted potholders, she moved the pot, swabbing at the still-hot cooktop with paper towels. *Good enough.* Glad nobody was home to chuckle at her foibles, Eve tried each burner in turn, but they merely clicked. They must've gotten saturated from the spill. If they didn't ignite after drying, she'd *never* live down wrecking the stove.

Her noodle dough was too sticky, so Eve took a handful of flour from the bag, dusting the counter as she'd been instructed on the online video. The bag fell over, a thick cloud of flour settling over everything in a two-foot radius. With a groan of frustration, she backed up, brushing flour from her apron and sleeves. After sweeping the kitchen floor, she got back to the task at hand.

While her pasta dried on the counter, Eve tried the main burner, relieved when it lit. Adjusting the flame to medium, she stirred the soup with the wooden spoon. When she turned, Wally sat on the counter, lapping at the spilled broth, his tail on the pasta. At Eve's outcry, he regarded her blankly.

Shooing him from the kitchen, she noted with a jaundiced eye the flour paw prints he'd left. Eve threw the furry noodles in the trash. The rest looked okay to her. She added them by handfuls to the steaming soup. As she wiped the flour and spilled broth with a damp sponge, the flour and liquid combined, making a glue-like smear on the tile. *Gah. This is ridiculous.* A glance at the apple-shaped wall clock showed her father due soon, and Jake, too. She hurled the sponge in the sink in a fit of pique.

Eve brought a spoonful of soup to her lips. The chicken was tasteless, and the noodles rubbery. *Where's the flavor?* When she shook salt in the pot, the lid dropped into the soup, and the contents of the shaker dissolved in slow motion. Eve's blood pressure skyrocketed. *Maybe once it's stirred in.*

Her father found her sitting at the kitchen table fifteen minutes later, her head in her hands. Biting his lip, he asked, "Can I help?"

Eve's gaze ran over the chaotic scene. She muttered, "Sure . . . call a priest."

CHAPTER TWENTY-NINE

Eve hastened to answer the door. Tall and imposing as ever, Jake wore his standard tailored suit and wool overcoat. He smelled fantastic. In her old clothes, with her hair mussed, Eve was at a disadvantage. Her cheeks suffused with heat.

"You've been busy." Jake indicated her soup-splattered sweatshirt, wiping a flour smudge from her nose. At his touch, her breath hissed through her teeth. Eve could tell he felt the jolt of electric current, too, by the way his eyes dilated.

She was breathless when she took his overcoat and jacket and hung them in the hall closet. "My soup was an epic fail. I hope you're hungry for pizza."

"Starving," Jake agreed easily, loosening his tie. His wicked expression told her food wasn't on his mind. Feeling her blush to the roots of her hair, Eve realized her dad had joined them in the foyer.

"Nothing better than pizza and football," Dad said heartily, and Eve gave him a grateful smile. He teased her mercilessly but was also her biggest cheerleader.

"Mr. Shawcross." Jake extended a hand.

Dad shook it, saying, "Please, come to the living room."

As any suitor ought to, Jake was friendly and deferential when talking to her dad. Perching on the arm of the sofa, Eve listened, her hands clasped in her lap to keep them from wringing. Switching on the TV to the pregame show, Dad commented on this season's quarterback. Eve expected a lengthy spiel and breathed in relief. Evidently, candid discussion regarding her and Jake would come later. She went upstairs to change.

Brushing her hair, Eve noted her flushed face in the mirror above the bureau. She chose a peach knit blouse with a square neckline that showed off her décolletage. Heart hammering violently in her chest, she was sure if she peered down, her chest would be lurching in time with the beats. *I need a highball of whiskey, stat.*

After coiling her hair into a bun at the nape of her neck, Eve applied lip gloss before descending the stairs. She found Addy home and involved in an animated conversation with Jake. Today's t-shirt said, *I'm Not Short, I'm Fun-Sized!*

Addy stood. "I'll get changed. Back in a jiff."

Feeling Jake's stare, Eve poured a whiskey at the drinks cart. She examined him as he interacted with her father, marveling at the difference in him now he was older. He was quite a suave man of the world.

The pizza was delivered as Addy returned, wearing a becoming burgundy sweater that brought out the red highlights in her hair. She and Eve went to the kitchen for plates and napkins. The counters were still smeared with flour, but Addy didn't comment. Instead, she said, "Jake's smitten with you."

"He's in lust with me, Addy, not love." Eve picked up the stack of paper plates, but Addy restrained her with a hand on her arm.

"The atmosphere between you two crackled when you came into the room." Addy fanned herself with a paper napkin, and Eve shook her head in aggravation. She wasn't in the mood.

Addy dished slices of pizza, and they watched the game while eating. Eve made a show of enjoying her meal, but every bite tasted of sawdust and her soda made her queasy. After dinner, she collected their trash and distributed another round of beer. Her dad was glued to the TV screen, but the compulsion to have the news in the open overpowered her. *If I don't get this off my chest, I may explode.* "Dad," she began, but their team scored a touchdown, and Dad and Jake cheered. At the commercial break, she tried again, her voice squeaky. "Dad?"

Jake raised a hand to stop her. "Allow me, Eve."

Uh oh.

Jake's expression was solemn, respectful. Dad used the remote to turn the volume down on the TV and he and Addy waited expectantly.

"I'm not sure how much Eve told you, but we've known each other for many years." After a beat, Jake added, "She's accepted my marriage proposal."

There was an awkward silence. Eve froze, knowing she must resemble a deer-caught-in-headlights. *Damn you, Jake Carter. Couldn't you have broken the news with more finesse?*

Addy prompted, "You say you've known Eve for years?"

"Yes." Jake nodded. "In fact, if she hadn't met Martin Pierce, we very well could be married already." Eve threw Jake a panicked look, but he shook his head almost imperceptibly as if to tell her he had it under control.

"I learn yesterday you two have been dating, and now you say you're *engaged*?" Dad asked, brows knit in dissatisfaction. "I'm not a fan of how swiftly events are progressing here."

"I'm sorry, Dad," Eve said with genuine regret. "I should've told you sooner."

"Damn right, you should have," Dad said. Eve bit her lip at the rebuff in his voice.

"My humble financial circumstances made me a poor option as a husband before. I can't blame Eve for choosing Martin Pierce instead." Jake's expression was impassive. *Bullshit.* If the atmosphere weren't so strained, she would've snorted.

"I'm disappointed, Eve. I always thought we could talk about anything," her dad said, as if Jake hadn't spoken. His words cut her to the bone.

"I didn't mean to — I didn't expect a proposal." Eve's eyes filled with tears. She blinked them back, wishing the floor would open and swallow her.

Addy volleyed her a sympathetic smile, reminding Dad, "Eve did say she worried you'd disapprove."

He scowled at Addy, snapping, "Don't tell me *you* knew of the engagement before *me*."

"Perhaps Eve confided in me because I'm not judgmental," Addy retorted. "Bloody hell, she was right to worry — look at the way you're carrying on. Making the poor mite cry. It's a time of joy and celebration, you pillock!"

"Oh, please don't fuss at each other," Eve begged, putting her hands to her face. "That's the last thing I want."

"Jim. Addy." Jake projected his voice. Eve imagined it was the same commanding tone he used at board meetings. "I won't lie to you and say Eve and I have a great unrequited love. It's not the way I'm wired."

Eve's throat crashed to the floor, convinced he made a tactical error. "Jake —"

"With all due respect, Eve made a mistake marrying Martin." Jake paused. "But she and I are a good match, and she realizes that now."

Dad shook his head, still frowning. "I don't understand. Are you in love with my daughter, *or not?*"

"We've always had feelings, and I know we have great compatibility," Jake assured him. *Talk about spin.* "Tradition dictates I should've asked for your blessing before proposing, but rest assured I *will* take care of Eve in exactly the manner she deserves."

Jake wasn't lying about their shared *feelings* and *compatibility*. She knew what he meant. Their *feelings* were lust, and their *compatibility* was in bed. *The manner I deserve?* Eve felt a pang of foreboding. What did he have in store for her?

"You may be my boss, young man, but you have a lot to

prove to me," Dad warned. Nonetheless, some of the chill faded.

"I relish the challenge, sir."

CHAPTER THIRTY

Restless in bed late that night, Eve disturbed Wally. He abandoned her pillow with a mew of protest, jumping to the floor to sleep on a vent. Though Eve's body was tired, her mind wouldn't settle. The events of the day replayed over and over. There was no way she could sleep. Giving up, she flung off her comforter and flicked on the lamp, then padded downstairs, where she grabbed a bottle of whiskey from the drinks cart and a glass from the kitchen.

Back in bed, Eve sipped her whiskey and thought. Opening the drawer in the nightstand, she pulled out the velvet jeweler's box. The stone glittered fire and ice when she turned it in the lamplight. She put it in the palm of her hand, testing its weight and contemplating how Jake would place it on her finger the following day. Disturbed, she put the ring away, pouring another drink.

Eve managed to fall asleep at dawn, sinking into deep slumber caused by over-imbibing whiskey. The alarm ringing on her phone pulled her from the murky depths. Poking a hand from under the toasty recesses of her comforter to silence it, she brought the phone to her face. It was twelve-thirty, and she was due at the courthouse at one. "Shit!"

She tossed back her blankets and leaped from the bed, her head pounding from a hangover. She was in danger of being late for her own wedding. Wind rattled the windowpanes, so Eve disregarded the dress she'd laid out the evening before and found a navy suit in her closet. Harried, she slipped into the pants, then a frilly polka dot blouse. Before tying the pussy bow at a jaunty angle at her neck, she slid her arms into the fitted jacket. Tucking in her blouse, she surveyed her hair, which was in the loose braid she'd done before bed. Eve snatched at the elastic band and combed her hands through her hair. It would have to do.

I'm getting married today. It seemed surreal. Negotiating the heavy downtown traffic on the way to the courthouse was a distraction. With time to dwell over her upcoming nuptials, she'd be in bits. Instead, Eve concentrated on finding a parking spot and reaching Judge Morrison's chambers as fast as possible. Climbing the flight of stairs, Eve checked her phone. She was ten minutes late. At the landing, she paused to collect herself. Shrugging out of her coat, folding it over her forearm, she tucked her hair behind her ears. *Breathe.* She heard voices around the corner. *Here goes nothin'.*

"Ah, this must be the bride," a woman in a judge's robe said. Jake wore his usual dark suit and a grouchy expression. Her tardiness clearly irked him. Beside him was Lex Carter. Eve tried not to gawk at Lex's goth-like attire — a sheer black sheath over a pleather mini dress which exposed tattoos on her arms and chest. At Eve's perusal, Lex's mouth screwed into a rebellious grin, her jeweled lip piercing catching the light. *Why didn't Jake tell me his sister would be here?*

She tore her gaze from Lex, giving the judge what she hoped was a winsome smile, though her lips were rubbery. "Sorry. Traffic."

"No problem," Judge Morrison assured her. "Let's head to my chambers."

"Ring?" Jake asked. Eve nodded, foraging in her purse. Her anxiety kicked in, making it hard to breathe. *This is happening.* Her hand trembled when she held out the jeweler's box. Jake frowned and took her coat, handing it to Lex. He chaperoned Eve to the waiting judge. *Does he think I'm gonna bolt for the door?*

Judge Morrison explained, "This ceremony's

straightforward. I'll ask you in turn if you're free to marry and you'll affirm you are. Then you'll endorse the marriage certificate. Shall we begin?"

Eve lost her ability to focus. The roller coaster approached a dizzying descent, and she braced for impact. She forgot to inhale and exhale. Jake nudged her when it was her turn to say, "I am." She was barely aware of Judge Morrison asking Jake for his affirmation. The flashy diamond ring was shackled on her finger. Eve looked up from the ring and met Jake's gaze. *Is this real life?* As Jake bent to kiss her cheek, his face was expressionless. Light-headed, she let the breath she'd been holding go.

Jake's manner threw her. He acted as if this was another day at the office, a deal brokered. *Is this a successful takeover? Isn't this what he wanted?* Eve signed the marriage certificate, reeling. *That's it? I'm married?* Clumsily, she handed the pen to Jake, searching his face for any indication of his feelings. His signature was bold, scrawled with no hesitation, but his face remained blank. *He's not the least bit bothered.* Jake held her coat for her while Lex signed as a witness. Eve disguised her bewilderment.

"I must return to the office, but since Alexandra was kind enough to attend, I thought it would be nice for you to take her for a meal," Jake said, buttoning his coat and draping his cashmere scarf around his neck. *Take Lex to lunch?*

Heart aflutter, Eve tied the sash to her raincoat. She couldn't keep her hands still. Did she want to have lunch with Lex? Not really, she wanted to *run*. She scrambled for an excuse, but her ingrained sense of manners won. "Does she know about our . . . arrangement?"

"Of course." From his pocket, Jake produced a black charge card with Eve's name on it. "Use this for lunch."

Without another word, he nodded his farewell. Eve closed her fingers over the card. Watching her new husband walk down the hallway without a backward glance, she wrestled with her confusion. Maybe that was Jake's plan—to leave her guessing, leave her wanting more. Was she relieved? Regretful? Indifferent? She would've been hard-pressed to answer if asked.

They were playing an odd game Eve didn't know the rules to.

She wasn't aware of Lex beside her until she said, "What a fuckin' charade. I've passed kidney stones less painful. The least you can do is buy me a T-bone for witnessing *that*."

Lex poured steak sauce on her meat with a heavy hand. Chewing, she glowered in Eve's direction. Eve pretended she didn't notice, squeezing lemon into her herbal tea. Unspent adrenaline coursed through her veins. Nauseous from her hangover, she hadn't been able to stomach the idea of food. Lex's rare steak revolted her. Another peep at the blood pooling on her plate, and she would be running to the bathroom, hand over mouth.

"I want you to know I'm *not* on your team. I'm team Jake, one hundred percent."

After a moment's hesitation, Eve murmured, "I'm sure I'm the villainess in his version of events."

"Did you abort my brother's baby so you'd be free to marry a rich man?" Lex's voice was strident, her expression a mixture of slyness and disdain. Tea slopped over the edge of Eve's cup, burning her hand. The couple at the neighboring table stopped their conversation and turned to gawk. Eve's face flushed with embarrassment. She glared at them until they glanced away, then placed her cup back on the saucer with a clink.

Her voice wobbled when she quietly asked, "Jake thinks I had *an abortion*?"

Lex sipped her wine. "We've discussed it."

Christ. What's happened to my life? Eve put a hand to her temple to rub away her headache, but it was hopeless. Did Jake think her capable of such cold-hearted deceit, or was it Lex's suspicions manifesting? She wondered what she'd ever done to deserve her misfortune. *It's gotta be bad karma.*

Lex hadn't any right to delve into her personal life, Eve decided, her mouth tightening. She wasn't sure she'd be able to gather the courage to discuss the miscarriage with Jake — she certainly wasn't going to with Lex. The diamond on her finger glittered. Eve quashed the urge to yank it off and put it in her purse, out of sight. Clinging to her tattered dignity, she said, "I believe in a woman's right to choose, but like I told Jake, I miscarried. And that's all I'm gonna say about that."

She couldn't tell if Lex believed her, but didn't care. Eve wanted to get up from the table and leave Lex to find her own damn ride home. She'd had enough of the Carter siblings. Sipping her tea and keeping her sentiments to herself took everything she had.

"I don't understand why my brother insisted on marrying you, but I suppose you can't be worse than any of his other conquests. You're ancient compared to most of 'em though," Lex told Eve with a casual wave of her hand.

"Gee, thanks."

"They were idiots. They reeked of desperation. They thought he'd fall in love with them, but that ain't Jake." Lex signaled the waiter to order dessert and coffee. Eve requested more tea, and sat back in her chair, crossing her arms. "They were out on their asses when they didn't play by his rules."

"Charming," Eve remarked in a dry tone. "And I was graced with a proposal? Wasn't I *lucky*?"

Lex laughed, and Eve was struck by how attractive she was. She and Jake shared excellent genes. Did Lex have men fawning over her, or did the shaved head and combat boots keep them at bay? Maybe she wore her pleather and piercings as a shield. Lex's lips contorted into a smile. "When they find Jake's off the market, they'll be devastated."

Eve rolled her eyes heavenward. "Perhaps they can form a support group to help them overcome their despair."

Veil of flippancy lifting for a moment, Lex appraised her without cunning for the first time that day. "You're an enigma to me, Eve. You're different than I expected."

"You mean different than your brother described me? I'm no *femme fatale*," Eve said. Their waiter arrived with tea on a silver tray for her, placing a cup of coffee and a slice of cake in front of Lex.

Lifting a forkful of cake to her mouth, Lex mused, "A money-grubbing climber with zero scruples, capable of doing anything to snag a rich husband? Or a woman whose biggest crime was to spurn my brother? Time will tell."

CHAPTER THIRTY-ONE

"So, the nicest thing I can say about her is her tattoos match," Eve said, sitting on the counter next to the fridge while Addy added more cumin to the pot on the cooktop.

"Put you through the wringer, didn't she? Blimey." Positioning the lid on the pot, Addy stretched for a mixing bowl from the cabinet. Ingredients for cornbread waited in a tidy row. Addy measured the dry ingredients before breaking an egg into the batter. She pushed the bowl over to Eve, along with a wooden spoon. As Eve stirred, Addy poured in a splash of milk.

"We're obligated to invite her to Thanksgiving," Eve said as Addy placed the cast iron skillet into the oven. The familiar squeak of the front door opening told her that her dad was home from work.

Settling at the kitchen table with a mug of coffee, he sniffed the air. "Chili?"

"Yes, with sausage and cubed beef. The way you like." Addy beamed, then added, "Remember, Sylvie and the children are coming to dinner tonight. She's giving Eve and me haircuts after. We also need to discuss wedding dresses." Dad said nothing while he drank his coffee. Addy tapped Eve's hand. "Mind fetching a pound of butter from the basement freezer?"

"Sure." Eve kept her tone light, but when she descended the stairs, her throat clogged with tears. Her father had barely spoken to her after the bombshell news of her and Jake's engagement. *He's probably worried about what else I'm hiding from him.* She thought of Barbee. *Dad's right to worry.* Stress made Eve's body ache like she'd been run over by a truck.

Eve was walking a tenuous tightrope, and no matter how carefully she tried to balance, she couldn't. She'd spent the afternoon ruminating over her courthouse marriage and the eventful lunch. In the end, she decided to hold off on bringing up the miscarriage to Jake. Dredging it up was unbearable. "Chickenshit," she mumbled in the silence of the laundry room.

Eve heard a noise coming from her father's den. Investigating, she found the normally closed door to Dad's darkroom ajar. Wally reclined on the base of the enlarger, the developer tray upturned. She expected to see spilled chemicals, but the tray must've been empty. *Thank goodness.* Wally blinked a grin, licking a paw and rubbing it over his face. She scolded, "This is a no kitty zone."

Putting the tray back where it belonged, Eve picked Wally up, noticing prints hung to dry on the clothesline. Scratching Wally under his chin, she studied them. There were snaps of Addy on the Staten Island Ferry with the Statue of Liberty in the background, the wind ruffling her hair and at Strawberry Fields, placing a bouquet of forget-me-nots on the Imagine memorial with tears on her cheeks. There was one in front of the fountain at Columbus Circle, with a mouthful of pretzel and a sheepish look as if caught unawares until the last second. Her skin was creamy, and her eyes twinkled. The sun shone on her hair.

The camera adored Addy, and heart-swelling, Eve realized her father did, too. The photos said it better than any love letter could.

Looks like Dad and Addy have some secrets of their own.

"Can you manage a wedding dress *and* the gown for the gala?" Eve asked while Sylvie combed her hair. In addition to working as a stylist, Sylvie wanted to open a dress shop. Last time she and the children had come for dinner, Eve had looked through the portfolio she'd brought along.

"It's the slow season. The wedding dress isn't a problem, but when's the gala?"

"The second Saturday of December. If you don't have time, I'll buy off the rack." Eve waited for Sylvie to unsnap her cape, checking her hair in the hand-held mirror. Moving to Addy's chair, Sylvie placed the cape over her shoulders with a flick of her wrist.

"Same as last time?" Sylvie asked, combing through Addy's shoulder-length tresses.

"Yes, ta."

Eve found another can of soda for Sylvie in the fridge, then popped it open and placing it on the table within reach.

Pushing back a lock of brown hair, Sylvie flashed Eve a smile, which lit up her face and transformed her from rather plain to cute. "I should be able to throw together a simple dress. What did you have in mind?"

"Simple," Eve assured her, flipping through Addy's issue of *Winter Bride* magazine. "Include a hefty surcharge for rushing. Jake can afford it."

"She likes vintage styles," Addy told Sylvie, then looked at Eve. "How about a nineteen fifties inspired bridal gown?"

It didn't matter. Why should it? Eve wasn't a typical bride. The wedding was for show. "Sure."

"I'll research it. Maybe I can do a three-quarter length sleeve, or make a capelet? Let me have a think." Sylvie checked Addy's hair for symmetry, scissors snipping. "Tell me about this gala."

"I don't know much." Eve lifted a shoulder. "It's in the city, at The Courtenay-Blake, for a charity Jake supports. I'm to meet his mentor, Arthur Tate. Jake says the Tates are to Port Breakwater what the *Kennedys* are to Hyannis Port."

"Port Breakwater? The Courtenay-Blake? These people are

rich," Sylvie said.

Addy added, "Everyone will be dressed to the nines."

Sylvie took a drink of her soda. "Jewel tones will be popular this time of year. What were you thinking of wearing?"

"I don't know." Eve shrugged. "Jake says there will be dancing, so I have to be able to move. Other than that, I'm open to suggestions. Your portfolio proves you know how to dress a woman's body, Sylvie. I'll leave the style up to you."

"I'll suggest light blue," Addy said. "Eve looks fabulous in that color."

"I've got my tape in my minivan. I'll take your measurements before I leave."

Addy put a hand on Eve's arm. "I researched reception venues on your father's laptop yesterday, and I think I found one. I'll call them tomorrow, and then I'll search for invitation ideas."

"Sounds like a plan," Eve said, grateful Addy had taken over the wedding planning. She couldn't care less. "Sylvie, are you still coming for Thanksgiving dinner?"

"Yes, my ex will have the kids and my parents are traveling to my brother's in Arizona." Sylvie unbuttoned the cape and lifted it from Addy. "I'll make a pecan pie."

Addy picked up the mirror. "Oh, scrummy."

Grabbing the broom and dustpan from the pantry, Eve swept hair while Sylvie went to her van for her tape measure. She'd finished jotting down Eve's measurements on a scrap of paper when five-year-old Aiden appeared in the doorway, rubbing his eyes. "Mommy, the movie's over. Gabby fell asleep, but I didn't."

"Okay, buddy. Put your coat on, and I'll be there in a minute." She assembled her supplies and set her empty soda cans on the counter. "I've got to get the kids home."

"I'll help get them into your van," Addy offered.

Eve peeked in the living room. Her dad was snoring in his

club chair, and Gabby was stretched out on the sofa. Eve pressed money in Sylvie's hand, giving the woman a quick hug of thanks.

"A hundred dollars! That's way too much." She handed some back, but Eve shook her head.

"Give it to Santa for the kids' Christmas gifts."

Chapter Thirty-two

The parade blared on the living room TV while they worked in the kitchen, listening to the host's commentary. The house was permeated with the smell of roasting turkey, and at the table, Eve and her dad peeled and diced potatoes from a ten-pound sack.

"Remind me to put the broccoli casserole in at noon, Evie," Addy said.

Eve nodded, then stilled. "Thumbs is coming."

They assembled in front of the TV to watch the balloons move down Central Park West. The cameras panning, Dad said, "He's wearing a bowtie and top hat this year."

Nostalgia swelled in Eve's heart, the memories of her childhood holidays warming her. For several minutes, they viewed the parade until the gray cat floated from camera range. Eve put her arm around her father, her head on his shoulder.

"When I was five, Dad took me to the city to see the parade," Eve explained to Addy, holding her arm out to encourage her into the fold. "It's not Thanksgiving at the Shawcross house until we see Thumbs."

"We'll have to go see the parade in person," Addy said, squeezing Eve's shoulder. The football game had begun when Eve spotted Jake's sports car at the curb through the living room window. Married over a week, it was the first time she'd see him since the courthouse ceremony. Eve's breath quickened when she checked herself in the hall mirror. She wore a black tunic over skinny jeans, a plaid scarf looped around her neck, and her hair was in a messy bun. The doorbell rang as she applied clear lip gloss.

"Got it," Eve hollered over her shoulder, adjusting her gold hoop earrings when she opened the door.

Lex held up a dark bottle of wine with a red foil label, her smile playful. "I pilfered Jake's wine cellar this morning. This is the good shit, sis."

Behind her, Jake held more bottles. Hair damp from a recent shower, he smelled of musk and citrus. *Talk about smoking hot.* A woman with less restraint would climb him like a tree and bite his neck, Eve decided. Speechless, she took Lex's crushed velvet cloak.

Dad and Addy waited outside the foyer for Eve to introduce Lex. Addy had changed into a shirt saying, *I'm Into Fitness – Fitten' This Turkey In My Mouth.* Though Eve had prepared her dad for Lex's fashion, his eyebrows lifted when he saw Lex's skimpy dress. Today her eyelids and lips were heavily lined in black.

Eve's mouth quirked at Lex's awkward reaction when Addy drew her in for a hug. "How lovely to meet you, darling."

Shucking his navy peacoat, Jake bypassed Eve to put it in the closet. *He's making himself right at home.* She was conscious of the magnetic buzz charging the air whenever he was around. It was the first time since she'd been back that he wore jeans, but he didn't need a suit to look good enough to devour. Jake's moss-colored shirt brought out the hazel in his irises and molded to his muscled chest and biceps. And his jeans hugged *all* the right places, Eve noted, as he shook her father's outstretched hand.

"Jake and Lex brought wine," Eve announced. Lex sprawled on the couch beside Sylvie. *She'd better behave herself.*

"Eve, it would be a good idea to open the wine to let it breathe," Jake said. "Come help me."

"Would you mind checking the potatoes while you're in there, pet?" Addy asked, intent on the game. Their team scored a touchdown, and Addy clapped with enthusiasm. Dad's affinity for football had rubbed off on her. "Now, Jim, they got six points for the touchdown . . ."

Pretending to inspect the stylized eagle on the label of the wine bottle as they went into the kitchen, Eve's interest was instead on Jake's firm backside.

He uncorked the first bottle with the sure, confident actions of someone knowing their way around a corkscrew. Slouching against the fridge, Eve feigned indifference, yet the air pulsated with sexual tension. Uncorking another bottle, Jake said, "Alexandra said you two had a good time at your lunch."

"It was super," she murmured. Aware of his scrutiny, she blushed. Briefly considering questioning Jake about what Lex asked at lunch, Eve lacked the courage. *Now ain't the time.*

He lifted the bottle. "This wine is good enough to drink right away, want some?" Dry-mouthed, Eve was suddenly desperate for a drink.

Jake splashed the deep garnet colored liquid into a wineglass, swirled it, then drank. "Mmm. My favorite wine and my favorite girl. Life doesn't get much better than this."

"Nobody's in here. You don't have to put on a performance." Eve threw him side-eye, but took the goblet from him, giving it a delicate sniff. She was no expert, but she detected notes of plum, blackberry, and perhaps currants. The wine was full-bodied, dry, and smooth on her taste buds. *Something this good deserves to be savored.* Eyes shut, Eve took another sip, holding the wine in her mouth before swallowing. When her eyelids fluttered open, she found Jake studying her, his gaze penetrating. She cleared her throat.

"A religious experience, isn't it?" Jake whispered, bringing a thumb to her lip to wipe away a drop of wine left behind.

He licked the moisture from his thumb, and Eve gulped, transfixed by the way he stared at her mouth. "I never got a proper kiss at the ceremony, did I?"

Breath hitching, Eve realized she'd been anticipating this moment since they last kissed. She didn't protest when Jake took the wineglass and set it on the counter. Cupping her face in his hands, he dropped his mouth to hers. Lips brushing hers, he lingered to inhale her breath. He did nothing else, waiting for Eve to yield, and yield she did, closing her eyes and seeking his lips so she could savor them the same way she had the wine. Jake tasted of chocolate, honey, and potent desire. The world dissolved away.

Even the knowledge she was playing with fire didn't stop her from responding when Jake's tongue teased hers. Eve opened to him, willing to give him anything at that moment. The power of her want was painful. Blood pounding in her ears, she twined her arms around his neck, pressing into him. A low sigh escaped her lips. His arousal through his jeans verified he wanted her as much as she wanted him.

Gently scraping his teeth against her lower lip, he captured it to suck on it. His fingers found the hem of her shirt, and he trailed his fingertips over the bare skin of her stomach. She made a sound like a hiss when he caressed his way to her breast, finding her pebbled nipple through her bra. Vaguely aware of jeers and boos from the living room when the opposing team scored, she felt reality come back as sure as two cymbals crashing. *What am I doing?* Eve wrenched away, touching a finger to her kiss swollen lips.

Leaning back against the counter and lifting the wineglass, Jake stared at her, his expression wolfish.

CHAPTER THIRTY-THREE

Dad carved the turkey at the head of the table. Eve was hyper-aware of Jake seated across the table. Her body was, too. Her pulse thrummed at her center, reminding her she needed satiation. Her hands trembled when she scooped broccoli from the casserole onto her plate. She avoided Jake's perceptive grin.

"My ex picked the kids up yesterday." Sylvie put her napkin in her lap. "Last night was the first solid eight hours of sleep I've gotten in months."

"I don't know how you do it." Addy spooned potatoes onto her plate and held the bowl for Eve. "Evie?"

"Sorry. Woolgathering," Eve mumbled, taking the dish. She'd been fantasizing about throwing Jake on her bed and having her wicked way with him.

"I won't be as busy once I finish my online business course," Sylvie said.

Eve asked, "How close are you to opening a shop?"

Lex heaped potatoes on her plate and drowned them in gravy. *That girl can pack it away.*

Sylvie replied, "I'm afraid it's a pipedream, since I have zero capital. I've researched grants and micro-lenders, but . . ."

"It's not unusual to have funding issues as an entrepreneur." Jake's voice was kind, and Eve scrutinized him from across the table, startled. Why did his kindness surprise her? "Have you completed your business plan?"

Sylvie pulled a face. "I'm working on it."

"Why don't you come by my office? I'll take a look at what you have so far and see if I can help," Jake said, and Eve smiled. He caught her eye and winked.

"That would be great. Thanks, Jake."

"The *pièce de résistance*," Dad announced, raising the platter, and they clapped, buoyed by wine and high spirits.

Her mind occupied, Eve nibbled absentmindedly as everybody dug into their food. When they helped themselves to seconds, Addy, an animated hostess, shared stories about her kindergarten students.

"Aiden says he's going to be an elf in the Christmas pageant," Sylvie said. "He has a striped hat and plastic ears to wear."

"I'm definitely coming to watch. Maybe we can all go to dinner afterward," Eve said, and Sylvie nodded, putting her fork and knife across her plate.

"When's the program at Consolidated?" Addy asked Eve.

"The Thursday before Christmas."

Jake frowned. "What program?"

Lex, who had been quiet and observant through the meal, ribbed him, "Guess you don't know *everything*, big brother."

Eve raised an eyebrow, asking Jake, "*I'm* in charge of the center, aren't I?"

Jake put his hands up.

Chuckling, she collected dirty dishes. "Flyers will be posted Monday."

"Oh, no, my dear. The men clean up." Dad pulled his napkin from the collar of his sweater, standing.

"You ladies relax, and I'll bring coffee," Jake said.

Reclining back in her chair and yawning, Addy stretched her arms over her head as Dad cleared the table. "I can get used to this."

The sound of clinking dishes and the murmur of Dad and Jake's conversation drifted into the dining room. Sylvie told

Lex, "It was nice of your brother to offer to help me with my business plan."

Lex grinned. "Jake has his moments."

Eve recalled their kiss. *I'll say.*

"You hens going Black Friday shopping?" Addy asked, and they chatted until Jake brought coffee. With his shirt-sleeves pushed past his elbows, he wore Addy's salmon-colored apron. His domesticity seeming so out of character, Eve bit back a cackle. His arch look told her he was affronted, but he bowed with flourish after depositing the tray on the table.

As he headed back to the kitchen, they chorused in unison, "Thank you, Jake."

"I'll play mother," Addy said, pouring coffee and distributing cups.

"I'm dying of curiosity." Lex tilted her head toward the mixed media sketchbook and basket of art supplies on the buffet. She reached for the book before Eve could protest. She wasn't sure how she felt about Lex flicking through it, though the drawings were innocuous enough.

Addy beamed. "Eve's our resident artist."

"I've taken classes, but I'm strictly an amateur." Eve crammed down nagging feelings of inadequacy. "I've been experimenting with watercolor over graphite."

Lex looked at Eve with a thoughtful expression, shaking her head. "These are good. I have a friend who's looking for an illustrator. Would you take on a commission?"

"What?" Eve laughed.

"I'll introduce you, see if you two click." Lex cautioned, "It won't pay much, but it'll help build a portfolio—if that's what you want."

"Let me see these masterpieces," Sylvie demanded. She studied a graphite sketch of a toddler at the shore, the muted watercolors highlighting the rolling surf and the chubby curve of the child's cheek. "Wow. You have talent, Eve."

Eve felt her face heat at the praise. Addy sounded proud when she asked, "Did you see the cardinal? She painted that last week."

Later, after the sun set low on the horizon and guests left, Eve lingered in the dining room, poring over her sketches. Were they good enough? Was she capable of illustrating professionally? She wasn't sure, but the prospect intrigued her. She'd think about it, but now all she wanted was to tuck up into bed.

Yawning, Eve went to put her cup in the dishwasher. Approaching the darkened kitchen, she came upon her dad and Addy in the shadows by the sink, arms wrapped around each other in a passionate embrace.

CHAPTER THIRTY-FOUR

Eve followed behind the butler, Charles, as he carried her luggage into one of the bedrooms of the beautifully appointed suite. The immaculate room featured an upholstered headboard, silk drapes, and vases of peonies. Turning to her after placing the luggage on the stand, Charles bowed in deference. "Shall I unpack? Or perhaps madam wants a bath drawn?"

"Uh, no, thank you." Eve tried not to look like a country bumpkin, pulling money from her wallet for a tip. She'd never stayed at a hotel with personal butlers. *Is twenty too much, or not enough?* He accepted the tip, bowing again before leaving.

"Gosh." Sylvie shook her head in awe from the table where she'd set up makeup and brushes. "This place."

"I know," Eve agreed, surveying the living room's velvet sofas, crystal chandeliers, and the floor to ceiling windows overlooking Central Park. "How the other half lives, eh?"

"How *you* live, now," Sylvie reminded her. Eve paused for a moment, flustered, but Sylvie was right. *Do I belong here?* Wearing her ring as Jake insisted, she was otherwise average looking, clad in jeans and a sweater, her hair in a ponytail. She *must* look out of place. Instead of luxurious and pampered, she felt outclassed and uncomfortable.

"I'm glad you agreed to be my stylist today," Eve said, trying to shake off her mood. "And I can't wait to see the dress you designed. I love surprises."

"I was tricky making you close your eyes during the fitting,

139

wasn't I?" Sylvie laughed.

During her manicure and pedicure, Eve's mind wandered. Jake had sent her a short email earlier in the week to let her know what to expect. He'd also forwarded her the confirmation email from The Courtenay-Blake with the reservation number, in case she needed it for check-in. It included the invoice for the suite. One night cost several thousand dollars. Eve, with her fiscally conservative upbringing, balked. If her father knew, he'd slump in a faint.

"You're bothered," Sylvie said, arranging Eve's hair on the top of her head. "What are you thinking?"

"This place is *too* swanky for me," Eve admitted, despising how transparent she was to those around her. "And I'm meeting so many new people tonight. It's daunting."

"I want you to look dewy. And I'll do a light lip." Sylvie applied the foundation on Eve's face with a sponge. "Wanna know what I think?"

Eve looked to the ceiling while Sylvie put mascara on her lashes. "Tell me."

"It's all about attitude. Fake it 'til you make it. I'm not being trite. It works." Sylvie found a pink lip stain, using the applicator to demonstrate how to tap the powder onto Eve's lips. When satisfied, she added a dab of shimmer on the center of Eve's bottom lip. "I'll leave this so you can reapply."

Eve glanced at the clock on the fireplace mantel. "If Jake doesn't get here soon, we'll miss cocktail hour."

"Let me get the gown, and I'll help you dress." Grabbing the garment bag from where it hung on the back of the bedroom door, she unzipped it. Eve saw flashes of icy blue material. "Don't look yet."

Humoring her, Eve averted her eyes. "All right."

"Okay, step in." When Sylvie zipped the dress, Eve was aware of two things—the luxurious material and the glove-like fit. Sylvie positioned her in front of the bathroom mirror.

"You can look."

Eve's gaze skimmed over the bateau neckline to the ankle-length skirt with its sexy thigh-high slit. *Wow.* She evaluated her reflection. Her hair and makeup were on point, and the gown was gorgeous. *Fake it 'til you make it, huh? I'll try my best.*

Sylvie's gaze met hers. "You like it? Be honest."

"I love it." Eve turned to check the back of the gown in the mirror. "You gave me an hourglass figure. Where have you been my whole life?"

Sylvie giggled. "I know you prefer vintage fashion, so I researched gowns from the nineteen fifties. This is my interpretation of an *Edith Head* design."

On the way back to the living room, Eve snagged a bottle of water from the kitchenette fridge, handing it to Sylvie. "You were right about these strappy silver heels. They're perfect. You're an artiste."

Laughing, Sylvie twisted the cap from the water bottle. "You're a good canvas."

"You probably say that to all the girls," Eve teased.

"I don't know if I'm supposed to tell you . . ." Sylvie said, and Eve raised an eyebrow. "I got a call from Jake. He wanted to buy you a necklace, so I gave recommendations."

Really? Eve glimpsed out the window. Heavy snow was falling over Central Park, creating a picture-postcard scene. Lifting the phone on the desk, she called Charles to carry Sylvie's bags. Before Sylvie departed, Eve reminded her to drive with care, handing her a generous payment for her services.

The wintry city landscape below beckoned Eve. She watched as a cab, stopping short, rammed another, dangerously close to slamming into the horse-drawn carriage toting tourists around the park. She wagered they'd close up shop soon due to inclement weather. Her thoughts turned to Jake. Was he driving his sports car to the city, or was he chauffeured? A moment later, the door to the suite opened.

Jake was in a tuxedo, fresh shaven, his hair slicked back. *Holy fuck. What's the word? Debonair.* He joined her at the window, a blue jeweler's box in his hand. She untied the red holiday bow, pulling off the lid. It was a choker of creamy pearls and sparkling diamonds. Her voice was husky when she said, "How beautiful. Thank you, Jake."

Eve's gaze rested on Jake's strong, capable hands when he lifted the necklace. She faced the window, and he fastened the clasp. When he brought his lips to the sensitive skin behind her ear, she gasped.

Jake whispered into her ear, "Legend says *Cleopatra* ground pearls into wine. She wanted to drink their beauty."

CHAPTER THIRTY-FIVE

How easy it would've been to give in to her hunger. It'd been too long since she'd felt *good*. All it would take was one kiss, and they'd be tearing off their clothes. Eve knew Jake's prowess in bed. It would be capital H-O-T hot. *Heart-pounding, intense, toe-curling.* She bit her lip as the elevator descended. *The Kama Sutra would have to publish a sequel.*

At the entrance to the ballroom, they paused. Guests mingled, drinks in hand. Most women wore dresses in jewel tones, as Sylvie predicted. The simple elegance and the color of Eve's gown made her stand out like a beacon, which she hadn't taken into consideration. Several people turned to their companions and whispered. She swallowed hard, pretending not to notice. On the far side of the ballroom, the orchestra performed a version of Leo Friedman's *Let Me Call You Sweetheart.*

Jake asked, "Dance?"

Why not? Eve wasn't ready to make polite chitchat, but she loved to dance and hadn't had the opportunity for many months.

Her face stinging with heat from the inquisitive looks she received, they made their way through the crowd to the dancefloor. Plastering on a demure expression, Eve was determined to keep the mask in place for the evening. *Fake it 'til you make it, right?*

In Jake's arms, everything vanished. It was only him—the satiny feel of the vicuna fabric of the tux under her fingertips, the bergamot of his cologne, and the possessive way his hands clasped her waist.

Bodies meshing like puzzle pieces, where she was soft, he was solid. It was innately sexual how their bodies communicated. Hips swaying to the music in a choreography of foreplay, the rhythm of dance mimicked the rhythm of sex.

She brought her head back to meet Jake's gaze. He watched her, nostrils flaring. The raw need she found made her melt. No longer under her own volition, Eve buried her fingers in his hair and pulled his mouth to hers.

A jovial voice shattered their bubble. "There you are, young man!" With an almost imperceptible groan, Jake straightened, nodding at the septuagenarian in a natty plaid bow tie and cummerbund. What hair he had on his head was white and combed over his freckled pate. Eyebrows dark and steeply arched, his smile tempered the harsh contours of his face. "What a fine pair of dancers you are. The guests are wondering who this fetching lady is."

Jake cleared his throat. "Eve, meet Arthur."

Arthur extended a large, warm hand to her. "Enchanted, simply enchanted."

"Hello." Eve was a trifle breathless, and her cheeks suffused with heat, but Arthur's expression was amiable. She shook off her embarrassment, returning his smile.

"Come greet my daughter-in-law. She arranged this shindig." An ash-blonde woman in her mid-forties was in a circle of people, speaking in a spirited fashion, hands fluttering. She wore a chic embroidered kimono and chunky jewelry. Nose blade-like and long, it touched her upper lip. It dominated her patrician-featured face, but Eve thought it lent her character. Her self-assurance was alluring, shouting *old money!*

"Hester," Arthur boomed. "This is Eve, Jake's fiancée."

Cornflower blue eyes pinned Eve. *Why does she look familiar?* Hester nodded cordially, indicating the man at her side, a younger version of Arthur but with more hair. "My husband, Thomas. And I see my reprobate brother. At last. Eve, allow me to introduce Hitchcock Grant."

"Hitch?" Her best friend was before her in the flesh. With a whoop, he seized her in a bear hug and spun her. Eve squealed, swatting at his arm to make him release her. Setting her down, he planted a smooch on her cheek. She noticed Jake's narrowed gaze on them.

"Evie! Here of all places. Let's dance and catch up." As if an afterthought, Hitch glanced at Jake. Pausing for an instant, Jake nodded assent.

Eve let Hitch guide her to the dancefloor. She felt Jake's hawk-like eyes tracking them while he visited with Arthur and Thomas. She stifled a groan when the orchestra started a rendition of *La cumparsita*. *If I know my show-off BFF . . .*

"Like we learned at our lessons? It's my favorite and I never get to." Hitch gave her pleading puppy dog eyes.

Jake will love the attention we'll receive. She warned, "I'm rusty."

"C'mon. For Ol' Hitch?"

In a nanosecond of impulsivity, Eve indulged him. *I deserve to have fun.* It had been eons since she let loose and dancing with Hitch was a blast.

In a provocative sashay, Eve walked behind him, then moved into him, snaking a hand around his side to rest a palm against his chest. Sliding to Hitch's side, as if to evade him, she focused on counting steps. She did the fancy footwork required before twirling into his arms. Choking back a giggle when Hitch slithered fingers up her side and down her arm, he drew her hand to his. Dancing with Hitch wasn't sexy—it was comical. How different it was dancing the waltz with Jake.

People viewed them with frank admiration, forming a semi-circle around them. With a roll of his wrist, Hitch whirled Eve away, pirouetting her in an elaborate display of exaggerated sensuality.

Hitch, with his lean athletic form, was light on his feet, and a superb dancer. Eve required concentration. She was in the zone, blocking all else out. Before the final dip, someone handed Hitch a long-stemmed red rose. Ham that he was, he played along, securing it between his teeth. He waggled his eyebrows, splaying her across his knee, Eve's head dangling over the floor. Chest rising and falling with exertion, she saw Jake where she'd left him, beyond the clapping spectators. His face dark, he looked pissed. *Oh-oh. Danger, Will Robinson.* Hitch brought her back to her feet and they curtsied to their fans.

"Exhibitionist," Eve teased, catching her breath, pretending to be unaware of Jake. Hitch handed her the rose.

"Guilty as charged." Hitch grinned, not even winded. Another song began, and they settled into a dignified foxtrot, which was far less flamboyant.

"I can't believe you're here. Small world."

"There's nothing smaller than the world of the super-rich, doll," Hitch said. Eve stole a look at Jake. His manner was indifferent, but she recognized the radiating suspicion. Clearly, Hitch Grant was a threat.

In normal circumstances, she would've chuckled, but Jake's mistrust sobered her. Knowing Hitch was gay would soothe the savage beast, but coming out was Hitch's choice. Eve wouldn't betray his confidence. Besides, she told herself, they were *just* dancing.

"That Jake is a *snack*. I've seen him at parties. We rich throw lots of those." Hitch said with a measure of self-deprecation, "When we feel bad for squandering money on parties, we organize more parties disguised as fundraisers."

Eve's laugh trilled. "I've missed you."

"Hester said Jake's fiancée was named Eve, but I never imagined it was you. You work *fast*."

Eve gave him an innocent smile. "I've known Jake longer than I've known you."

"If looks could kill, I'd be in an urn in the Grant family mausoleum. Is he always so caveman?"

"I've never paraded a handsome playboy in front of him before," Eve kidded, batting her lashes.

The orchestra struck up another song. "How do you like Arthur?"

"He's a sweetheart."

"He is. Thomas is a decent enough guy, too, although he dresses as if his life is one long brunch." Hitch rolled his eyes.

Eve giggled. "Anything else I should know about the Tates?"

"Arthur has two daughters. One is mind-numbingly dull but harmless enough. Watch out for the younger one, Siobhan," Hitch cautioned.

"Why?"

Hitch clicked his tongue against his teeth. "'Cause Siobhan's a sneaky little hussy. And she's been trying to stick her talons in your man for *years*."

CHAPTER THIRTY-SIX

"I believe that was *three* songs," Jake's said coldly, taking Eve in his arms and steering her to the opposite side of the room.

Her forehead creased into a frown. "You were rude to my friend."

"*Friend*? After that spectacle? I'm no fool." Jake's voice was tight, a muscle working in his jaw. "No man would want to be *friends* with you."

"What happened to keeping emotions in check? Are you jealous?"

"You're my wife," Jake reminded her in a calmer tone. "You were all over each other. I won't be made a fool."

"Making you look foolish isn't what I intended." Eve searched his eyes. *If I asked him about Siobhan Tate, what would he say?*

"This function is important to me, Angie. Come along. Dinner'll be served soon."

They were at a round table at the front of the room, near a podium on a raised dais. Hitch, Hester, and Thomas were across from Eve and Jake. Arthur was seated on Jake's left. An obese woman with a golf ball-sized sapphire brooch on her caftan was beside Eve. Chatty, she was an agreeable dinner companion.

During the multicourse meal, Eve drank too much wine. Mind wandering, she mulled what Hitch had said about Siobhan. Something akin to apprehension gripped her. Why? *It's not like I'm possessive . . . am I?* After coffee and dessert

were served, Hester rose and repositioned her orange kimono. As she stood behind the podium, her smile encom-
passed the entire room.

"Thank you for attending The Grant Collaborative's Sev-
entieth Anniversary Fundraiser. As many of you know, the
foundation was the brainchild of my namesake, my paternal
grandmother, Hester Vanderkellen-Grant. It was her fervent
wish every woman and child, but especially those living in
poverty, had resources in times of crisis. We continue her mission today by providing help for those who need it most . . .
with healthcare assistance, food vouchers, job training . . . and
more." The crowd applauded and Eve joined in. Hester nodded, clapping her hands toward the guests as if to recognize
their patronage. Eve volleyed Hitch an impressed look, and
he lifted his palms in a gesture of modesty.

Hester continued, "I'm pleased to announce an additional
initiative, Fostering with Support, spearheaded by the substantial financial assistance of my friend, Jake Carter, of Carter
Consolidated. Jake, please come up and say a few words."
What? Eve's mouth dropped open. *Jake Carter, benevolent
philanthropist?* He got up to applause. Approaching the podium, he shook Hester's hand, his manner gregarious and at
ease. The room quieted enough to hear a pin drop while he
spoke.

"Although it's not a topic I discuss, as a child I endured
profound abuse and entered my first foster home on my elev-
enth birthday. Since I wasn't the easiest foster child, I didn't
last long at placements." Eve scanned the faces of patrons at
neighboring tables. They looked as shook up at his revelations
as she was. Jake smiled. "In case you're waiting with bated
breath to see if the story has a happy ending, allow me to reassure you, I managed to do okay."

There was a smattering of laughter and Jake chuckled before continuing, "My success wouldn't have been possible

without help. Fostering with Support's guiding principle is not merely does it take a village to raise a child . . . it also takes a village to sustain loving foster families. Fostering with Support will offer resources and mentorship beginning this spring in Old Hillbury. Philanthropy is the lifeblood of the Grant Collaborative, and I thank you for your continued contribution."

After Jake's speech, he ordered a scotch on the rocks from the bar, downing it neatly. Perhaps sharing his past had cost him, Eve mused, but he hid it well. When guests left, she stood by Jake's side while he glad-handed, ever the host. By the time they bade the Tates goodnight, her cheeks hurt from smiling.

Exiting the elevator and walking down the hall to their suite, Eve turned to Jake, but he lifted an indifferent shoulder. "Don't look so stunned, Angie."

"I *am* stunned," she assured him.

"Why?"

"Because, Jake, we're *married* and I know nothing about you." Waiting for him to hold the key card up to the sensor to unlock the door, Eve questioned why she was perturbed. Perhaps it was his laissez-faire attitude. "Don't you think I should know you were an abused child? That you grew up in foster care?"

He didn't answer. Tossing his jacket aside, Jake poured them whiskeys at the sideboard. Handing her a glass, he untied the bow at his neck. Eve slipped off her silver sandals and buried her sore toes in the plush pile of the rug. Dropping to the sofa, she curled into a corner, reflective.

Jake's reticence caused nagging tentacles of dread to tickle her gut, which, to her chagrin, manifested to agitation. Why wouldn't he let her in? And what about Arthur's daughter?

Tone sharp, Eve demanded, "Tell me about you and Siobhan Tate."

CHAPTER THIRTY-SEVEN

Jake flopped into an occasional chair across from Eve, drink in hand and a derisive expression on his face. "I see Grant's been telling tales. He's not above shit-stirring when it benefits him."

"I asked him about Arthur's family, and he mentioned Siobhan." She battled to be reasonable. "What can Hitch possibly have to gain by sharing that?"

"You didn't see the way he looked at you while you were dancing."

"It was for show. I knew what would happen when we tangoed, but I won't apologize for my decision. Truly, it was in jest." Eve put her whiskey down on the table, leveling him with a solemn look. "I wanted to . . . let loose. Have fun, for once."

"Hmm." Jake traveled a thumb across his lower lip. "Are you saying I'm not *fun*?" His tone held a hint of innuendo.

Intense, exciting, and unreadable, maybe. Eve's gaze locked on the dimple in his cheek. She knew what kind of *fun* Jake meant. She cleared her throat. "I'm saying you have nothing to fret about. I'm not attracted to Hitch. And, as you said, I'm *your* wife."

"Siobhan Tate and I have history." Eve's eyes widened at Jake's unexpected candor. He said, "She's a spoiled little girl who doesn't wish to accept it was over before it began. I see her because she's Arthur's daughter. End of."

Eve got the decanter of whiskey from the sideboard and topped off their tumblers. Before she moved away, Jake reached for her, pulling her onto his lap.

He took the decanter from her, setting it on the floor. "I belong to you," Jake promised.

Her breath hissed when she looked into his eyes. High voltage current zapped straight to her loins.

In a trance, heart skipping, she lowered her face to his. His supple lips were gentle but insistent. The hands gripping her waist tightened when the kiss deepened. A moan escaped Eve when his lips left hers, moving to her neck to suckle the responsive skin there. His fingertips roved up her ribcage to the bodice of her dress, eliciting goosebumps as he fondled her breasts through the fabric.

Pushing the strap of her dress down her arm, Jake brought his mouth to Eve's bare shoulder. Trailing his tongue over the soft flesh before nipping her, he scraped his teeth against the curve of her shoulder. When she gasped, he made a sound deep in his throat, his nimble fingers finding the zipper to her gown. Eve felt his arousal poking at her bottom. She shifted in his lap, finding the waistband of his trousers with confident fingers, emboldened by his groan of satisfaction to open the snap—

The buzz of the suite's doorbell brought them back to earth. Dazed, Eve pulled away from Jake, who panted as she did. Realization of how dangerously close they'd been to having sex sobered her. Trembling, she scrambled from his lap. She ignored the throbbing ache between her thighs and the way her body begged for release. Jake growled. Smoothing his disheveled hair, he fixed his trousers as he went to the door.

Eve collapsed on the sofa. She brought a shaky hand to her cheek, feeling the heat emanating from it. She was burning. How had she let things go so far?

Jake returned, glowering. "A hotel guest had the wrong room."

"I'm glad we were interrupted," Eve said quietly, not

meeting his gaze. "I'm sorry, but I'm not ready, no matter what my body may say."

Jake lowered to the sofa, reaching for her hand. He laced his warm fingers with hers. "I know you need *more* from me, Angie, but my past is tough to talk about. The mention I made in the speech tonight was the most I've ever shared, and that's thanks to you."

"Really?"

He nodded, bringing her hand to his lips to nuzzle it. "Of course."

"Jake," Eve whispered. "You don't think I had an abortion, do you?"

Jake sighed. "Lex?"

"Yes, but you have to know . . . I'd never—"

Jake was silent for a moment, as if struggling to find the right words.

Eve's heartbeat thumped against her ribcage. *Why's he hesitating?*

"I don't believe you lied about the miscarriage."

"You don't sound too sure."

"I did wonder, once," Jake admitted. "The more I get to know you, the more I realize you're nothing like I thought you were."

"Boy, you must've really hated me." Eve picked up her whiskey, knowing she'd be hungover if she didn't cool it, but not caring. Her voice was husky when she said, "It was an awful thing to go through alone."

Jake's hand worked the back of his neck and he sighed again. "If you would've turned to me—"

"For some reason, I always think I have to handle everything on my own. If I could go back, I'd do a lot of things differently, believe me." Eve finished her drink, setting her empty glass on the table. She took a fortifying breath. "I had a second miscarriage early in my marriage."

Jake said nothing, but once more, he lifted her hand to kiss it, his eyes compassionate.

"I found afterward I have medical issues . . . it was a miracle I got pregnant at all." Eve gave him a tremulous smile, endeavoring to look blasé but failing miserably. "At least when we do have sex, we won't have to use protection."

Jake's mouth pursed. "Let me guess. Pierce wasn't open to adoption?"

Eve shook her head, blinking back tears. Jake gathered her into his arms and held her, kissing her forehead. "He was a damn fool," he said, his voice gruff.

CHAPTER THIRTY-EIGHT

"That was . . . eventful." Jake maneuvered his car through commuter traffic in downtown Old Hillbury.

"Preschool holiday programs can be," Eve murmured, rubbing her hands together to warm them in front of the dash vents.

"Where are your gloves, Angie?" Jake scolded, pressing a button to switch on her seat heater. "The parents were complimentary — despite technical difficulties."

"The CD worked fine earlier," Eve grumbled. "*Naturally*, it acts up at performance time."

"You handled it."

"Try to be the lone singer in front of fifty people and tell me how painless it is," Eve muttered. "The teachers could've sung louder to help me. I'm no *Rosemary Clooney*."

"I think you established that," Jake teased.

She clucked. "Hey, zip it, you."

Jake laughed, tuning the radio to Christmas music as he drove to Rockwater. Eve studied his profile in the glow of the dashboard, the familiar sexual pull tugging. Since the gala, he'd been downright beguiling. As time passed, she thawed, overlooking her misgivings and how bitter he'd sounded during their first meetings. She sent up a silent prayer that her trust wasn't misplaced.

In the darkness, the lit windows cast swathes of warm yellow light over the glittering lawns of the snug homes. Thick snow fell, adding magic to the night and reminding Eve of Christmases past. At her mew of happiness, Jake turned to

155

her, an eyebrow raised, "You okay?"

"Oh, waxing nostalgic about my childhood. Rockwater still looks exactly the same, you know." Eve took in the adorable houses on Yankee Drive, thinking they would be perfect in a holiday movie. Jake pulled to the curb in front of Dad's Tudor. He put the car in park and swiveled in his seat, studying her.

Eve's voice became wistful with remembrance. "I was ten — the first year Dad put the nativity scene in the front yard. It looked as you see now — and we'd returned from Christmas Eve services at church. Dad parked and said, *What's that wiseman holding instead of frankincense?* When I ran to look, I found a crimson velvet box with a green tartan bow. The tag read, *For Beloved Eve.*"

When she paused, Jake asked, "What was it?"

"A gold heart-shaped locket, and inside were pictures of my parents as babies. It was so beautiful, so special." Eve swallowed the emotion in her throat. "I lost the locket when I was in middle school, and I never forgave myself."

"Your father didn't replace it?"

"I didn't tell him. I felt terribly guilty." Eve shook herself from her reverie, giving Jake a smile. "We'd better go inside. Addy told me she'd have a full house and needs help."

They stepped over the threshold, meeting pandemonium, along with the pungent aroma of burned food. A red-faced toddler sat on the floor in a pool of red wine, wailing for her blanket, which Dad was using to dab at the spill.

Aiden and his three-year-old sister stood on the sofa, in a tug-of-war over a toy. Aiden's cheeks were flushed with exertion. Gabby howled in indignation. Aiden gave one last tug, and Gabby lost the battle. Her howls turned to ear-splitting shrieks, piercing Eve's soul.

Through it all, a smoke detector alarm pealed, insistent, from the hallway.

Jake prodded Eve to action, opening the hall closet for a

broom and waving it in front of the detector. She bent to the screaming toddler, whisking the baby into her arms. Shushing her, Eve found a toy to appease Gabby. When the alarm ceased, the room was still.

Eve bit her lip to keep from tittering. "Hiya, Dad."

The banging of cookery drifted from the kitchen, along with Addy's voice. "Bloody prehistoric bloody stove!"

Aiden's eyes went big when Addy's language became more colorful. Jake winced, throwing Eve a look of amused astonishment. Mopping sweat from his brow with a handkerchief, Dad opened a window. He sputtered before admitting in a small voice, "I am not much of a babysitter, apparently."

Eve held the baby on her lap, positioned on the sofa between Aiden and Gabby to discourage any further skirmishes. She giggled when her dad sagged in his club chair, his expression stupefied. At the drinks cart, Jake collected club soda, salt, and a cloth napkin. He knelt to attend the carpet. Patting the baby's back, Eve watched his actions with rapt absorption. Seeing Jake doing chores around the house made him even sexier. She imagined the headline in *The Times – Billionaire Tycoon Transforms into Domestic God!*

Absently, Eve kissed the baby's silken head, asking, "What's her name?"

"Annie. But I prefer to call her *The Terminator*."

"Dad," Eve chided. From her peripheral vision, she saw Jake's shoulders shaking in silent laughter.

Addy emerged from the kitchen, hair mussed and apron askew. "You two are lifesavers. Evie, can you change Annie? Jim, get your shirt and Annie's blankie in the laundry before the stain sets." Turning, she called over her shoulder, "Dinner will be slightly delayed."

Eve found a corduroy dress embroidered with yellow ducks in the diaper bag on the side table. She laid Annie on the carpet and blew a raspberry on her tummy. Annie rewarded Eve with a squeal. Order was restored by the time

Sylvie arrived. Shedding her parka, she sat on the sofa, pulling Aiden and Gabby close. "What a day."

Eve rose, baby on her hip. "I'll grab you a soda." In the kitchen, Addy whipped potatoes on the stovetop, looking flustered. "Can I help?"

"No, pet. Mind Annie. I bit off more than I could chew when I agreed to babysit her, too, but I couldn't say no to a neighbor in need."

Going back into the living room, Eve handed Sylvie the soda. After a long drink, Sylvie said, "We've become a permanent fixture in this house. Hope you're not sick of us."

"If I were, I wouldn't have asked you to be in the wedding," Eve pointed out.

"I don't want to wear out our welcome. When my parents come back from Arizona after the New Year, I won't need Addy to babysit as much."

"You're still coming to Christmas dinner, aren't you?"

"We wouldn't miss it," Sylvie said.

"Soup's on," Addy announced. They filed into the dining room, settling the kids at the table while Addy dished chicken and potatoes. Eve set Annie on her lap and fed her tiny morsels of food. When she felt Jake's scrutiny from across the table, she realized this was the first time he'd seen her interact one-on-one with a child.

"We need to talk wedding plans," Addy said. She'd insisted on winter-themed nuptials with all the trimmings. Privately, Eve thought it was a waste of time and money. After all, their marriage wouldn't be *real*, would it?

"The final fitting for my dress is the day after New Year's," Eve told Jake.

Addy squeezed Sylvie's shoulder. "Your designs are heavenly. You've done us proud. Jim, wait until you see my maid of honor frock. Ruby velvet." Addy speared a piece of chicken with her fork. "Weren't we fortunate Lex's friend was able to paint those invitations so quickly?"

"She did a beautiful job," Eve agreed, giving Annie a spoonful of mashed potatoes from her plate. She flailed her tiny fists in the air in approval. Eve laughed, kissing Annie's forehead.

"Hand-painted invitations?" Her father shook his head. "Bet that was costly."

"I spent less on my first motorcycle." Jake smiled. "Addy, have you been to Elk Mountain Lodge yet to meet with the executive chef?"

"Yes. They need your final food selections to make sure they have time to order everything in. And you need to choose your linens and china. I have swatches and photos of your options in a folder for you."

"Where's this lodge?" Sylvie asked.

"Forty minutes from Old Hillbury, at the foothills of Elk Mountain," Eve said. "Dad took me there when I was in eighth grade and I fell in love with it. We stayed for a week during the summer."

Addy enthused, "Stone fireplaces, wood beams, and a hall that'll accommodate hundreds of guests complete with antler horn chandeliers. I've tasked the event coordinator with draping tulle and fairy lights between the chandeliers. We're shipping in upholstered chairs, too."

"Dreamy," Sylvie said. "What are your flowers?"

"I'm letting Addy decide," Eve said.

Addy beamed. "I've settled on Mister Lincoln roses, which are deep red, and smell fantastic. Each table will have an arrangement."

After dinner, Eve and Sylvie cleared the table and started the dishwasher, then went to join everyone in the living room. Dad pointed to his chair, a mischievous look on his face. "Why, Aiden, you forgot to check under my chair cushion today, son."

It was a game they often played together. Earlier, he'd hidden coins for the child to *find*. Aiden foraged for buried treasure, then Dad helped him sort the coins. As Dad explained the difference between a penny and nickel, Eve confided to Sylvie, "We played this when I was little."

"Jim's gonna make an awesome grandfather."

Sylvie's innocent words were a dagger to Eve's heart. *How do you tell someone you're barren?* Her smile slipped. Sylvie didn't seem to notice, but she caught Jake regarding her with a grave look.

Jake pulled Eve into the dining room under the guise of reviewing Addy's folder. He closed the pocket doors, giving them privacy.

Eve wilted into a chair, exhausted. She mused, "After all these years, a casual comment still wrecks me."

Jake sat across from her, elbows on the table. His face was impassive. They stared at each other for several minutes. "Would you like a child, Angie?" he asked in a gruff tone.

The abruptness of Jake's question threw her for a minute, but Eve recovered enough to ask drolly, "Do you plan on ordering one online?"

"It's a sincere inquiry." His gaze never left hers. She felt like he saw into her soul, exposing the chinks in her armor.

Eve looked away, not sure how to respond. When she spoke, her voice quavered. "Are you saying you want a *normal* marriage? That you love me? Because a child needs two parents who love each other, Jake."

"You know that's not the way I'm programmed. I can't even guarantee I'd be a conventional sort of father." He was apologetic but firm. "But if you want a baby, you'll get one."

"Oh?" Emotion gripped Eve. Disappointment. Despair. What did she expect him to tell her? That he wanted happily-ever-after? Heart sinking, she accepted he didn't. *I have no other choice.* The knowledge of it made her sound angry when she asked, "How?"

"IVF, a surrogate . . . hell, I'll buy you one if that's what it takes," Jake growled.

"Because you're contractually obligated to keep me appeased?"

A line formed between his brows. "Don't be that way, Angie. You knew the score when we got married. I'm trying, but don't push me."

Eve bit the inside of her cheek to quell her displeasure. No matter how much she wanted to be a mother, she wouldn't choose to bring a baby into a loveless marriage. At best, Jake would be a reluctant father.

How was that fair to a child?

CHAPTER THIRTY-NINE

"Happy Christmas! Where's Alexandra?" Addy asked when she took Jake's coat. She wore a red Santa hat trimmed in white and a matching sweater that declared *I'm Not Short, I'm Elf-Sized!*

"She's spending today with a friend." Jake crossed the living room, carrying a bag. Opening it, he held up bottles of the same wine he'd brought for Thanksgiving. Eve blushed, remembering the wine—and the kiss they'd shared in the kitchen that day. In many ways, it seemed ages ago, but his effect on her was as potent now. Fidgeting with her dress, she came forward to take the bottles. Jake whispered in her ear, "You look good enough to eat."

"Addy's prepared a feast." Dad held his hand out for Jake to shake. "Come have eggnog and watch *It's a Wonderful Life*, son. It's compulsory Christmas viewing in this family."

"The prime rib's almost finished roasting and Sylvie's due any moment," Addy announced, asking for Eve's help in the kitchen. She brushed butter on rolls while Addy checked the veggies steaming on the stovetop.

The doorbell rang and Addy, eyes shining, clapped her hands. "Sylvie and the kids."

Dad had set up the Christmas tree the night before and stacked gifts under it that morning. Like bees to honey, the kids were drawn to it. As soon as they took off their winter coats, Aiden and Gabby knelt at the base of the tree, shaking packages.

"Now you two leave those be," Sylvie scolded lightly,

before running back to her minivan to get a stockpot of oyster stew, her contribution to the meal. She placed the pot on the stove while Eve poured glasses of Jake's wine. Handing Addy and Sylvie each a glass, she lifted hers in a toast. "Merry Christmas, ladies."

Eve swirled the garnet liquid before drinking, identifying the hints of blackberry and currant. The wine again brought back remembrance of Jake's kiss, and a pang of longing hit her. She and Jake had barely spoken since the night of the center's program. It was inconceivable that in a few short weeks they'd be living together in his house.

Addy plated thick slices of meat while Eve brought side dishes into the dining room. Sylvie ladled oyster stew into bowls. Soon everyone was seated around the table. The meal proved both delicious and festive. Addy got to her feet, tipsy and face red from too much drink, and said, "I have an announcement I'm busting to share." Eve caught sight of Sylvie's grin. "I've had such a jolly good time putting together the wedding that Sylvie and I have teamed up to open Elite Bridal and Events. She'll run the dress side, and I'll do the event planning."

Sylvie chimed in, saying, "We're leasing space on Carolina Avenue, and our soft opening's in February."

"Congratulations." Eve came around the table to kiss Sylvie, then Addy. "You know, my house is set to close in early January. Are you looking for investors?"

"You bet," Sylvie said.

Jake added, "I'd be happy to invest, as well."

Addy lifted her wine. "We'll take it."

"I'll gladly come help you set up or paint—anything." Eve put her arm around Addy's shoulders.

"Are you sure you'll have time? You've taken on the commission from Alexandra's friend for that children's book, plus you work full-time," Dad reminded her.

"And you'll be a newlywed," Sylvie said in a coy voice. "You probably won't want to leave your love nest."

Eve's cheeks went pink. "I'll find the time." Grabbing the bottle of wine from the center of the table, she refilled glasses for a toast. "To new beginnings."

"To new beginnings," Jake said, meeting Eve's gaze. He motioned to her with his glass, saluting her.

Well, that's kinda confusing. He says he's not programmed for a real relationship, but then, he does stuff to make me second guess him.

When they were sure they couldn't eat another bite, Addy cut generous portions of Christmas pudding swimming in custard. After dinner, Dad put holiday music on the stereo in the front room and stoked the fire in the fireplace. Lounging on the sofa, Jake crooked a finger to Eve in invitation. She sat, tentative, but his arm snaked around her waist, pulling her against him. The scent of bergamot from his cologne was hypnotic. Nestled into his side, Eve felt her inhibitions dissolve. Being there, with Jake, felt *right*. She was falling for him, and there was nothing she could do to stop it.

They watched the children unwrap their gifts, and while they entertained themselves with their new toys, the adults exchanged presents. Eve and Jake gave her father a sweater and imported tobacco for his pipe, and Addy a pearl necklace and earrings.

Jake whispered, "Put your hand out, Angie, and close your eyes." Eve looked up at him, brow furrowed. His dimple flashed. "Go on."

Lowering her eyelids, Eve felt the weight of something placed in her palm. When she opened her eyes again, she found a crimson velvet box with a green tartan bow. The tag read, *For Beloved Eve.*

At a loss for words, she felt her eyes pool with tears.

He put his lips to her ear, whispering, "Merry Christmas, baby."

CHAPTER FORTY

Eve woke bleary-eyed after a restless night. Slipping into her robe, she peered out the window over the backyard, as she often had as a child. Her intestines were knotted, and her hands damp with perspiration, but the winter scene soothed her. It'd snowed during the night. The tree branches were crystalline. The backyard was a glistening carpet of diamonds in the morning sun. A cardinal flew from the icy branch of one tree to another. The day was to be glorious, crisp-cold and blue-skied — the ideal backdrop for a winter wedding.

My wedding.

"Try to eat, pet," Addy urged an hour later, setting glasses of juice and plates with buttered muffins in front of Eve and Sylvie.

"You look pale. Wedding day jitters?" Sylvie asked, and Eve nodded, pushing the plate away.

Addy put a motherly hand over hers. "Everything will go smoothly. After all, you have Elite Bridal and Events to make sure of it."

Eve managed a wan smile. "There are so many people invited. All eyes will be on me."

"As Jake's wife, you'll have to get used to that," Sylvie told her.

Eve pulled a face, but Sylvie was right.

"He says he's taking you to Fiji for your honeymoon. You must be thrilled," Addy said brightly, sitting down at the kitchen table with a coffee.

Eve nodded. *And apprehensive, and unprepared, and bothered.*

Her pulse accelerated at the idea of being alone with Jake on a long trip. She wouldn't be able to deny herself much longer. Since Thanksgiving, he'd been sweet and sexy and appealing. Still, nerves fluttered at the thought of Jake seeing her naked. Would he be disappointed she was no longer a nubile virgin?

"Where's Alexandra?" Addy asked, dragging Eve from her thoughts. As if on cue, the doorbell rang, and Addy hastened to the foyer.

Lex was already in her bridesmaid dress. Eve hadn't seen her since November, and she looked gorgeous. Today she sported a becoming pixie hairstyle — and no piercings. "I honored my brother's request," Lex snarled, "to tone it down."

"Watch out, it might hurt your reputation," Eve said facetiously.

Sticking her tongue out at Eve, Lex plopped into a chair.

Addy put a cup in front of Lex. "Here's some coffee, darling."

Unearthing a flask from her leather purse, Lex splashed booze in her cup. She bestowed a look on Eve like she dared her to say something. Eve beamed, refusing to take the bait.

Listening to the others chat while Sylvie styled her hair into an updo and applied her makeup, Eve's mind was elsewhere. She was startled when it was time for Addy and Sylvie to change, leaving her alone with Lex.

Eve accepted Lex's proffered flask, adding vodka to her juice. "You haven't been around much."

"I live my own life." Lex shrugged. "Jake and I ain't attached at the hip."

A peek at the clock told Eve it was late and she needed to get into her gown soon. Swigging her juice, she wished she'd added more vodka. "I thought you were close."

Lex laughed. "We are, but I live my own life and Jake likes his space. You'd be wise to remember that."

Irritation flickered. She had enough to deal with today and

166

didn't want a verbal sparring match with her sister-in-law. "Oh?"

"Jake can't help being thoughtful, which gives his conquests the wrong idea." Lex shrugged again. "Women tend to fall for him."

"Are you implying I've *fallen* for Jake?"

"I don't know, Eve." Lex fixed her with a hard stare. "Have you?"

Eve met her stare but didn't answer her question. Instead, she asked, "What if I did?"

"He's like me — he'll retreat. I saw women grasp and cling harder, but he was outta there. It's his own fault. He shouldn't lead them on." Lex drained her coffee and lifted the flask to drink directly from it. "Watch yourself."

Eve pretended to examine her manicure, not wanting Lex to see her words had stung. From the living room, Sylvie said, "Eve?"

Glad for an opportunity to escape, Eve rose but kept her face blank.

Waiting for Sylvie to zip her gown, she wrangled her emotions. So, she was being treated to Jake's *Don Juan* routine, was she? The generous gifts, the seduction. One woman in a long line of women, she'd do well to remember she wasn't special.

"It's you," Addy said.

Eve twisted to look in the mirror above her father's dresser, giving Sylvie a radiant smile. It *was* lovely. The bodice featured an Alençon lace overlay, and the Sabrina neckline added a 1950s flair. Full skirted, it had pockets to stow lipstick.

"Vintage fashion's fun to design." Sylvie checked the garment for wrinkles. "Lots of brides chase trends, and then wedding photos look dated. This is timeless."

"I want to see the full effect. Do you have the cape?" Addy

asked, and Sylvie nodded, pulling a white faux fur capelet from a wardrobe bag and draping it over Eve's shoulders. "How pretty."

They heard her father call out from the living room. He'd stayed the night at Jake's to give the ladies free rein of the house. Eve shed the capelet as she, Addy, and Sylvie joined him. Propped against the doorway to the kitchen, Lex observed with cynical eyes. Eve acted like a normal bride, but with Lex lurking, it proved challenging.

"Dear, you look delightful." Her father kissed her on the cheek and produced a velvet case from his suit pocket. "Jake sent your wedding gift along with me."

Eve flipped the lid, finding a sparkling ruby necklace and earrings. Sylvie and Addy gasped. *Whoa.* Eve took the pearl earrings from her ears with trembling fingers, replacing them with the rubies. Addy stepped forward to help remove the gold locket at Eve's neck so Dad could fasten the ruby necklace in its place. Eve ignored Lex's smirk as she stood before the hall mirror, meeting her dad's loving eyes in the reflection.

Addy's voice was tender when she hugged Eve. "I couldn't be any prouder of you than if you were my daughter, luv." Eve held Addy tight and got control of herself. What a peculiar charade this was.

Sylvie picked up Eve's bouquet of fragrant red roses from the coffee table. Before taking the flowers, Eve embraced her, whispering, "Thank you, Sylvie—for everything."

"The photographer and the limo are here," her dad said. "We'll take some pictures before heading to St. Luke's."

It wasn't easy to remain detached while the ivory-colored wedding car made its way to the stone cathedral. Their marriage might not be a genuine one, but Eve was as jittery as a real bride. She wondered with chagrin if her terror would be obvious in the photos they'd taken before leaving the house. It was happening too fast. Her father held out a hand. Eve gripped it like it was a life preserver. *Breathe in, breathe out. Breathe in, breathe out.*

Soon they were at the curb in front of the picturesque church. Intricate stained-glass windows glinted in the winter sunshine, and a blood-red carpet extended from the sidewalk to the carved wooden doors. Eve's stomach quaked when she spotted the shivering press snapping publicity photos. It was a stark reminder that Jake was society column fodder. Dad tendered his arm to assist her from the car. She looked up at him, wide-eyed, feeling like a fraud. He whispered, "You've got this."

Eve greeted Jake's groomsmen in the church's vestibule. Caine and Jed worked security for Consolidated, and Geoff was Jake's friend from the gym. She had met them before, but now her nerves made her inarticulate. The atmosphere in the vestibule became strained as Sylvie touched up Eve's lipstick. Addy's chatter helped, and Eve volleyed her friend an appreciative look. Soon Geoff gave Lex his arm and they started down the aisle, followed by Sylvie and Jed, then Addy and Caine.

The strains of *Wagner's Bridal Chorus* began, and her father smiled at her. "Ready?"

The pews were packed with guests, but Eve was aware only of the fine-looking man at the altar. The ambiance of the cathedral was intimate and rosy. Light filtered through the stained-glass windows, reflecting prisms onto the floor of the old stone church. Making her way to the nave, Eve never broke her gaze from Jake's.

His green eyes glowed. He wore a tailored tux that highlighted his tall, muscular body and broad shoulders. His coal-black hair was slicked back from his face. Electric anticipation tickled Eve's spine when she took Jake's hand. She allowed herself to be swept up into the pretense that they were a couple in love.

When it was time for their vows, Eve's voice was low. It was surreal to hear Jake pledge to love and cherish her. Scrambling to focus on the officiant reciting a reading and leading them in prayer, Eve reflected that time was water. Before she knew it, Jake placed a diamond-encrusted wedding band and the engagement ring on her finger, and they were pronounced husband and wife. His lips were warm on hers when they sealed their oath. Eve was officially Mrs. Jake Carter.

I need a bloody drink.

CHAPTER FORTY-ONE

At Elk Mountain Inn, Eve's mouth dropped open. Miles of white tulle and fairy lights were strung between the antler chandeliers, as Addy intended. There were floral arrangements and silver candelabras on the long wooden trestle tables. The gleaming china, shining crystal, and the tufted chairs added elegance to an otherwise rustic room. Woodsmoke from the stone fireplaces flanking the hall scented the air. Addy's vision was realized—it was dreamlike, enchanting.

"Incredible," Jake said.

When they were announced, the guests applauded. The room was full of people Eve didn't know. She looked up at Jake and gulped. He escorted her around the hall for a meet and greet. She clung to his arm, stunned at the multitude of new faces. Claustrophobia clawed at her breast, but she didn't lose her mega-watt smile. Snagging a glass of champagne from a passing waiter, she downed it. When dinner was served, Eve caught sight of her coworkers in the crowd. Grateful to see familiar people, she lifted a hand in greeting. Taking her seat, she felt she was on a roller coaster, clinging on until the ride slowed. Champagne helped.

The multi-course dinner lasted an eternity. *Vichyssoise* was served after guests took their seats. The gourmet meal was a feast for the eyes as well as the stomach, but Eve picked at her lobster thermidor. The bridal party seemed to be having a good time. Jake and Caine were deep in conversation about Consolidated. Even at his wedding, work apparently

171

dominated Jake's mind.

Addy caught Eve's eye and winked as the next course was set in front of them. The salad dressed with an orange blossom champagne emulsion looked tempting, but Eve feared she'd end up with watercress wedged between her front teeth. Instead of eating, she refilled her glass from the bottle of bubbly on the table and grew giddy at the absurdity of the occasion.

Hitch sat with the Tates across the room. He raised his flute, and Eve blew him a kiss. Lex watched, a sardonic twist to her lips. Turning away, Eve ignored her with a giggle. Bolstered by drink, she was determined to have a good time. It was her party, wasn't it? She wasn't going to let Lex spoil it for her.

Red velvet wedding cake with hand-painted fondant was displayed on a round table near the orchestra. When Addy told Eve it took eighty hours to decorate and cost as much as a car, Eve nearly swooned. Now she and Jake posed for photos in front of the confection. Buoyed by spirits, she enjoyed the ritual of cake cutting.

"What a marvelous day," her dad told her during the father-daughter dance. "I've never been to a fancier wedding. Addy's done an admirable job."

"She has. She's a special woman." Eve looked up at her father through her lashes, her head spinning though her tone was diffident. "But I think you know that."

"I—er, that is, yes." He flushed, then changed the subject. "You've found a good match with Jake."

"Have I?" Eve swallowed her mirth. *Is this really happening?*

Her father nodded. "Still waters run deep."

"I'm starry-eyed, Dad."

He smiled indulgently. "Jake's a different animal than you or me. Remember, he came from another world — one nothing like your solid middle-class upbringing. In spite of his difficult past, he's assimilated into *this* world."

A moment later, Jake was at her side. The orchestra began a rendition of *Wild Horses* for their first dance. Lights dimming, he drew her into his arms. Eve exhaled, and woozy from drinking, she leaned in. He whispered against her hair, "You're exquisite."

"I'm *drunk*. I must've put away a magnum of champagne."

"You might want to slow down, or you'll be hungover for our flight."

"Our *flight*?" Eve said, "I'm not packed."

"Addy's got you covered."

"Mmmm," Eve said drowsily.

"You *are* plastered, aren't you?"

"How else am I to survive the reception?"

"My big plan for our consummation may be in jeopardy, huh?" Jake's tone was dry, and Eve laughed.

"About that—"

"Our wedding night?" Jake asked, voice full of innuendo.

"Yep. I thought—we've been getting along great, and maybe tonight's the night. But Lex opened her trap."

Jake made an aggravated noise in his throat. "What did she say?"

"Oh, pfft, don't worry. I'm not," Eve slurred. "Maybe I need to go with the flow more. Have a good time. Not feel. I ought to drink to excess more often—it's *freeing*."

Jake sounded troubled when he said, "Angie."

Hitch sidled up to them. "A dance, doll?"

Jake's expression tightened. He looked like he wanted to ignore the request, but nodded. He growled with warning, "No tangos tonight, Grant."

"Yessir." Hitch grimaced in jest, bringing his hand up in a military salute to Jake's retreating figure before fixing his cornflower blue eyes on Eve. "You make a damn good-looking bride."

"Gee, thanks." She batted her eyelashes. "I'm glad you're here. I wasn't sure you'd still be in town."

"I don't hang about for long, do I?" Hitch twirled her around the dancefloor to the up-tempo beat of the music.

"Slow down, *Astaire*. I've had a lot to drink."

Hitch snickered but adapted the speed of his steps as another song started. "I've decided to renovate my apartment in the city so I'll be here over the summer—"

Arthur was at Eve's elbow. "May I cut in?"

"Sure thing, Art," Hitch said good-naturedly, bowing before moving off. "Laters."

"It's been a heck of a party," Arthur thundered, taking Eve's hand in his. His style of dancing proved as vigorous as his manner. Her stomach flip-flopped as he steered her around the ballroom, but Eve pasted on a bright smile. *I knew I was gonna regret that last gallon of champagne.*

She bit back a hiccup. "I'm glad you're enjoying it."

"I told Jake to bring you up to my house in Port Breakwater. And to our yearly Hamptons jaunt to my daughter Aoife's place on the beach. I'm looking forward to getting to know you."

Her head swam while she tried to keep up her end of the conversation. "Jake says he owes everything to you. How long have you known each other?"

"He was thirteen when we met—it's a funny story I don't usually tell . . ." Arthur chuckled, then leaned in, conspiratorial. "He stole my car."

"Oh?" Eve tittered. She could picture it.

"I was restoring a classic car and it was parked outside a body shop overnight. Jake hot-wired it. Took it for a joyride. He was smart as a whip but had no place to channel his energy. I liked the lad. He had fire in his belly."

"And you got him started in construction?"

"I arranged for some jobs. Tested his mettle. He finished

his degree, and I invested in his business when it came time for that. I've never seen a man more hardworking or determined to succeed."

"Old softie." Eve kissed him on his weathered cheek. Arthur blustered, and she smothered her snigger.

"Jake did the hard work," Arthur said gruffly, adding, "I remember when he met you. He talked about you often."

"Really?"

"I see folks are departing. And here comes Jake to fetch you." Eve was disappointed. She wanted to pump him for more information.

As Jake piloted her toward the guests preparing to leave, she murmured, "I need another glass of champers to get through this."

He frowned down at her. "I don't think that's a good idea."

CHAPTER FORTY-TWO

"Do you remember anything about last night?" Jake asked during their flight to Fiji.

"Other than I passed out on the sofa once we were in our suite?" Eve snorted. Her head pounded with a hangover. She was grateful they were flying on a Consolidated jet. Every time she flew commercial, she was invariably seated between a colicky baby with a loaded diaper and a sweaty fat man in a stained wife-beater. Wealth definitely had its perks.

"You said you'd decided to *go with the flow*. Is that how you feel today?"

"I suppose." Eve stared out the window and over the clouds. She wished she was the type of woman who could charge forward with abandon. Be less cautious.

"Look, why don't we set everything aside and try to enjoy our trip?" Jake suggested.

Eve wanted nothing but to nurse her hangover. "I'll try."

After the fifteen-hour flight, the jet landed in Viti Levu, Fiji, at noon local time. Hot, humid air hit Eve when they disembarked. The searing sunshine shocked her senses and made her sweater stick to her back. She adjusted her sunglasses and hoped Addy had packed cool clothes. Set on a cleared parcel of land bordered by palm trees and mountains, the airport was a low, modern structure. The sky was azure blue, the clouds puffy cotton. A dark-skinned man with a dazzling white smile hurried across the tarmac, colorful plumeria leis looped over his forearm.

"*Ni sa bula*, Mr. and Mrs. Carter." Smile never wavering, the man draped the aromatic leis over their heads. "My name is William, and I'm here to facilitate your visitor visas."

Jake responded, "*Vinaka vaka levu.*"

Naturally he speaks the language.

Jake took their passports from his overnight bag, handing them to William as they walked into the building.

"We're issued visas here?" Eve asked.

Jake nodded.

William gave them VIP treatment, opening a velvet rope in front of a line of travelers. Eve felt the scrutiny of the people queued to receive visas and get passports stamped at the counter. Jake's natural self-confidence turned heads despite his casual dress. She heard the murmurs behind them.

"They must be *somebody*," an Australian-accented woman in a polyester pantsuit said to her companion, and a flush stained Eve's cheeks. The woman used her phone to snap their photo. *Rude.*

William furnished a folder with their paperwork moments later. Exchanging American currency for Fijian, he handled it with the same unruffled efficiency. He directed them to a canary yellow helicopter with *Bliss Island Resort* painted in black script on the door.

Mimicking Jake's actions, Eve snapped herself into the seat harness and slid the bulky headphones over her ears. The pilot's voice came over the headphones, welcoming them, and explaining the flight would be thirty minutes to Bliss Island. Lifting, the helicopter veered to the right. There was a gaily painted building in the distance, and the pilot explained it was Sri Siva Subramaniya, the largest Hindi temple in Fiji. Eve looked with curiosity over the landscape. She'd been to the South Pacific, but not Fiji. Turquoise blue waters and palm tree-fringed beaches beckoned. In the distance, waterfalls were set amongst the leafy green of the rainforest.

"Fiji's home to over three hundred islands." The pilot's

accent was lilting and musical. "Two-thirds are beautifully unspoiled."

During the trip, he indicated landmarks and attractions. Telling them a brief history of the islands, he listed some popular recreational activities — hiking, kayaking, and shark feeding. Jake laced his hand with Eve's and she gave him an enthusiastic grin as the pilot said, "There are spectacular coral reefs to explore at Bliss Island Resort. We also have a top-notch spa available if you'd like a massage. The oils are made from local fruits and nuts."

They came upon an island partially surrounded by an aquamarine lagoon. Centered on the isle was a wide building with a right and left wing. Traditional bungalows of wood and straw were set apart from the hotel, each accompanied by a pool. The pilot eased the helicopter down on a helipad behind the main building, and a porter hurried to meet them.

While Jake checked them in, Eve's gaze drank in the fashionable lobby with its Polynesian art. The mosaic tile floor was a tribal motif. Shutters on the windows were open to allow in the sea breeze. On the left and right side of the reception desk, wooden staircases curved, meeting at the top.

"Andreas will show you to your *bure*." The cheerful clerk nodded to a dark-skinned man in a uniform of canary yellow shirt and khaki shorts. "Your lunch will be set up on the beach shortly."

"I want to purchase *sulus* first," Jake said. "They're available onsite, aren't they?"

On their way to the shop in the East wing, Jake explained swimsuits and resort wear was an acceptable dress code while on Bliss Island, but when sightseeing off-island, the custom was to dress modestly. A salesclerk showed them a selection of *sulus* in flamboyant colors. Eve chose a few, hoping they'd match the suits Addy packed.

Andreas shepherded them from the main building and

past the beach. A breeze blew in from the lagoon, making Eve sigh with gratitude. The sea sang its siren song. She couldn't wait to get into the water. They were ushered through a lushly overgrown path to their private *bure*, a traditional thatched roof bungalow. After briefly showing them the hut's amenities, Andreas bowed formally before departing.

"How divine!" Eve said, running fingertips over a primitive black-and-cream patterned vase on a rattan stand. The *bure* had a pitched ceiling and woven wall coverings. The muslin drapes at the jalousie-style windows flapped in the breeze. A romantic canopy bed swathed in mosquito netting was in the middle of the hut. Eve imagined a photo of it in a honeymoon brochure, the caption declaring, *A Tropical Backdrop for Connubial Coupling.*

Eve had said she'd try to *go with the flow*, but once confronted with a bed, it wasn't so straightforward. She covered her unease by opening the sliding shutters to the private patio. She feigned fascination with the wicker furniture and plunge pool. When she turned to face Jake, he smiled like he'd read her mind.

"You were too keyed up to eat on the plane. You must be starving now." He pointed to the bathroom. "Why don't you change in there?"

Her skin prickling, Eve murmured a shy word of thanks and slipped into the tiled bathroom with her suitcase. Addy had packed her favorite coral-colored bikini. Her hands shook when she dressed. Wrapping the coral and turquoise *sulu* sarong style around her hips, she ignored her bothersome feelings of inadequacy. *Jake will have to accept me as I am, dammit.*

As she left the bathroom, twisting her hair into a clip, Eve caught sight of Jake, bare-chested, pulling on swim trunks. His tanned muscles rippled in movement. Mouth dry, she swallowed and averted her gaze, not wanting to gawk. She packed towels into a straw beach bag along with sunscreen.

Eve peeked at Jake. Hands on his hips, he regarded her with unabashed hunger. She felt a suffusion of crimson bloom on her neck and chest, and he grinned. Picking up the camera Dad and Addy gave them for Christmas, he held out a hand.

"Lunch is set up *on* the beach."

Eve looked over her sunglasses at the umbrella-shaded table set into the sand where the water met the shore. They collapsed into their chairs, the warm water moving over their bare feet.

Waiters in canary yellow polo shirts toted platters of icy drinks, grilled fish, and cut tropical fruit. Eve's gaze feasted on the artistically arranged fruit. Her stomach growled, demanding appeasement. Nectar dribbled down her chin as she sank her teeth into a piece of colorful melon. Never had anything tasted so vibrant. Eve savored the burst of flavor, wiping her chin with a cloth napkin.

"Need a moment alone?" Jake teased, and she laughed, self-conscious.

They devoured grilled snapper and prawns, trying a national delicacy of *kokodo*, a ceviche of mahi-mahi marinated in coconut milk and lime, and sipped iced tea spiked with rum. After lunch, a beach attendant set up lounge chairs for them.

"May I help you put on sunscreen? I'm very thorough," Jake assured her, roguish smirk in place.

I'll bet, Cassanova. "Uh, no thanks. I've got it." Yawning, Eve pulled the clip from her hair, and she wilted into the thick cushion of her chaise. The lunch with its rum drinks, the tropical breeze, and the sound of the surf lulled her into deep sleep.

Jake shook her shoulder an hour later. "Let's swim, sleepyhead."

Eve yawned and stretched, then shed her sarong, reluctantly baring her bikini-clad body. Jake whistled in appreciation. Linking hands, they ran together into the crashing surf, frolicking like children. She dove into the crystal-like water, causing a small school of silver fish to scatter. Surfacing, she scraped her hair from her forehead and floated leisurely on her back, eyes closed to the brilliance of the afternoon sun. Jake swam to her and grabbed her ankle, yanking her underwater. He waited for her when she regained her balance, water dripping from his eyelashes and a playful grin on his lips. With a squeal of mock indignation, Eve dove away quick as a dolphin, and the chase was on.

Breaking the surface, she settled into a swift breaststroke, only to be caught a moment later when Jake effortlessly overtook her. Grabbing her, he smothered her laugh with a kiss that made Eve's toes curl. When he pulled away, his expression was ardent and voice husky. "Will you let me take you to bed?"

Throwing caution into the wind, Eve nodded.

Chapter Forty-three

Once Jake pushed the shutters to their hut closed, second thoughts plagued Eve. He came to her, cupping her face in his palm, thumb scraping her lips. "It's like riding a bike, you know."

"What if you're . . . disappointed? What if it's not as good as it used to be? What if I'm not?" Eve asked in a tiny voice, but Jake laughed as if that was the most ridiculous thing he'd ever heard.

"I'm not worried." He sobered, and his expression turned smoldering. "You trusted me the night I took your virginity, will you trust me again?"

Eve took a deep breath and nodded, remembering his patience, his restraint. Jake gathered the hair at the nape of her neck and wound it around his hand the way she'd fantasized. He gently tugged until she tilted her head to the side, exposing the delicate curve of her neck. When Jake nuzzled her there, Eve gasped, biting her lip. He slithered his tongue from her neck to behind her ear. She felt goosebumps in response. He hadn't forgotten what she liked.

"Okay?" Jake asked, pausing until she nodded again. As he kissed his way down to her shoulder, Eve felt his free hand explore her breasts through her bathing suit. She was sure her heart would explode through her chest at any moment. Breath ragged, she lost her ability to think. Snaking his hand around her waist, he spun her, bringing her hard against his pelvis. The ridge of his arousal prodded the small of her back, and she felt her body quicken. Eve's moan proved she was no longer in control.

"More?" he whispered, before pushing her bikini top aside to cup her bare flesh. Eve craned her neck to kiss him, shattered by the sight, sound, and taste of him. It was sweet surrender. She couldn't remember wanting anything the way she wanted Jake inside her. She leaned her back against his bare chest, putting her hands over his when he kneaded the sensitive flesh of her breasts, head tipped to encourage his kisses at her neck. Jake's nimble fingers found her nipples, playing with them until they were hard as pebbles.

"Angie," Jake murmured thickly into her hair, his hands everywhere. Eve turned to face him once again and presented her lips. He kissed her thoroughly, and Eve felt his tongue tease hers, flicking over her lower lip, sucking. Jake's fingers moved to her spine then cupped her bottom, lifting her pelvis against his manhood. Their bathing suits were the only barrier between them. Eve's sex throbbed with her pulse, aching for a release she'd denied too long.

He shucked his swim trunks, and then Jake was before her in naked glory. Eve caressed her palms over his shoulders, muscled chest, his tight abs, leaving goosebumps in her wake. His breath hitched and she became aware of her power over him as a woman. It was a high. She put a tentative hand on him. He was a contrast of velvet and steel.

"If you keep touching me that way, I won't last long at all." Jake groaned, pulling away to slide Eve's bikini bottoms down her legs. As he trailed his fingertips back up to her mound, his experienced fingers delved into her folds, which were slick with arousal. He made a sound low in his throat, telling her he approved. She felt the subtle shift in power return to Jake as she lost herself in his touch. She came fast and hard, looping her arms around his neck to keep from falling. Eve hadn't yet caught her breath when he laid her on the bed beneath the mosquito net.

"I'm not nearly done with you yet," Jake vowed huskily, pushing her thighs apart and kneeling before her at the edge of the bed. He brought her ankle to his mouth, kissing his way to her inner thigh. Nipping with his teeth, he left her gasping. Tongue explorative, he teased her slit, finding her engorged clit, sucking, licking. Eve bucked. Gripping her legs, he jerked her back into position. When she continued to squirm, he restrained her by bracing his forearms against her spread thighs.

"Stay still, or I'll bend you over my knees and give you a proper spanking," Jake said against her, his voice full of innuendo.

Ooh, kinky! Eve moaned at the thought of lying bare assed over his lap. He rubbed his thumb against her nub until heat radiated to her toes, and then Eve felt his tongue lap at her folds. With surprise, she felt her body tightening with another climax. Back arched, her hands clenched the bedspread as unbearably exquisite waves of pleasure radiated from her center through her body.

She was weak as a kitten. Chuckling, Jake settled his body between Eve's thighs, his forearms braced on either side of her head, his forehead touching hers.

"I have waited so long for this," he said against her lips, entering her in one smooth measure. His thrusts were calculated and controlled as he filled her, pulled out slowly, and drove hard into her again and again. Heavy-lidded, she watched him in the dim light of their *bure*, finding his face a study of intensity. Eve cried out when she felt him swell, knowing he was on the verge of release.

With a guttural moan, Jake went over the edge.

Eve felt herself blush from the roots of her hair to the tips of her pink-painted toenails when Jake joined her at their private patio, a tray from room service balanced on his palm.

Hello, Adonis. Unshaven and sleep tousled, Jake was hotter than ever. Unwinding the towel from his lean hips, he let it drop to the ground. His chuckle told her he noticed her quick intake of breath.

"Coffee?" Jake placed a cup of thick brew and a plate with a croissant in front of her. Butterflies fluttered in Eve's stomach. She avoided the food and took a tiny sip of her coffee while Jake wolfed down three pastries. He smiled at her under his coal-black lashes, wiping his mouth with a napkin. "I worked up an appetite."

She lobbed him a timid look. "Sorry, I guess I'm not good at pillow talk."

"There's no reason for you to be shy, Angie. I don't want any barriers between us."

"Don't you?"

"Of course not," Jake told her, matter-of-factly.

"Are we to make-believe we're carefree newlyweds?" Eve slipped on her sunglasses to escape his scrutiny, folding her arms over her chest.

His posture was relaxed. "Sure, why not?"

Biting her cheek, she was silent for several seconds before whispering, "Because I'm not good at pretending, Jake."

"You certainly weren't pretending to enjoy yourself last night," he teased, pouring another cup of coffee. "Relax."

"Relax?" Eve muttered, laughing without humor. "I'm not good at that either."

He plucked the white hibiscus from the vase on the tray, then leaned over to tuck it behind her ear. Jake's eyes were emeralds in the morning sunshine. His expression was earnest when he said softly, "Evangeline, my beautiful island girl. Humor me. I only want to give you the world."

"Oh, you *are* good," Eve breathed, her tone cynical. How many other women had he said such things to? Still, she was susceptible to his charms.

She cursed her weakness as Jake winked at her and lifted the camera from the edge of the tray, gesturing, "Come here. Sit on my lap. I want to remember this moment and how you look."

Eve looked meaningfully at his naked form. *"Sit on your lap?"*

"I'll behave," he promised. "On my honor as a *Boy Scout*."

"You, a *Boy Scout*? As if!" Eve put her head back and laughed at the thought, which seemed to tickle him and broke the tension in the air.

Once she was on his lap, Jake stretched out his arm, tilting the camera. "I have an idea of how we could have fun with this camera." His lips were on the bare skin of her shoulder. "But we have a scuba lesson."

Eve and Jake assembled with other guests at the lagoon, filing onto a launch that would take them to a broad band of coral reefs. Wearing tanks, flippers, and goggles, they dove from the launch to explore.

As she swam, Eve made sure her tether, which would lead her back to the launch, was secure. There were coral reefs in hues of rose, orange, and purple. Unconcerned by her presence, fish swam around her. She lifted the underwater camera on loan from the resort and took photos. They would never equal the vibrancy in person. Eve wished she could bottle up the sensations of calm weightless underwater solitude, where just her muted breathing could be heard, to be relived later at home.

Following the blazing radiance of the tropical sunset, they relaxed on the beach with other tourists. The natives performed a *meke*, a traditional dance. Afterward, there was a ceremony where the performers walked over burning coals, urging guests to join them if brave enough.

Jake looked at her, questioning. She said in a wry tone, "I

think not."

He nodded to the buffet set further up the beach. "Ready for dinner?"

Fish, pork, and chicken had been placed underground with taro and sweet potatoes and covered with kelp and coals to slow cook. The *lovo* was eaten from palm leaf plates and washed down with rum. Famished from the physical exertion of the day, Eve ate heartily.

Later she and Jake sat with the other vacationers around a bonfire. A communal bowl of *kava* was passed. Unsure, Eve brought the bowl to her mouth. The potion, made from the root of a pepper plant, was earthy and bitter. Tongue tingling, she probed her numb lips. When the *kava* was passed again, she was less hesitant and drank deeply. Within minutes, Eve's limbs grew leaden, and she hunched against Jake, eyelids drooping.

"You've had a full day. Off to bed with you," he said, scooping her into his arms and carrying her to their *bure*. Aware of the crisp bedsheets and the ceiling fan spinning lazily from the beamed ceiling, Eve heard the mosquito netting swoosh to the floor.

CHAPTER FORTY-FOUR

They dined on a boat anchored at sea and then were brought inland to sightsee on Vita Levu. Eve put Jake in charge of snapping photos. "My guidebook says not to take pictures of villagers without permission," she reminded him.

They perused fruits and handicrafts for sale at open-air markets, Jake standing by ever tolerant while Eve searched for mementos. There was a wooden mask and a pottery bowl she thought her dad would like, and t-shirts and miniaturized sets of *Lali* drums for Sylvie's kids.

Late that afternoon, outside a jewelry shop, Jake said, "I think Sylvie and Addy would want something from here." Eve bit her lip, looking over the trays of jewelry, spoiled for choice. She picked the same gift for both women — a black pearl pendant on a dainty chain. Jake pointed to a bracelet of black pearls, telling the proprietor, "I'll also take that for my wife."

"You've already given me so much," Eve protested, but Jake dismissed her with an unconcerned shrug. He fastened the bracelet around her wrist and brought her palm to his lips, tongue running over her mound of Venus. Sparking current flowed directly from Eve's hand to her heart, wreaking havoc with her respiratory system.

"Thirsty?" Jake asked, his mouth still on her palm, and at a loss for words, she bobbed her head. They drank coconut water and snacked on slices of cold melon at a stand a few yards away. When the genial fruit seller took their photo in front of her booth, Eve's smile was genuine.

A peek at her phone showed the time had got away from them, and they raced to mail her postcards. In a hastily scrawled script, Eve described the blue of the sky and the brine of the sea air, the turquoise hue of the water, the powdered sugar-like sand, and the friendliness of the Fijians.

On the walk back to the pier, a sign on a table of carved souvenirs attracted Eve. She put a hand on Jake's forearm to stop him, bringing him over to the stall for a closer inspection. The macabre nature of the wooden oddity was a talking piece, especially for those who liked dark humor. Eve looked up at him with an impish grin. "I know who'd like one of these."

Cannibal fork, the hand-lettered placard said, *Same design used by cannibals until practice outlawed in the mid-19th century.*

Jake chuckled, meeting her gaze. They said in unison, "Lex."

As the vessel cut through the water on the way back to Bliss Island, they stood shoulder to shoulder at the bow at sunset. The sky gradually changed from orange to fuchsia to lavender, the tangerine orb of the sun dipping beyond the horizon. Jake moved to stand behind her, his arms circling her waist and his chin resting on the top of her head.

"Spectacular." Eve sighed in reverence.

"Yes," Jake whispered into her hair. "You are."

Later, while Jake arranged room service, Eve disrobed and slipped into their private pool, feeling decadent and slightly sinful. The night seemed magical. The air was soft, and a balmy breeze carried the fragrance of gardenias and plumeria to her nose. After a long, hot day on her feet, she found the water delicious. The contact of the cool water on her heated flesh made her skin rise in goosebumps. She groaned, sinking lower and lower.

The sky had darkened to star-filled velvety blackness when Jake emerged from their hut, the light spilling from the doorway revealing his nakedness. Eve's pulse raced, her gaze turning greedy at his approach. *I know what we're gonna do.* A charcuterie board in one hand, his other was closed around the neck of a bottle of wine. Wading into the pool, he placed the board on the wide ledge.

"Here." Jake passed her the uncorked bottle. "Let's be savages and not bother with glasses."

She downed a generous glug. It was no revelation that the wine was an excellent red, dry and semi-smooth. It made her taste buds come alive. "Mmmm," Eve said, giving the wine back.

"Not bad," Jake agreed after a swig, setting the bottle on the ledge. He put a wedge of cheese partway in his mouth and leaned in to feed her. Desire pooling in her belly, she nibbled the cheese, then accepted a morsel of salami from his deft fingers. He handed her the wine. The moonlight reflected on the surface of the water, allowing Eve to meet Jake's gaze. She felt bold. The wine had a heady effect on her.

When he offered her a chocolate, Eve let it melt on her tongue, capturing his finger with her teeth. At the same time, she put her free hand underwater and groped him. Jake gasped, slowly removing his finger from her mouth. His tone was thoughtful when he murmured, "Aren't you cheeky?"

Eve smirked when he swelled in her grasp. She took another drink from the bottle, not looking away. Jake's arousal was like a drug. She watched with satisfaction as the skin tautened over his cheekbones from her ministrations, his breathing labored. With a flick of his wrist, he snatched the wine from her, flinging it to the grass. He hauled her hard against him. Voice rasping, he confided, "Woman, you are a sweet surprise."

"You like?" Eve whispered, inhibitions forgotten.

"I like." Jake brought his head down to seal his lips over hers, his fingers meandering to seek her slippery cleft. She whimpered into his mouth, bucking against him. He said with approval, "I definitely like."

Pushing her until she was against the tiled wall of the pool, he spread her thighs and pounded into her with one fierce thrust. Eve groaned, head flung back, her fingernails gripping his arms. She wrapped her legs around him and locked her ankles around his waist.

Setting a leisurely pace, Jake rocked back and forth in a slow, measured rhythm, leaving Eve desperate for more. She bit her lip to keep from crying out, her breath going from unsteady to short pants. Burying her fingers into the hair at the nape of his neck to bring him closer, she trailed her tongue over the column of his throat to taste the salt of his sweat. Nibbling at Jake's neck where his pulse thudded, she sank her teeth into his flesh. He made a low growl in the back of his throat, hands spasmodic on her hips.

Elevating her pelvis to meet every methodical plunge of his powerful hips, Eve urged him to increase his tempo. He brought her close to the edge, then slowed, repeating the honeyed torment again and again. His game was pleasure spiked with pain, leaving her wanting.

Jake asked against her mouth, "You want me to make you cum?"

Eve groaned, urging him by undulating her pelvis.

"Tell me."

Her whisper was a plea. "Yes."

Jake drove into her with hard, quick strokes until Eve felt herself open to him like a blossoming flower.

CHAPTER FORTY-FIVE

The following week, after an outing to Natadola Beach, they were ferried back to Bliss Island. Stepping onto the pier, Jake told Eve their belongings had been moved to new accommodations in their absence. At first, Eve was disappointed to lose the snug *bure* where they'd spent many fiery nights. "Will we be staying in the main building?"

"We're gonna sleep with the fishes."

"Like *Luca Brasi*?" Eve threw Jake a look of mock horror, and he laughed, explaining Bliss Island had underwater accommodations.

As they descended underground via elevator, he said, "There's a two-year-long waiting list. I pulled strings to get a room for the week."

The lobby was pod-like. It was climate controlled, and the heat radiated off Eve in surges. Two-thirds of the curved room was glassed in. Spotlights beamed over the ocean floor, allowing an expansive view of sea-life. *Denizens of the deep*. An octopus floated past while Jake got their room keycard.

"Quite the place, isn't it?" he asked, navigating down the central hallway past a nightclub, a restaurant, and a movie theater to their room, a self-contained chamber attached to the main structure. He allowed Eve to enter first, flipping a switch that bathed the room in mellow light.

A rounded glass wall dominated the room. There was a king-size bed angled toward it. A seating area was to one side, a *Jacuzzi* on the other. Tucked into the back of the room was a luxurious bathroom tiled in stone. Kicking off her sandals,

Eve exhaled, her feet sinking into the carpet. In a closet by the bathroom, she located their clothes hanging neatly on wooden hangers, organized by color.

"Watch," Jake instructed when she lowered beside him on the sofa. He used a remote control to turn on spotlights outside the glass, illuminating multi-colored coral reefs and schools of fish. With a push of a button, bits of chum dispersed. A sea turtle swam up to the glass and Eve leaped from her seat for a better vantage.

While she took in the view, Jake filled the *Jacuzzi* with water and stripped off his clothes. He held a hand out to her, and, under his spell, Eve took it. Movements deliberate, he loosened the necktie of her cotton peasant blouse, pulling it over her head. Now accustomed to intimacy with Jake, she didn't hesitate to shimmy from her skirt and panties. Twining her arms around his neck, she lifted her face.

Caressing her arms and back as he kissed her, he then moved his lips to the crook of her neck. Hungrily, he suckled her throat and breasts, his hands roaming possessively over the curves of Eve's bottom. By the time he helped her into the swirling water, she was his captive.

Easing into the tub, Jake situated her between his thighs. She leaned into him, nestling her back against his solid chest. Eyelids flickering, Eve concentrated on his touch. Proof of his arousal was evident against her spine as he fondled her breasts. After gathering her hair in one palm, Jake wrapped the tendrils around his fist and tugged until her neck was exposed. She quivered when he brought his mouth to the nape of her neck, then to her ear. His tongue traced the curve of her earlobe, and she whispered his name.

Jake's other hand moved down her torso until his fingers found her center, circling her clit lazily until she hissed, her back arching. He lifted Eve and hovered her over his burgeoning manhood, lowering her until her walls fully sheathed him.

Breath hot on her shoulder, Jake guided her hips as she rode him, undulating wildly. Unchecked, water sloshed over the sides of the tub and to the floor. With a sob, Eve came hard, collapsing against his chest.

"You're mine," he pledged, lips against her ear when his seed spilled in her.

Over the subsequent week, they explored the islands when the weather allowed, leaving Bliss Island by a private cruiser and returning in the evenings to watch the sea-life beyond the glass wall of their room. Shopping at an open-air market, Eve snapped photos of Jake playing soccer with native children, looking happy and boyish. Later they met fellow guests from the resort and dined together, posing for a group photo outside the restaurant for a memento. Several shots were also taken of exotic species of flowers at the Orchid Gardens.

They went hiking and mountain biking, and on a boat safari up the Sigatoka River on a chugging craft that reminded Eve of *The African Queen*. Days were spent at the beach, swimming, or dozing on cushy deck chairs. Once, they went by seaplane to a golf course, where Jake easily beat Eve, a competent golfer, by several strokes.

During their lighthearted fun, Eve brushed aside Lex's words of warning like they were cobwebs. In private moments when she was able to catch her breath and think, she acknowledged she was hopelessly in love with Jake. How could she not be? He was the perfect man, a mixture of thoughtful, intense, indulgent and playful. And, the sex.

If I ask Jake if he loves me, will he withdraw? Eve told herself that after the expense and care of planning their honeymoon, he must feel as she did, despite assertions theirs was a marriage of convenience. Apprehension jabbed at her when she wondered what life would be like when the honeymoon was over. Home seemed far away, with its cold and snow — and its uncertainty.

Their last day at Bliss Island arrived in the blink of an eye. Over a light breakfast in their room, they savored the view of their coral reef. The resort kitchen provided a basket lunch, and they were flown by helicopter to an uninhabited island to have a picnic beside a waterfall.

Completely alone, they swam in the tranquil pool at the base of the cascading falls, their clothes abandoned on the grassy bank. Afterward, they stretched out on a blanket, sipping wine and feeding each other bites of cheese and fruit. They made love and swam again. When the helicopter came back to fetch them late that afternoon, they were dressed, blanket neatly folded.

Eve greeted their pilot by name when she got into her seat, buckling her harness like a pro.

As they approached another island, Jake squeezed her hand. A dwelling with a wide veranda and a solar-paneled roof was in the middle of the isle, a kidney-shaped pool with a cabana behind the house. At the shoreline, a sailboat and a speedboat were moored at a dock attached to a boathouse. She glanced at Jake with a question in her eyes, but he gave her a blank look. When she frowned, he grinned, the dimple showing in his cheek.

"See you at pickup." The pilot called over the noise of the blades when they exited the chopper with their suitcases. Soon the crashing surf was the solitary sound in the secluded paradise.

"This is gorgeous. Did you rent this place through Bliss Island?" Eve asked, distracted by the view.

"It's yours."

She turned to Jake, forehead creased. "Huh?"

"It's an early birthday present—your own private island."

CHAPTER FORTY-SIX

"What?"

"It's an early birthday present."

It came out of nowhere and caught her off guard. An internal dam holding her insecurities and fears in check creaked with pressure, needing release. Eve realized, with a whoosh of alarm, she was losing control. The freezing grip of dread was a band tightening on her ribcage until she couldn't get air. She said in a strangled tone, "It's too much."

"I thought you'd be pleased," Jake replied.

Her mind raced with a million thoughts, but she couldn't fix on any particular one. Eve knew what was happening — she was having a panic attack. Her vision dimmed, though she was cognizant of Jake at the fringes. She brought her hands up to cover her face. She couldn't let him see her this way. *Why now?* "No, no, no."

"I am *not* Pierce, Angie." It was as if he meant to reassure her, but when his words weren't effective, Jake's exasperation became clear. "If I want to buy you ten more houses, I damn well will."

Eve spun away, facing the beach. She hadn't suffered a panic attack in years, but they were terrifying — the first time she'd experienced one, she thought she was dying. Vaguely, she was aware of the waves lapping the shore without a care in the world. Eve summoned the energy needed to meet Jake's eyes again.

"You've thrown money like confetti since I've been back . . ." She lifted a visibly shaking hand. "This ring, paying

millions for my debts, the wedding, the honeymoon. Now —
an island. When does it stop?"

"I don't understand. You knew what you were getting
into." He added in a contemplative way, "Correct me if I'm
wrong, but most women would envy what you have."

"I'm *not* most women." Eve began, but her voice was
shriller than she intended. She choked back her hysteria. "I
told you when we were in your kitchen hashing the details.
Paying my debts was enough for me — more than enough."

"I'm simply fulfilling my side of the bargain the best way I
know how."

She whimpered in defeat. *Jake will never understand.* About
to bawl, she lurched forward to the beach, biting back anguish — *her* beach. Eve had fooled herself into playing make-
believe, but they weren't normal newlyweds, and nothing
would ever change that.

Deliberating Jake's solemn vow to love, honor, and cherish
her, she recalled how easily the words fell from his tongue.
The whole trip was a statement. He was giving her the lavish
lifestyle he'd promised. Eve felt sullied. *Fulfilling his contractual obligations. Buying me. How demoralizing.*

Ignoring the dark clouds predicting a storm, she sank
down to the powdery sand and pulled her knees to her chin.
Staring out to sea, she salvaged a modicum of self-control,
keeping her tears at bay. Jake followed. He dropped alongside
her, his expression puzzled.

He trickled a handful of sand through his fingers. "You are
a mystery to me sometimes, Angie."

The wind blew Eve's hair in her eyes and she tucked the
strands behind her ears with impatient fingers. She bit her lip,
compelled to open to him, but the easy relationship they'd
forged over the last weeks was a tenuous one. She remembered *Don Quixote* and the futility of tilting at windmills —
once spoken, words couldn't be taken back. "I have all these

feelings . . ."

"Okay, tell me," Jake said. "You don't have to pull any punches with me."

"I don't? You truly have no idea what I've been through the last six months, do you?" The words came out in a torrent, agony making Eve's tone harsh. "Husband slaughtered. Running cross country to evade his debts — do you know about the allegations of fraud at Martin's lab? Here's something I bet you don't know — he was stockpiling money to flee the country. I don't know who he planned to take with him, but it wasn't me!"

Jake proffered a hand, but she smacked it away. She cried in earnest, a raindrop falling on her nose.

"I can't be strong anymore." Sick with self-loathing, Eve put her hands over her face. "Do you think I've dealt with the trauma of what happened? I haven't. I push it away, but it's there, underneath the rage. I *hate* Martin, his lies, and his schemes with the heat of a thousand burning suns."

"I *am* sorry."

Rain came down in sheets now, drenching Eve's clothes and hair, but she didn't notice. "I keep it together, but it'll take *one* tiny little thing to push me over the edge and I think falling in love with a man who sees sex as a transaction may do it."

"Christ." Jake sounded horrified. "Is that what you think?"

Eve took her hands from her face and pinned him with a hard look. "Well, isn't it? Tell me how you feel about me."

As if caught off guard by her request, Jake's lips parted. "What?"

"I said — tell me how you *feel* about me. You don't love me. Do you at least like me?"

"I *like* you. I enjoy your company very much."

Eve nodded. *Spoken like a man with tender feelings.* "Do you ever see yourself loving me? Ever wanting a family — with me?" When he hesitated, she vaulted to her feet. His hesitation told her more than words ever could.

Jake sprang up. "Angie—"

"We really are light years apart." She steeled herself, her heart aching in her chest. "We're trying to run before we learn to walk. I'm sorry, Jake. Oh, Lord. I've made so many mistakes . . . I-I thought I could do this . . ."

He grabbed her wrist, and her gaze cut to his. Eve shivered, remembering a similar scene at his apartment at the Maxwell Arms. Jake raised his voice to be heard over a crack of thunder. "Goddammit, if you think I'm gonna let you go again, you're fuckin' wrong."

Resentment bloomed in her chest. Eve looked to where his fingers gripped her wrist. "Don't fret. I'll keep my end of the bargain."

"Meaning what, precisely?" Jake's face was set, a muscle working in his jaw.

"Meaning," she shouted, wrenching away. "I'll play your game. I'll run your estate and I'll wear fancy clothes and be a perfect mindless little wife. Isn't that what you wanted?"

"I want more," he growled.

"Sex?" Eve censured him with her glare. "I'm worthy of love—I *deserve* it! I deserve a real marriage."

She started for the house, ignoring the blackness threatening the edges of her vision.

So . . . this *is what dying feels like.*

CHAPTER FORTY-SEVEN

Finding an unlocked door, Eve slipped into the house, going from room to room until she came to a bedroom. Stripping off her wet clothes, she got into bed, making a cocoon with the quilt.

When she woke late the following morning, she was heavy-headed and nauseated as if hungover. She was surprised to see her damp luggage neatly placed on a stand at the end of the bed. She hadn't heard Jake bring it in. Misery and embarrassment washed over her as Eve thought about her meltdown the day before. *The honeymoon's over, sweetheart.*

After showering, she slipped a sundress over her head and twisted her hair into a topknot. Seated at the kitchen table, Jake had his laptop open in front of him. When Eve pulled out a chair, he looked at her like she was a ticking time-bomb that might detonate at any second. "You all right?"

She swallowed. "I pushed a lot of feelings under the rug for far too long. At some point, they were bound to erupt. This island was the proverbial straw." Eve stared at her folded hands, her voice unsteady. "I know I agreed to be a billionaire's wife, but I don't relish you tossing your money around. It makes me feel like I've been purchased. That's foul."

"Eve," Jake said, but she held up a hand.

"About yesterday. I don't regret what I said. I needed to say it. I just wish I could've been calmer. More concise." Tears pooled in her eyes and she sniffled. "The first time I had a panic attack was after my second miscarriage. I'd hinged everything on that pregnancy and I coped poorly with the loss.

I've suffered from bad anxiety since, but it's been years since an episode. Even when Martin was killed, I was lucky enough not to have one. I think everything's built up on me, and I'm at a-a breaking point." Eve bit her lip hard to keep from crying. "I tell you this because I've come to the conclusion I cannot keep burying unpleasantness. At some point, I gotta deal with it. I thought I was strong, but I'm *not*."

"Tell me what you need, and you'll have it."

"I don't need you to *buy* me anything. I'll find a therapist. You should do the same."

Jake scoffed, "I don't need therapy."

Eve scanned his face and lifted a shoulder in resignation. "If you say so."

Reclining back in his chair, he crossed his arms. "I've given you everything I thought you wanted."

"But I don't want a sugar daddy. I want the white picket fence, two point five kids, dog, station wagon. The whole ball of wax."

"I've been honest with you since the beginning," Jake argued, frowning.

"I can't fault you there. You've made your stance crystal clear." She put up a hand in a conciliatory gesture. "It's *my* fault. I may be frustrated with you, but I blame myself. I thought I could handle this, but . . . I've learned I'm someone who's looking for happily-ever-after. The heart wants what it wants."

"Get your head out of the clouds, Angie. The concept of happily-ever-after is a fuckin' *illusion*. It's manufactured to trick women into buying romance novels." His voice was harsh, his mouth tight.

"Ah, there it is." Eve shook her head, lips curving into an unhappy smile. "I know there's a guy somewhere who'll be able to give me what money can't buy — love."

His expression turned to a scowl of displeasure. "I don't

like that."

A flash of anger made Eve snap. "You're actually jealous. You have some gall."

Jake pushed up from the table and left the room.

For the remainder of the trip, they were two strangers, seeing each other in passing and barely speaking. Jake was aloof. Perhaps he was angry or hurt. He wasn't the man of the last weeks. Eve felt his absence every moment, longed for the easy rapport they'd shared. While he spent hours alone in the library with the door shut, she had plenty of time to think. Her mind was the sharpest it had been in months.

Each day she reclined on a chaise by the kidney-shaped swimming pool, her sketchbook in her lap unopened. Eve recalled, with a shudder, the aftermath of Martin's death—his bitter betrayal, which made her grief turn to hatred, and the horror of the allegations of financial fraud, worrying about money, and being hounded by creditors. Had the mugger really made off with over two million dollars? Eve had so many questions and so few answers.

She looked around at her island paradise. It was a privilege to be surrounded by beautiful, shiny things, but she'd give them up without a second thought—for her own family. Tears hidden behind sunglasses, Eve felt different grief, a fresh realization—if she stayed long term with Jake, she might *never* have a loving husband or children. The pain of the last months was a necessary learning curve. She resolved to make changes.

The mood was somber on the flight home. Looking in the mirror of the jet's lavatory, Eve was startled. Her colorful sundress clung prettily to her curves. Her sun-streaked hair and bronzed skin made her blue-gray irises a vivid blue. She looked every inch a relaxed newlywed.

Appearances are deceiving.

Landing, Eve saw a Carter Consolidated driver waiting to

whisk them home. She stared out the tinted window of the limo at the dreary winter landscape, longing for the sweltering heat of Fiji. Old Hillbury was depressing as hell.

Once unpacked, Eve set about fulfilling oaths made. She ordered a new wardrobe of designer clothes and searched for a therapist. She was fortunate to find a doctor with glowing online reviews and an immediate opening. Her first session went well, and Eve agreed to weekly appointments with Dr. Ryan at her downtown office.

"How are you since we first spoke?" Dr. Ryan asked, surveying her with perceptive eyes.

Deliberating, Eve shifted in her seat, crossing her legs. "We've been home for such a short time. I don't see Jake much. His workday goes from dawn to dusk. I think, maybe, that isn't a bad thing. I need space."

"You haven't been intimate?"

"No. Jake isn't happy, but I'm trying to keep everything businesslike. Sex leaves me wanting more than he's willing to give."

Dr. Ryan nodded. "Has he initiated?"

"Once. I told him my feelings haven't changed." Eve shook her head, sighing. "Our agreement was clear-cut. We should abide by it. Keep the mood friendly, detached."

"But, can you see how withholding intimacy may seem punitive?"

Eve groaned, rubbing a hand over her face. "That's not my intent. It's self-preservation. *I* can't handle the intimacy. I need breathing room to work on my own issues."

"How was Valentine's Day?"

Eve shrugged. "The fourteenth was also my birthday. Jake wanted to take me to Vermont for a skiing weekend, but I got sick with the flu."

"Have you kept busy?"

"I've cut down my hours at work because I'm whipping the house into shape. On Saturday, I finished illustrating the children's book. The author's happy with my work, so . . ."

"Didn't you mention your friends are opening a shop?"

Eve tucked her hair behind her ear, nodding. "Their soft opening's coming up and I was over there yesterday to unpack and organize fabric."

Dr. Ryan put on her reading glasses and consulted her notes. "At your first session, we discussed your art as a helpful addition to your therapy. Let's talk of some coping strategies for when you feel overwhelmed . . ."

CHAPTER FORTY-EIGHT

The following weekend Dad, Addy, Sylvie, and the children were invited to dinner. Eve meant to give them their souvenirs from Fiji. Dressing carefully in a cocktail dress and heels, she reminded herself she needed to accept her role as Jake's wife for what it was—a job. She applied lipstick when the doorbell chimed.

"My goodness, I love your outfit." Addy gave Eve a hug, considering the new paint and furniture in the foyer. She examined a floral motif *vide poche* on the hallway table. "Ooh, posh."

"Rather," Eve quipped in her best plummy English accent. She greeted the kids, then said, "The painters are coming Monday to do the upstairs rooms and I've ordered wallpaper for the dining room. Things are moving along."

Dad held up a bakery box. "I bought a cake to celebrate your birthday."

Eve gave him a kiss on the cheek, taking the cake. "Thanks, Dad."

"Shame you were sick for your thirtieth," Sylvie said. "Wow. This is an awesome house."

"It's your first time here, isn't it?" Eve asked, bringing the group into the kitchen and inviting them to sit.

Sylvie settled Aiden and Gabby at the section of the kitchen table not covered with towering piles of wedding gifts. Taking coloring books and crayons from a knapsack, she set them on the table, along with a tablet. There were footsteps on the back stairs by the pantry, and Jake appeared. He wore a close-fitting sweater and jeans faded from laundering. Heart leaping as it usually did when he was near, Eve observed him with mixed emotions. *Huh. Not so easy to keep feelings impersonal, is it?*

"Hallo, Jake." Addy lifted a bottle of white. "Anyone want wine? I've got a throat dry as *Gandhi's* flipflop."

Eve realized she still held the bakery box. She set it on the counter. "Sure."

"Yes, please," Sylvie said. Jake shook Dad's hand and then reached into the fridge for beer, handing a bottle to Dad before joining him at the island.

"We were too busy when you were over helping at the shop to talk much. Tell us about your trip," Addy said, handing out the wine. "The postcards were delightful." Never one to stand still long, she sliced the loaf of bread on the cutting board while Eve checked the frozen lasagna baking in the oven.

Leaning back against the counter, Eve described their activities, where they stayed, and the people they'd encountered during the trip, feeling Jake's brooding gaze on her the whole time. She brightly ended with, "And Jake bought me an island for my birthday." Without waiting for their reaction, Eve took bagged salad from the fridge's crisper drawer and emptied it in a bowl.

"Say again?" her dad asked, his beer bottle stalled at his lips. Sylvie's eyebrows rose. Addy looked over to Eve, her brown eyes wide and her mouth opened to form a perfect *o*.

An emotion akin to agitation passed over Jake's face before he said in a blasé tone, "It's an investment. If you ever want to vacation in Fiji, it's there for your use."

"Well," Addy finally said. "We may take you up on that someday. Do you have pictures from your trip?"

"We can look at them on the TV in the den after dinner," Eve said, asking over her shoulder, "Jake, can you move the gifts from the table? I started opening them today but didn't get far."

Sylvie insisted, "Let us."

"You can pile them on the floor." Eve took containers of salad dressing from the fridge door.

"Cor blimey! What's this?" Addy held the framed *Rembrandt* lithograph the Tate family had given them as a wedding present.

"That insignificant trinket is an example of the sort of gifts billionaires give," Eve replied tartly, giving Jake side-eye. He'd been offhand about the expensive present.

Addy handed the artwork to Dad, and he whistled through his teeth. "This puts our chip and dip set to shame."

"I liked your gift," Eve insisted, wondering if she'd ever be comfortable living a lifestyle of excess.

"Arthur sure thinks a lot of you." Addy put her hand on Jake's shoulder.

He gave her a smile. "He's the father I never had."

"He's darling," Eve agreed. "We're invited to Port Breakwater for St. Patrick's Day weekend. The whole family will be there. They make a big deal of the holiday."

"Tate's not an Irish name, is it?" her dad asked.

"No, but Arthur's mother was an O'Brien," Jake explained.

"Arthur extended the invitation to you and Dad, Addy," Eve said. "So, if you can get away from Elite, you guys should come."

"A weekend off can be arranged," Sylvie replied. "My mother will fill in. An invitation to Port Breakwater shouldn't be passed up. It's the wealthiest region on the East coast."

"Is it?" Eve asked, considering. "I wouldn't be surprised."

"This is unusual paper for a wedding pressie," Addy remarked, holding up an unopened box emblazoned with golf balls. "It has your name on it, pet."

"I don't remember that." Eve put the tray of lasagna on the stovetop with oven mitts before coming around the island to take the gift from Addy. She pulled the taped-on card from the box. *Here's to the memories of halcyon days past. All my love, Hitch.*

"Aww, it's from Hitch." Eve tore the paper and opened the box, giggling as she pulled out a squirrel figurine.

"I don't understand." Sylvie's brow knit in puzzlement.

Eve said mildly, "He's an idiot."

"What is it?" Jake hadn't looked overjoyed when Hitch's name was mentioned, and after reading the card, his face darkened.

"Just a stupid inside joke." Eve knew he wouldn't like that but didn't care. "Once, when Hitch and I golfed together, a squirrel chased us from the eighteenth hole to the clubhouse. We barely survived with our lives. We'd had drinks before the round. It's worth noting that five piña coladas can make *anything* hysterical."

"I can see the headline now, *When Good Squirrels Go Bad,*" Addy said, and Dad chuckled.

"If Hitch were here, you'd be in stitches. He's a better storyteller than me." Putting the figure back in the box, Eve peeked at Jake. "It's a gag gift."

"It certainly made me gag," Jake muttered under his breath.

Eve pretended she hadn't heard, keeping her face expressionless.

Over the meal, the conversation centered on Elite. The final fixtures they'd been waiting on had been installed the day before.

"I can't believe our soft opening's in a week," Sylvie said. She and Addy looked at each other and beamed.

They sang *Happy Birthday* to Eve and she cut slices of chocolate cake for everyone. When they went to relax in the den, Jake pulled up the photos on the TV. Eve had organized a folder of twenty photos. Images scrolling on the screen, she gave a quick narration, then handed out souvenirs.

Banging the sticks against their *Lali* drums, Aiden and Gabby squealed. Sylvie volleyed Eve and Jake a baffled look. "What have I *ever* done to you two to deserve *this*?"

Eve flinched playfully. "Sorry. I didn't think."

She and Jake walked their guests to the door, exchanging hugs and waving until Sylvie's minivan disappeared down the winding driveway. She loaded the dishwasher, and Jake went to work on his laptop in front of the fire.

Eve picked up on the irritation emanating from him. She planned to give him a wide berth. She was too exhausted for a confrontation.

CHAPTER FORTY-NINE

The following week Eve met Hitch to watch a mid-morning revival of the *Marx Brothers' Duck Soup* at the multiplex in uptown Old Hillbury. Snickering like schoolchildren, they ate handfuls of buttery popcorn and shared a bag of red licorice while sipping soda. She enjoyed Hitch's happy-go-lucky personality. He was a diversion.

Afterward, they dawdled at one of the round tables by the arcade in the lobby of the theater with refills of soda and split a pizza, talking until Eve was hoarse. She told Hitch about the trip to Fiji and the island Jake purchased for her, showing him photos on her phone.

"You know," Eve said coyly. "Jake's terribly jealous of you. He thinks you have the hots for me."

"Really? I mean, I know he loathes me, but that's awesome!" Hitch's enthusiasm made Eve chuckle. He teased, "You have that girl-next-door *thang* going for you. If I were straight . . ."

"I'm average looking," Eve shrugged, but smiled. "However, I never refuse a compliment."

Hitch sobered. "I know it's appalling of me to ask a married woman—but are you willing to continue being my beard a little longer?"

"I'm hardly your *beard*." Eve put a hand on his. "But, I'll never out you, not to anyone."

"Jake would tell Arthur, and . . . I'm not ready for it to be common knowledge." Hitch lifted a shoulder, apologetic.

"It's not my story to tell."

"Thanks, doll."

Eve took a drink of soda. "How's the apartment remodel going?"

"Ugh, slow as molasses." Hitch rolled his eyes. "Delay after delay."

"Are you going to Arthur's for the holiday?"

"Eh. I was invited, but probably not." Leaning back in his chair, stretching his arms behind his head, he seemed unaware a group of teenage girls entering the theater tittered in his direction. His blond surfer looks were youthful, but what made him attractive was his carefree attitude. "I can't—ugh, Siobhan is *bad* news."

"Right. Jake's ex-flame."

"She's trouble with a capital T. You'll see what I mean when you meet her. Last year she dated Steve Santinelli, but she dropped him like a hot potato with the scandal. Since then, she's set her sights back on Jake. That he's married probably won't be much of a deterrent."

"Who's Steve Santinelli?"

"You know. CEO of Big Santi's Pizza? The one who killed Ginger the Giraffe while big game hunting in Africa?"

"Ahh." Realization dawned and Eve wrinkled her nose. She had no issue with hunting for food, but the idea of rich men gunning down majestic animals for sport, especially ones in an enclosure, was revolting. "Siobhan dated *him?*"

"Hester says his trophy hunting perturbed her, but I think she was more perturbed by the bad press, especially when they hounded *her*."

"Oof."

"Enough about her." With a sly grin, Hitch asked, "Did you and the macho man do anything for your birthday slash Valentine's Day?"

Eve shook her head. "I got sick. I wasn't in the mood to go anywhere. I've been busy. Every night I tumble into bed, spent."

"Here." Hitch produced a shopping bag. *"Feliz cumpleaños."*

Eve looked at him through her eyelashes. "I wondered why you brought that with you into the theater." Opening the bag, she hooted.

"It reminded me of our days at The Palms. Maybe you want a collection?" Hitch twinkled. "Love it, don'tcha?"

It was another squirrel statue. This one wore a Hawaiian shirt and held a tropical drink. Eve threw her arms around Hitch, hugging him. *"Where do you find these?"*

Jake's car was parked by the front door. Eve glanced at the clock on the dash. It was early afternoon. He hadn't been happy when she'd told him her plans to see Hitch. Had he come home early to pick a fight?

Eve parked in the garage. Approaching the service door, she detected the smell of pot. Jake was loafing at the island, looking casually sexy in a cable-knit sweater and jeans. A blunt sat in a glass ashtray. She put her handbag on a stool and scanned his face. "Why are you home?"

"To talk to you." He picked up the blunt and took a drag.

"I didn't know you still smoked."

He held it toward her in offering.

"No, thanks. I'm nauseous."

Jake slowly exhaled smoke from his lungs. "Helps me unwind. You sure? It'll settle your stomach."

"No, I'm okay. But you go ahead. I'm not bothered by weed. What do you want to talk about? Is something wrong?"

He surveyed her, heavy lidded. "I haven't been happy this past month, in case you didn't notice."

"Oh, I noticed, but I'm not your keeper." Eve smiled to lessen the sting of her words, watching him bring the blunt to his lips. "I've been handling my shit, and it's up to you to handle yours, Jake."

Jake exhaled. "Kitten has claws." His mouth curved in the semblance of a smile for the first time in weeks. He put what was left of his blunt in the ashtray. "You've been freezing me out. I don't like it.",

Eve tilted her head. His face was drawn, and his energy was worlds apart from his normal crisp vitality. "I wouldn't say *freezing you out,* but I have kept my distance."

"I want to fix that," he said frankly, with the confidence of a man proficient in fixing problems.

"You know how I feel." Eve brought a hand to her forehead, rubbing her temple, suddenly drained. The junk food she'd eaten at the theater lay like a rock in her stomach. "We've been through this."

"I'm not saying everything will be perfect—hell, I'm not sure I'm capable of being the kind of man you deserve . . ." Jake rubbed a thumb across his lower lip. "All I know is I miss you."

She looked at him in shock, eyes wide. "You've never opened up to me like this before."

"I've never felt this way before." His voice was thoughtful. "I'll even see a shrink if that's what it takes."

"But I didn't ask you to do that for me. You need to for yourself."

Jake nodded. "Yeah." He ran a hand through his hair. "Angie, if I had the power to change what I am for you, I'd do it in a second, but I can't."

Eve crossed to him, heart softening, and knelt in front of his stool. She put her hands on his. "I don't expect that. Just let me in."

"You have no idea the shit I've been through. It's ruined me . . . there's no coming back from it. I'm damaged goods," he said gruffly.

"Don't say that," Eve cried, standing and wrapping her

arms around him tight, wanting to bear some of his distress. At first, Jake's arms stayed at his sides, but then, he buried his head in her breasts and returned her embrace for several moments.

"Let's go up to my a-frame in Stowe. Let's escape everything, and be alone. No distractions, no phones, no laptops. Just you and me and a bed," Jake coaxed, bringing her palm to his lips.

Eve play-acted that her heart wasn't knocking like a jackhammer at the thought of intimacy, and she gave him a look. "Remember what I said about us not running before we learn to walk?"

"I can call my pilot and he can file a flight plan." His smile was lopsided. "We can be in the air in an hour and in Stowe by dinnertime."

"Jake." She shook her head, but her resolve flagged.

"I have the bag with your new ski clothes sitting in my closet, and I know a friendly little Italian restaurant where we can have supper by candlelight. We're young and rich. Let's be wild and crazy."

Eve sighed, thawing. She hoped she wouldn't regret her weakness.

CHAPTER FIFTY

"Tell me about Stowe," Dr. Ryan said.

"Jake set about wooing me, and he succeeded. His a-frame has a breathtaking view of Mount Mansfield. He made a fire, and it was cozy. Romantic. He's an excellent skier and reined himself in to match my speed. I'm not good. He skis as well as he does most things. Sometimes, I'm in awe. It's like Jake can do *anything*." Eve's voice trailed off, and she stared into space for a moment, lost in thought.

"Were you intimate?"

"Yes." Eve admitted dryly, "Maybe I'm easily seduced, but he knows *all* the right moves."

"Do you regret it?"

"I certainly didn't at the time." Her chuckle was self-deprecating. "He opened up to me before we left, which swayed me. In the aftermath, I do have *feelings*—they're hard to articulate, but I guess that's why I'm here, right?"

"You've talked of *learning how to walk before you run* when it comes to your relationship with your husband. Explore further."

"It means getting to know each other outside the bedroom—we've done everything backward. I'm trying to change course." Eve shook her head, frustrated.

"From what you tell me, you and Jake are getting to know each other."

"We are, but—" Eve conceded, but her exasperation was clear. "Maybe I'm overeager. I know it takes time. I've been thinking about what we discussed at my last appointment—

about punishing Jake. Ugh, why is this so hard?"

"You're doing fine. Let words pour from you in a stream of consciousness."

Eve took a deep breath, trying to gather her thoughts. "Well, Jake said I've been *freezing him out,* but I told you—punishment wasn't my goal." She waved her hand before continuing,

"Let me back up—I wasn't necessarily *angry* when we returned from Fiji. That's not accurate. I *was* angry and frustrated during our blowout at the beach, definitely, but in the days after, the anger and frustration evolved. When we left, I was disappointed, introspective, and resigned to the fact I need to accept Jake as he is. I decided I'd keep to our agreement and put in my time. At the end of the year, we'd go our own ways.

"We have a duty to ourselves to try to . . . I don't know . . . carve out what happiness we can. When I was a girl, I always saw myself someday being a wife and a mother. It's all I ever wanted. I have one life. I won't live forever. My marriage with Martin was a failure. It was time wasted. In Fiji, I came to the conclusion I didn't like the trajectory of the path I'm on."

"Tie that back to Jake," Dr. R said.

"Okay. If somebody is adamant regarding their goals and your goals don't mesh with theirs—isn't it madness to invest your time, energy, and heart into a relationship destined for failure? I think it's short-sighted to enter into one thinking you can change your partner. He's been honest with me. I've made a commitment for a year. The problem is I fell in love with Jake. I had to decide if I could handle a casual sexual relationship without intimacy. Loving someone who says they can't, and won't, love you back . . . ." Eve bit her lip and her eyes filled with tears.

"Here," Dr. Ryan said, holding out a box of tissues. With a quick smile of thanks, Eve pulled several tissues from the box.

"Before we left for Stowe, Jake opened up to me, and any resolve I'd built up after Fiji vanished. That's why I agreed to go. It gave me hope maybe—someday, somehow—we can have a future. This year, I'm gonna use my time constructively as I can. I want to try to make a go of my marriage."

"Do you credit your distance as the reason he opened up to you?"

"I suppose."

"How so?"

Eve lifted a shoulder. "If I hadn't spoken up for myself and insisted on some space, would Jake have opened up to me on his own, eventually? I don't know—maybe he would've, maybe not—but we both had a taste of happiness on our honeymoon. Jake realized he missed me, so—look, it's enough for now. With some compromise, maybe our marriage can survive."

"For a compromise to succeed, both parties have to meet in the middle, and you're asking your husband to make a lot of changes. How will *you* change?"

"Does it seem like I expect Jake to do the heavy lifting, and I do nothing?" Eve asked, dismayed. Dr. Ryan didn't answer. "I have so many flaws and so much baggage. That's why I'm here." She looked out the window behind the doctor's desk, shaking her head.

"Tell me what you're willing to work on."

"I've got an agenda. Personal growth . . . and that will spill over into all areas of my life." Eve met Dr. Ryan's eyes. "I need to change how understanding and patient I am. I need to work on speaking up for myself and confronting painful subjects head-on, rather than retreating. Not isolate. Reaching out. Try to . . ." A fat tear rolled down her cheek and she swiped at it, biting back a sob. "I have to be vulnerable and work on trusting again."

"Heavy stuff." Dr. Ryan looked at her wristwatch. "Why

don't you spend the remainder of your session telling me how you feel regarding the upcoming visit where you'll meet your husband's ex."

Eve exhaled, appreciating the break. She blew her nose, then rolled her eyes heavenward. "Lemme tell you about this chick and you'll see why I'm not looking forward to this weekend . . ."

CHAPTER FIFTY-ONE

"Come in for a bevy before we drive to Arthur's," Addy said, voice high-pitched. Dad was behind Addy in the foyer, a goofy grin on his face. He held a bottle of champagne.

"What's going on?" Eve asked, shedding her sweater and adjusting the skirt of her wrap dress as she entered the living room. Dad poured the champagne. Accepting a flute, Jake took off his sunglasses and tucked them in the open neck of his polo shirt. Eve shot Addy a questioning look, but she only turned pink.

"Eve, Jake." Dad puffed out his chest and raised his glass. "I'm pleased to announce Addy's consented to be my wife."

"Oh my God!" Eve whooped, grabbing Addy into an enthusiastic hug. Dad shook Jake's hand and she beamed at her father over Addy's shoulder.

"You are pleased, aren't you, pet?" Addy asked tenderly, pulling away.

"I'm on Cloud Nine." Eve kissed her dad's cheek, teasing, "I saw you two snogging at Christmastime."

Dad blushed.

"Let's see the ring," Eve urged. Addy presented her hand and she admired the emerald set among a cluster of diamonds. "It's perfect. Addy, I can't believe you're going to be my step-mother."

Dad put his arm around Addy. His adoration was obvious when he looked down at his fiancée.

"We were thinking of August for the wedding, depending

on how busy the shop is. I want to buy a suit and a posh hat," Addy confided while Jake drove them to Port Breakwater. "Naturally, you and Jake will be our witnesses."

Eve thought her father and Addy made love seem easy. *But look how long it took for them to find each other.* Recalling her father's loneliness during her childhood, she was delighted Addy would officially be family. Weepy with emotion, Eve made the pretense of watching the scenery out the window, blinking away tears.

Two hours later, Jake maneuvered the vehicle through a gate and up a hill to Arthur's seaside estate. The rambling white clapboard-sided Colonial with forest green shutters was surrounded by immaculately landscaped grounds, with a view of the Long Island Sound. Various luxury cars were parked on the brick paver drive beside a bubbling fountain. Jake stopped behind a sporty convertible with a vanity plate that said, *Siobhan.*

Dad whistled. "This mansion makes my Tudor look like a shanty."

"Everyone's here," Jake replied, setting his sunglasses on the dashboard.

Slipping her cardigan on and taking hold of her purse, Eve braced to meet Siobhan. *Be open-minded. Draw your own conclusions.* Still, a mild zip of warning made her stomach clench.

"Ready, luv?" Addy asked.

Nodding, Eve affectionately linked arms with Addy, who looked attractive in her fuchsia linen shirt and white capris, a print scarf knotted around her neck, and her Christmas pearls in her ears.

A uniformed maid answered the door, but Arthur came into the foyer to receive them in his cordial way. "Welcome, welcome." Accompanying them to a formal living room tastefully decorated in beige and peach, he said, "Our guests have arrived."

Hester and Thomas hugged them effusively as if they were old friends. Thomas introduced their sons, ginger-haired twins in their teens who reclined in a window seat, scrolling on smartphones.

"My daughters and son-in-law were in Aspen for the holidays, or you would've met them at the wedding," Arthur explained, indicating Aoife and Jameson Conroy. Aoife was dressed in a matronly flowery shift, her coppery hair cut in an unflattering bob. She held a fussy baby on her lap.

Eve greeted Aoife, then Jameson, a tall, studious looking man wearing spectacles and a tweed sport coat with leather patches at the elbows. The couple nodded and smiled.

"This is Mary-Alice," Aoife said, and like a honeybee drawn to nectar, Addy went to the child.

"And meet my youngest daughter," Arthur's voice thundered. "This cute little gal is Siobhan."

"You saved the best for last, Daddy." A striking woman with calculating eyes posed at the fireplace, a martini in hand. Her green dress was a perfect foil for her red hair but left nothing to the imagination. A blood-red color coated her lips and talon-like fingernails. Siobhan's blue-eyed gaze lasered into Eve, her hostility radiating in surges.

Arthur gestured to the sofas. "Please, sit. How was the drive?"

"Quite pleasant," Addy said. Eve found an unoccupied chair beside the long sofa her dad and Addy shared with the Conroys. Jake plopped down on another sofa by the fireplace, crossing an ankle over his knee.

Eve's gaze followed Siobhan as she sashayed to sit beside Jake. *That dress is so tight, girlfriend's feet are probably blue.* Saying something in a low tone to him, she ran a fingertip across his knee. Eve felt a stab of annoyance when he answered, his smile friendly. Siobhan giggled, and Addy's raised eyebrows told Eve she had her number, too.

Perching on the arm of Eve's chair, Arthur handed her a cocktail, which she sipped to be polite. He asked, "How was Fiji, young lady?" For several minutes, they discussed the islands, the food, and the culture.

"It's hard to believe we've been home six weeks. I can't wait to go back." Eve smiled, her attention covertly on Jake. Catching sight of framed photos on the bookshelf beside her chair, she got an idea. "I see pictures with you astride horses. I didn't know you rode."

"I have a few geldings and an Arabian I keep stabled up the road. Don't tell me *you* ride? How marvelous."

"I had an Arabian, but I sold him when I moved west. I wouldn't mind owning another someday. Tell me about yours. How many hands?" Eve asked, hoping to occupy Arthur so she could spy on Siobhan and Jake. As Arthur warmed to the subject, Jake tipped his head back and laughed. Eve recognized what she felt—jealousy. She'd never been prone to it, and she didn't like it much.

When dinner was announced, the group stood, Eve holding back to wait for Jake. She was vexed to find Siobhan clinging to him.

"Oh, Eve," Siobhan trilled in apology. "I'm *so* sorry to monopolize your husband, but Jakey and I haven't seen each other in ages and we have *so* much to catch up on! You don't mind if I take your place beside him at dinner, do you, sweetie?"

"He's all yours," Eve said dryly. *Jakey? Barf.* She didn't meet Jake's mocking eyes.

"Oh, that's *so* precious of you." Siobhan batted her eyelashes. "Jakey, you're so lucky to have an *understanding* wife."

Her father and Addy joined Eve. Addy poked her with a discreet elbow, and they shared a look.

Fine china and crystal were set on a table long enough to seat twenty people. Eve sat on the opposite side of the table from Jake and Siobhan, beside her dad and Addy. She feigned interest in her food and Addy's chatter. In high spirits during the meal, her dad told the Tates about his and Addy's engagement and proposed a toast.

"*Sláinte!*" Arthur lifted his wineglass. "I also salute Aoife and Jameson, who're expecting another child this summer. Here's to a wonderful St. Paddy's weekend." Eve pasted a contented expression on her face, sipping from her water goblet. The idea of spirits nauseated her.

The group, minus Aoife, who went to put the baby down for the night, went out to the patio to enjoy after-dinner drinks. Staff turned on patio heaters to keep the chill off. Steam from the pool hovered like mist, and the twins stripped to trunks and cannonballed into the deep end. Water splashed to where Jake and Siobhan were talking. Siobhan recoiled like a scalded cat, and her face reddened with fury. Whirling to her nephews, she snarled, "You two little shits better watch it."

Eve was taken aback by Siobhan's wrath. The teens were engaging in harmless fun. It hardly warranted the overreaction. *Yikes, I wouldn't want to really piss her off.*

Later that night, Eve was shown to a guestroom while Jake finished a game of billiards with Siobhan in the library. A consummate host, Arthur encouraged Eve to sleep late if she wished. He'd told everyone at dinner he arranged brunch at his country club, then an afternoon of recreation. "There are squash and tennis courts, or the indoor pool. They have a spa if you ladies prefer," Arthur added deferentially.

Slipping a white cotton nightie over her head, Eve surveyed the spacious accommodations. There was every amenity guests required, including a bookshelf. Settling in the antique four-poster bed with a book, she was on chapter two when Jake came into the room. Dropping his trousers to the floor, he pulled his polo shirt over his head, his muscles rippling with movement. Putting on a pair of black lounge pants, Jake went into the bathroom, yawning when he returned.

"What's on your agenda tomorrow? The spa?" Jake asked, drawing back the duvet on his side of the bed. When Eve didn't answer, he focused on her for the first time. She shot him a look.

"I do believe you're jealous, baby." He grinned at her, the dimple in his cheek flashing.

Since their shaky truce in Stowe, they'd kept things light. Eve rolled her eyes, not answering. He prompted, "Well?"

"I suppose it depends on what your simpering little girlfriend decides to do," she replied, half-joking. "I shouldn't let you out of my sight with her around."

"Siobhan's harmless."

"She did everything but bite your neck."

"I like it when you're possessive." Jake chuckled, coming around the bed and climbing onto the mattress. Situating between Eve's thighs, he balanced above her, his arms on the headboard.

"Really?" Eve whispered, her heartbeat picking up speed.

"Speaking of necks . . . yours is my favorite," he murmured, gaze hungry. Setting his arms down on either side of Eve's pillow, he brought his lips to her throat. She shivered as he nibbled from her throat to her collarbone.

"Mmm, I could do this all night. You taste good . . . like honey." He pushed her nightie up to her stomach, finding her naked. He mused, "I wonder what other parts of you taste like? One way to find out . . ."

CHAPTER FIFTY-TWO

"This is the dog's bollocks," Addy said, the masseuse working her shoulders. She and Eve were face-down on massage tables, opting for a day of pampering while the others swam or played squash in the indoor courts.

"You deserve it, after the work you've been doing at the shop. The grand opening was a hit, especially the fashion show. I'm sorry I got sick and missed the end of it."

"Speaking of sick. You looked off-color at dinner last night. I figured it was because of that horrid girl."

"Ugh, wasn't she disgraceful?" Eve laughed. Her masseuse rubbed her calves and ankles, and it felt heavenly.

"Perhaps you should see a doctor. You may be anemic." Their masseuses placed warm stones on their backs, leaving the room.

"Oh, I'm fine. We've *all* been overworked. You and Sylvie opening Elite, and me working *and* decorating the house, which is a full-time job itself."

"I'm glad to have this weekend with you. We never see each other anymore!"

Later, they sat side by side getting mani-pedis, discussing Siobhan. That morning she'd insisted on sitting beside Jake in the limo and at brunch in the club's restaurant, making Eve feel like a third wheel. He indulged the girl and told Eve he was merely being courteous when she'd called him out on it.

"She's had work done," Addy said.

Eve tilted her head, thoughtful. "You think so?"

"At least a nose job and butt implant, I'd wager."

"I wouldn't be surprised, I guess." Eve shrugged. "The Tates aren't good-looking people. Their warmth is what makes them attractive."

"My point is everything about that tart is fake from her fingernails to her eyelashes. She's a nasty little slapper. She needs to lay off those martinis, too. They don't make her more likable." Addy sniffed.

The house buzzed with activity on St. Patrick's Day. The cooks prepared a corned beef and cabbage lunch, and after a rest, Arthur planned an evening on the town for everyone. Eve read her novel outside in the garden gazebo on an upholstered chaise, waiting for lunch. The wafting smell of corned beef made her stomach growl. Thinking of her waistline, she'd eaten a light breakfast and planned to devour lunch. A cold breeze carried from the Sound, reaching her through the open gazebo windows.

Eve slipped her feet back into her leather moccasins for the short stroll to the pool, where she'd left her sweater on a patio chair. Walking along the side of the house, she was about to turn the corner when she heard female voices in a conversation. Aoife and Siobhan were on the patio. She slowed, not wanting to intrude.

"That Addy," Siobhan said nastily. "What a lard ass. I thought a tidal wave was gonna follow her into the living room."

Little snot. Anger rose in Eve's ribcage on Addy's behalf, her pulse gathering speed as she considered confronting Siobhan. When she heard her name, she became rooted to the grass, as if paralyzed.

"I don't know why Jake's carried a torch for her all these years." Siobhan's tone was derisive. "Her pussy ain't lined in gold."

"You're a brat. Daddy's annoyed," Aoife admonished her younger sister. "Eve's got a fun sense of humor, and she's very pretty. I can see why Jake's attracted to her."

"Did I say she's *hideous*?" Siobhan asked, then her voice took on a whiny quality. "All I've heard is how gorgeous she is. I'm *so* fucking sick of it."

"Jake's a good guy. He deserves happiness."

Don't listen. Move. Move. But Eve's legs wouldn't work.

"I remember how pissed he was when she dumped him for that other guy. It only made Jake want her more. When he realizes she ain't special, I'll be there to comfort him."

"I think you have a long wait ahead of you."

Siobhan argued, "Jake needs a wife from a wealthy family, someone with class and upbringing, who can give him sons."

"The Pierces are hardly white trash." Aoife laughed.

"Before we left for Aspen, I heard Daddy on the phone with Jake. Turns out perfect Eve ain't so perfect. She can't have kids."

Eve bit her cheek hard to keep from crying out. That little bitch knowing she couldn't bear children was a twisting knife. As Eve sagged against the house, her vision shimmered.

"We have a past. I *know* Jake still wants me. He needs her *out* of his system, once and for all." Siobhan's tone turned conspiratorial. "That man loves pussy — the things he can do with his tongue. He's *so* creative. And, it doesn't hurt he's hung like a *stallion*. Once, he used scarves to tie me — "

Heaving, Eve scurried back to the privacy of the gazebo overlooking Long Island Sound, hand clasped tightly over her mouth. Bending out a window, she vomited into the bushes until spent. Sitting down heavily on a bench, she wiped her mouth with the back of her hand, but the nausea persisted. She put her head between her legs. Humiliated both by *what* she heard and how *much* she heard, she should've turned around the second she realized they were talking about her. It was like coming upon a train wreck — the things Siobhan said. Eve wanted to die when she thought of Jake doing the same things in bed with that catty little madam as he did with her.

"There you are. It's nearly lunchtime — pet, what's wrong?" Addy lowered to the bench and put an arm around Eve. "Are you feeling lurgy?"

She detailed what she'd overheard. "When Siobhan enthused about Jake's technique in bed, I felt sick. I trucked outta there."

"That sneak admitted to eavesdropping on her father's conversations with Jake?"

"I did some eavesdropping myself," Eve said, rueful.

"It's hardly the same. That nasty little chippie needs a wallop across the chops." Addy bristled like an angry little hen. "I've half a mind to go tell her a thing or two."

Alarm panged. "No, Addy. Just leave it."

"I can't believe a chap as fine as Arthur fathered such an offspring."

At the dining table, Eve acted normally. Her pride wouldn't allow anything else. The meal was served family-style, and there were bowls of potatoes, carrots, and cabbage. She looked greedily at the platters of sliced corned beef, surprised the earlier upset hadn't affected her appetite. Slathering Irish butter on a slice of crusty soda bread, Eve waited for the food to be passed. The conversation centered on that evening's plans.

"I've something special in mind." Arthur twinkled, pouring a tumbler of whiskey.

"Daddy, I know a club downtown that's *so* perfect." Siobhan knocked back her cocktail and went to the sideboard to mix another. "It's exclusive, but I know the owner. We can dance."

I'll bet the only dancing that girl knows is the dirty variety.

"No, no. I've already made plans," Arthur said. "I've bought us boxes at The Grosvenor for tonight's performance of *The Playboy of the Western World*. I hope that's amenable to the group."

"Very amenable." Hester took a swig from her bottle of stout. "The twins can stay behind and babysit Mary-Alice."

"Aw, Mom," Peter groaned.

Patrick demanded, "Why can't we go?"

"You'll stay behind and mind the baby," Thomas said, his lips twitching when he added, "I don't need my sons watching a play glorifying patricide."

The ginger-haired boys sulked the remainder of the meal but didn't argue any further.

"I can't wait to wear my new dress," Addy said, sipping her whiskey and ginger ale.

"Me, too," Eve agreed, imagining Jake's reaction to the demurely sexy dress she'd packed. A delicate quiver of longing coursed through her.

CHAPTER FIFTY-THREE

That evening, the men had an aperitif in the living room while the ladies dressed.

At the stairway landing, Eve gave Siobhan a chilly smile, politely gesturing for her to go first. The woman wore a too-small purple dress pulling at the seams and heavy make-up. Her red hair was a tousled mass of curls flowing down her back. Eve thought she looked vulgar when she preened in the hallway mirror.

Stepping into the room, Eve felt Jake's eyes rake over her. The ivory chiffon frock she wore cost a fortune, but she'd bought it because it reminded her of *Marilyn Monroe*'s dress in *The Seven Year Itch*. It showed plenty of skin, but she carried a pashmina shawl. Sitting beside Jake on the sofa, Eve crossed her legs. He put his arm around her, his lips caressing her bare shoulder.

"You're breathtaking," he said huskily. Eve stole a glance to where Siobhan conversed with Hester. The color high in her face, her eyes shot daggers at Eve. Loving the feeling of one-upping Siobhan, she gave Jake a kiss, fading into him. When he withdrew, he nodded to the silver high-heeled sandals with the ankle strap she wore, whispering against her lips, "Wear those to bed tonight, and nothing else."

Squirming in her seat, Eve felt red-hot desire zap through her body. She visualized being bent over the edge of the bed, facedown, Jake's hands on her hips as he thrust deep into her. A blush settled on her cheeks, and he chuckled.

Sipping the drink that Arthur handed her, Eve listened to

the conversations around her. Siobhan's contemptuous gaze was blistering, but she kept her face blank, refusing to let Siobhan under her skin. When Jake's fingers brushed lazily up and down her bare arm, Eve's attention shifted and reasoning evaporated.

Soon the limousines arrived, and the group split. Arthur steered Siobhan to the limo with the Conroys and Dad and Addy. "There's more space in that car, honey," Arthur said, ignoring Siobhan's scowl. Eve hid a smirk when she followed Hester to the second limo, her mood buoyed by Siobhan's absence. Jake settled beside her on the leather seat as Arthur uncorked a bottle of champagne.

As they were chauffeured to the theatre, Jake rested his hand on her knee, discussing boating with Thomas. His stroking fingers, coupled with the champagne, made Eve float on a cloud. Hester turned to her, "When you come to Aoife and Jamie's place in the Hamptons this summer, we'll sail. Have you ever?"

"No." Eve shook her head regretfully. "Since we have a sailboat at our house in Fiji, I intend to learn. Right now, all I know about sailing is *hoist the mainsail* and *three sheets to the wind.*"

"Jake's the man to teach you. He's a first-rate sailor," Thomas assured her. Eve smiled and glanced at Jake, unsurprised. Thomas asked him, "What's that saying? *The first time you think of reducing sail?*"

"The first time you think of reducing sail, you should," Jake quipped, and everyone except Eve laughed. She figured people who sailed would get the joke.

"Thomas," Hester said, and he turned to her.

"I'll teach you how to sail." Jake nodded amiably. "I spent a whole summer learning knots." He leaned in to purr in Eve's ear, "Some are ideal for bedposts." Gulping, Eve felt her face heat at the pornographic images flitting through her mind.

"Jake," Arthur boomed from across the aisle. "What do you say to The Hamptons in August?"

Eve waited for her pulse to slow. Jake had to say but a few words, and she was a wreck. His sexual power over her was a potent drug. She was hooked. Then it occurred to her, sobering her. Siobhan had made a comment about scarves. Had Jake practiced his sailor's knots on her? Prickly awareness roiled in Eve's gut. *Nope, don't like that.* The unwelcome feelings lingered until the limo pulled up to the theatre, but she pushed them aside, trying to be rational. *I can't be upset with Jake for having sex with Siobhan before we were together, can I?*

Arthur mentioned he'd bought private boxes for them, and as they came into the lobby, Eve looked around. The Grosvenor resembled other theatres she'd frequented — high-ceilinged, ornately gilded, and swathed in burgundy velvet. Waiting their turn to be shown to their seats, Arthur said, "We have five loges so each couple has their own. Siobhan shall sit with me."

Thanks, Art. Eve bit her tongue to keep from smiling at the dissatisfied glower Siobhan lobbed at her father. She caught Eve's expression and Eve coughed, busying herself with her pashmina. *Surely, she can't seriously think she'd share a loge with Jake?* An usher in a black uniform led Eve and Jake upstairs to their opera box facing the stage. A chandelier dimmed to candlelight strength was suspended above a settee, leaving the enclosure shadowy.

"Isn't this comfy," Jake said after the usher closed the double doors. Shucking his jacket, he loosened the tasseled ropes holding the drapes back on either side of the loge. He pulled the curtains so they were further cloistered. Falling to the settee, he invited Eve into the crook of his arm. Burrowed into his side, Eve decided it *was* comfy — secluded in their own little world, they were shut away.

At the end of Act One, Jake leaned in to suckle her neck,

his mouth voracious. By the start of Act Two, his fingertips rucked the material of her skirt, hiking it up and flicking it aside to bare her naked thigh. Gasping, Eve was deliciously scandalized. Though she'd never been one to engage in public sex, knowing they could be discovered *in flagrante delicto* left her feeling wanton.

With her body sizzling, arousal pooled at Eve's center. She twitched, the blood pulsing in her clit matching her heartbeat. She'd long given up on what the *Widow Quin* said to *Christy Mahon* when Jake skimmed a finger under the elastic of her panties.

"Open your thighs, Angie," Jake whispered against her ear, and she obeyed, mesmerized. Eve bit her lip to keep from crying out when he teased her sensitive nub the way he knew she liked—tickling and circling with light pressure. Removing his finger, brought it to his mouth, licking the moisture away with a murmur of approval.

Eve watched him in the low hazy light, dizzy. When Jake returned to his ministrations, she tipped her head back. He made her tingle in all the right places. Lost in his touch, she honed, trance-like, on the frenzied tension building low in her belly. She pushed her pelvis against his hand. Sealing his mouth to hers, he increased the pressure of his thumb on her clit, sliding two fingers in her slick opening. Hips bucking, she shattered into a climax, moaning into his mouth.

As she came back to earth, Eve lay back for a minute to catch her breath.

With a wicked grin, she trailed a hand languidly from Jake's thigh to his crotch, rubbing her palm against the bulge she found there. Meeting his eyes, she licked her lips to show him what she planned.

"That so?" His breath hissed when Eve unzipped his trousers, fingertips explorative. Stroking the length of him, she reveled in the contrast of rigid and pliable, and the way her actions left Jake gasping. With a quick glance around to ensure she wasn't seen, she slipped down to the floor and knelt before him. Bringing her tongue to his tip, she flicked away the moisture beaded there, raking her nails over his balls. He jerked, making a strangled sound low in his throat.

Eve looked up to him, purring, "You know what I want."

When she took the length of him into her mouth and sucked, Jake buried his hands in her hair, thrusting his hips. Savoring the feel of his hard cock and the groans of pleasure he couldn't suppress, Eve increased the rhythm of her movements. He tasted amazing, and she felt drunk with power. It was a rush. Deciding to lay claim on him, she wanted him to lose control. The skin of his balls tightened in her palm. He was on the precipice.

Jake moaned her name as his body convulsed, warm seed spilling on her tongue. Noting his heavy-lidded gaze and heaving chest, Eve swallowed his offering, then licked him clean.

CHAPTER FIFTY-FOUR

"Did you talk to Jake about what you overheard Siobhan say to Aoife?" Dr. Ryan asked.

"It was uncomfortable for me, but once we returned home, I did. I'm proud of myself, because normally I'd let something like that go. I kinda felt unsatisfied by his reassurances, though."

"Why?"

"Because Jake said he puts up with Siobhan for Arthur's sake, and I've *got nothing to worry about.*"

The doctor's pen readied at her notebook. "Elaborate."

"It was *surface.* He pushed my concerns aside. I don't think he truly realizes what a troublemaker Siobhan is." Eve shrugged, but she was perturbed. "Jake apologized for her knowledge of my fertility issues. He says he confides in Arthur, but she's a snoop. Ugh, she's terrible. She kissed my husband *on the mouth* when we left."

"Bold," Dr. Ryan conceded.

Eve gave her a look. "I get the impression that girl's been around the block more times than the ice cream man."

"Jake's relationship with Arthur means you'll be in Siobhan's company often. How'll you cope?"

She lifted an indifferent shoulder. "I'll tolerate her. What else can I do? If she crosses the line and Jake doesn't put his foot down . . . I won't be happy."

"Awkward position for Jake."

"Sure. He doesn't want to offend Arthur, but I can tell Arthur's embarrassed by her. She's in her late twenties, but she acts like a spoiled teenager."

"You can't control how others behave, and neither can Jake. Or Arthur." Dr. Ryan fixed her with keen eyes. "We're only responsible for how *we* react to behaviors."

"Look, I don't blame Jake for the shit Siobhan pulls. My problem's with him encouraging her. We're getting along, and I don't want anything to screw that up."

"What about your friendship with Hitch Grant?"

Eve frowned. "What of it?"

"It causes conflict."

"It's not the same at all."

Dr. Ryan tilted her head. "Why not?"

"Intent. Siobhan loathes me and wants Jake. Hitch is gay."

"But Hitch's closeted."

"Yes, but we aren't being inappropriate."

"Jake doesn't know Hitch's gay. Naturally, he sees him as competition."

"I *won't* out Hitch. Not to anyone."

"Okay." Dr. Ryan put her hands up. "Just understand there *are* parallels between the two situations."

Eve gave her side-eye but nodded. "You have a point. I'll keep it in mind."

"That's all I ask. When will you see Siobhan again?"

"The Tates are coming to stay a weekend with us early April. That's my deadline to have the house finished."

The day the Tates were due, Eve strolled through the house. *It looks good. Like a real home.* No expense spared, she'd spent two million furnishing it. Pausing at the stone fireplace in the living room, she adjusted the framed wedding photos on the mantel and the arrangement of orchids in a copper *Teco* vase. After fixing the throw pillows on the tufted sofas and the rocking chairs so they looked carelessly elegant, she stood back to admire them. The brocade, canvas, and satins in earth tones tempered the angular modernist-style of the house. Without intending to, she'd branded the house her own.

Dad and Addy arrived late afternoon. They hadn't visited in weeks, and Addy insisted on a tour. Her dad settled into the den with Jake to watch TV and drink beer until the Tates showed up.

"You've been busy." Addy looked around the kitchen with her hands on her hips. Sliding the pocket doors to the formal dining room, she ran a hand along the cherrywood dining table and leather armchairs. "Gorgeous."

"Vintage designer. Not cheap." Eve indicated to the blue and cream geometric wallpaper. "It's a reproduction of a *Wright* drawing for the *Price* house in Arizona."

"You've done your homework." Addy pushed another set of doors apart on the other side of the room attached to the formal living area. "Usually, I don't care for mid-century décor, but you've made it homey."

"The transitional style furniture helps soften it. The rugs and drapes help, too." Eve followed Addy as she climbed the stairs. The wall along the stairway showcased photos of their honeymoon, arranged in an informal collage spanning the entire space. The largest photo was Eve and Jake's selfie in their private courtyard at Bliss Island. She wore a bikini and a hibiscus was tucked behind her left ear, he was sexy and barechested with a just-woke-up stubble on his chin. Posed cheek to cheek, they smiled, their eyes vivid in the morning sun. Eve thought that day seemed a thousand years ago.

"You make a lovely home, pet." Addy complimented when they came back downstairs. She stacked plates and silverware on the kitchen counter. "That horrid creature coming today?"

"Yes." Eve double-checked that there were enough bottles of red wine in the countertop rack. She'd purchased steaks for Jake to grill. Addy had made a scrumptious looking fruit tart with a shiny glaze. Eve's mouth watered with anticipation.

Pouring glasses of lemonade, they went outside to sit. Nodding to the new patio furniture, Addy asked, "What's it like being able to buy *whatever* you want?"

Eve took a seat on a chaise and crossed her legs. "I didn't really economize in California . . . not that we had Jake's kind of money."

"Sky's the limit now, innit?"

"You know flea markets and tag sales are my thing." Eve brightened. "Remember the mercury glass Christmas ornaments at the junk shop in El Segundo?"

"You always had good fortune when scouting. What happened to them?"

"They were sold in the estate sale, along with most of my treasures."

"Shame. You had some lovely pieces." Addy's voice was kind. "So, do you miss the house in California?"

"Sure, and my garden."

"You've plenty of room here to plant one."

"Maybe what I miss most about that life was the boring predictability of it." Eve's mouth turned down, but she lifted a shoulder, trying to be pragmatic.

"How are you and Jake?"

"We're figuring it out," Eve said, and Addy placed a motherly hand on hers.

The patio doors opened. It was Jake with the Tates. Eve had difficulty looking away from Siobhan's outfit. The cheap satin dress in a splashy red print made Eve's 1950s inspired floral frock appear plain.

Addy rose. "Jim and I'll get drinks."

"The house looks superb." Hester's cornflower eyes crinkled with her smile.

"You've got flair, young lady," Arthur bellowed. "You ought to do consulting!"

"Who'd hire an amateur?" Siobhan muttered, and Aoife elbowed her.

Eve handed out glasses of lemonade from the trays her dad and Addy brought. Peter and Patrick scrolled on their phones, not joining in the adults' conversation. Addy was sociable as ever. Cuddling Mary-Alice on her lap, she led the conversation from topic to topic, filling the group in on the progress at Elite.

"I've got a job for you." Hester described a party she wanted to have planned, and Eve's mind strayed to Jake at the grill, his well-worn jeans hugging his backside. Siobhan lolled against the stone countertop beside him, drink in hand, coquettish. *She's thirsty.* To Jake's credit, he seemed disinterested in the girl. As if sensing Eve's stare, he turned.

He caught and held her gaze. She knew what the searing heat in his eyes meant. Eve's face flushed, her body responding immediately to the naughty images running through her mind. She swallowed and shifted in her seat, and Jake smirked. Eve winked at him, blowing him a kiss.

"My father mentioned you owned a horse in California," Thomas said, and Eve tore her attention from Jake. "Did you ever do any jumping or dressage?"

"No, I didn't have him long."

"Eve," Jake called over his shoulder, flipping the steaks on the grill. "I think this fall we should look into buying a couple of horses so we can ride together. There's a farm two miles away from us where we can stable them."

"Daddy got me a gelding." Siobhan beamed. "After you purchase a horse, I'll bring the trailer down, Jakey."

"It'd be fun to have you and Arthur join us," Jake agreed, as if deliberately obtuse. Siobhan's smile turned to a frown.

"Evie, can you help me inside?" Addy closed the kitchen door, shaking her head. "Siobhan's acting true to form, but at least Jake's not tolerating her nonsense."

"We discussed her." Eve peeked out the window. They remained at the grill, Siobhan's hand on Jake's arm as she spoke. "He's respecting my feelings by not encouraging her. Thankfully."

"Jake's a decent bloke." Addy clucked, saying, "Blimey, Hester and Aoife look like they stepped from a magazine advertisement, but can you believe Siobhan's frock? Talk about tragic."

"Oof, I know. She resembles a blood clot."

CHAPTER FIFTY-FIVE

The evening passed pleasantly. The Tates were charming, animated company. The group had a lively discourse about books, theater, and films over drinks. Jake and Thomas debated which *Rocky* movie was superior. Addy and Hester chatted about musicals. When the sun set, Jameson put Mary-Alice to bed, and Jake turned on the patio heaters. Peter and Patrick went inside to stream the first *Rocky* movie in the den.

Jake selected music on the sound system while Arthur stacked firewood in the pit to make a bonfire. When the strains of *Angie* came over the speakers, Eve became pensive. Meeting Jake's eyes across the fire, she smiled. Whenever she'd heard the song during their separation, she'd thought of him—his charisma, his intensity, and his ardor. Was he re-membering the past, too?

As Jake sang the lyrics, Eve's heart constricted. God help her, but she loved him. The depth of emotion was almost a physical pain. She blinked back tears. Siobhan leaned over to talk to Jake, and he looked away, breaking the spell. Resent-ment mounting, Eve watched their interaction, Jake's raven head next to Siobhan's coppery one. Her hand with its ugly, talon-like nails on his forearm. When the intro to *Wild Horses* played, Eve went inside, craving solitude. Tidying the kitchen, she wiped the counters, trying to overcome her an-noyance.

Behind her, the patio door opened, then closed. The over-powering perfume wafted and clung to Eve's nostrils. She didn't need to turn around to see who it was but did anyway.

With a polite smile, she asked, "Need something, Siobhan?"

Sashaying over like she owned the joint, Siobhan helped herself to a wineglass from the rack, filling it from an open bottle on the island. She peered at Eve over the rim of the glass, the color high in her face. "You should know the first time we fucked was the day after you broke up."

Time slowed. Her parted mouth belying her incredulity, Eve heard the beating of her heart in her ears. *"Excuse me?"*

"Yet Jake continued to burn for *you*." Siobhan slurred, "Don't you wonder how long it'll be before he gets you out of his system once and for all?"

Silent for several seconds, Eve murmured, "Aren't you a little ray of pitch black." Cheeks on fire, she kept her cool. *Remember Dr. R's advice on how we can only control how we respond.*

"I understand Jakey. More than you ever could, *sweetie*." Lips slanted in a cunning smile, Siobhan tapped on the wineglass with her red-painted nails.

Eve ignored the clammy feeling building in her gut. "Those who know the least usually have the most to say."

"I know him intimately, don't worry about *that*."

"Yet *I* received a proposal. Telling, isn't it?"

"There's nothin' special about you. He'll see soon enough," Siobhan snarled, as if incensed Eve wouldn't be riled. "You're dull as dishwater."

The words hit home, echoing what Eve told herself many times. Insides quaking, she kept her expression composed. "You should eat some of the make-up you cake on your face so you can be pretty on the inside, too."

Siobhan sat the wineglass hard on the counter, glowering. "You wish you were as hot as me, bitch."

Stomach gurgling, Eve bit back her nausea. She'd be running for the toilet soon. Her fingers gripped the sponge in her hand, reflexively. She flung it in the sink and took a steadying breath. "I'm gonna give you a free pass this time because I don't want to embarrass your family, but if you *ever* come at me again, you'll regret it."

Siobhan looked flabbergasted when Eve walked away. Perhaps she'd assumed Eve would rise to the bait and make a fool of herself. Perhaps she hadn't predicted her poise. Opening the door and poking her head out, Eve called cheerfully, "I'm off to bed. See y'all in the morning."

She strolled past Siobhan without a second glance. *One point for me.*

Locking her bedroom door with urgent fingers, Eve rushed to the bathroom, where she lost her dinner. After, she leaned back against the wall, shaking, feeling miserable. If Siobhan wanted Jake, let her go for it. All she wanted was to be left alone to enjoy a hot shower, a cool bed, and not to see Siobhan's hateful face for eight hours.

She stood in the shower for a long time. Wearily, Eve toweled herself in front of the steam-fogged mirror. Taking another towel from the closet, she wiped the mirror, studying her reflection. She looked tired. Had she gained weight? *Can this day get any better?*

Tugging on a cotton nightie, Eve plaited her hair into a braid. When she opened the door, she gasped, finding a bare-chested Jake leaning against the doorjamb. "Why'd you lock me out, Angie?"

"Siobhan and I had a chat—or should I say *spat*? I needed to be alone." She moved past him to put her towels in the hamper. "She was drunk, but I think maybe she was stoned, too."

"Why do you say that?"

"I used to work with a woman named Becca who abused prescription medication. Siobhan's pupils were pinpoints, plus she slurred her words. Becca was the same way."

"What did Siobhan say?" Jake demanded.

"Oh, that you two *fucked*—she's so eloquent—the day after we broke up, among other things." Eve pulled the bedcovers down. Stilling, she tilted her head, considering him. "I don't hear denials."

He ran a hand through his hair. "She's been after me for years. If I'd wanted to be caught, I would've been."

"Are you denying a relationship with her?"

"*Relationship*? We *fucked* a few times. It meant nothing to me."

"Cute."

Jake's expression was aggrieved. "Christ, Angie. It was *you* I wanted, but you chose Pierce. Siobhan offered pussy on a silver platter. What would you ask me to do, be a monk until you were free again?"

"Of course not, but *her*?" Eve questioned, then said huskily, "She's in love with you, you know."

"She loves herself," he stated, matter-of-factly. He came to join her. His voice warmed her when he brought his hand to cup her cheek. "Don't waste your compassion on her. She'd sooner scratch your eyes out."

Eve covered his hand with hers. "I hope this isn't a come-on, because you can forget it, *Genghis*. You're not conquering me tonight. I'm bloody exhausted."

Jake nuzzled his lips against her forehead. "I want to hold you. Be close to you."

"I'd like that."

Later, as Eve succumbed to sleep, Jake whispered against her hair, "Sweet dreams, baby."

CHAPTER FIFTY-SIX

On Friday, Eve unpacked a shipment of material at Elite and prepared the week's takings for deposit. Sylvie, Eve, and Addy chatted at their cars after closing.

"Come out to my place for a birthday drink tomorrow before we go out," Eve said to Sylvie. "Since I'm *not* feeling booze, I'll be your designated driver for the night."

"Sure. I'll get a taxi to bring us to your house, though I don't think being a designated driver sounds like much fun," Sylvie said. "*You'll* drink, won't you, Addy?"

"I'll be tired from working at Elite, plus I'm babysitting early Sunday. So I better not." Addy unlocked the door to Dad's sedan, throwing her purse and the zippered bank pouch on the passenger seat.

"Wanna meet at Eve's?"

"No, at the club. I'll text you."

Eve drove home at an unhurried pace, listening to *All Things Considered* on *NPR* while traversing the quiet secluded roads. Chilled, she thought longingly of a hot shower and a BLT in front of the TV.

Roused from her thoughts, Eve noticed headlights coming up fast behind her. A glimpse at the speedometer revealed she was well under the speed limit. *Move.* She accelerated but the car was already abreast her. The sedan edged into the lane before clearing Eve's SUV. She blasted her horn and slammed on the brake, but wasn't able to avoid impact. There was a crunch when the back-passenger side of the car connected with her SUV's front driver's side.

"Fuck!" Eve barked, hands clenching the steering wheel. The sedan pulled to the shoulder, and she did the same, feeling as if adrenaline leaked from her ears.

In the gathering twilight, a hulking figure of a man emerged from the car. Turning on her hazards with shaky fingers, Eve dug in the glove compartment for her insurance card. She sent up a silent prayer that the guy wouldn't be an asshole.

When she looked again, he was back in his car and taking off like a bat out of hell. Eve stared, mouth agape, as the vehicle fishtailed around the curve of the road, the passenger-side taillight out. *What in the world?* In the rearview mirror, she saw a station wagon stop behind her SUV.

The bent figure of an older man exited the wagon. He had a shuffling gait and moved at a snail-like pace. Eve got out of her vehicle and used the time to gather her composure.

"Aren't you Mrs. Jake Carter? I'm Alfred Mayer, your neighbor." He shook her hand, noticing her trembling fingers. "Are you okay? My wife and I were on our way home from supper and saw that man sideswipe you."

Alfred didn't look a day younger than ninety. Eve gave him a sheepish look and projected her voice in case he was hard of hearing. "I'm mad at myself. I should've been more alert."

"It was unavoidable. I'd wager it was perhaps even intentional," Alfred said, his liver-spotted brow knit in concern.

No, surely not. Eve shook her head. "I should've let him pass without speeding up." They checked the front of her SUV for damage. There was a small dent on the bumper and the headlight housing was cracked. The pitch of her voice indicated her relief. "Oh, that's nothing."

"A lot of peculiar folks on the road nowadays. I'll follow you to ensure you get home safely. Close your gate, will you?" With a call of thanks, Eve waited until he was in his car, and put her SUV in gear. She continued down the road, careful to keep Alfred in her sights. He idled his station wagon until the gate clanged shut behind Eve and, with a honk, went on his way. She told herself she was humoring him by securing the gate, but his assertions the collision was premeditated made worry tingle.

Jake got home an hour later, tossing his keys in the *vide poche* on the foyer table before joining her in the den. Pouring a scotch at the bar, he asked, "Why was the gate closed?" Eve described the fender bender, trying to downplay the incident. Bringing his drink to the sofa, Jake frowned. "Alfred thought it was *intentional*?"

"It's ridiculous, Jake. I'm sure he's a darling man, but he probably breathes conspiracy theories."

He put his glass down. Leaning forward, he cradled Eve's face in his hands, searching her eyes. "You need to be careful."

"I realize that. I shouldn't have been daydreaming."

"Damn right," Jake snapped. "Do I need to hire you a driver?"

"What? Cool it. My independence is *everything*." Mildly indignant, Eve pulled from his grasp. "You're overreacting."

"Maybe, but I'm certainly not comfortable with you driving a damaged vehicle."

"It's a tiny dent." She declared, "It'll be perfectly fine for Sylvie's girls' night."

"What girls' night?"

"I told you last week. Tomorrow's Sylvie's birthday, and I'm driving."

Jake let the matter drop, going upstairs to shower.

The following afternoon, a shiny SUV was delivered to the house. When the courier handed her the key fob and left in the waiting courtesy car, Eve shook her head at Jake. He said, "You can sell your vehicle or give it to Addy. Whatever you like."

"What I *like* is my car. I know it's old, but it's in great shape. I don't need a new one."

"I've worked very hard in the last ten years to be able to provide, and I *will* provide."

Eve looked at the sporty gray SUV, then back at Jake, conflicted. It *was* beautiful. Should she accept the costly gift? It seemed self-indulgent, but the caring expression on his face made her surrender. "Ugh, I'll *never* get used to spending so much money at the drop of a hat."

Sylvie buzzed from the gate at six that night. When Eve opened the front door, it was clear the four scantily-clad giggling women had already started celebrating.

"Eve, this is Mara and her sister, Maxine, good friends of mine." Sylvie indicated the two Asian women beside her. Then, putting her arm around the shoulders of a slim strawberry blonde, Sylvie said, "And this is Ivy, my cousin, who we *dragged* out." They laughed as if Ivy's introversion was a long-running joke.

Eve led them to the kitchen, where they climbed onto stools at the island. Pouring champagne, she made a toast. Plucking a package wrapped with polka dot paper from a shelf, she handed it to Sylvie.

Grinning, Sylvie tore the paper, squealing like a teenager when she lifted the lid on the box. She slipped her feet from her ballerina flats and into the heels. "You heard me talking about these stilettos. You knew I couldn't afford them . . . gosh, Eve, they're expensive. Are you sure?"

Eve laughed. "Yes."

There were footsteps on the basement stairs. Jake entered, wearing basketball shorts and nothing else. His bare chest glistened with perspiration from a workout in his downstairs gym. He propped easily against the pantry door. "Happy birthday, Sylvie."

Introducing Jake to Sylvie's friends, Eve evaluated their reactions with amusement. She didn't blame them for being impressed. She often felt the same around him. *Eat your hearts out, girls.* Refilling flutes, she said, "I'll change, and we'll go."

Eve went up the back stairs to her dressing room. She'd been inclined to put on jeans, but after seeing their cocktail dresses, she opted for a pale charmeuse dress overlaid with black lace. A sexy little number, it molded to her curves. Sliding her feet into black stilettos, Eve found a matching clutch. She left her hair down, her only jewelry her pearl earrings and wedding rings. Applying her lip gloss, she entered the kitchen.

Jake's eyes flicked over her, his expression greedy, like a hungry man eying a juicy steak. Liking that look, Eve puckered her lips and threw him a kiss.

As Sylvie and her friends got into the new SUV, Jake stopped Eve with a hand on her arm. In one fluid movement, he pulled her inside and backed her up against the foyer wall, out of the sight of the others, bending his head to kiss her hard. When he pulled away, they were both breathing heavily. Eve knew what Jake's kiss conveyed. *You are mine. Men may see you tonight and want you, but it's my bed you'll be in tonight.* "Later," he promised.

Eve's lips tingled during the drive to town. The windows were down to let in the silken night air, and *Amy Winehouse* blasted on satellite radio. *Life ain't too bad, is it?*

"*Valaraaaay,*" Sylvie emoted off-key, and Eve giggled.

The club was busy when Eve pulled the SUV up to valet parking shortly after eight. Addy waited for them inside the doors. Eve evaluated the crowds with trepidation, mentally reviewing techniques she learned from Dr. Ryan to combat her anxiety. *Here goes nothin'.*

It was 80s Night. Eve hurried to the dancefloor when she heard the strains of *Prince's Purple Rain* begin. The group danced nonstop for an hour. When *Footloose* by *Kenny Loggins* wrapped up, Addy waved the white flag of defeat, snagging a high-top table in the bar area. Eve ordered club soda and joined Addy, raising her voice to be heard over the pounding music. "It feels later than nine-thirty."

"I'm not as young as I used to be," Addy hollered back over *Billy Idol*'s *White Wedding*, putting her hands over her ears and contorting her lips. Eve laughed. Sylvie and her friends were enthusiastic dancers. They ground against each other and other clubbers. "Can you imagine what your father would say if I did that?"

"He'd be scandalized."

Sylvie zigzagged over to their table. "Let's go to The Clockworks. Maxine knows one of the DJs there."

"I better scoot home to bed, luv."

Sylvie pouted. "The night's still young, Addy!"

"But, I'm not." She patted Sylvie's arm in apology and kissed her cheek.

At The Clockworks, Eve danced for a while, but she couldn't get into the techno-style house music. Weary, she found an empty seat along the bar and rotated her chair to watch Sylvie and her friends. Eve envied their tireless energy. She felt the flesh on the nape of her neck rise in awareness and discovered a tall, handsome man beside her.

He bent down near her face, his breath smelling of bubblegum. "Want to dance?" Eve shook her head, giving him a diffident smile. Fighting her anxiety drained her. The undulating mass of intoxicated people made her tired. Her gut warned she was being observed, but Eve dismissed it as paranoia. Overcome by the stale heat of too many bodies and her bladder full, she decided a bathroom break was in order.

Emerging from the restroom, Eve spied an exit down the hall. Thinking wistfully of a refuge from the smothering crowds, she poked her head out the door. The shadowy alleyway served as an employee parking lot. An inadequate security light above the door threw little light, but the air was refreshing. Making sure the door wouldn't lock behind her, she rested against the building, breathing deeply.

Wishing she was home, she yawned, shutting her eyes, blissfully unaware of her vulnerability.

The door beside her opened with an ominous creak.

Within seconds, she was in an iron grip. A strong hand clapped a sickeningly sweet-smelling cloth over her face. Mouth opening to scream, Eve gagged on the rag. The attacker's arm slithered around her waist, pulling her against his chest. Suspended off the ground, she fought, twisting and turning, to unsuccessfully wriggle from his grasp. Kicking fruitlessly against his shins, she lost her heels.

The man had the advantage of size and brawn. The skirmish continued for no more than minutes but felt like hours. Eve knew she wouldn't have the strength to continue struggling.

Realizing he was duck-walking her away from the building, she panicked. *He's taking me somewhere. I can't get away.*

The cloying odor of the rag made acid rise in her throat. Limbs growing heavy, she saw stars. Eve comprehended she was losing consciousness. There was the distinctive sound of a car trunk opening. With the last bit of strength she possessed, she flailed her arms against her captor, her fists connecting solidly with his chin.

The exit door burst open. Eve was hazily aware of the sound of running feet and a man's voice yelling, "Hey!"

She was released, plummeting to the blacktop. Head spinning, she heard the roar of an engine as a car sped away, tires squealing. Eve squinted at the retreating sedan. The passenger side taillight was out.

Darkness closed in.

CHAPTER FIFTY-SEVEN

"Angie! Angie, wake up." Jake knelt on the pavement, chafing her wrists. Her head and shoulders rested against his thighs. His phone rang, and Eve rolled away, retching.

"Caine, give me good news . . . that's not what I want to hear." He growled in frustration. "Okay, meet me back here. And call Jed. I want him at the house. No, I'll drive her." Jake stowed his phone in his jean pocket, placing a palm on Eve's back. "Baby, I'm here, and you're safe."

"What happened?" Eve shook her head to clear it, and the bile rose in her throat again. She heaved until empty then collapsed against Jake, panting. He used the hem of his t-shirt to wipe her mouth.

"Time to get up." He gracefully got to his feet and lifted her into his arms, carrying her to an idling SUV.

"How is she?" A man asked.

"She'll do." Jake put her in the passenger seat and removed his leather jacket, tucking it around her. Eve's head cleared, but she felt wretched. She feebly listened to the conversation between the two men, brain sluggish.

Is this real life?

The man sounded grimly satisfied. "You were right."

"Yeah." Jake didn't sound happy. "I'll sort her friends and talk to management." He pulled out his phone. As he walked away, Eve heard, "Jones, sorry to wake you, but I need you to chauffeur some ladies — "

Shivering, she looked over at the driver, pulling the coat

closer. It was Jake's groomsman, Caine, who oversaw security for Carter Consolidated. "He was big and strong as an ox. Smelled like one, too," Eve said hoarsely, shuddering when the memories flooded. She recalled the smell of unwashed skin, the garlicky stink of his breath. Hysteria tore at her throat. "He wanted to put me in a trunk!"

"You're okay now, Eve," Caine reassured her kindly, squeezing her hand.

"I know the car." She took a shaky breath. "It's the guy who sideswiped me last night."

"What make and model?"

"I don't know what kind. Older, maybe dark blue? Busted passenger-side taillight."

"Jake called Alfred Mayer. He's ex-law enforcement, so Jake trusts his judgment. He recommended keeping an eye on you."

Eve frowned. "But Jake didn't know where we were going."

"He installs GPS locators in his vehicles," Caine explained. "I saw you heading to the restroom, and figured you'd return in a few minutes. I didn't expect you to go out the back exit."

"Oh."

"Will you be okay for a minute while I check out the scene?"

She nodded. Caine walked through the parking lot. A few minutes later, Jake was back, and Caine met him at Eve's door. Jake tilted his head toward the building. "It's sorted. Management says you can view their CCTV footage. I have Jones on his way with a limo for Eve's friends."

"Look what I found." Caine lifted a scrap of cloth daintily by the corner and brought it to Jake's nose. He shook his head.

"Chloroform. Fucker's read too many cheap detective novels." Jake handed Caine a key fob. "Drive Eve's SUV back to the house after reviewing the CCTV—it's out front, by the valet stand. We'll take this."

"You packing?" Caine asked, and Jake pulled something from the waistband of his jeans.

Eve's appalled gaze fixed on the gun in Jake's hand. He cupped her chin to make her meet his eyes. "It's precautionary."

He got behind the wheel, placing the firearm on the center console between the front seats. She looked warily at the weapon as if it might spontaneously fire.

Jake shifted the SUV into gear. "Don't worry. The safety's on."

"*Don't worry?*" Eve asked faintly, incredulous. He drove aggressively, on the lookout for anything unusual. Bringing her hand to her mouth, she stared, sightless, out the window. Since Sal and Iris's initial visit in California, this situation was exactly what she feared.

"Talk, Angie."

Eve shook her head. The last thread of control unraveled, and she sobbed silently, her body wracking. Jake reached over and put his hand on her leg.

"Don't cry. Talk to me."

Choking on her terror, she whispered, "Dr. Ryan and I discussed this—the fear I wasn't fully done with Martin's bullshit."

"We don't know this is connected to Pierce."

"I've waited for the other shoe to drop." Eve wiped at her nose with her forearm. Tone strangled, she blubbered, "I thought I was scared before . . ."

"I'm a wealthy man. Kidnapping for ransom's a possibility."

She wouldn't have it. "It's connected to Martin. I feel it."

"Fuck. I'm sorry," Jake said, turning onto Route 9.

"Why are *you* sorry? I should've listened to Alfred Mayer—and my own instincts."

"My investigators double and triple checked to make sure they found all of Pierce's debts."

"They missed one. That's not *your* fault. This is Martin's fault. That *bastard*," Eve said around the chattering of her teeth. "Don't be sorry."

Jake growled. "Well, I am."

As they drove up the driveway, apprehension kept them from speaking. He parked in front of the garage and swiveled to her, looking solemn. "I've failed you. Knowing that, do you believe me when I tell you as long as there's breath in my body, no harm will come to you?"

"I don't hold you responsible." Eve brought a trembling hand to her forehead. "Ugh. I need sleep."

"Not until you've been evaluated for injuries."

She didn't have the strength to open the car door. Jake grabbed the weapon from the center console and tucked it in his waistband, coming around the vehicle to help her. His gaze roved the grounds and Jed, Jake's employee and friend, unbolted the front door for them.

"Can you take Eve upstairs and check her over? I have phone calls to make." Jake turned to Eve. "Jed's a trained medic."

She meekly allowed him to take her arm. He spoke of innocuous subjects, his Southern accent soothing. Shivering at the edge of her bed, Eve submitted to a physical exam, answering Jed's questions in a halting voice. She was barefoot. The skirt of her cocktail dress was ripped, and her tights shredded.

"You gotta goose egg on your noggin', but no signs of concussion," Jed said in his slow drawl, putting the penlight he used to check her pupils in his shirt pocket. "You're gonna be mighty sore in the AM, I reckon."

"Sleep. Please," Eve beseeched. Head pounding and lethargic, her mind didn't work right. All she could think about was sinking into bed and slumbering for days.

"Need help undressin'?"

Eve shook her head, and Jed left. She got under the covers fully clothed, falling asleep immediately. Several times during the night, someone peeked in to check on her, hushed voices conversing in the hallway.

It was sunrise when Eve woke, completely alert. She threw back the covers. Padding to the bathroom, she was aware of her stiff muscles and the scrapes on her knees and palms from the pavement. Catching a whiff of the traces of vomit in her hair, Eve wrinkled her nose. It didn't smell of roses. Stripping, she dolefully observed the pile of destroyed garments. *There's three grand in the crapper.* Scrubbing with her favorite citrus body wash in the shower, she rinsed off the filth of the night before.

Once dressed in yoga pants and a long-sleeved t-shirt, Eve felt more like herself. She stretched, evaluating her injuries. Though sore, she'd expected worse, and now her headache was but a dull throb. Her stomach growled, demanding breakfast. She heard the murmur of voices in the kitchen when she went down the back stairs. Jake, Caine, Jed, and two others were at the kitchen table, each with a yellow legal pad lined with notes. They quieted when Eve came in.

With fatigued eyes, Jake looked her over, assessing. "How do you feel?"

"Hungry." Eve reddened under the scrutiny of the roomful of people. "Anybody want cereal? Toaster pastries? I'm not a good cook, but I can put toaster pastries in the toaster."

"You don't need to prepare food," Jake said, but she saw the cups of coffee littering the tabletop and deduced they'd worked through the night.

"If you have the fixins, I make a mean *huevos ranchero*," Jed piped up, grinning.

Eve returned his smile, grateful for a measure of normalcy.

"Let's check the fridge."

Jed topped the warmed tortillas with fried eggs. She heated jarred salsa and spooned it on the eggs. The kitchen was soundless while everyone single-mindedly ate.

Plate empty, Eve put her hands around her mug for warmth, studying those assembled. There were four men — Jake, Jed, Caine, and Markus, who Jed referred to as their *computer geek*. There was also a diminutive reserved redhead named Sara Montague, who they called *Monty*. Eve looked at each person in turn before speaking. "What's the plan?"

Jake poured more OJ in his tumbler. "The house is secure. The wall's not easily breached. We have video surveillance set up, which will be monitored. Caine, Jed, or Monty will always be with you, and they're armed."

"What about my job?"

"I don't care about your job. Your safety's priority one. Anytime I feel it's warranted, you'll be on a Consolidated jet to Fiji," Jake replied, his tone firm.

"I'll have bodyguards when I go out?"

Jake's mouth was set in a grim line. "If it's up to me, you'll never leave this house again."

CHAPTER FIFTY-EIGHT

Eve slouched down in her chair and put her tablet in her lap. "This is our third video appointment in as many weeks. How are you coping with your confinement?" Dr. Ryan asked.

"I have cabin fever. I've binge-watched TV, read books, sketched, cleaned the house, and baked *almost* edible cupcakes." She said unhappily, "Call me *Rapunzel*, 'cause I'm locked in a castle."

"What about the journaling I assigned you?"

Eve clicked her tongue against her teeth. "The other twenty-two hours in the day are the problem, Doc."

"You haven't found another book commission?"

"Not yet, but my sister-in-law said she'd ask around. She was actually pleasant when I called her, for once."

"How's your relationship with Jake during this trying time?"

Eve shrugged. "He has an important merger he's working on with a foreign company. He's not around much."

"How do you feel about that?"

Biting her lip, she took a minute to ponder before answering. "When I married Jake, I expected him to put work first. He got to where he is by working round the clock. I have Caine, Monty, and Jed for company."

"We talked of how it's not weak to need your husband. Make sure you reach out for support. On that vein, have you explained what's going on to friends and family?"

Bobbing her head in assent, Eve brightened. "I asked my

friend Sylvie over last night. The visit broke the monotony."

"Let's talk about your safety. Is there an imminent threat?" Dr. Ryan asked.

"I don't know. I'm not allowed out. I missed Addy's Easter ham for the first time in seven years."

"And how's the investigation going?"

"It's going nowhere. The CCTV at the club was blurry. It's a waiting game . . . I won't pretend I'm not scared, but how long am I supposed to live this way?"

Dr. Ryan gave her a sympathetic look. "I'd never suggest you go against the wishes of your security team, but at some point, you must leave the house for your mental health. You've made strides with your anxiety disorder by using Cognitive Behavioral Therapy, but this is a setback. The longer you're confined, the more difficult it'll be to resume a normal life."

"I know, but the idea of going out *is* terrifying. The recurring nightmares reinforce the fear. They're almost a prophecy." Eve chewed a nail, her expression disturbed.

"Tell me."

"It's always the same. I'm in a bed, but it's not *my* bed . . . it's pitch-black, but I hear hissing and then snakes are *all* over me—everywhere! I fling them away but there are too many. One twists around my neck, squeezing." She put her hand to her throat as heaviness settled on her chest, making breathing difficult. "Literally, the writing is on the wall in neon—*something's going to happen.* Monty heard me screaming from downstairs this morning. She thought somebody was in my room." Rubbing a palm against her sternum, she attempted to coax away the constriction.

"Sounds dreadful. But don't read too much into it. Dreams don't foretell. Your subconscious is advising caution." Dr. Ryan peeked at her wristwatch. "Time's going fast. Why don't we review your techniques for when you feel panicky?"

When the session concluded, Eve shut the cover on her tablet and put her head back. Doc was right. She needed to leave the house for her own sanity. Possibly, the failed abductions weren't connected to Martin—the guy could be a garden variety stalker. Maybe he'd given up. It would take courage to leave the house, even with bodyguards, but rebellion mounted. How *dare* some wacko make her subsist in fear?

Later, she and Jed played cards at the kitchen table. He always had a redneck joke to break Eve's mood when she turned melancholy. Husky, with a nose that looked like it had been broken more than once, he had an engaging smile. He dealt the cards, his tanned hands big but nimble. She put down a card, thinking of Sylvie's visit the evening before.

Jed was on duty until seven, consequently he'd been there for Sylvie's visit. They'd both been part of the wedding party, but Jed met the kids for the first time. Aiden warmed to him right away. Shy Gabby came around. Jed was as good with the kids as he was with adults because he was entertaining. Sylvie had stolen glances at him beneath her lashes. He caught her gaze and turned scarlet. Evaluating the interaction with perceptive eyes, Eve detected attraction. She'd excused herself to give them privacy under the guise of checking on the kids, who watched TV in the den.

"You scooted fast when Caine showed up for his shift last night." Eve asked without guile, "So when are you taking Sylvie out?"

"Ain't you slicker than snot?" Jed's mouth puckered when he put down an Ace and swept the cards into his pile. "Saturday."

Eve sang *Matchmaker* from *Fiddler on the Roof*, feeling upbeat for the first time in a long time. Jed ducked his head in an *aw, shucks* sort of way. She turned serious. "Jed, things are quiet. When can I leave the house for a few hours?"

Chapter Fifty-nine

The next night, Eve and Caine watched reruns of *The Office* in the den. *Michael* had hit *Meredith* with his car when Eve's phone pinged. It was Hitch. *Lunch tomorrow at the Courtenay-Blake? I'd like you to see my place afterward.*

She bit her lower lip, asking Caine, "Did Jed talk to you about an outing?"

"Yes, and he and I discussed it with Jake this morning." Caine's keen hazel eyes met hers.

"Jake had a video conference with his lawyers in Asia late last night. I didn't hear him come in or leave. What did he say to the idea?"

"He hated it, but I told him he couldn't lock you away forever. Where do you want to go?"

"A friend invited me to lunch in the city tomorrow. It isn't too short notice, is it?" Eve gave him a winsome look, and Caine chuckled.

"If I were cooped up, I'd be climbing the walls, too. Go ahead and make your plans. I'll figure it out."

Caine spent thirty minutes on the phone dealing with logistics. When he put his cell away, Eve apologized for being difficult, but he waved a casual hand. "You're hardly *difficult*. You made me cupcakes."

She grimaced. "Who knew boxed mix could be so tricky?"

"Lemme tell you about a difficult client. Once, I was assigned to a diplomat's teenage daughter. Talk about a pain in the ass. She shinned down an oak tree during my shift and snuck off to a frat party. I found her and dragged her home by her scruff. Her father chewed her out, then me, then her again."

"You don't have to worry about me sneaking out," Eve assured him, a shiver going down her spine at the thought.

"Good."

Once Eve decided to push for an excursion, she'd forged ahead with bravado. Now that plans were made, she wondered if she'd been hasty, even reckless. *Talk about second thoughts!* Tension making her stomach somersault, she looked at Caine for reassurance. "Am I making a mistake pushing for this?"

He tactfully said nothing.

"You're nervous as a whore in church," Hitch commented, waving away the *maître d* and pulling out Eve's chair himself. He looked chic but casual, wearing dark jeans with a sharp crease and a linen shirt open at the neck, his feet in loafers with no socks. Although Jed was nearby, Eve felt exposed. She checked the restaurant entrance compulsively.

Feeling crisp in her white shirtdress with the wide brown belt when she'd left the house, Eve now wilted. She wiped the perspiration from her lip with jittery fingers. "I *am* nervous."

"Perhaps we should go." Hitch placed a comforting arm around her. "It's too soon."

Dragging her gaze to him, Eve shook her head. "I have to face it. In time, it'll be easier . . . I hope." The waiter asked for her drink order, and after he left, Eve admitted, "As big as Jake's house is, I'm going stir-crazy."

"I'll bet."

Eve motioned toward Jed. "There's security at the exits, too."

"Wow. Your own *Secret Service* detail."

She lifted a shoulder, trying to summon her usual good humor. "Marry a billionaire and live a life of glamour, you know."

"Heh. How's Jake handling you being in peril?"

"Apparently, he's not thrilled I'm in public," Eve said. Nerves made her heart palpitate, but she pasted a pragmatic look on her face. "I don't see him much. I catch a glimpse of him arriving home late at night or leaving early in the morning. There's no time for heart-to-hearts."

"I envy his ambition. A mogul's life ain't for me, doll," Hitch said when the waiter brought her sparkling water.

Mouth parched, she drank, her attention cutting again to the entrance. "I sometimes wonder if I should go to the house in Fiji, but it's so far away."

They ordered shrimp salads, and once alone, Hitch turned to her in earnest. "If it gets too hot to handle, and you need someplace closer, my family's got a home in Aquinnah. Flying my *Cessna*, I can have you there in an hour."

Eve realized she fidgeted. She put her hands in her lap. "Aquinnah?"

"Martha's Vineyard. *Jackie O* had a house there for years," Hitch replied. "Our place belonged to Grandmother Hester's folks. It's private, on the beach, and rarely used."

Touched, for a moment, Eve was speechless. Prone to emotions of late, tears pooled. "That's kind. Thank you." She sniffled. "Before I liquify to a puddle, tell me what's going on in *your* life."

For twenty minutes, Hitch chatted about the renovations at his apartment, bringing up his interior designer's name often. Their salads were brought to the table, and Eve was relieved her anxiety had somewhat dissipated. Suddenly ravenous, she fell upon her food.

"Your appetite hasn't suffered," Hitch said in a droll voice.

"Be polite," she scolded lightly, but his expression was troubled and he didn't eat. She put her fork down. "What's going on?"

"I need to talk to you."

Heart sinking, Eve put her hand in his. "Oh, no. Are you all right?"

He moaned. "No. I'm in love."

"That's wonderful. Or isn't it?" She shook her head at him, confused.

"Yes, and no. I'm gonna have to come out, because I'm smitten with my decorator."

Eve tipped her head back and laughed. "Ah. No wonder you mentioned him so often. That's great."

Hitch opened his arms and she hugged him, maintaining contact for several seconds. When she pulled away, she pecked his cheek. He smiled down at her and, impulsively, Eve embraced him again.

Over Hitch's shoulder, she discovered Jake seated in the far corner of the restaurant, surrounded by business associates. He was watching them, his back rigid and mouth harsh. *I guess he's keeping tabs on me. Well, fuck.* Though innocent of wrongdoing, Eve felt instantaneous guilt. The hugs and kiss she'd shared with Hitch certainly made them *look* guilty. Alarmed, she intended to go to him and explain, but it was like Jake sensed her objective. He shook his head, and his face was forbidding, dark with a scowl. "Jake's here."

"Shit," Hitch said *sotto voce*, turning to look. "He saw us canoodling. Do you think my death'll be painful and lingering?"

"Don't rule it out." She flashed him a contrite smile, but her lips were rubber. "I'll explain it to him later."

"Tell him I'm gay and have a boyfriend. I'm comin' out anyhow." Hitch shrugged. "Why continue with pretense?"

As they left, Jed nonchalantly followed. Eve looked over her shoulder to gauge Jake's mood. His eyes shot daggers.

Fifteen minutes later, an elegant man opened the door to

Hitch's apartment and drew Eve into his arms. "I meet you at last, sugar."

Julian Haverford had the honeyed accent of a Savannah native. He was tall and rail thin, dressed impeccably in dark gray. His black hair was slicked back into a ponytail, and when he smiled, Eve noted perfect teeth. Hitch's laissez-faire surfer looks complemented Julian's dark sophistication.

Hitch was as spirited as a child on Christmas morning. "Let me show you what we've done."

Putting aside her distress over what happened at the restaurant, Eve tried to pay attention to the tour. The living room's walls were creamy white and the bamboo floors gleamed. There were ecru upholstered furniture and a sisal rug. Rusted metal signs and folk-art pieces were artfully displayed.

"I'm relieved you didn't buy those severe sofas you were considering," Eve teased, striving for light-heartedness. Hitch ushered her to a kitchen with salvaged cabinetry, concrete countertops, and a wooden trestle table with mismatched chairs. She ran a hand over the humped-back mint-green fridge. "Very cool."

"It's Jules's influence. Fair enough, since he'll be living here, too." He put an arm around Julian.

Eve grinned with natural warmth. "Julian, you have great taste . . . in décor *and* in men."

Epitomizing Southern charm, Julian served Earl Grey from a *Majolica* tea service. Hitch contentedly leaned back against the nubby cushion of the canvas-covered sofa with his tea while Julian offered Madeleines on a plate. Eve took a cookie, forcing cheer in her voice when she marveled, "And he bakes, too."

An hour later, with regret, she put her cup and saucer down on the steamer trunk they used as a coffee table. It was time to face the proverbial music. Eve had an irate husband to contend with.

"Don't let him go full Neanderthal on you," Hitch advised at the door as if predicting her thoughts. "He won't be angry once he knows I don't like the ladies. And don't forget Aquinnah!"

CHAPTER SIXTY

Eve didn't hear from Jake all afternoon. At five, Jed removed the marinating zipper bag of chicken from the fridge.

"The buttermilk makes for some mighty fine Southern fried chicken," he explained, dipping poultry into an egg wash laced with hot sauce, then seasoned flour. He dropped a thigh in shimmering peanut oil.

The kitchen filled with the scent of good food and Eve said, "I'm glad *somebody* in this house can cook."

After dinner, she made a plate for Jake and covered it in foil. He'd not answered her text whether he'd be home to eat. *That's how it is, huh? Childish.* Trying to concentrate on a rerun of *Parks and Rec* in the den, she became queasy. Would Jake ever come home? Vexed, Eve decided to head to bed.

Eve woke with a start when Jake came into the bedroom and shut the door late that night. Clicking on the bedside lamp, she squinted at him while he undressed. "Where were you? Why didn't you answer my texts?"

"I was busy eating dinner."

Eve's nose scrunched when she caught the wafting stench of a familiar perfume. The flowery fragrance tickling her throat, she sneezed. She didn't bother hiding reproach when she demanded, "Were you with Siobhan?"

Jake lifted an indifferent shoulder. "She bought me a burger in the city."

"Payback for Hitch? That's mature."

"Arthur met us there." His tone became surly. "I didn't

throw myself at Siobhan the way you did Grant, that's for damn sure."

Eve sneezed again. "I didn't *throw* myself—"

"Your first time leaving the house—against my objections, mind you, and you meet *him*. I don't understand the allure unless you prefer old money to mine?"

"That's enough!" She snapped. "Listen to me, Jake, Hitch—"

Jake's jaw clenched. He held up a hand. "Save it. I don't wanna know."

"But—"

"It's late, and I don't have time for this shit. I've got meetings early tomorrow. This is an important takeover. I have to be on top of my game."

Eve's frustration welled. It was juvenile, but she was riled. *Let him chew on this.* "I'm working at Elite tomorrow."

Jake raked a hand through his hair. "This house is the safest place for you. How can I keep you safe if you won't stay put?"

"This house is becoming a prison."

"I'm sleeping in the den."

Nothin' like a churlish billionaire.

"Here," Jed said the next afternoon outside Elite as Eve prepared to exit the SUV. A silver charm bracelet hung from his index finger.

"What's this?"

"You said it wouldn't be fittin' to have us lingering about in Elite. This is insurance. The starfish charm has a panic button on the underside." Jed demonstrated how to slide a tiny mechanism. "See, here's the switch."

"Let me try." Eve attempted to open the panel. It was fiddly.

"It takes practice. The globe charm is a GPS tracker, just in case. I'll be here. Monty's posted at the alley exit. You press that button, and I'll come runnin' — I'll move faster than a jackrabbit on a date."

The afternoon was uneventful. It was a relief to be able to pretend things were normal, and Eve loved spending time with Sylvie and Addy. Time flew. Before she knew it, Jed drove them home. "I figure that Mississippi pot roast's ready in the crockpot," he teased when Eve's stomach grumbled.

Eve was getting out plates and silverware when Monty rushed into the room, her manner urgent. She offered her tablet with the live feed from the camera posted at the highway turnoff to the property. "A vehicle's approaching the gate. Do you recognize it?"

On the screen, a green sports car halted at the intercom and they heard the buzz when the call button was depressed. "It's my sister-in-law. It's unlike her to drop by."

"I'll take the golf cart down and check it out before I let her in," Monty said.

Eve shrugged at Jed as the service door closed behind Monty. They waited, wordless, until she returned, Lex in tow. Today, Lex's hair was styled into gelled spikes. Her outfit consisted of a black t-shirt and a mini-skirt, and her usual combat boots. Piercings glinted in her lip, nose, and eyebrow and a studded leather collar circled her neck.

"Good, I made it in time for dinner," Lex said breezily, swinging a shopping bag from her wrist. She opened it and held up each item for Eve's perusal — a charcoal set, sketchbooks, and erasers. "You told me the other day you were bored. I come bearing gifts."

"Hmm. Considerate of you."

"Don't look at me like that, sis." Lex snatched a warm roll from the basket on the island. Chewing, she mused, "It's almost as if you think I don't like you."

Pink-cheeked, Monty dished up food while Jed poured drinks. Eve leaned in toward Lex so the others wouldn't hear.

"I thought you were *Team Jake?*"

Lex's mouth moved into a lopsided grin, making her look like Jake's twin. "Maybe you're growing on me like a fungus."

Eve shook her head, not disguising her amusement. "Ditto."

Lex ate as if famished, then heaped seconds on her plate. Usually reserved, Monty was bubbly, asking her, "You went to Hillbury High? When did you graduate? I don't remember you."

"Eight years ago. I spent my days in the art room or STAC." Lex promised, "You would've remembered me if we'd met."

Eve asked, "What's STAC?"

"It's what they called detention," Monty explained absent-mindedly, her eyes drinking in Lex.

"Lex? Detention?" Eve deadpanned. "Shocker."

Lex curled her lip in Eve's direction. "What's for dessert?"

Jed chimed in, "Bread pudding. My meemaw's recipe."

Eve lingered over her dessert, content to eavesdrop on Monty and Lex. She'd never seen either woman so talkative. Later, when she prepared to leave, Lex pulled Eve aside. "Do you know what flowers Sara likes?"

Eve looked at her in consternation. *Sara? Not Monty?* "I don't know her well. Why?"

"Because I'm gonna send her some . . . I think roses with the thorns removed. I'm inviting her to dinner at Chez Michel."

Chez Michel was an intimate French restaurant on the outskirts of Old Hillbury, known for *poulet chasseur* and booth seating concealed by toile screens.

CHAPTER SIXTY-ONE

Sylvie called Thursday evening.

"Can you work for a couple of hours tomorrow afternoon? Aiden has a doctor's appointment and Addy's babysitting for a friend."

"This weekend's the Founders Days celebration, right?" Eve asked. "You aren't closing the shop early?"

"I planned to, but there's a chance there'll be foot traffic from the parade-goers. You know me. I hate to risk a sale."

Eve hesitated. *Better not commit 'til I get permission.* "It should be fine, but let me ask Jed."

"If the shop's dead, will you organize the loft? The work-room's messy."

"Sure. Hold on a sec."

Eve poked her head into the kitchen, where Jed was reading a magazine at the table. "Sylvie's in a jam and needs me to cover the shop tomorrow. I said I'd talk to you first."

Jed nodded. "I'll guard from the street. Monty'll take the alley exit."

Sylvie gave Eve a quick hug. "Thanks for holding down the fort."

"I'm happy to help. Why don't you say hi to Jed before you go? He's parked in front of the ice cream parlor at the corner. We didn't realize Carolina would be blocked off for the parade."

The din of the paradegoers drifted into the showroom. Eve stood at the door, watching Sylvie weave through the throng

271

of people camped on the sidewalk in front of Elite. A pair of kids chased each other around a trash bin. Others flapped hand-held flags or ate popcorn from paper bags stained with butter. She went up to the loft when a brass band playing a jaunty ragtime tune made its way down Carolina Avenue.

Messy didn't adequately describe the workroom. It was a disaster. Bolts of lace and tulle were haphazardly stacked on the tables instead of stowed in the racks where they belonged, and there were piles of fabric scraps on every surface. Eve was on the floor on her hands and knees collecting spools of thread beneath the worktable when the front door chimed and a woman's greeting floated upstairs.

"I'll be right down," Eve called, scooting from underneath the table. Loose threads clung to her pleated skirt and frilly blouse. She picked at them, scrambling to her feet. Preoccupied with her task, Eve didn't see the woman coming upstairs until she stopped at the landing.

It was a virtually unrecognizable *Jillian Caldwell.*

Her clothes were rumpled, her steel-gray hair greasy, and her silvery eyes *wild.*

She was so out of place, Eve blinked, then squinted, expecting her to be a mirage. Martin's polished colleague from the lab had lost weight. The skin of her neck hung loose, giving her jowls. Without makeup, she looked haggard. Ugly. Gone was her usual smart pantsuit and heels, making her resemble a modern-day *Joan Crawford.* Her dark sweatshirt and baggy chinos desperately needed laundering.

This isn't right. Eve's instincts warned *run, run, run* but her feet were glued to the carpet.

Jillian trilled, "I'm a blast from the past, aren't I?"

The drumming of Eve's heart was an uncomfortable tattoo. "What are you doing in Old Hillbury?"

"Searching for *you.*"

"*For me?*" Eve shook her head, perplexed. *Something's very wrong here.* "Jillian . . . you look awful. Are you all right?"

"Now that I've got you, I'm fine." Jillian reached in the kangaroo pouch of her hoodie, brandishing a revolver. She twirled the firearm around her finger like a Wild West gunslinger.

Is this real? Eyes widening in astonishment, Eve held up her hands, backing away until she bumped into a wall. Voice quavering, she demanded, "What is going on?"

Jillian sneered, "Trust you to land on your feet like a cat with nine lives. Snagged yourself a billionaire, no less."

Eve summoned a pacifying tone. "Tell me what you want."

"The money, bitch. Martin procured over two million dollars."

"H-how do you know about that?"

Jillian ignored the question. "What did you do with it?"

"The police think the mugger who killed Martin took the money."

"Mugger? *Mugger?* There was no mugger." Jillian leveled the gun at Eve, and Eve yelped, dropping down and bringing her hands up to cover her head.

Time fluxed, became liquified. Eve's chest rose and fell in measured beats. With a spark of cognizance, the puzzle pieces clicked into place. Her arms fell to her side as she stood up. Eyes filling with tears, Eve whispered, "*You* killed Martin." She implored, "But, *why*, Jillian? I always thought you loved him."

"A mistake," Jillian agreed in a friendly way. "Martin was a two-timing sonofabitch."

"I-I don't understand."

"You never were swift. *I* was falsifying records at the lab. I have a gambling problem, sweet cheeks. I confessed my misdeeds to Martin when things got hot and asked him to leave the country with me. He drained accounts. Got loans. He said . . ." Jillian's voice cracked. "He said he loved me."

"It was *you* he was going to take to Cape Azul." Eve put her hand to her chest to subdue the anguish rising in her breast.

"Quit. *Quit it.*" Jillian waved the gun to punctuate her speech.

What if it fires accidentally?

"Bitch, you don't get it. He two-timed me."

She listened, slack-jawed, as Jillian disclosed, "When I confronted him at his car a few nights before we were supposed to leave, he admitted lying to me. He said I'd *destroyed his life.* He wasn't taking *me* to Cape Azul.

"He was wrong to fuck with me. My switchblade sure shut him up. I showed him." Jillian's lips twisted into a grin while her chest puffed with self-importance. "I'm smart. Meticulous. I cover my tracks. I'd destroyed camera footage countless times."

"*You* left the threatening note vowing to make me pay," Eve murmured with sudden clarity. "*You* broke into the house, looking for the money."

Jillian took a step closer. "I thank my lucky stars the day I came across you and your stud's wedding photo in a gossip magazine. I found you!"

"But I swear—I don't have the money." Eve tore her gaze away to hunt for an escape route. Jillian blocked the stairway. Maybe she could dart to the hallway and into the breakroom? It was the only option.

"Eyes here," Jillian ordered. "Carter's loaded. He'd better pay, or *you'll* be sorry."

Wake up. Press the button for help. The button on the charm. How had she forgotten? Eve found the charm, but her fingers trembled and she couldn't open the cover. To buy more time, she said, "He'll pay. How much money do you want?"

Jillian chortled. "Enough to make up for the trouble you caused my baby brother. He failed to catch you twice. *Twice.* But you won't get away this time, my pretty." Using a singsong voice, she swiveled her head slowly back and forth. *She's certifiable.*

The panel on the underside of the starfish gave way. With a surge of relief, Eve jabbed the panic button with a frantic finger.

"Vinnie? Come on up, little bro. It's time." Jillian gave Eve a smug look. "Don't count on the redhead in the alley. Vinnie's got my switchblade. He took care of her."

Eve felt like she'd been slugged in the gut. She slumped against the wall. "No."

Jillian smiled.

Monty had glowed when she told Eve about her date with Lex. White-hot guilt coursed through her. *If Monty's dead, it's my fault. Please, God, let Sara Montague be alive.*

A massive, sweaty man with a cherubic face climbed the stairs with lumbering movements. He licked his lips and giggled when he saw Eve. Vinnie said in a high-pitched childlike voice, "You said I could play with her soon as we're back, Jilly. You pinky-swore. Remember, Jilly?"

This cannot be happening.

In a matter of seconds, there were two quick, loud reports as gunshots rang out. Reflexively, Eve ducked.

A crimson stain spread across Vinnie's filthy shirt. His body crumbled, collapsing to the floor in slow motion. His expression was dumbfounded.

He stared, his mouth slack. He twitched and then stilled.

Bright blood spread on the carpet under Vinnie in an ever-widening circle. Its heavy metallic tang perfumed the air.

"Vinnie, no!" Jillian shrieked, bending to him, and Eve seized the opportunity. She made for the hall, gagging at the pungent odor of spilled blood. Conscious of Jillian's lusty roar, she stumbled into a run.

Chunks of plaster from the wall by Eve's head exploded as Jillian fired in her direction.

Slamming the breakroom door shut, she pushed the lock in

the center of the knob with her palm. Thrusting an urgent hand into her skirt pocket, she rummaged for her phone. It wasn't there. With a gush of despair, Eve remembered she'd left it downstairs by the cash register.

Jillian pounded on the breakroom door, screeching like a banshee. Shrinking into the corner of the room, Eve stared at the door banging against the jamb, hypnotized.

She was trapped. She needed a weapon.

Her gaze juddered to rest on the heavy lunch table. She thought fast. Adrenaline providing superhuman strength, she lifted the table so the top was pressed against the door.

It would merely slow Jillian.

I'm already dead.

Where can Jed be?

CHAPTER SIXTY-TWO

From beyond the breakroom, there was the muffled sound of a man commanding, "Lower your weapon. Now!"

Jed?

Multiple gunshots reverberated. Eve dove down, praying as she'd never prayed before.

At last it was quiet. Through the ringing in her ears, Eve heard Jed's voice. "It's over. The five-o's on the way. Open the door."

The dregs of adrenaline allowed her to wrench away the table and open the battered door. Jillian's prone figure lay at the threshold. Eve cowered, but Jed was there to cajole her out, his arm outstretched, his gun holstered, and his composure unruffled.

His eyes widened when his gaze skittered over Eve's face. Dazed, she looked down. Her shirt was stained with blood. Lifting a tentative hand to her ear, she unnecessarily said, "I'm bleeding."

Jed pulled her to the loft, where Vinnie's body was in a heap at the landing of the stairs. The blood soaking the carpet was a livid crimson. The air was thick with the grisly smell of death and vibrated with energy. Eve recoiled with a whimper of revulsion, hysterics threatening to devour her.

Hoisting her over his shoulder, Jed carried her downstairs, depositing her on the settee by the dressing rooms. With rapt absorption, he examined her for injuries. "A few inches over and your jugular would've been hit. Holy hell, you're one lucky gal to come away with a grazed ear."

"I am?"

"Yes, ma'am." Jed found a box of tissues on Addy's desk and pulled out a fistful, placing the wad in her palm. "Use this to stanch the wound."

"Can you call Jake?" Eve asked, teeth chattering. "I need him."

"He would've been alerted when you pressed the panic button. Since Consolidated's four blocks away, I reckon he'll be here lickety-split."

Monty. The pulse hammering in her temple made her light-headed, but she clutched Jed's arm, "Vinnie stabbed Monty. Go to her."

Yanking a curtain from a dressing room cubicle, he wrapped it around Eve's shoulders. "Keep warm. You're going into shock. You'll be okay on your own?"

"Go!" Once alone, her body bore the aftermath of trauma. She disconnected, becoming heavy-lidded with exhaustion. Her stinging ear unnoticed, Eve curled into a fetal position.

"Angie." Jake was beside her what seemed moments later. She heard the approaching whine of sirens as he folded her in his arms and cradled her against his solid chest.

"Monty?"

His lips were on her forehead and she felt the steady, reassuring beat of his heart through his shirt. "She's alive."

Eve whimpered with relief.

"Let me see your ear." Jake's expression was tender. "I was so scared. I jogged all the way."

Eve babbled, "They're upstairs. Dead."

"Shh, Angie. Just rest."

"You don't understand —"

Uniformed police officers entered the shop from the alley door, escorted by Jed. Their faces were grim.

It was a quiet night in the ER. After a short wait, Jake

maneuvered Eve's wheelchair into an exam room, where her vitals were taken. He was clearly alarmed by the elevated reading of her blood pressure, but the nurse said, "It's not unusual for a patient's BP to have a trauma response. We'll monitor it. When was your last period, Eve?"

Fuzzy-headed, she looked at the slight woman in bewilderment. Her thoughts were fixated on Monty, who was in surgery, and Jed, who waited outside the operating theater. Monty had lost her spleen, would she lose her life, too? *Has somebody let Lex know?*

"Eve? When was your last period?"

She murmured helplessly, "Maybe before Christmas?"

"Is there a chance you're pregnant?"

Eve's focus sharpened. She looked at Jake, finding his face an inscrutable mask. She shook her head. "My cycle's irregular."

The nurse said, "Conception tends to be rather slim with your medical issues, but it *can* happen."

"I'd like a test administered," Jake said evenly.

The nurse nodded. Leaving the room, she assured them, "The doctor will be in shortly."

"You're fortunate," the doctor said, stitching Eve's ear. "This could've been much worse. We'll give you a script for antibiotics, but keep the wound clean and you shouldn't have further concerns."

After supplying a urine specimen at the lab, Eve waited with Jake for the results. With her tongue cemented to the roof of her mouth, she was jolted by the notion of unintended pregnancy after years of infertility. Incapable of asking Jake for his thoughts, she wondered what his response would be when the test came back negative. Relief?

Eve looked up to find him observing her. She fiddled with the pleats of her skirt, face heating. "Why don't you go see how Monty's surgery's going?"

The air was charged with something undefinable. "I think

I'll stay."

Resting her head against the wall, Eve identified it. It was a vague flicker, but it was there, a glimmering sliver. Hope. She snuffed it out. *You know what the chances are.* Her eyelids drooped, her body demanding slumber. The room was warm. She fought to stay alert.

The doctor knocked on the door and Eve's lethargy vaporized.

"Congratulations, parents-to-be."

CHAPTER SIXTY-THREE

Eve engaged the alarm out of habit. The house seemed too quiet, with the security team conspicuously absent. Biological demands propelling her, she moved as if in a trance, opening the fridge for a bottle of water. She gulped it down. Her body required food, too. With unsteady hands, she grabbed soda crackers from the cabinet and shoved one in her mouth. Chewing, she noticed Jake at the kitchen table, his brow knit and hands clasped.

A zap of unease reengaged her with reality. Eve sagged into a chair, asking, "You okay?"

He brought a thumb to his mouth, rubbing his lip. "I should be asking you that. It's been a day."

"Tell me about it." She crossed her arms over her chest. Though lucidity seeped slowly back, she remained detached. She'd have to sort out what happened later when she could reflect. Eve's voice was small when she said, "I'll probably miscarry, Jake."

"You heard the doctor. Once past the first trimester, viability reaches ninety percent," he reminded her. "You've not gotten this far before, have you?"

She shook her head.

Jake viewed her with clever eyes. "That wasn't the stomach flu on your birthday. You likely conceived in Fiji and are safely in your second trimester."

Eve couldn't latch onto a logical train of thought. She'd dismissed bouts of illness and fatigue. There was the sporadic nausea. The heightened aversion to liquor and strong smells.

The few pounds she'd lamented gaining. She muttered, "I guess with the goings-on, I overlooked the signs."

"Guess so," Jake said, and she frowned, not understanding his tone.

"Are you *upset* I'm pregnant?"

He lifted a hand to work at the back of his neck. "I'm not sure how I feel."

"Wait—*you're* the one who broached the subject of kids at Christmastime. You were willing to pacify me with a baby then. What's changed?"

Appearing unmoved by Eve's riled tone, he said, "That was a concept. This is reality."

"You think?"

"Angie." His look was pointed. "I'll provide the best medical care money can buy, and you'll have my full support, but I'll never be the kind of father Jim is. I'm not capable of it."

"I wouldn't—all I'd want—" She swallowed, trying to shake her exasperation. "All I'd ask is for you to try. Can't you pledge that—to *try*?"

"Let me show you something." Jake bent to remove his shoe and sock. He brought his foot to the table. Stretching forward, he spread the digits one by one so she could see the angry scars on the tender flesh between each toe.

Eve looked at him, puzzled. "I never saw that before. What happened?"

"My old man liked to put his smokes out there."

"Jesus." She intended to rise, but Jake put up a hand.

"I don't want pity. I'm telling you the type of father I had. I want you to understand my . . . limits."

She shook her head, throat clogging. "It's not *pity*. It's empathy."

"I don't want it." Jake was unyielding. "You've been through a lot today. We should save this discussion for when you're calm."

"Don't patronize me. Talking's what we need. I want to *know you*. The good, bad, and ugly."

"Enough."

She retorted, "Don't talk to me that way. I'm not some lackey at Consolidated who'll scurry away at your command."

"Then stop pushing."

Eve's anxiety escalated, but she didn't care. "Am I to be satisfied with the crumbs you toss my way? Grateful, even?" She stopped and took a breath, reining herself in. "My heart aches for the abused child you were and the damaged man you are, but we must consider the needs of *this* child now." She put a protective hand on her stomach.

"Did I suggest otherwise?" He scowled, his mouth tight. "I told you—you'll have anything you require. The best money can buy."

There's no reasoning with this man. Resentment reared its head. "I wish you'd give a fraction of the nurturing you give Consolidated to *our* relationship."

"You know how important this takeover is to me."

"And in a few months, there'll be another important takeover. Then another. There'll *always* be another."

The set of Jake's face became mulish. "You knew the score when you married me."

"Change the record. We're *way* past that now." Eve was severe when she added, "You told me you'd find a therapist. Have you?"

"I've been occupied with more pressing matters."

"Our marriage should be priority one—as should this baby—it's a goddamn miracle!"

She smacked her palm hard against the table, startling herself as much as him. She didn't bother hiding her discontent. "Look here, Jake. It's time for some plain-speaking. You better get with the program, pal, or you'll lose us both."

"Whoa." Dr. Ryan shook her head.

"Yep," she agreed. "Crazy, right?"

"Have you processed it?"

Eve looked exhausted. She had seen the dark circles under her eyes in the mirror that morning. "Not really. Not yet. With Martin's death, I learned how to put my problems in a metaphorical box so I could deal with the here and now. Using those coping skills is how I'm getting by without ending up in a straitjacket."

"Are you and Jake pulling together, or pushing apart?"

Eve shifted in her seat. "In romance novels, what happened at Elite would be the climax the main characters needed to realize they belong together. They'd ride off into the sunset, happily-ever-after."

"Not like real life?"

"Not that I've ever noticed," she said, becoming pensive. "I've been experiencing a concerning emotion, one that's unusual for me — apathy."

"Elaborate."

"I have tunnel vision. All I want is a healthy baby. I'll sacrifice *anything* for that."

"Even your marriage?"

Eve frowned. "Are you asking if I love my baby more than Jake?"

"We'll explore that further later." Dr. Ryan paused. "Right now, let's talk about your pregnancy. Are you high risk?"

"No. I've had tests and sonograms and ultrasounds showing the baby's fine. It helps I've got more than a full trimester behind me — but anything can happen."

"What's the problem with Jake? Doesn't he want children?"

"Good question. I can't get him to talk. I push, he retreats. He's surly with feelings he obviously can't articulate. I see traces of fear, insecurity, annoyance." Eve was clear-eyed. Resolute. "But I can't bother with him anymore. As I said, my focus has shifted."

"Do you think you two can find your way?"

"All I know is I can't reach him right now. It makes me feel—look, I've cried more the last couple of days than I *ever* have." She rubbed her temple. "I'm so tired. I think I need a break from everything. Be alone to think. Get perspective."

"Would Jake want that?"

"I'll suggest it. Soon." She lifted a shoulder, trying for detachment, though her mouth trembled. "Maybe we need to see once and for all if absence does indeed make the heart grow fonder."

"Regardless, I urge you to continue your counseling sessions. The fallout of Martin's murder left you with mild PTSD. You were making strides until Jillian's appearance. Remember, I'm available for emergency sessions. We can do it by video like we did before. I'm here for you."

Eve's lips curved, some of her usual humor surfacing. "That's the most I've heard you say at once, Doc. Don't worry. I won't stop therapy. It keeps me sane. There was a time when I couldn't say *murder* without flinching. Now I understand it was a trigger for me. I'll need you while I work through everything." She hesitated. "Do you think a sabbatical's unwise?"

"If you truly think it'll help, then go for it. You're capable of deciding."

"Well, I try to respect my gut but I don't know if I can trust it anymore—I'm floundering."

"What's happened with the fraud investigation?"

Eve picked at her nail. "I had a visit yesterday from an investigator. Apparently, the Feds were onto Jillian but lacked solid evidence. I suppose she was desperate for money and wanted to disappear before something concrete was uncovered. Anyway, the case died with her."

"And Martin's lab?"

"The building he was once proud of sits abandoned." Eve threw her therapist a matter-of-fact look. "You know, his aunt did say she thought the person who committed the fraud was the one who killed him."

"Have you contacted his family?"

"No. I sent them a Christmas card, but we weren't close. Martin was our link. California's another life, a million years ago. Now, I feel conflicted. *Raw.* I have questions. What if Martin wasn't cheating? What if he always did intend to take *me* away? Maybe he was protecting me by keeping me in the dark 'til the last second. Was I wrong to feel so much *rage*?"

"You managed the best you could with the information you had at the time," Dr. Ryan pointed out.

"I suppose, but I believed the worst of him, easily. I spent months thinking he was a lying, cheating fraud. And maybe he was. He'd definitely changed the last years of our marriage. When he told me out of the blue he'd decided he didn't want kids—that felt like betrayal in itself. Shit, there could've been a *third* woman we don't know about. He could've been double-crossing both Jillian and me. I'll probably never know the whole story."

Doc smiled. "Right. That old adage of hindsight being twenty-twenty doesn't apply."

"Indulge me. Let me play devil's advocate," Eve proposed. "Let's say Martin was completely innocent of wrongdoing—that Jillian asked him to run away with her, but he never planned to. That he was always gonna take me. That he wanted to avoid the fallout of *her* misdeeds . . ."

"Go on."

"Look, even if Martin was *completely innocent,* he should've gone to the police when he learned about Jillian committing fraud. He didn't, so that taints his actions. But I can't help wondering—if he'd come to me," Eve said slowly, swallowing with difficulty. "And put his cards on the table . . ."

"You'd have gone to Cape Azul?"

"Looking back, I can't see our marriage surviving much longer, but . . . maybe I would've gone? I certainly would've *thought* about going."

"That means you wouldn't ever cross paths with Jake again, right?"

Eve's expression was pained. "I'm . . . confused. I don't know up from down anymore."

"Some clarity will come, with time."

"Jake asked the same thing—would I have gone to Cape Azul if given the chance? I didn't know how to answer him, either. He told me he wouldn't try to compete with a dead man. And we've barely spoken since."

CHAPTER SIXTY-FOUR

Eve woke late the next morning. Disquiet took hold as she remembered her plans to discuss a separation with Jake at dinner. Contemplative, she lounged in bed, palm at her stomach. Though she'd slept ten hours, Eve remained drowsy. She considered sleeping for another hour. Her phone trilled from the bedside table and she answered, resigned. No putting off life any further.

"You sound sleepy."

"I just woke up," Eve admitted, a trifle embarrassed.

Addy said, "Kip all you can. You've been through a lot. And after the little one comes, you won't have the luxury."

"Agreed."

"I bought some thingummies for the layette."

"More?" Eve teased. Addy took her role of expectant grandmother seriously, lavishing her with both store-bought and hand-knit baby clothes.

"Sylvie's friend sews cloth nappies . . . Oh, bugger. A customer. I'll ring you back, luv."

Eve yawned and stretched, deciding to shower. When the phone rang again a minute later, she answered right away. "That was quick."

"Huh?"

Frowning at the screen, she couldn't place the number with the five-one-six area code. "Sorry. I expected somebody else. Who's this?"

"It's Siobhan, sweetie."

Eve stiffened. She was *not* in the mood. She didn't keep her disdain from her voice. "What do you want?"

"I've been out of town. Imagine my shock when I got back yesterday and heard about the skirmish at Elite."

I'll bet. "Thanks for the call, but I need to go."

"Wait. There's a secret I've been pondering sharing."

Eve didn't like Siobhan's sly tone, but her curiosity was piqued. "A secret?"

"Far be it from me to cause upset between you and Jakey — "

Eve shook her head, biting back a laugh. "Oh, absolutely."

Her sarcasm seemed lost on Siobhan, who continued, "You see, one woman to another, I thought you should know. I've deliberated about it. It wasn't an easy choice."

Eve frowned. "Have you been drinking?"

"Maybe." She giggled.

"At ten in the morning? Whatever — it doesn't matter — get to the point."

Siobhan let silence drag for several seconds, probably trying to ramp up the drama. "You probably aren't aware of Jake's scheme."

"*What?*" There it was — a prickle of forewarning. Eve heeded it and sat up against the headboard. "Stop talking in riddles or I'll hang up."

"He told me years ago. He was gonna make you regret tossing him aside. Jake's ego doesn't take kindly to such treatment, you know."

Engulfed by quicksand, Eve didn't speak. Siobhan continued, "There was talk of framing your father for embezzlement at Consolidated. Another possibility was good 'ol revenge porn. Posting lewd videos of you online. *Nobody* fucks with Jake Carter."

Eve's teeth set at Siobhan's ugly laugh. Aware only of her breathing, all else diminished. Was Siobhan honest? Could Jake really be that diabolical? That vindictive? Eve remembered well her reservations concerning Jake's proposal. Her intuition cautioned her, but she'd flouted it.

Siobhan's voice was spiked with mock concern when she asked, "Are you there, sweetie?"

Not allowing Siobhan the satisfaction of thinking she'd gotten to her, Eve collected herself and unearthed a carefree tone. "Oh, that? Jake told me. We laughed about it."

Silence. "I don't believe you." Siobhan's voice was practically unintelligible.

"I don't care what you believe."

Flinging her phone to the nightstand, Eve put her head in her hands. *My Lord.* Siobhan might be a drunk, but she was no liar. Eve wagered her father's employment at Consolidated had been manipulated by Jake years earlier. Her job at the daycare certainly was a setup. Was Jake some sort of Machiavellian mastermind? If she hadn't come back to Old Hillbury, would he have gone ahead with her dad's frame-up? *But I did come back.* Was revenge porn something he still intended? Was there a camera concealed in their bedroom? Eve felt sick—mortified.

She evaluated whether Siobhan's claims were plausible, recalling Jake's behavior at their first meetings—his simmering resentment, calculated barbs, and casual contempt. But he wasn't the same man he'd been when they were first reunited. Eve knew him now, didn't she? She'd seen him happy, sad, vulnerable. Though broken from his abusive childhood, Jake was a good man. How many times had he demonstrated his benevolence? Too many to count. From his gift of the locket at Christmas to spearheading Fostering with Support to helping Sylvie with her business plan and investing in Elite, he must be some actor.

How could Eve reconcile the Jake she knew with Siobhan's description of a spiteful man seeking vengeance? God help him if she found there was substance to Siobhan's claims.

There was only one thing to be done.

She would go to Consolidated and demand answers.

Dressing carefully, Eve selected an ivory dress. The signature band of navy and red accentuated her still-slender waist, and the golden buttons glinted at her elbows. She saw she was pale and pinched when she put on her makeup. When she bumped her injured ear with her hairbrush, it stung, reminding Eve she was alive. Slipping on matching heels, she grabbed a navy handbag and made her way to her SUV, which was parked in the furthest stall of the garage, near the vehicle Jake had bought her.

Single-minded while driving, Eve summoned her compartmentalization skills. Concentrating solely on arriving safely at Consolidated, she wouldn't, *couldn't*, allow any other thoughts. Her control dangled by a frayed thread.

Jake's car was in its designated spot in the parking ramp, evidence he was there. It was early afternoon, a time he usually did paperwork in his office. Eve left her SUV in the reserved VIP parking. Her heels clicked as she stepped into Consolidated's lobby. Managing a cheerful greeting to the receptionist, she strode to the employee elevator, her manner no-nonsense.

Swiping her employee badge, Eve noted her fingers were sweating. She pretended she was fearless and marched into the elevator, wiping her hands on the skirt of her dress.

Please, please, please . . . let Siobhan be lying.

Jake's perfectly coiffured assistant, Martha, was at her desk. "Hi, Eve. How are you?"

Please, let Siobhan be wrong. Eve's lips twisted into a smile. "I'm swell. Jake in?"

"Yes, let me buzz and let him know you're—"

"Not necessary," she insisted breezily, hurrying past Martha to Jake's inner sanctum. He looked up when she closed the door. She made her expression impassive, straightening her spine for combat. Jacket draped on his chair, his shirt-sleeves were rolled up to reveal tanned forearms. Jake was gorgeous. Even in her misery, she found him appealing. Scanning his face, Eve searched for a sign. *Who is this man?*

"Unlike you to stop by, Angie," Jake commented, shutting his laptop.

Approaching his desk, Eve noted his strong hands, his fingers tapered and capable, his wedding band catching the light. Those hands had brought her to the heights of ecstasy many times, so effortlessly. Her gaze traveled back up to his face to rest on his sensual mouth. She knew how those full lips felt on her skin. Worshipful. Eve tamped down her body's traitorous response. "I had a phone call from an obviously intoxicated Siobhan this morning."

Jake's brow furrowed as if he distinguished the tension emanating from her. When he began to speak, she held up a finger. "Answer this — did you tell her you intended to marry me as part of an elaborate conspiracy to . . . destroy me?"

Jake didn't respond. He didn't need to. Eve drank in his posture shifting, his shoulders drooping. Eyelids lowering, he shook his head. Lifting a hand to his chin, he rubbing roughly. He looked *trapped.* "Fuck."

"That's what I suspected," Eve whispered, his treachery cutting her like a dagger, the blade sharp, deadly. Her chest rapidly expanded and contracted as she fought for air. The aura was there, the smothering sensation alerting her to a looming panic attack. She curled her fists, her fingernails digging in her palms.

Jake's skin blanched white. "I *can* explain."

"Shut up." She brought a hand to where her pulse hopped at the base of her throat. *Calm down . . . the baby.* Her tone surprised her. Though agonized, she sounded emotionless when she said, "Our marriage is built on a lie. It's sown on the seeds of animosity and reprisal. I trusted you. I loved you." She swallowed the ache in her throat and bit her cheek until she tasted blood. She refused to look at him. "I'm a chump."

"Angie," Jake coaxed. "I—"

Eve snarled, "Shut up."

As she turned to leave, she heard the squeak of Jake's chair when he stood. Eve whipped around and met his eyes.

He didn't follow.

CHAPTER SIXTY-FIVE

The weathered wood-shingled house was sprawling by Cape Cod standards. Feeling empty, Eve exited the taxi. She was vaguely aware of the crashing of waves, and the briny scent of the sea.

"Nobody will trouble you here." Hitch turned on lamps and adjusted the thermostat. The house smelled of lemon wax and clean linen. "Maybe you should've packed a bag. I'm not sure you'll find any clothes in the closets, although you're welcome to use what's there."

"Nothing—not a single object—belongs to me at Jake's." Eve dully surveyed the comfortably worn furniture and built-in shelving filled with books and model ships. Normally, she'd find the enormous oak-beamed kitchen with its hanging pot rack over the cast iron *AGA* range charming. An over-stuffed blue and white plaid couch was positioned on a braided rug in front of a stone fireplace. Windows overlooked the lawn and the darkened beach beyond.

"You've been essentially catatonic," Hitch grumbled. "Tell me what's going on."

Sinking onto a stool, Eve could hear how reedy her voice was when she spoke about Siobhan's call that morning and her exchange with Jake at Consolidated. Hitch first looked bewildered, then his face blackened with anger. When she trailed off, eyes vacant, he captured her in a bear hug. It wasn't long until the dam broke and she wept.

Hitch shook his head. "What was he thinking?"

"I don't know. I don't know who he is."

"He's a fuckin' monster."

She slumped against the breakfast bar. "He needs help."

"I'll say."

Swallowing, Eve murmured, "I-I don't want to discuss Jake anymore."

"Okay, doll." Hitch's voice was sympathetic.

Sniffling, she gave him a wan smile. "Thank you."

"You know I owe you my life." He laced his fingers with hers.

It was something they didn't discuss. Five years earlier, after a fling ended badly, Hitch called Eve in the dead of night, disoriented and weeping. He'd washed down tranquilizers with a vodka tonic. She dashed over in her pajamas and let herself into his condo with the spare key he'd given her.

He'd passed out in the kitchen, but he was breathing. Half-carrying and half-dragging him, Eve put Hitch in the shower and doused him with icy water. When he came to, he'd refused to go to the ER and have his stomach pumped, fearing his family would learn about his attempted suicide. She made him put his fingers down his throat, then tucked him into bed.

Setting up camp alongside the bed with phone in hand in case she needed to call paramedics, Eve had monitored Hitch through the night, waking him at intervals and forcing him to drink water to flush his system. She'd been fraught with worry, but he'd survived the night. When dawn broke, they held each other and wept with relief, the experience frightening them both.

"Peaceful, isn't it? You can use the car in the garage to get around. There's a fleet card in the glove box for fuel and for the ferry."

"I can pay for my own gas. It's the least I can do."

"It's no big deal. And stay as long as you want." He looked through cabinets and the freezer, taking stock. "There's no fresh food, I'm afraid, since I didn't call ahead to the caretaker."

Opening one of the doors on the front of the cooker, Hitch used the touchscreen to preheat the baking oven and one of the hotplates. He sat a hunk of aged cheddar by the stove to defrost.

"I haven't eaten. No wonder I feel wretched."

"It's seven." Hitch scolded when he put a frozen loaf of French bread in the oven, "You need to take better care of yourself, Momma."

"I will. I'll use my time here to get my head on straight."

Pouring canned soup in a saucepan, Hitch pulled up the insulated cover to set the pan on the hotplate. "I think I'd better stay the night."

"Isn't Julian waiting for you in the city?"

"Yes, but you need me."

Eve said firmly, "I'll be fine. Once you leave, I'm off to bed."

"Here, come stir the soup."

Hitch went out the kitchen door to gather split firewood from the stack against the house. He kindled a fire that warmed the room. He then set out napkins and Eve ladled hot soup in crocks. During the meal, the only sound was the crackle of the fire and their spoons against the earthenware dishes.

"Before I arrange a taxi — you're *positive* you don't need me?"

Eve yawned. "Yep."

"You make sure you call your therapist tomorrow."

"I will."

"Let me know if you need anything."

After he left, Eve found a first edition *Agatha Christie* on the bookshelf in the living room. Three pages into chapter one of *At Bertram's Hotel*, her eyelids grew heavy. She pulled the afghan from the arm of the kitchen sofa up to her chin, slipping into slumber, and dreaming of a little girl with black hair and green eyes.

The fire had burned out and watery morning sunlight streamed in the kitchen windows when the ringing of Eve's phone woke her.

"You didn't come home last night." Jake was accusatory.

Her throat was parched and her ear stung from being slept on. She probed her earlobe with a careful finger. "After learning what you plotted, I may not be back."

"Where the fuck are you, Evangeline?"

"If you keep yelling, I'll hang up and *never* accept your call again." The silence on the other end was palpable.

"I'm coming for you right now. Where are you?" Jake bit out in measured tones.

"I need to be alone. I have a child to think of now. I will not lose my baby, Jake."

"*Our* baby. Goddammit, I have rights."

"That's a first. What about yesterday . . . what about Siobhan's call?" Eve heard him exhale a frustrated breath.

"Christ, when I said that shit to Siobhan, I was drunk and high, and you'd married Pierce. I was a fuckin' mess. If you would've listened, I would've told you that yesterday."

She wanted to believe him. "Vengeance never crossed your mind once I returned to Old Hillbury?"

There was a beat of silence. "Not after I got to know you."

"Took some time, did it?" Eve snorted. "Whatever . . . I've had enough. *I'm done.*"

"What in the actual fuck are you saying?" His tone was deadly calm.

Eve reminded herself to keep to the matter at hand. "I'm saying what matters to me is the health of my baby. Leave me alone. Give me space. Don't try to find me. Do you understand? Leave. Me. Alone."

"You're my fuckin' wife."

"Yes, I am. But you've made a fool of me. You've hurt me. I need to go now."

"Don't you dare hang up on—"

"Goodbye, Jake." Before she changed her mind, she blocked his number and shut down her phone.

Eve stared at the ashes in the hearth, which were as cold and dead as she felt.

CHAPTER SIXTY-SIX

"I don't even know him, Dr. R." Eve chewed her fingernail. "And I'm *pissed*."

"Understandable."

"He said once he got to know me, he reconsidered, but what type of person schemes like that? Because I *dared* to end our relationship? I mean — *what the fuck*."

"When did Jake reconsider? Recently?"

"Does *when* matter?"

"Shouldn't you give him the opportunity to explain?"

Provoked to close the cover of her tablet and end her session, Eve demanded, "Shouldn't you be on *my* side?"

"I am," Dr. Ryan reassured her. "But Jake said that to Siobhan years ago when he was intoxicated. People often say things when inebriated they later regret."

Eve mewed in frustration. "I'm not overreacting. Do you want me to be a doormat?"

"It's my job to help you gain perspective."

"Hmm."

"I can see you're hurting," Dr. Ryan said softly. "I want you to know your feelings *are* valid."

"Part of my anger is because I'm pissed at myself. My gut warned me when he proposed — I should've listened to it. I know it's small of me," she admitted. "But I want Jake to feel as bad as I do — I want him to *suffer*."

"An eye for an eye?"

"I'm not proud of it."

"You'd get self-satisfaction from making Jake suffer, but

how's it helpful in the long term?"

"*It's not.* Don't you think I know that?"

"At some juncture, you need to open the lines of communication," Dr. Ryan said. "Effective communication's paramount. Either you forge ahead *together*, or it's already over."

"But that's the problem. He'd wheedle my location from me. If Jake materialized, I'd crumble. I'm defenseless when it comes to him. He can play me like a violin. We'd end up in bed. And the problems, the disagreements, the dysfunctions . . . would never be resolved."

"Understand that by continuing to refuse his calls, you *are* making a decision."

"I'm teaching him he can't treat me shitty. You tell me, is it unreasonable to ask him to undergo counseling?"

Dr. Ryan shook her head. "It's not unreasonable. He knows your expectations?"

"Yes."

"So, the ball's in his court."

Eve took a breath. "Look, I'll open those lines of communication, like you suggest, but with caution. When it feels right."

"What's your plan?"

"To take care of myself. Be at peace. Thrive. Since Martin's death, my life's been off the rails."

"How long will you stay at your friend's house?"

"I'm in no hurry." Eve lifted a shoulder, unconcerned. "I don't want to see Jake."

"Not easy facing someone who's wronged you."

She sought the right words. "Given the option of fight or flight after our confrontation, I chose flight. Was that spineless?"

"Aren't both options about survival?"

Eve nodded thoughtfully as the doctor said, "Between now and your next appointment, I want you to weigh up whether you truly *want* your marriage to survive. Is it worth fighting for?"

Once the video call disconnected, Eve allowed herself a moment to think of Jake during happier times. The sound of his laugh, the sun as it glinted against his jet-black hair in Fiji, his whispers of desire, the feel of his hands reverently running over her flesh, worshipping her. *Okay, enough. Stop.*

Eve forced herself back to reality. She needed to find an obstetrician, buy clothes, toiletries, and groceries. She'd have to call Addy, too, and explain why she'd left town. Cleaning up the best she could without a comb or toothbrush, she went to the garage. There was a silver station wagon with the key fob on the dashboard. The GPS navigation was a lifesaver in the unfamiliar surroundings.

Using the debit card from her personal bank account, Eve bought what she needed. At the market she loaded a cart with fruits, vegetables, and meat. Her purchases in the hatchback, she returned to the house.

She changed into a sweater and maternity jeans from the shop in Chilmark. After brushing her teeth with her new toothbrush, Eve watched an online instructional video to help her prepare lunch. She slipped off her sandals and put her feet on the sun-warmed stones of the patio while she ate. There was a slight breeze and the day was bright. After lunch, she stretched out on an upholstered lounger, spreading the afghan she used the night before over her knees. Reading until she felt sleepy, Eve indulged in a nap.

Later, she walked across the lawn and down to the private beach, barefoot with pant hems rolled up, the afghan a shawl. Mindful of sharp rocks, she picked her way to the shore. The water was frigid, but she didn't care.

That night, she spoke to Addy, which was an ordeal. She hated rehashing Siobhan's phone call. Addy urged her to come home, and Eve became defensive. Afterward, trying to shake off her disturbing mood, she carried her shopping bags upstairs and chose a bedroom. The spacious room had indigo blue walls and an ocean view. A four-poster bed was piled with needlepoint throw pillows. French doors led to a balcony, a wicker chair with a table situated in the corner. She sat there and breathed in the brackish stink coming off the water. Mists of thick, rolling fog suspended in the air, leaving her hair and skin and tinged with salt. Her outfit became damp from the humidity, but she stayed a long time.

Later, Eve hung her clothes in the closet, stowing underwear and bras in the antique dresser across from the bed. After a leisurely shower, she lay on the bed, mindful of her ear, inhaling the scent of lemon furniture wax and the sea.

Her hand curled over her abdomen. In spite of everything, the pregnancy survived. Clearly, the baby was a fighter. She willed her child to be born full-term, strong and healthy.

Eve was out for a walk, casually looking for seashells and driftwood along the long expanse of sandy shore behind the house, when her phone trilled from the pocket of her jeans.

"Your Neanderthal husband's here. He's threatening me with bodily harm if I don't tell him where you are. He's drunk as a damn skunk!" Eve heard a scuffle on the other end, as Hitch and Jake argued. Then the phone fell, disconnecting the call. *Oh my God.*

Hands shaking, she dialed back.

"That troglodyte punched me," Hitch whined. "He about broke my jaw. What a barbarian."

"I'm sorry! Give him the phone, Hitch. Let me talk to him."

There was more racket before Jake's voice came on the line, his breathing uneven.

"Where are you?"

"*What the fuck,* Jake? Jesus. Leave Hitch alone and I'll call you in a few minutes on your cell."

Eve disconnected, sinking to the sand. Her jeans soaked up

icy seawater like a sponge but she didn't notice. She brought her knees to her chest, horrified Hitch had been dragged further into their drama. Steeling herself, she reluctantly rang Jake back.

"You're tearing me apart, Angie." His voice was almost incoherent. Hitch was right. He *was* drunk.

"You shouldn't have confronted Hitch, and you shouldn't have punched him. I asked him not to disclose where I was. He was honoring my wishes." She imagined him running his hands through his hair, his eyes bloodshot, and her heart squeezed.

"What else was I supposed to do?" Jake asked harshly. "You won't take my calls. Even Addy and Jim don't know where you are. I knew *he would*, that fucker."

She sighed. "How many times must I tell you Hitch is *not* your rival?"

"Yet you ran to him. Open your eyes, Angie, no man wants friendship with a woman beautiful as you."

"No, you need to open *your* eyes. Hitch. Is. Gay."

There was silence on the other end of the line.

"I tried to tell you before, but you didn't want to know."

"Oh, Christ. I've gotta see you. I need you so bad it hurts." He indeed sounded as if he was in pain.

Eve felt her resolve flag and toughened her stance. She whispered, "Not yet."

"Then, when? When can I see you?"

"If you want us to ever have a chance in the future, you *must* see a therapist."

Jake's speech was garbled when he insisted, "I need you. You're all I ever needed."

"After you've had a couple of sessions . . . we'll talk, okay?" Tears coursed down Eve's cheeks, unchecked.

"You know you're everything to me, Angie. I'll get counseling. Come home."

She wiped her nose on her sleeve and cleared her throat. "I'm sorry, but I don't trust you to not put off therapy again. I don't want to fall into the same dysfunctional cycle as before."

"I need you home. We belong together."

"I can hardly understand you. Lay off the booze, Jake. And arrange for a car. You can't drive in your condition."

Eve sat for a long time, staring out at the choppy surf. The wind was formidable, causing the sea oats by the shore to whip to and fro. Her hair was a messy tangle. Before the call, she'd found tranquility, and now she felt incredibly worn. Fathoming it was her typical biological response to stress, Eve trudged up to the lawn and went into the house through the kitchen door. The stairs to her bedroom seemed insurmountable, but she winched herself up by using the banister as a tow line.

Wrapping in the quilt, Eve collapsed onto the mattress, not bothering to strip off her wet, sandy jeans and not waking until morning.

CHAPTER SIXTY-SEVEN

Eve functioned as an automaton. Hollow, she robotically went through the necessary motions to satisfy her biological requirements. Sleeping, waking, and forcing down nutritious meals at the appropriate intervals marked the time. She continued therapy. Getting plenty of sun, she went on strolls for exercise. Her ear no longer pained her. By degrees, Eve appreciated the sea air again, the warmth of the sun, and the taste of food she ate. Life's simple pleasures again became pleasurable.

Enrolling in courses in Chilmark, Eve learned the basics of cookery and advanced watercolor techniques. She visited the library and checked out classics she hadn't time to read before. Settling into a routine, she cleaned, did laundry, and prepared meals in the mornings while listening to music or streaming *The Office*. She spent her afternoons reading, drawing, or attending classes. She talked to Hitch, her dad and Addy, and Sylvie on the phone. Once in a while, Lex texted to keep Eve up to date on Monty's recovery. Days meandered to weeks, and soon more than a month elapsed.

Thoughts turning inward, she looked in the full-length mirror in the bathroom and noted the transformation of her physique. She now sported a recognizable *baby bump*, hips broadening, her breasts fuller. Eve's obstetrician praised her for taking her health seriously and encouraged her to continue, reassuring her she'd made the right choice leaving Old Hillbury.

After her latest checkup, Eve dialed Addy's number using

the buttons on the dash of the station wagon while she drove, and Addy answered with an affectionate greeting. "I miss you, pet. Now that you've disclosed your location, Jim and I thought we'd visit over the Fourth of July. I know it's still a while away, but I figured you'd be chuffed."

"I can't wait. You probably won't recognize me. Learning to cook can be really fattening!"

Eve finished loading the dishwasher with her dinner dishes when her phone pinged from the counter. It was an email from Jake. A flurry of emotions flew through her — worry, excitement, yearning. Perching on the edge of the sofa, she read with anxious eyes.

May 28
Angie,
The last month has been fucking unbearable.
I see Dr. Fletcher at least once a week now . . . I don't know why I resisted therapy. Maybe I thought it'd prove I'm not man enough to handle my shit. It sucks to confront my issues but I know there's nothing I won't do to have you in my life again. I've sat at my laptop many times trying to write this . . . I wonder if I'll make any sense. I'll go for it, and plunge in —
It's been torture reliving my childhood, but I'm lighter after a session. I'm optimistic there can be some measure of healing. Part of my homework is to share a bit of what I went through. My shrink says we need to be vulnerable with each other. He's right, and I long to share closeness with you, Angie, please know that . . . no matter how much I withdraw. You are everything to me, and I want to be everything for you.
I know you planned to reach out first, so I hope you'll be receptive to this. Shit, I'm not sure you'll open this email. I know you're angry and hurt. I know I fucked up because I am fucked up. I don't think I know how to relate to people, to be soft . . . but I need to ponder more before I broach the subject with you.

Remember when you asked if I'd mind if you brought your cat to live with us and I said no? Well, that's because I remembered stuff from when I was a kid. I realize now I'd had a flashback when you brought up the subject. That's why I was terse with you, not because I was irritated with you. I'm sorry if I seemed that way.

I was in Kindergarten when a mutt followed me home. I'd never been allowed a pet, but I liked him and wanted him. I knew my father would be mad. I hid the dog in the woodshed and stole food to feed it. It wasn't long until it was discovered. My father pulled me outside by the ear and walloped me, hard. That poor flea-bitten mongrel came to my defense. He nipped at my old man. I was made to watch while my father beat that unfortunate beast to death with an ax. To this day . . . I'm haunted by the sight, sounds, and smells of it. Writing this – I want to throw up. I'm sweating. Shaking. I'm that defenseless kid again.

That story is one in a long line of incidents that traumatized me growing up. I remember many, but I'm also sure I've repressed some . . .

Mom was still around then. Lex was a toddler. Mom took a lot of beatings for us kids, but one day she vanished. Even now, I don't know if she escaped, or if my father strangled her to death. He often choked her until she lost consciousness. So, either we were abandoned by choice, or her devotion to us was her undoing. I'll never know for sure. I've mulled over hiring investigators to look into it, but I'm not sure I can handle the truth.

Once Mom was gone, I became Lex's protector. It was a mercy when the old man went on a bender and we had a few days reprieve. It wasn't easy being an elementary schoolkid responsible for another person, but I managed. The old man didn't lay a finger on Lex. He didn't really notice her much. Most of her injuries were from him pushing her aside to get to me. He liked hurting me. It angered him when he couldn't break me, but it never made him stop trying. I don't know if it was mental illness or just alcoholism, but he was a ruthless, twisted fucker.

I'm not sure I could say this stuff out loud to you . . . writing it makes it easier. But I'm about at my limit . . .

I've seen the tenderness you have for me shining in your eyes. I catch the way your mouth curves into a gentle smile when you look at me. I value your admiration and approval, Angie. You are so loving, so innocent, so good. The idea of you reading this shit kills me. I don't want the evil to taint you the way it has me. That you may view me any different is a punch in the gut — it knocks the wind right out of me.

I ache for you. The bed is a cold, lonely place without you.

When you're ready, please reach out, and let me know if you need anything . . .

Always, Jake

Phone in her hand, Eve sat back on the sofa, staggered. *My God.*

CHAPTER SIXTY-EIGHT

During her next video appointment, Eve told Dr. Ryan about Jake's email.

"Did you respond?"

"Yes. I told him about our sessions and what we talk about. Jake was right. Doing it by letter made it possible. I'm not sure I could've if we were face-to-face, either."

"How did you *feel* when you read his email?"

"So many emotions." Eve rested her chin on her hand and looked at Dr. R on the screen of her tablet. "I was revolted by what I learned. I understand Jake more now, and Lex, too. I can't imagine growing up the way they did. Their father was a psycho! Those poor kids. If that asshole weren't dead, I'd hunt him down and kill him with my bare hands."

"Quite different from your own upbringing?"

"My father may be a reserved man, but he's kind, generous, fair." Eve shook her head in wonder. "I didn't have a mother, but I had a terrific upbringing. Imagine, a decent childhood like mine, and still needing therapy. How do Jake and Lex function? They're successful in their careers and at a young age, too. I'd expect them to struggle more."

"But how do their personal lives measure up?"

"Hmm. You're right, of course. Something's gotta give. I know there's more to Lex than meets the eye. From her texts, I gather she and Monty are on and off, and look at Jake and me . . ."

"But you're brighter than you've been in a long time. I can see receiving Jake's letter motivates you to salvage your marriage. Are you going home?"

"Not yet. This is working. I'm going with it." Eve's phone chimed on the table, and she quickly glanced at it. "Oh my gosh. Hitch and his boyfriend are on their way for a surprise visit."

"It'll be good for you to have your friends there. Let's finish up so you can prepare for your guests."

Eve was reading a paperback on an Adirondack chair by the front door when a taxi turned onto the crushed clamshell lane of Sandpiper Drive.

While Hitch paid the carfare, Julian gathered her into a hug. "Hey, sugar. You're looking fine."

"You aren't too shabby yourself." Eve smoothed the skirt of her empire-waisted sundress, feeling far from fashionable. Wearing fitted trousers and a button-down shirt, he looked casual but chic, like a model in a cologne ad. A sweater was thrown carelessly over his shoulders, his black hair in its usual ponytail. Hitch, clad in t-shirt and board shorts, joined them, a large box in his arms.

"Is that an expectant mother I see?" Hitch bussed her cheek.

"The baby's the size of an acorn squash." Eve beamed, then nodded to the carton. "What's *that*?"

"Baby shower in a box," Julian said as they entered the house and went to the kitchen. Eve lowered onto a stool. Hitch doled out fried chicken, sliced cheese, and salads from a picnic hamper. Julian took a cake from a bakery box, then unpacked an assortment of wrapped gifts. Eve laughed when Hitch draped a purple feather boa around her shoulders and Julian affixed a plastic crown on the top of her head.

They carried their plates to the patio table. She filled them in on how she was doing between bites of food. The men made the atmosphere celebratory. Hitch streamed music through his cell phone. Julian oversaw refreshments, mixing a pitcher of vodka martinis, and handing Eve a *Shirley Temple* in a plastic party cup. Using a long-stemmed cherry to stir her drink, she thanked them for coming. They were tactful enough not to mention Jake.

After the meal, they made a fuss over Eve, watching her open the beautifully wrapped gifts. The items included a hand-knit yellow sweater and booties, bibs with funny quips, and a sterling silver piggy bank. Grateful tears came to Eve's eyes when she looked at her friends.

"No waterworks now, doll," Hitch scolded, handing her a box from the pocket of his shorts. "Jules says baby gifts are exciting, but Momma shouldn't be neglected."

"I hope you like it. We found it at an antique shop on Tybee Island when we visited my grandmother in Georgia last month," Julian said. Eve lifted the hinged lid. It was a vintage pin set with purple and blue crystals.

Her voice showed her delight. "Oh, I love peacocks."

"Hitch said you're a fan of nineteen fifties fashion. The pin's of the same period," Julian explained.

"I have a dress that it'd be fabulous with . . . not that it fits anymore." Eve's laugh was rueful. "I'll try to find something I can wear it on for my father and Addy's wedding. I don't know where time went. It's but a few months away. By then, I'll be huge."

Hitch raised his martini in a toast. Julian cut wedges of decadent chocolate cake with thick marmalade filling, which Eve devoured with ferocity surprising even her, making little noises of pleasure while she ate. After her last bite, she said, "That made my dreams come true."

Julian winked, serving her another slice. Later, Hitch went inside to the hall closet and brought out board games. They played a trivia game, Hitch turning on the patio heaters when the air turned cold. Eve prepared cheese and crackers for them to nosh on when they were ready for a snack. It was late when they made their way upstairs to bed.

The sun was high in the sky when the aroma of cooking sausage wafted its way up the stairway and tickled Eve's nose. She tossed back the covers and put her hair up with a clip, wondering how she could be hungry after all the food she'd eaten the night before.

At the *AGA*, Julian was turning frying sausage links with tongs, looking suave. Studying him, Eve acknowledged he'd be ordinary if not for his sensational style. Not many men could put together an outfit, but Julian sure could. Whisking pancake batter, his slim, elegant hands moved deftly. He lobbed her a smile and indicated a bowl of fruit salad.

"So," he said over his shoulder while he flipped pancakes. "You're doing really well, aren't you?"

Eve swallowed a bite of melon. "I am. I'm taking classes and learning a lot about myself. I'm finally going to be a mother. I'm excited about what the future holds."

"You don't feel isolated?" Julian put the sausages and pancakes on an earthenware platter and closed the insulated covers on the cooktop.

"I keep busy. Plus, I still connect with everyone at home." She filled her plate with hot food and doused it with maple syrup.

He sat beside her and fixed his plate. "I don't suppose you're attending Arthur's birthday festivities later this month in the Hamptons?"

"No, although Elite's planning it. Addy'll be there overseeing it. Jake will probably be there, too, as a guest. I wonder what he's said to people about me leaving."

"Evidently, they've been told your doctor prescribed a respite. Jake's been discreet."

"But I'm sure he's confided in Arthur, seeing how tight

they are." Eve shrugged. She didn't have control over what others did.

Julian took a drink of juice. "I sure wish you were coming to the Hamptons. Hitch's family's attending and I wouldn't mind having a friend in my corner, since this'll be my first time meeting them."

Eve put her fork down and placed a hand on Julian's arm. "Hitch told them about you?"

"I did," Hitch broke in from the doorway, pushing fingers through his recently shampooed hair. "I came out to them last month."

"And?" Eve prompted when he sat on a stool on the other side of the island.

"I give them credit for their grace. Even Grandfather Caulfield took it in stride. That's progressive for a fella still calling Asian people *Orientals*." He shuddered delicately. Eve smiled as Julian reached across the island for Hitch's hand.

Chapter Sixty-nine

June 20
Angie,

I appreciate your reply more than I can ever express. I've been walking around like a new man since reading your email . . . it's given me renewed hope, though it often wavers.

There's no other way to say it, but plainly — you've brought me to my knees.

The first days after you left, I was rabid — and let me say, your leaving was a tactical maneuver I never anticipated. It fucked me up — I thought if I gave you a few days or a week, you'd be back, but you held steadfast. You think you aren't strong, but you are. Or, perhaps you had no problem cutting me out. I think I always needed you more than you needed me.

I've respected your wishes . . . got a counselor and threw myself into work to stay occupied. As I work sixteen and eighteen-hour days, I've come to the conclusion you're right about the nurturing I've given Consolidated. I still want to keep a hand in, but Consolidated's robust and I have more money than I'd ever need. Would it please you if I promise to concentrate more on us? Work nine to five? You know I don't make promises lightly — I am willing to make big changes.

It's late as I write this letter on my laptop in bed. The house is a lonely place without you. Impersonal. You brought everything to life. Made things sunnier by being here. I used to roll my eyes at your constant re-watching of The Office. Now I stream episodes to feel closer to you. I play your music — Van Morrison, Norah Jones, John Mayer — for the same reason. I'm soothed by the memories of you singing Rosie's Lullaby when you prepare yet another

meal of sandwiches. I wish you were here to tease . . . I'd give any-
thing to hear you sing off-key right now. To hold you. Be inside you.

Your absence has taught me I'm not resilient enough to be happy
without you.

To say I've done soul-searching is putting it mildly . . . you men-
tioned your pregnancy's going well, and it makes my thoughts turn
to fatherhood. I've never failed at anything I've put my mind to, yet
you have no idea how much I dread the idea of failing as a father.
I've been a poor husband, what if I'm a worse father? I know I'm
exposing my insecurity typing this . . . but what if you become de-
voted to the child and lose interest in me? I'll never not want you . . .
what if you no longer want me? I've always had confidence in my
ability to seduce you, to satisfy you.

I know our sexual compatibility is my hold over you. I admit to
using it to my advantage, but now I see it's not enough to bring you
home. You're learning you don't need me. Can I hope to hold onto
you? I'm so unworthy of you.

In your letter, you wanted answers about my plan to exact
vengeance. *Yes, I've done things I'm ashamed of, but I don't think*
it's nearly as diabolical as you fear.

It's getting late now, but soon.
Always, Jake

"That's wonderful," Dr. Ryan said after Eve read Jake's letter aloud. "He's trying."

"I know. When I wrote back, I gave him props. But what if
we *can't* communicate *in person?*"

"It'll be awkward—at first. That's to be expected, but Jake's
laying himself bare to you. You've grown, but he's made *huge*
strides."

Eve nodded. "Like he said, he isn't the type of man to fail
something he's set his mind to."

"Are you ready to go home?"

"My father and Addy are coming to visit in a few weeks.
I'll move back after I finish my classes in early August. The

wedding's the ninth, and Jake and I are to be witnesses. The ceremony will be at the courthouse downtown, and there's a reception afterward at a restaurant on the Hudson."

"When's your due date?"

"Early October, so I won't be tiny when I see him. I've told myself I can eat what I want and worry about it later, but I've gained too much weight." Eve looked down at her bust and hips, volleying Dr. Ryan a sheepish look. She said dryly, "Maybe Jake won't be sexually attracted to *me* anymore."

"I'm sure that's crossed your mind since you've spoken of the intense physical relationship you share. But Jake thinks *you* won't want *him*."

Snorting, Eve shook her head. "*Me not want Jake?* That's ridiculous, and I told him that when I wrote back. I've never had sexual chemistry with anyone the way I do with him. Martin and I didn't have any problems in the bedroom, but our attraction was unlike the fiery *lust* I feel for Jake. Lemme tell ya, Doc, once you've experienced it, you notice its absence."

"Your sexual chemistry may be undeniable, but elaborate on your feelings *outside* the bedroom."

"You mean, how do I know I love him and I'm not infatuated?" Eve propped her chin in her palm while she thought. "The pull's still there eleven years on, but the emotion behind it is hard to verbalize. It's a million different reasons. I think I've always loved him. It's more than how he makes me *feel*. I know he'd have my back. There's nobody else you'd want in your corner more than Jake. No doubt, he's made his mistakes. Yet, I do respect him. At his core, he's decent. He does care about people. He says he fears softness, but he can be soft. When it comes down to it, I want to spend every moment with him."

"If you feel that way, then why not fly back home tomorrow?"

"Because I want to see this through."

"But, you sound pretty certain you'll reconcile."

Eve bit her lip. "It's that niggle of worry I have—that it'll be different in person. It gives me pause."

"Understandable."

"This past weekend was Arthur Tate's birthday party in The Hamptons. Hitch texted me yesterday. He was thrilled to tell me his family accepted Julian with open arms. They had a lobster boil on the beach at Aoife and Jamie Conroy's. Aoife gave birth last week, but the baby was premature and had to spend a few days in the NICU. The celebration was extra joyful because they brought him home from the hospital Thursday."

"Aoife is Arthur's daughter, right?" Dr. Ryan asked.

Eve nodded. "When I talked to Addy, she mentioned Sylvie's in charge of the Fourth of July party at Arthur's estate. It's huge for Sylvie, because Addy'll be on vacation, visiting me, and two hundred people will be there. A fortune's been spent on entertainment and fireworks." Eve rolled her eyes. "The super-rich and their endless string of parties."

"Have you had any further communication with Siobhan Tate?"

"Oh, my stars!" Eve smacked her forehead. "I cannot believe I didn't tell you what Hitch learned from his sister, Hester—Siobhan's in *rehab*."

"For?"

"Opioid addiction and alcohol." Eve tamped down a distinct whoosh of *schadenfreude*. She didn't want to be that way.

"Really. Does that information offer perspective about her behavior toward you in the past?"

"I suspected she had substance abuse problems and brought the subject up with Jake." Eve paused, remembering. "She kept it together at social events, though."

"Addicts become adept at hiding their addictions."

"But I wonder if she was self-medicating. It's crossed my mind Siobhan might have a personality disorder. Granted, I'm no expert."

"It's a possibility," Dr. Ryan conceded. "She'll be assessed at the treatment facility."

Eve said, "You know how villains in fiction are able to find redemption? Like in *Wicked*? Where you can appreciate the witch's perspective and empathize?"

"Sure?"

"I always viewed Siobhan as a one-dimensional villainess with zero redeeming qualities. But she must have a few, right?"

CHAPTER SEVENTY

"Luv!" Addy hugged Eve close. "You look like a fertility goddess."

"I do see similarities between my figure and *The Venus of Willendorf*," Eve deadpanned, then grinned at Addy's red t-shirt. It proclaimed in a glittered script, *Five-Foot-Tall Firecracker!*

Dad lugged suitcases from the trunk of their rental car and put them on the front steps before embracing Eve in his reserved way. "How are you keeping, my dear? You look well. And your ear's completely healed."

She gave her father a bright smile. "I'm great."

Her dad wore a short-sleeve yellow polo shirt and coordinating pink and yellow plaid shorts, which tickled Eve. It had to be Addy's influence. She couldn't imagine him choosing such an ensemble.

She led them inside and upstairs to their room. Addy was talkative, as usual. "This is exactly how a house on Martha's Vineyard should look. The ferry took forever! Have you enjoyed your stay? When will you come home?"

Eve laughed at Addy's mile-a-minute questions, reminded again of how much she'd missed her friend. "Let's get a drink and sit out on the patio. We'll catch up."

When it was time to prepare dinner, Addy insisted on cooking.

"I've learned a lot from my lessons. We did a whole unit on grilled meat," Eve argued, but Addy wouldn't hear of it. Shaking her head with resignation, she asked her dad about work, avoiding any mention of Jake or their separation. Dad brought the subject up a few minutes later.

"Hitch was kind to offer his family's home, but will you reconcile with Jake?"

"I'm still deciding. After we see each other, I'll know. I hope."

Her dad's voice was mild when he said, "He's told me how important it is for his child to not be borne of a broken home."

Eve's eyebrows lifted involuntarily. "When did you have that conversation?"

"We've had lunch weekly since you came up here."

"Really? Jake's never said. Come to think of it, neither has Addy."

"I never shared with her." He looked guilty. "It's not a secret, but I worried you'd think me disloyal."

"It's okay, Dad. I don't think that." Eve put her hand in his.

"He's a good person. So are you. Every relationship has its ups and downs."

"Yours and Addy's doesn't—other than the hiccups at first, I mean," Eve said.

"We did have some issues to tackle beyond that. You and Jake can overcome your obstacles as Addy and I did." Her father met her eyes. "In five short weeks, you two will be together in the same room for the first time in months. Do you feel out of your depth?"

She nodded. "I'd be lying if I said I wasn't nervous."

Addy came out of the kitchen door with a platter. After placing steaks on the preheated grill, she plopped into a chair, then poured more tea in her glass. "I'm chuffed. I love this place."

The conversation turned to Sylvie and her kids and the shop. Addy proudly told Eve they'd hired more help. "I feel cheeky taking time off during the busy season, but Sylvie insisted. She's head over heels for Jed. The kids adore him, too."

Addy smiled at Dad. "Would you mind checking the ribeyes, sweetheart?"

"Sylvie and Jed make a great couple," Eve agreed as her father rose. "What do you guys want to do while here?"

"Fireworks on the Fourth is compulsory," Dad said from the grill.

"Naturally." Addy turned to Eve. "What should we see?"

"The Cliffs, and Gay Head Lighthouse. There are bikes in the garage, if you want to ride. There's an antique shop I've been meaning to check out. And Hitch told me about a place that makes yummy lobster rolls."

Addy's manner was enthusiastic. "I want to do the lot."

"I hope you'll set aside some time for relaxation, honey," Dad said.

"I will." Addy gave him a bright smile. "You can stay back tomorrow and read your book while Eve and I go dress shopping."

Eve's face set in a grimace. "A tent may fit me."

Dad brought the platter to the table, putting a well-done steak on Eve's plate. She thanked him, then asked Addy, "Blue, or purple? I want to wear the pin Hitch and Julian gave me."

"Either's fine," Addy said, dishing up potato salad. "Incidentally, Jake sent along a gift."

Her heartbeat accelerating, Eve put her fork down.

Addy laughed. "Don't fret." She rifled in her purse, which hung from the back of her chair, and produced a small gold bag. "Jake says it's a push present."

Eve recognized the distinctive embossed insignia of an up-market jeweler. "*Push present?*"

"A gift a husband gives his expectant wife. There's a card in the bag, too."

Eve fished out a jeweler's box and opened it. It was a striking platinum and diamond ring with a glittering stone the color of the ocean. "It's October's birthstone."

"I wonder what that sparkler costs. I'm nosy enough to look it up online, but I bet that place isn't the sort that tells you outright." Addy said, "Try it on."

"It may not fit. My wedding ring's gotten snug." Eve forced it over the knuckle of her right-hand ring finger.

Addy threw her a look. "That's a lovely bit of all right, innit?"

That night after her dad and Addy were asleep, Eve sat on her bed and tore open the envelope.

> *June 25*
> *Angie,*
> *In the past, you've told me you don't care for gifts given as a gesture of appeasement or to fulfill obligations. Believe me when I tell you that isn't the case with this gift. This is pure sentimentality. I chose the ring because tourmaline will be our child's birthstone. I've sent it as a tangible expression of how much I care. Please wear it next month at Jim and Addy's wedding.*
> *Always, Jake*

CHAPTER SEVENTY-ONE

Eve brought the pin along when they shopped for her matron of honor dress. Wanting a gown that would wow Jake, she couldn't find anything flattering. She felt fat and clumsy in every garment and knew in the weeks leading to the wedding she'd become even more so. Entering another store, Eve dolefully questioned whether she should have sampled so much fudge during the confectionery unit of cooking class.

"Don't get disheartened. Try this one." Addy handed Eve a blue dress, cajoling, "Give it a chance, pet."

She went into the fitting room, begrudgingly. Moody and uncomfortable from the heat, she felt as dainty as a pork chop. Stepping in the chiffon frock, Eve pulled the bodice over her swollen abdomen with a tug. She'd need to go up several sizes, but the color flattered her and matched the stones in the peacock pin.

Turning her head, Eve surveyed herself in the angled mirrors. Her midsection was cute. The generalized weight gain from overindulging rich food wasn't. *Oof. Baby got back.* There was no way the frock could be zipped. Her breasts strained at the seams of the bodice and the material dug into her flesh. She fought the compulsion to yank the garment off and wave the white flag of defeat, but Addy wanted to see it on. *Let her clap her eyes on this travesty.*

As she emerged from the cubicle, Addy said, "Oh my."

"If there were a soundtrack to my life, *Milkshake* by *Kelis* would be playing at this very moment," Eve grumbled.

"Hmm. Well. Your bust is quite..." Addy hesitated.

"Magnificent. Let's try a larger size."

A few minutes later, Eve exited the dressing room, wiping the perspiration from her brow.

"You're positively glowing."

"That's *sweat*, Addy. I know because I have a trickle of it traveling down the back of my calf." Vowing never to dress shop ever again, all she wanted was a cold drink.

"Now, now," Addy clucked like a hen. "It's lovely. It matches the pin, and the chiffon's light and airy."

"Except, there's no place to put the pin." Eve indicated the deep neckline of the off-the-shoulder empire-waisted design.

The salesclerk suggested, "You can put your hair in an updo and attach the pin there."

"Sold," Eve said with relief. "Addy, how about a lobster roll, on me?"

They loafed on a park bench, watching kids frolicking at the playground. Eve demolished her sandwich, breadcrumbs dusting the skirt of her printed sundress. Using a paper napkin to wipe butter from her fingers, she considered buying another roll. She thought of how big her butt looked in the dress shop's mirrors and instead sipped from her plastic tumbler of iced tea. "Have the Tates sent back their RSVPs?"

"Yes. The lot are coming. Lex has a gallery show, so she won't make it, but I expect a good turnout." Addy crumpled her sandwich wrapper and threw their trash in a bin. "I considered renting a marquee and having the reception outside, but it's too bloody hot." Addy shooed a fly away. "Not to mention the bugs."

"Did you reserve the entire space?"

Addy nodded. "I used The Riverside Grill for a client last month. I'm fortunate to have snagged it. It's the finest restaurant on the Hudson."

"Do you think Siobhan will come?"

"In deference to Arthur, she's invited, though I'd prefer she doesn't. Perhaps she's a changed woman after treatment."

Eve gave her a look. "*A changed woman*? That's asking a bit much."

"I'll be stroppy if she makes trouble on my wedding day."

Eve raised an eyebrow. "Maybe she's gotten a prescription for mood stabilizers."

Addy laughed. "One can hope."

"How did Jake look when he stopped by to give you my gift?"

"Tired. But in good enough spirits. I think he's excited about the upcoming nuptials because it means seeing you. Are *you* excited?"

"Yes, and anxious," Eve admitted, observing a child swing from the monkey bars. She was envious of his boundless energy. Yawning, she said, "I have no stamina anymore. I need a siesta."

Scooting to the edge of the bench, Addy held out her hand to help her stand. When they walked to the wagon, Addy said, "I was thinking the other day about the missing money. Where did Martin hide it? Will it ever turn up? It would make a nice nest egg for the baby's education, wouldn't it?"

"That amount of money would cover more than college." Eve eased in behind the wheel. "It's probably hidden somewhere nobody'll *ever* find it."

The remainder of her father and Addy's visit passed quickly. On Independence Day, they brought folding chairs to the park, watching fireworks at dusk while eating hoagies and potato chips from a wicker picnic hamper. There were bike rides and swimming, board games on the patio, and an evening bonfire on the beach.

The day before her dad and Addy were to leave, Eve took them to Gay Head Lighthouse. The tour was fascinating, and despite Eve's indolence, she climbed the stairs to the top of the red brick lighthouse. She was rewarded with a spectacular view of Vineyard Sound. They ate lunch at the delightful restaurant nearby, then shopped for pottery created by artisans belonging to the *Wampanoag Tribe.*

Eve waved until the rental car disappeared down Sandpiper Drive, feeling left behind. She was ready to return home.

CHAPTER SEVENTY-TWO

A*ugust 1*
Angie,

It's time for me to lay it on the line. I know I'll ramble, and who knows if it'll be logical, but . . .

Jim and Addy's wedding approaches, and in dark moments I fight to remain confident you'll return to me. As much as it pains me to write this – if you don't wish to reconcile . . . then, the house is yours. I cannot fathom the idea of living there any longer without you. You don't know it, but I built it for you. I remember many years ago you made an offhand comment that you'd visited **Fallingwater** *and liked it. I built it to demonstrate I can give you what you want. It'll break me if you want a divorce, but you'll never need for anything for the rest of your life. What I have is yours. If it's not enough, I'll get more.*

I've made mistakes. Raised the way I was, I didn't know what a proper relationship was. When we were first together, I thought we were a normal *couple. Now, I know our sole connection in bed made it impossible for you to see that what we had as more than sex. We didn't hold hands or cuddle. There wasn't intimacy or shared dreams. I didn't take you to dinner or dancing or introduce you to my friends. I realize now – I should have. When you told me you were pregnant, it came at me like a bolt of lightning. I had to marry you to hold onto you. I knew I couldn't live without you. Perhaps I'm wrong, but I remain steadfast in my belief that if you hadn't met Pierce, we would've had our ups and downs but eventually found our way.*

At one time, I put you on a pedestal, but I've come to learn you're the real deal. You aren't merely beautiful. You have many other commendable qualities. You're funny. Smart. Playful. Vibrant. Sweet. Caring. Lovable. I could go on all day listing your virtues. Even your so-called flaws are endearing. You can't carry a tune. Or cook. You're often late. You're obsessed with slapstick comedies I shake my head at. I'm streaming your music while I write this . . . By Your Side *by Sade is playing, and it makes me long for you in my arms. To tell you how much you mean to me is difficult . . . I wish I had the chance to show you.*

I never felt worthy of you, Angie. When you left me for Pierce, it cut me deep. My worst fear was my insecurity regarding you, and by leaving, it reinforced I'd never be good enough. In all else, I had supreme self-confidence . . . but never when it came to you.

I faltered. I stopped working, didn't go to class. I drank too much bourbon and smoked too much weed. I got in fights at bars. I put a guy in the hospital. And I hooked up with Siobhan more than once. These things, I profoundly regret. I did anything and everything to make me forget my pain. I was lost. I hated you, but I hated myself more.

My body ached for you, yet I contemplated revenge . . . it was easier than admitting I was dying inside. I wanted to hurt you, make you remorseful. During benders, I said things to Siobhan I shouldn't have. I tell you, not as an excuse, but as an explanation – that I was fucked up beyond recognition.

Almost failing business school was a wake-up call. I pulled myself up by my bootstraps. I was gonna prove myself to you, come hell or high water. I figured someday we'd cross paths again. It was fated. We have some sort of – I don't know how to describe it – but I liken it to a spiritual connection. It may be a romantic notion from a man who doesn't deem himself a romantic, but I always thought we were destined to be together – I've told you that.

Yes, I did make a plan. I was single-minded in everything I did . . . hiring Jim was part of it. Building the house was part of it. I was biding my time, hoping for an opportunity to meet you again and rekindle our relationship. When I learned you'd returned to Old Hillbury, it was my chance – I had to act. I enticed you to Consolidated for a job, but you know that. The minute you arrived in my office, I wasn't merely meeting the past, I'd come face to face with my frailties, my shortcomings. It stirred up so much shit . . . I struggled. Seeing you again made it not cut and dried anymore.

Yes, I did keep tabs on you. When I learned Pierce left you owing millions to the wrong people, I used the knowledge to my advantage. I liked the idea of having you under my thumb. I was calling the shots, but still — you controlled me, even if you didn't realize it. I would've done anything to have you back in my bed. And, yes, I resented you . . . at first. Your cool blonde beauty always made you untouchable — but that's because I didn't know you. I was at war with myself as I did. I'd built you into what you weren't . . . a cold, shallow woman, a social climber. By Thanksgiving, I found I was terribly wrong. My instincts had never failed me so miserably. It jolted me. So, I reminded myself whenever I caved — hold back. Deep down, I discerned you'd someday realize the truth, that I was a white-trash punk who made it big. That's why I was wild with jealousy over your friendship with Hitch. He has class. Even with my steadfast belief that we're meant to be together, I feared you'd wise up and decide he was better for you. From the beginning, I used everything in my arsenal to pull you in but kept you at arm's length. I'm aware of how fucked up that is. By God, if I could go back, I'd do things differently.

When you were shot at Elite, it frightened the hell out of me. I needed to open up to you, make amends. But then we learned about the pregnancy, and my uncertainties bubbled up. There's nothing I fear more than becoming my father. I know I retreated. I didn't know what else to do. I needed distance. After learning the truth about Pierce, I saw you were destroyed. You grappled with how you would've responded if he'd asked you to go away with him, even if it meant we never would've reunited. It about killed me. I feared you'd choose him again, if given the opportunity. I was wounded by the notion you preferred to be Pierce's grieving widow rather than my wife.

I'm a man accustomed to getting my way. I'm intense. And when it comes to you, I've always been possessive. The idea of you with another man . . . maybe it's a failing, but I fight for and protect *what's mine at all costs. Simply, I want you, Angie, and the child you carry. Tell me what you require, and it's yours.*

I'm still wrestling with how my life will change with the birth of a baby. And remain unsure what kind of a father I'll make, but you better believe I'm gonna be part of that kid's life. The sex may be earth-shattering, but I know it's not enough to keep you . . . you don't care about my money much. Maybe I'll never deserve you, but that doesn't mean I'll ever stop trying to be what you need me to be. If nothing else, will wanting our child to have a full-time father be enough to bring you back to me?

You've been straightforward. You want love. I don't know why that's fucking hard for me to say, but let me tell you — if there were ever somebody I wanted to be able to say it to, it would be you, Angie. If we divorce, we'll always share a connection through our child. I take some measure of comfort in that knowledge.

On the matter of Siobhan — she was never important to me. She was there when I needed someone, but I told her I intended to get you back one day. That's hard for her to accept, but she doesn't care about me. Siobhan's out for number one. She's got a lot of problems. I'm sure you've heard she's in rehab. I spoke to Arthur after you left and told him your suspicions about her addiction. He's hit hard when faced with the truth. The intervention aged him, but he wants her healthy. I'll admit I liked knowing you were jealous of the attention I gave Siobhan, but I did her no favors by indulging her, even if it was primarily for Arthur's benefit. I regret it. She's nothing to me. It's only you, Angie. It's only ever been you. You're my past. You're my future.

Always, Jake

CHAPTER SEVENTY-THREE

Wordless while Hitch drove her from the airfield to Dad and Addy's in his sports car, Eve viewed the neighborhood with fresh eyes. She'd been gone for three months, but everything seemed different. *Or, perhaps it's me that's changed . . .*

"Iced coffee?" Eve asked when he put her valise on the living room sofa. They sat at the enamel-topped table in the yellow kitchen. Addy wouldn't be home from work until lunchtime, and the house was cold without her friendly presence.

"It's weird to be back." Eve took a deep breath and gave Hitch a grateful look. "Thank you, from the bottom of my heart."

"Don't become sappy, doll," he said, but he smiled.

"Why don't you stay for lunch? Addy's promised chicken salad."

"I can't. There's a board meeting in the city later that's *mandatory.*" Hitch moped, mouth turned down. "Can you believe I actually have to put on a suit for it? I fuckin' hate New York in August—it's almost as bad as Calcutta in June."

Eve helped at Elite the next morning. Dad and Addy's wedding was the following day, and tasks needed attending to before Addy took time off for her honeymoon. By lunchtime, Eve was beat. She drove her dad's car home, promising to pick Addy up after she napped.

Bleary-eyed from slumber, Eve scratched Wally's chin while she texted Jake to let him know she'd decided to pick up her SUV. Within seconds, he responded. *I can be at the house in an hour.*

Eve paused before replying. Butterflies flapped their wings in her belly at the thought of seeing him, but she looked at her rumpled dress and put a hand to her pillow-mashed hair. She'd daydreamed of the first time they'd see each other again—and looking like a frump wasn't what she pictured. She asked if he'd be willing to hold off until they met at the courthouse, and he reluctantly agreed.

Addy waited in the driveway while Eve let herself into Jake's house. How strange it was to be back. It was familiar yet alien at the same time. She took a second to look around. Tidy, it was much as she'd left it. Using the service door, Eve found her vehicle in its usual stall beside the SUV Jake purchased for her. The tires looked flat from sitting. She'd have to check the air soon. Briefly, she worried the battery would be drained, but her vehicle fired right up.

Trailing Addy down the driveway and through the iron gate, Eve turned the air conditioning to high and cranked up the radio. She cheerfully sang along to *Why Georgia* by *John Mayer*. Halfway back to town, there was a loud bang and Eve gasped, clutching the steering wheel tight. Recognizing the *flap, flap, flap* of a blown tire, she navigated the vehicle to the shoulder. After making a U-turn, Addy parked behind the SUV. Eve contemplated the tire with a bemused expression, giving Addy an aggravated look when she joined her.

"Damn. I guess I'll have to call a tow truck." Eve wrinkled her nose and swatted away a mosquito.

"I can change a tire. I saw a video online. Easy-peasy. The lug nuts may stop me if they're tight, though."

As Addy popped open the trunk, Eve shot her an impressed look. Mopping her brow, she watched Addy lift the carpeted panel to locate the jack and spare tire. Addy jerked away as if burned. "Bleedin' heck!"

Shaken, Eve demanded, "What's wrong?"

Addy stuttered but was unable to speak.

"What happened? Did something bite you?"

Addy lifted a hand to point a finger at the trunk. Eve stared as she fanned her face. "Look. Dosh!"

"Huh?" Steeling herself, Eve lifted the panel, flicking it aside. She drew a sharp breath, shaking her head in disbelief. She put a hand to the vehicle for support. *Holy Shit.*

Rubber-banded cash was stacked in neat rows where the jack and spare tire should've been.

Eve turned to Addy, her face drained of color. "You solved *The Case of the Missing Money, Nancy Drew.*"

"You aren't going into premature labor, are you?" Addy asked, her voice reedy.

Eve laughed. "I think I pissed myself."

"It was here the whole time."

They hooted with mirth until tears streamed down their faces at the absurdity of the discovery.

Addy flittered about nervously like a bird in her ivory wedding suit. Sylvie came to the house to help her get ready. She curled Addy's shoulder-length hair in an off the face style and placed a fascinator with feathers and netting atop her head.

"Addy, you look radiant," Eve said, giving her a hug before sitting for Sylvie to style her hair.

Gathering Eve's tresses into an updo, Sylvie affixed the peacock pin. "Putting the pin in your hair was a stroke of genius."

"I wish I could claim credit for the idea." Eve winked, looking at her reflection in a handheld mirror. She looked good. Eve felt a tremor of nerves when she thought of Jake seeing her heavily pregnant. Brushing the feeling aside, she lifted her juice tumbler to toast Addy, then pulled a package from her purse. "Here's your something new *and* something blue."

Addy opened the box to find an aquamarine ring. "Oh." She gave Eve a brilliant smile, tears glistening in her chestnut eyes.

"And, the something old, and something borrowed." Sylvie handed Addy an antique gold bracelet. "It was my grandmother's."

After Addy put on the jewelry, they shared a group hug.

Eve looked at the clock. "Oh my gosh, it's time to go already."

As they left, Sylvie said, "See you at the reception."

Jake waited at the courthouse, looking better than any fantasy Eve had conjured. He was tall and handsome as ever in a dark suit and crisp white shirt. Her breath caught. She faltered for a second, her legs wobbling like gelatin.

His gaze swept over her, pausing at her swollen midsection. When she approached to greet him, his expression was solemn. Circumspect, he leaned down to kiss her cheek, resting a hand on her bare shoulder. His touch sent sizzling heat blazing to her core. Eve twitched, meeting Jake's gaze. He stilled. He must feel it, too.

Her dad and Addy were at the door of the judge's chambers, holding hands. Dad called, "Come along, you two."

During the short service, Eve knew Jake's hungry stare never left her. She could barely concentrate on the vows. She was remembering their wedding. When she caught him watching her, his mouth curved into a lopsided smile showing his dimple. *He must be thinking the same.*

Once rings were exchanged, the bride and groom were instructed to kiss. Eve whooped, clapping. The buzzing sensation at Jake's nearness made her flush head to toe when she congratulated the newlyweds. Addy blushed prettily, her eyes bright, and Dad looked proud. He glanced at his watch, his new wedding band glinting. "We'd better get to the restaurant. Our reception starts soon."

"I'll give Eve a lift," Jake said, his voice smooth as silk. Her heart leaped at being alone with him.

After Dad and Addy drove away, Jake opened the car door for her. With some awkwardness, she folded into the leather seat. He came around and turned on the vehicle, setting the air conditioning to high. Exhaling as cold air gusted from the vents, Eve found him intently regarding her.

She plucked at the chiffon skirt. "I look *different*, don't I?"

"You're beautiful."

"I'm not. I never was. I'm just—ordinary."

"Never ordinary. Extraordinary," Jake whispered, bringing her hand to his mouth to nuzzle her knuckles. Yearning pooled in Eve's belly, making her inhale swiftly. They didn't break eye contact. The only sound was the air conditioner and their breathing.

Looking out the window, Eve coughed away the awkwardness she felt. "Addy found Martin's money yesterday. It was hidden in my SUV. I want you to have it. I owe you for paying his debts."

Jake made a noise low in his throat, bringing shaky fingers to her face. He forced her to meet his eyes again. "You owe me *nothing*. I don't care about the money. Don't you understand that?"

Slanting forward in his seat, he brought his lips to hers. At first, the kiss was tentative and gentle, but when Eve responded, he deepened it. His hands were everywhere—caressing her face, exploring her breasts, running up her thighs. She was carried along a wave of desire, all else forgotten.

"I want to take you home, baby." Jake's lips were at the curve of her neck, his voice thick. "Fuck. You have no idea how I've hungered for you."

She laced her fingers in his. "We can't miss the reception."

"I know." He closed his eyes for a moment before withdrawing and putting the car in gear.

CHAPTER SEVENTY-FOUR

Eve expected her usual crippling crowd anxiety to manifest but was surprised to find it barely noticeable. *I guess that therapy stuff works.* The restaurant wasn't much cooler than outside, and a bead of sweat rolled down the back of her knee.

Posing for photos, Addy said, "I'm oozing through my wedding suit. I'll ask the staff to turn the AC up."

As Hitch and Julian approached from across the room, Eve gave them a bright smile and did a *jazz hand* to highlight the peacock pinned in her hair.

Julian volleyed her a grin. "I do declare."

Sylvie waved at Eve from where she sat with Jed. Giving Julian and Hitch each a quick kiss, she excused herself, explaining, "I'm being summoned."

Hitch was good-natured as always. "Later."

"Stay sweet now, sugar." Julian winked.

Jed stood at once and swooped her into a hug. "You look ready to pop!"

Eve winced at the image his words evoked.

"Jed, don't say that," Sylvie admonished lightly. She told Eve, "Don't listen to him. Pregnancy becomes you."

"It surely does. Howdy, Jake." Jed held his hand out for a handshake, and Eve turned to find Jake beside her.

"Congrats, daddy-to-be." Sylvie kissed Jake's cheek, then suggested they get together for dinner soon. When Eve spotted Arthur at the bar ordering a drink, she slipped away.

"You look enchanting!" Arthur boomed. His face baggy, he had pouches under his eyes. He'd aged ten years since she'd last seen him. "How are you?"

"I was told I look ready to pop. Other than that, I'm fine." Eve grinned. Arthur ordered her a club soda, then ushered her to an empty table, setting their drinks down. Gallantly, he helped her into a chair.

He took a sip of his whiskey. "When did you get back to town?"

"A few days ago."

"I've missed seeing you. You'll have to come to Port Breakwater for Labor Day."

"I'd like that. I've thought about you a lot lately." Eve gave Arthur a compassionate smile. "Jake told me about the intervention. That must've been tough on you. I'm sorry."

Arthur swallowed, his shoulders drooping.

Eve's heart constricted and she put an encouraging hand on his arm.

"She got home Wednesday, swearing treatment helped. I didn't want her tempted by everyone drinking here today, but she insisted upon coming."

"Siobhan and I have our issues, but I do wish her well. Truly."

Arthur smiled at her when an announcement was made that luncheon was served. Standing, he held out a hand. Eve gave him a smooch before taking her seat beside her father, Addy, and Jake. The food was light fare, but for once, she had no appetite. She was overheated, and her chair made her tailbone ache. Sipping iced water, she people watched. Siobhan was seated with the Tate family, wearing a garish orange print dress. She met Eve's gaze and sneered before turning away. *I guess some things never change.*

When Jake tapped his champagne flute with a knife, Eve waited, eager to hear his speech. He broadcast a smile encompassing the room. "I'm a fortunate man to be part of the Shawcross family. I'll forever be grateful for how Jim and Addy

welcomed me into the fold. They're special people and a perfect couple. I'm gratified to be here to celebrate their love.
Raise your glasses to Jim and Addy."

Touched, Eve felt the sting of tears. Addy patted her hand.
"Those pregnancy hormones are making you broody." It *had*
been an emotional day. Though the air was dense with humidity outside, Eve needed a minute of solitude. Sneaking
away as soon as was decent, she leaned against a tree at the
riverbank. A breeze stirred, and she lifted her face.

The familiar cloying floral perfume told her she was no
longer alone. She opened her eyes. Siobhan's face was set in a
glare, her stance hostile. Skin prickling, Eve braced for the ug-
liness sure to come.

"You should've kept your fucking mouth shut."

"Cool it, Siobhan."

"Telling your suspicions about my opioid habit to Jake
started a rash of shit. I can stop taking pills anytime, if I want
to. I'm no junkie."

Eve cocked her head to the side. "Aren't you? Even now,
you're slurring. Have you been using?"

Siobhan's gaze flicked over her, her mouth curling with
distaste. "You're fuckin' *fat*."

Eve's fingers itched to smack away Siobhan's sneer. She
curled her hands into fists to resist the urge. "I'm *pregnant*."

"It's nothing a good kick wouldn't take care of."

Controlling her temper, Eve said, "You need help. I pity
you."

"You think it's an accomplishment letting Jake cum in you?
You're too tubby for him to want now." When Eve walked
past her to leave, Siobhan grabbed her arm.

Striving to look uninterested, Eve said, "Let go of me."

Siobhan tightened her grip. "Make me, lard ass."

In one smooth movement, Eve wrenched her arm away,
then brought a palm across Siobhan's face with a resounding

slap.

From the corner of her eye, she saw Jake sprinting across the grass. She moved back instinctively when Siobhan advanced, her fist raised.

Inserting himself between them, Jake wrapped his fingers around Siobhan's wrist. His voice was deadly calm when he said, "I *know* you weren't gonna punch my pregnant wife."

Adrenaline flowed through Eve's veins, making her dizzy. She slumped against the tree to keep from crumpling.

Siobhan was defiant, lifting her chin. "She assaulted me."

Jake's eyes narrowed. "Eve wouldn't have slapped you unprovoked."

"She's unbalanced. She attacked me!"

He looked at Siobhan, releasing her wrist. "You're high, aren't you?"

"It's to take the edge off," Siobhan insisted.

"You haven't been out of rehab a week." Jake shook his head in disbelief. His voice was severe when he asked, "How many times do I have to tell you *nicely* that I love Eve?"

Siobhan stroked his cheek. "But—"

Jake jerked away from her, face reddening with anger. "Read my lips. I love my wife. *I don't want you.*"

Siobhan's mouth moved, but no sound came out.

Jake took Eve's hand. He guided her to the parking lot and helped her into his car. Getting into the driver's seat, he shook his head. "She's high as a fuckin' kite."

Eve whispered, "*You said you love me.*"

"Yeah." Jake's short laugh was tinged with irony. "I thought I wouldn't be able to say it, but . . ." He scanned her face. "You look done in."

Eve pulled Jake's head to hers, kissing him with unabashed hunger.

Later that afternoon, a Carter Consolidated jet taxied down

the runway, then lifted. Eve waved until it was fully airborne. "Sending Dad and Addy to the house in Fiji for their honeymoon was thoughtful."

Jake bent to kiss her. "Let's go home."

When they came into the kitchen through the service door, he said, "Why don't you go upstairs and see if your bikini still fits?"

Eve frowned. "Why?"

"Look."

She went to the window. An inground pool had been installed beyond the patio, the water sparkling. Jake stood behind her. He brought his lips to her ear. "I'll meet you outside."

CHAPTER SEVENTY-FIVE

After wading into the delectably cool water, Eve floated on her back with eyes closed. There was a splash when Jake dove into the pool. Droplets of water landed on her face when he broke the surface and shook his hair. Eve opened an eye, finding his expression determined. He reached for her, lowering his lips to hers. Soon, she clung to him.

They necked like teenagers. The hazy heat of the day zapped her energy, but Eve was buoyed by passion. When her stomach gurgled, Jake asked, his tone amused, "Hungry?"

"A little," she admitted.

"I'll make us a sandwich."

Normal swimming impossible, Eve doggy paddled to the tiled stairs. Making her way to a lounge chair, she tugged her too-small swimsuit over her breasts. Jake handed her a bottle of water from the fridge by the grill as she toweled off.

He was back ten minutes later with two turkey sandwiches on a plate. He handed her one and lifted the other to his lips, observing her while he chewed.

Once finished, Eve said, "Thanks. For the sandwich, the swim, everything."

"You commented once you've always wanted a pool."

"You do have contractual obligations to fulfill, don't you?" she teased, then waited a trifle uncertainly for his reaction.

"Damn right I do," Jake replied, a smile in his eyes. He lay back on his lounger, putting his arms behind his head. Eve's gaze traveled from the fine silken hairs of his armpits to his muscled torso and lower. She swallowed with difficulty. Jake cleared his throat and she jumped, blushing.

He watched her watching him, his face earnest. "Let's go to bed."

Eve matched his ardor, her tongue moving with his when he kissed her. Her hands explored his chest and abs, shaking with urgency. She pushed his swim trunks from his lean hips. Jake pulled away, peeling her wet suit off with fevered movements. Lowering her to the bed, he lay beside her. He took his time, moving his mouth over the sensitized skin of her neck, shoulders, and breasts the way that made her bones melt. Eve quivered, her flesh tightening into goosebumps when Jake ran a possessive hand over her stomach. He trailed lazy fingertips to her hip, then her inner thigh. Eve mewed with impatience before he finally delved into her cleft and found her center. Gasping, she arched her hips toward his featherlight touch. Jake's lips were on her forehead. Her eyelids flicked open and she met his brilliant green eyes.

"You're so fucking beautiful."

Eve searched the depths of his eyes, tracing the contours of his lips with the tip of her finger. She brushed her mouth to his, hesitating a second before whispering against him, "I love you, Jake."

Jake's lids fell. He inhaled, then exhaled. Eve put a hand on his cheek, stroking him tenderly. When he opened his eyes again, she saw raw vulnerability. His voice was thick when he breathed, "I love you, Angie."

They shared another lingering kiss before Jake got up and knelt between her thighs. Eve tangled her fingers in his hair as he teased her swollen sex with his tongue. She throbbed, her pulse roaring in her ears and feeling the familiar tickle guaranteeing she was close.

Whispering Jake's name, Eve arched when spasms flowed

down to the tips of her toes and back, leaving her panting. She clenched her thighs together, savoring the heady feeling of satisfaction when he collapsed beside her. Pulling her against his chest, he made a sound of contentment low in his throat.

"The doctor said we can. It won't hurt the baby."

"Are you sure?"

Eve nodded. He settled between her thighs, bracing his arms on either side of her head. She shifted her legs to accommodate him, but it was cumbersome with her stomach in the way. They shared a laugh, then Jake re-situated. He entered her slowly as if to make sure he wasn't hurting her, his gaze never leaving her face. "You okay?"

"Better than okay," Eve murmured, concentrating on the pleasure he gave. He sank deeper by degrees, settling into an unhurried tempo that wrought a climax from her moments later. She stole a glance at him through her eyelashes, drinking in the warm look in his eyes when he smiled at her.

Her name was an oath on his lips when he went over the edge.

When Eve woke, the bedroom was dark. She thumbed through Jake's closet and found his robe, belting it around her girth. She twisted her hair into a clip. When she walked down the back stairs, she heard *Beast of Burden* playing in the kitchen.

The kitchen table was set and Jake was at the stove, emptying a colander of drained pasta into a pan of Bolognese sauce and singing along with the song. After their earlier intimacy, Eve suddenly felt shy. She sat at the island without saying anything.

Jake adjusted the song's volume using the touchscreen on the wall. When he greeted her, his manner was welcoming and easy. "About time you woke up, sleepyhead."

She blushed. "I can't go long without a catnap these days."

Jake's dazzling grin made Eve's heart skip a beat, and her bashfulness evaporated. He nodded to the stove. "I went to the market while you slept."

"It smells great. I'm ravenous." Her stomach growled on cue.

After they ate, Jake used the screen on the living room wall to choose music. *Sade*'s soulful voice sang *Kiss of Life* as he dropped beside Eve on the couch. She bit her lip, remembering Jake's letter — how he listened to her music in her absence, and longed for her.

Eve cleared her throat, keeping her tone light. "So, umm. You *love* me?"

Jake wrapped his arm around her and brought her to him, putting his lips to her forehead. "You heard right. More than anything."

Eve asked, "Is this the same man who swore he'd keep emotions from our marriage?"

He entwined his fingers with hers. "I was a damn fool. I loved you from the minute I saw you at The Roadhouse all those years ago. I just didn't realize it."

"Your letters were amazing." Eve's smile faltered when she added, "I was worried you'd hold back once we saw each other again."

"Old habits do die hard," Jake admitted. "But I assured you I'd try, and that's what I'm gonna do." He took a deep breath. "This is new territory for me, Angie."

Eve brought his hand to her mouth and kissed his knuckles, emotion making her voice hoarse when she said, "For me, too. We'll figure it out."

He murmured, "If you give me a chance, I'll spend the rest of my life proving how much I love you."

EPILOGUE

October fifth, Eve's water broke. After seventeen hours of labor, she birthed a healthy baby girl. Jake, her father, and Addy joyfully handed out boxes of Cuban cigars in the waiting room.

Hitch and Julian arrived with a bouquet of peonies, and later Jed, Sylvie, and the kids brought the baby a teddy bear. Lex and Monty stopped by to visit, Lex tossing Eve a pink onesie emblazoned with black skulls, her smile impish.

The day after Eve was discharged from the hospital, Arthur came to the house, a truck behind his car. While Jake escorted the deliverymen to the nursery, Arthur visited with Eve in the den, his manner subdued. He looked drained. She missed his usual jovial personality. "I thought you'd enjoy a rocker for the baby's room."

"You're thoughtful."

"Siobhan's almost done with another thirty-day stint at the Port Breakwater Center. This time may stick," Arthur said gruffly. "I saw her last weekend. She's terribly embarrassed by her behavior."

Is she really? Time would tell . . .

"I wish her the best," Eve said with sincerity. The baby fussed from her bassinet alongside the sofa and Eve gathered her up in her arms. She flashed Arthur a warm smile. "Do you want to hold her?"

"With that black hair, she already resembles Jake," Arthur said, cuddling the baby against his chest. "So, you've settled on Amelia Adeline?"

Eve nodded. "After my mother and Addy."

Jake stepped into the room. "Thanks for the rocking chair."

"I'm glad you like it. Well." Arthur handed Amelia back to Eve and got to his feet. "I won't keep you. I simply wanted to deliver the gift." He clapped Jake's back affectionately, saying heartily, "She's a beauty."

"Before you leave, I have a question for you," Jake said. "Would you be Amelia's godfather?"

Arthur's eyes became misty. He swallowed hard, overcome. "I'd be mighty honored, son."

After he left, Eve cradled Amelia to her breast. The baby rooted, making snuffling noises. Eve mused, "I guess somebody's hungry."

Jake's expression was tender when he caressed Amelia's silky head. He lowered his mouth to Eve's and they kissed. He whispered against her lips, "Christ, I'm the luckiest bastard alive."

YOU MAY ALSO ENJOY THE FOLLOWING FROM EXTASY BOOKS INC:

Escaping to Virginia
Daralyse Lyons

Excerpt

When they arrested my boyfriend for murdering my sister, I was there. I watched out his bedroom window as the police affixed handcuffs to his thick, strong wrists and took him away. As he got into the back of that squad car, I was certain of two things: First, that Thomas Emanuel Callahan was guilty and, second, that I loved him enough to tell anyone who would listen that he wasn't.

Marnie and I used to be close—back when we actually asked our mother to buy us matching dresses and begged to be allowed to sleep in the same bed. Before we grew up.

In our house, World War III was waged silently. Like so many other wars, it began with a quiet catalyst that radiated outwards. Shrapnel embedded itself deep within flesh, bombs were detonated, and hostages were assassinated. In the end, there were many casualties in my war against my sister. I refused to let Tommy become one of them.

In our house, a piece of pie was never just a piece of pie. It was a measure of our mother's love. Any discrepancy between the sizes of our slices telegraphed the difference in our worth.

I'm not sure exactly when it began to bother me that—other than on my birthday—Marnie always got the bigger portion of dessert. But I remember the first time I spoke up about it.

I was eleven. Marnie was twelve. We were Irish twins at only eleven months apart. It was the same day Dad announced he was walking out of our lives forever. Mom didn't even cry.

"He'll be back," she said, even though no one believed her.

Dad had already met someone else. Her name was Ruth. She smelled of pine trees, youth, and betrayal. Mom smelled like bacon grease and bossiness.

Ruth had a job offer in Tampa. Dad was going with her. When Marnie and I said goodbye under our mother's watchful gaze, my sister was smart enough not to let her arms linger too long around our father's waist. I have never been overly discerning, especially when it comes to matters of the heart, so I folded my body into Dad's and refused to let go until he pried my fingers loose.

"Hey!" He laughed. "It's not forever."

Dad was a good liar. I believed him long enough to let him go.

That night, when Mom served us pie, Marnie's slice was at least an inch wider than mine, and topped with twice as much whipped cream.

"How come she always gets the bigger slice?" I whined. "It's not fair."

My mother spun around from where she was standing at the kitchen sink, rinsing the dinner dishes. Her glower was a bullet straight to my chest. "Life isn't fair, Virginia. Get used to it."

Even though my mother was the one to fire that first shot, I blamed my sister. Why wouldn't I? Mom had chosen Marnie as her ally. I hung my head, ate my meagre ration of pie, and silently plotted my revenge. Later that night, I entered the battlefield of Marnie's bedroom and performed my first enemy act. I was discovered of course — tried as a traitor and grounded for a week.

My sister never understood why I stole her sterling silver charm bracelet (especially since I had one of my own), and I wasn't about to explain. Not to her anyway. The truth was I just wanted to feel superior in some small way. Maybe if I'd gotten away with my petty thievery, I'd have felt vindicated and a larger crisis would've been averted.

Not likely.

The great sage, Ramana Maharshi, once said, "Whatever is destined not to happen will not happen, try as you may. Whatever is destined to happen will happen, do what you may to prevent it. This is certain."

Marnie's and my rivalry was etched into the tablet of fate, as inevitable and unpreventable as a sneeze, and just as explosive. After I got caught with Marnie's precious bracelet, my sister started locking her bedroom door to keep me out. Fine by me. I'd already locked my heart and there was no way I was letting her inside.

Thomas and I grew up together, but we weren't friends or anything. He lived three houses down from me and our mothers hated each other. Even if I had been inclined to play with boys, or he with girls, our friendship would have been forbidden. When I was really young, out of obedience to my mother, I walked across the street just to avoid passing by Mrs. Callahan's house. That was before I discovered how good it felt to be disobedient.

According to Mom, the Callahans were a bunch of degenerates. Marnie and I had better stay away from them. The Callahan boy — a year older than Marnie, two years older than me — was taller than my father, and always struck me as being standoffish. He sat by himself in the back of the bus — too imposing for the cool kids to intimidate, too much of a loner to be inducted into the back-of-the-bussers' group. Those guys were the perfect mixture of popular and badass. They smoked clove cigarettes and went to make-out parties. Like me, their parents were divorced. Unlike me, they had two sets of full homes instead of one mostly empty one.

I envied them.

When we learned about Rosa Parks in the fourth grade, I never could wrap my head around the irony that, at one point, the front of the bus had been considered desirable.

Marnie sat in the back. It wasn't surprising. Even out of the house, my sister was everybody's favorite.

I sat in the middle. I was neither popular nor unpopular. I just sort of was.

It wasn't until a few weeks before my sixteenth birthday that Tommy Callahan talked to me.

Marnie and I were waiting at the bus stop. I checked my watch. The driver was late, as usual, in picking us up.

"He'll be here." Marnie—impatient about my impatience—stooped to scrape sidewalk gum excrement from the bottom of her shoe.

"I hate standing around doing nothing," I complained.

"Oh yeah, 'cause your life's so fucking interesting." She disposed of the gum, then withdrew a clove cigarette from its pack and sniffed the slender stick. She'd had that same pack for nearly a year. I never once saw her smoke.

I was about to tell my sister what a colossal idiot she was for thinking a pack of cigarettes would make her like the rest of her friends—the ones who chose to wear ripped jeans and vacationed in Jamaica. Our jeans were worn so bare they were practically falling apart. And, as for beach vacations, our once-a-summer trips to the shore didn't count. I didn't though. Just then, Thomas Callahan pulled up in his dented beige Camaro.

He rolled down his window. "Hey, Virginia."

Even though we'd never spoken, my name sounded familiar coming out of his mouth.

"Hi, Tommy."

That was the year I'd gotten breasts and I found myself wondering if he'd noticed the plush, melon-like mounds beneath my white V-neck t-shirt. He told me later that he'd noticed them, couldn't stop noticing them, in fact. But that was after he'd come to know each and every contour of my body, kissed the warm, wet place between my thighs, and inserted himself deep within the core of me, splitting me in half so that my entire life became divided into two distinct periods: BT, before Tommy, and AT, after Tommy.

"Want a ride?"

I glanced at Marnie. My sister pretended not to care that he'd only extended his offer to me.

"Sure." I climbed into the passenger seat. I didn't ask if Marnie could come along. I wanted to be alone with Tommy, just as he seemed to want to be alone with me.

My sister sucked the damp end of her unlit cigarette and scowled.

"Bye!" I waved at Marnie. By that point, we'd already come to despise one another, but I didn't want Tommy to think I was the kind of girl who hated her own sister.

Marnie glared at me. Then Tommy and I were off—heading towards school in the car that duct tape built.

Neither Tommy nor I came from money. Maybe that was part of our problem. Money buys you choices. If Tommy and I had had money, we could have afforded a different kind of escape. If Tommy and I had had money, he wouldn't have had to kill her.

About the Author

Quirky hermit. Crazy cat lady. Writer.

With degrees in education and psychology, Anne Lucy-Shanley is a novelist based in the American Midwest. An enthusiast of all things romance, she also dabbles in dystopian, young adult, and non-fiction writing. Her contemporary second-chance-at-love novel, Meeting the Past, spans multiple genres and showcases her unique voice.

Some of Anne's pastimes include drinking whiskey, sniggering at dirty jokes, and coming up with captivating storylines while soaking in the tub. When not embracing the quiet life with a book and a cat on her lap, she occasionally travels with her husband of twenty years.

Anne loves connecting with her readers. She can be found at these links:

https://annelucyshanley.com/
https://www.facebook.com/anne.lucyshanleywrites
https://www.instagram.com/writer_annelucyshanley/

Made in the USA
Monee, IL
25 April 2022

95371472R10197